MAYOR GOOD BOY

TURNS BAD

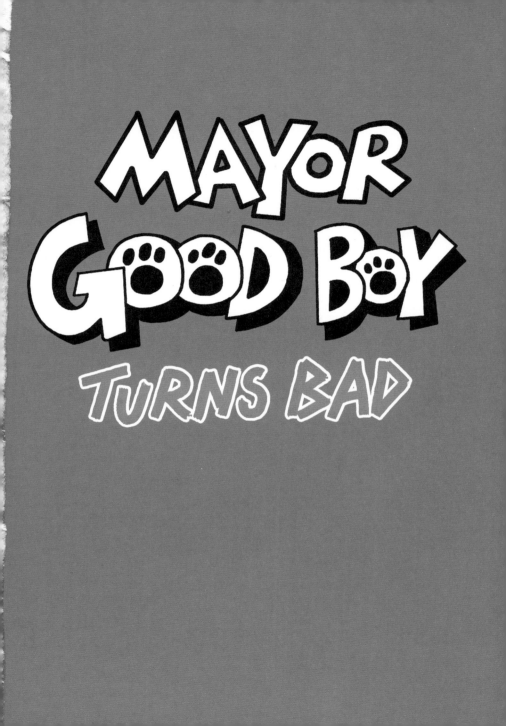

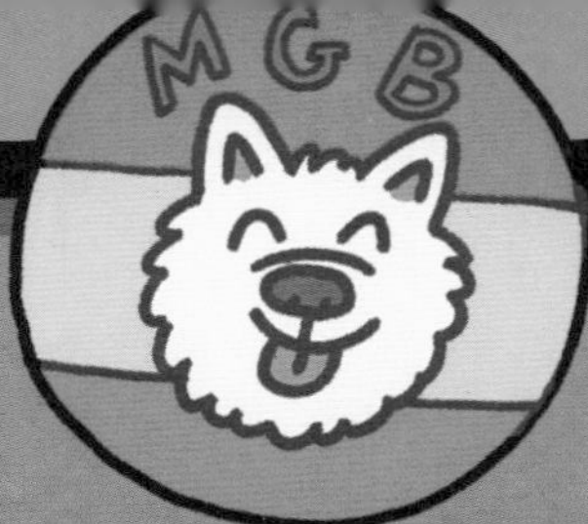
MGB

ALSO BY DAVE SCHEIDT AND MIRANDA HARMON

Mayor Good Boy

Mayor Good Boy Goes Hollywood

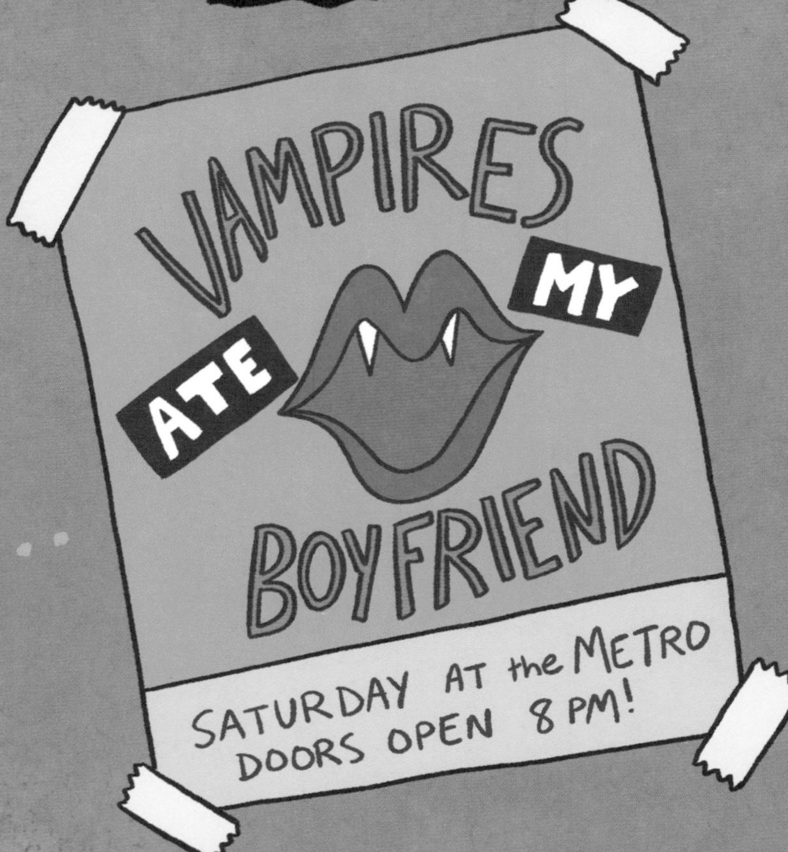
VAMPIRES
ATE
MY
BOYFRIEND
SATURDAY AT the METRO
DOORS OPEN 8 PM!

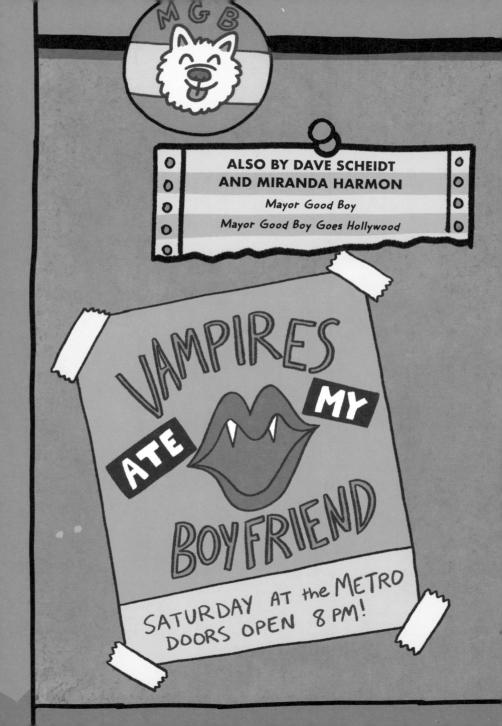

MAYOR GOOD BOY TURNS BAD

Written by Dave Scheidt
Illustrated by Miranda Harmon
Colored by Lyle Lynde

VAMPIRES ATE MY BOYFRIEND
The METRO
ADMIT ONE
ADMIT ONE

RH GRAPHIC
NEW YORK

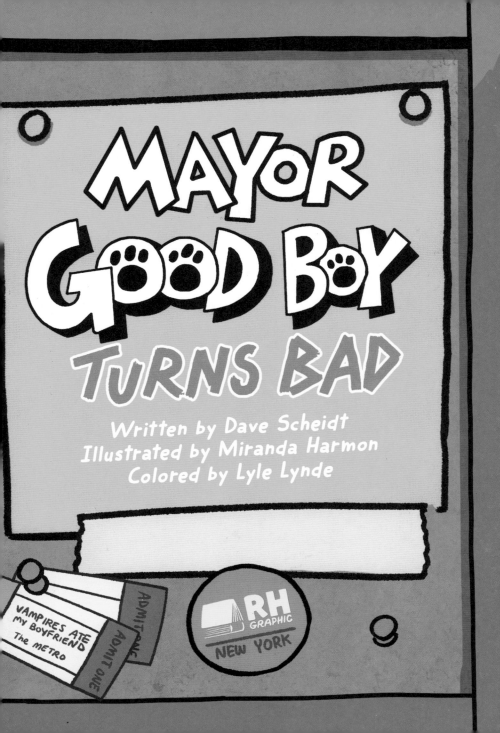

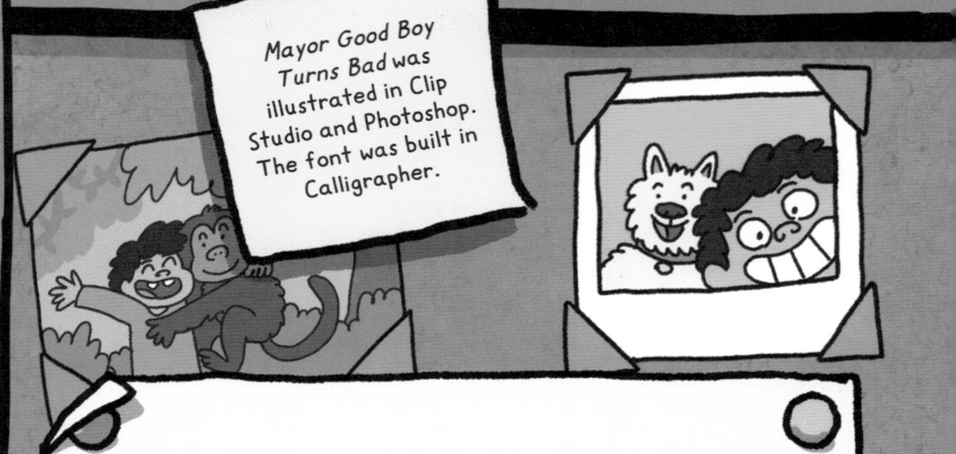
Mayor Good Boy Turns Bad was illustrated in Clip Studio and Photoshop. The font was built in Calligrapher.

This is a work of fiction. Names, characters, places, and incidents either are the product of the creators' imagination or are used fictitiously. Any resemblance to actual persons, living or dead, events, or locales is entirely coincidental.

 Published in the United States by RH Graphic, an imprint of Random House Children's Books, a division of Penguin Random House LLC, New York.

RH Graphic with the book design is a trademark of Penguin Random House LLC.

Visit us on the web! RHKidsGraphic.com • @RHKidsGraphic

Educators and librarians, for a variety of teaching tools, visit us at RHTeachersLibrarians.com

Library of Congress Cataloging-in-Publication Data is available upon request.
ISBN 978-0-593-12491-8 (hardcover) — ISBN 978-0-593-12607-3 (library binding)
ISBN 978-0-593-12492-5 (ebook)

Designed by Patrick Crotty
Colored by Lyle Lynde

MANUFACTURED IN CHINA
10 9 8 7 6 5 4 3 2 1
First Edition

RH GRAPHIC
A comic on every bookshelf.

For my family
—M.H.

To Mom, Dad, Eric, and Sarah
—D.S.

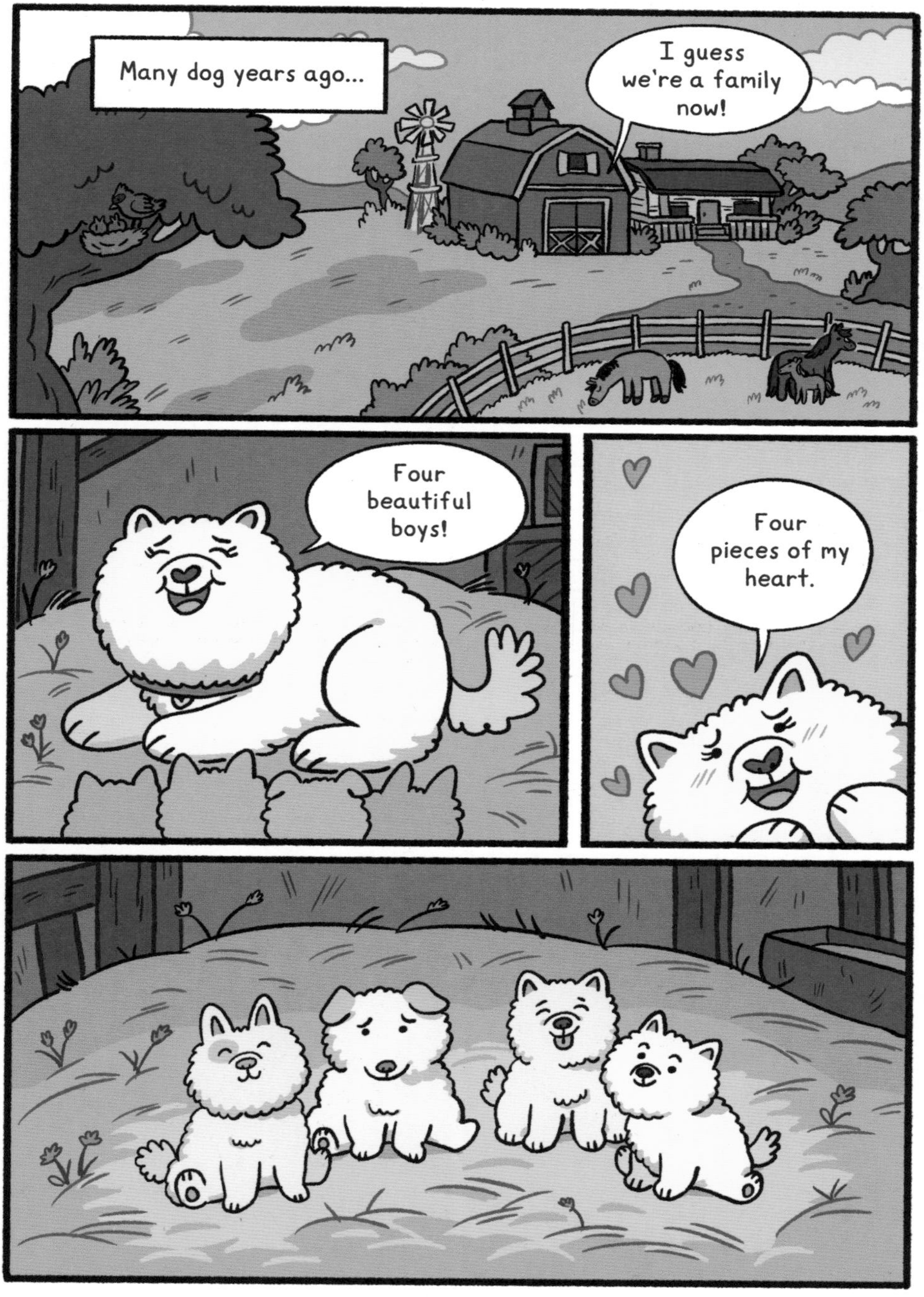
Many dog years ago...
I guess we're a family now!
Four beautiful boys!
Four pieces of my heart.

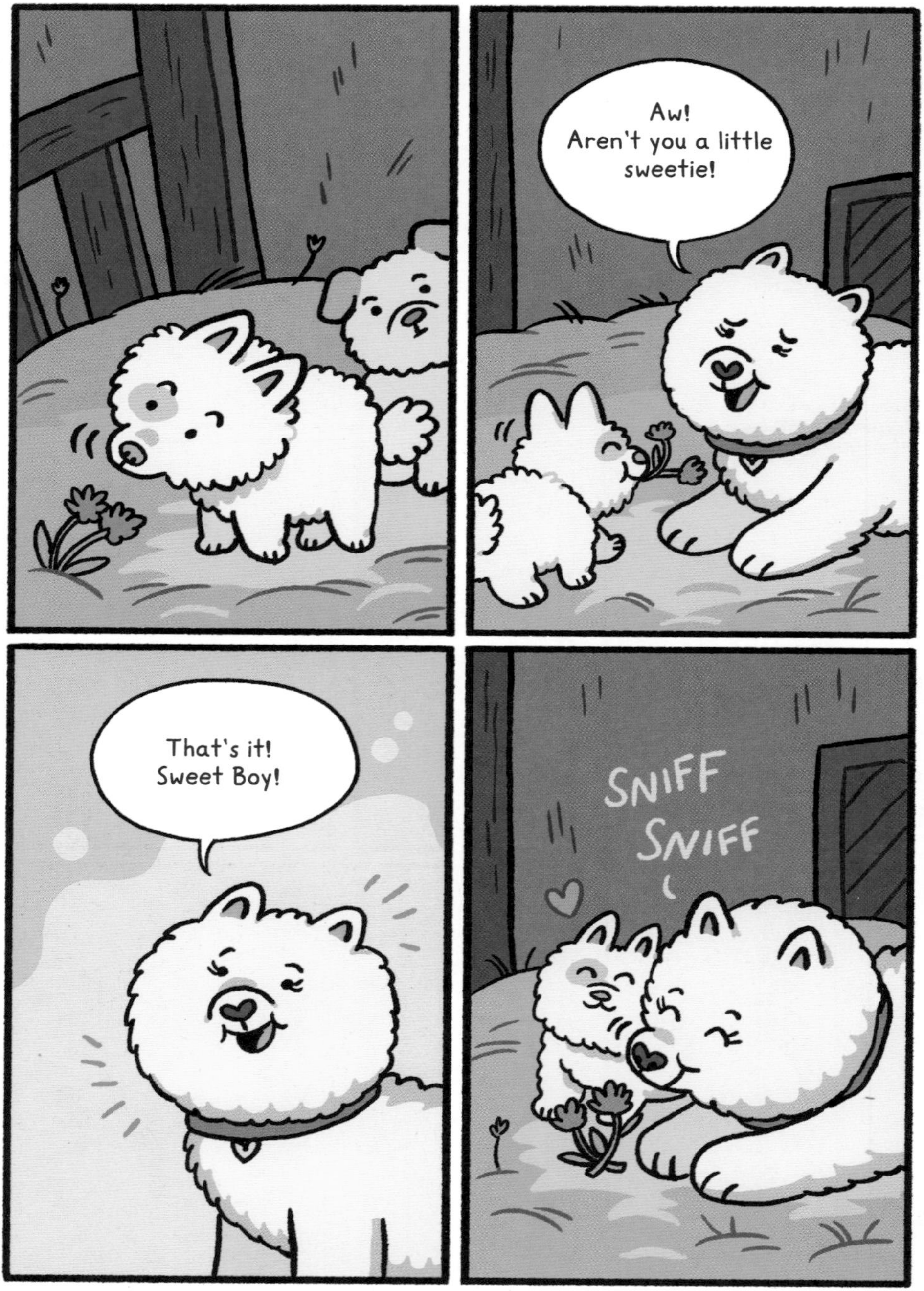
Aw!
Aren't you a little sweetie!
That's it!
Sweet Boy!
SNIFF
SNIFF

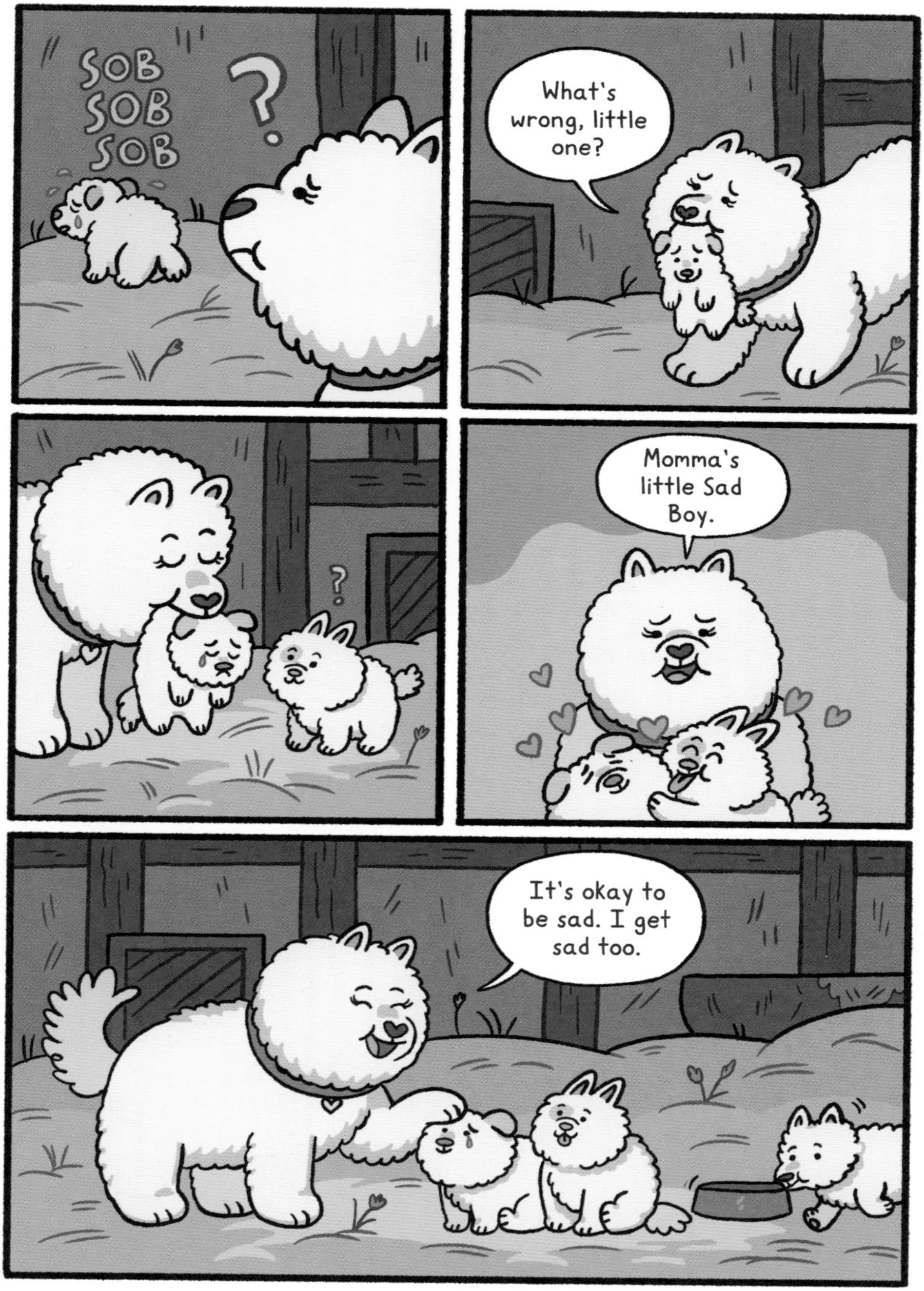
SOB SOB SOB
?
What's wrong, little one?
?
Momma's little Sad Boy.
It's okay to be sad. I get sad too.

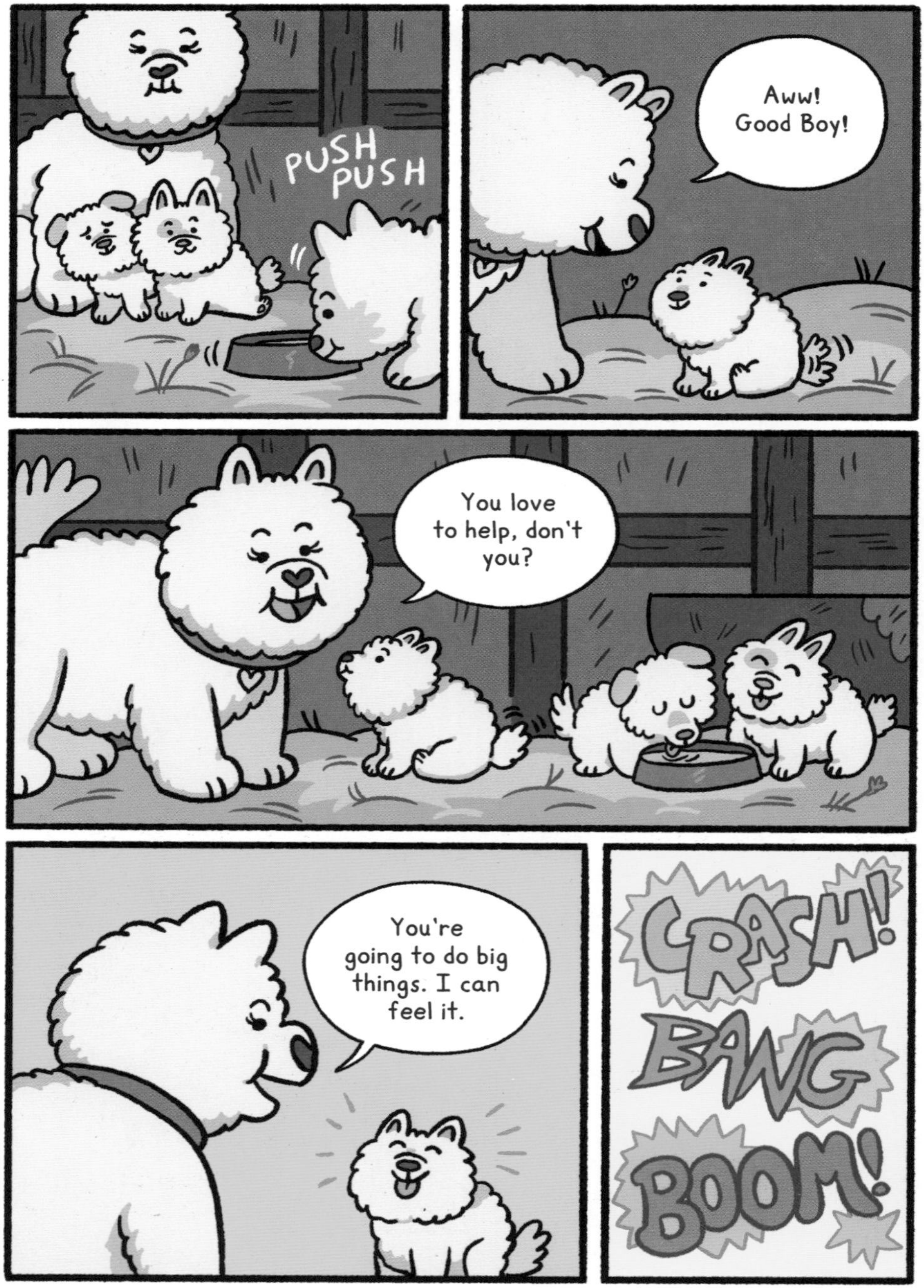
PUSH
PUSH
Aww!
Good Boy!
You love
to help, don't
you?
You're
going to do big
things. I can
feel it.
CRASH!
BANG
BOOM!

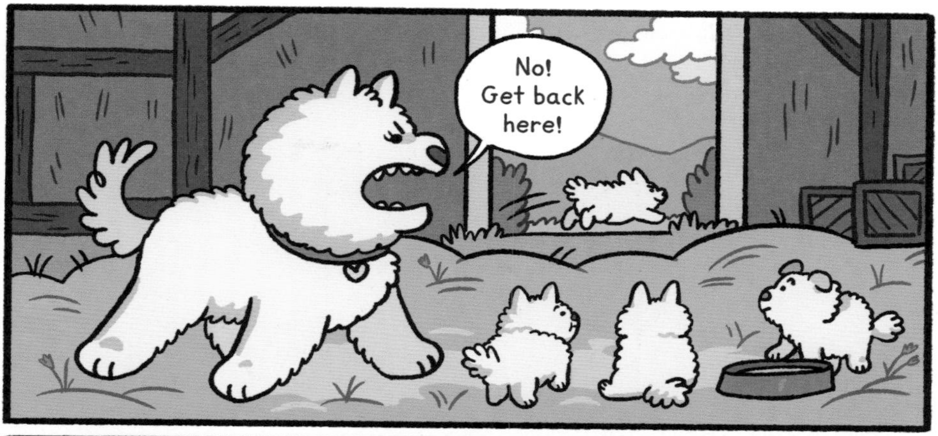
No! Get back here!

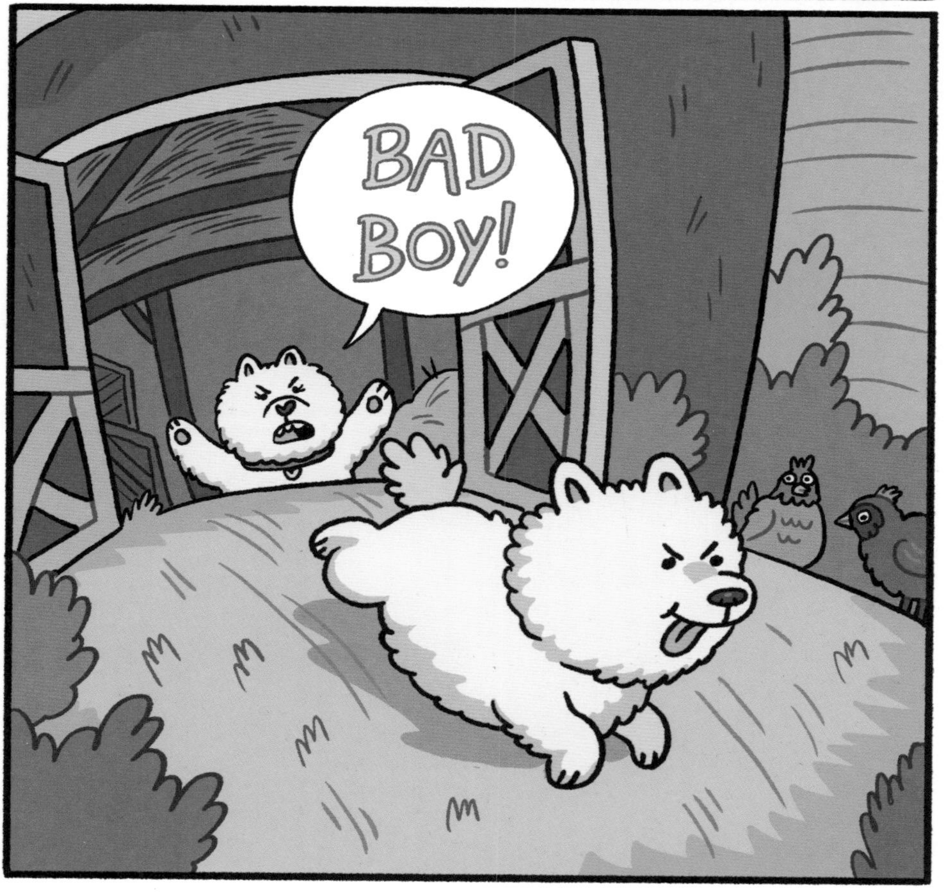
BAD BOY!

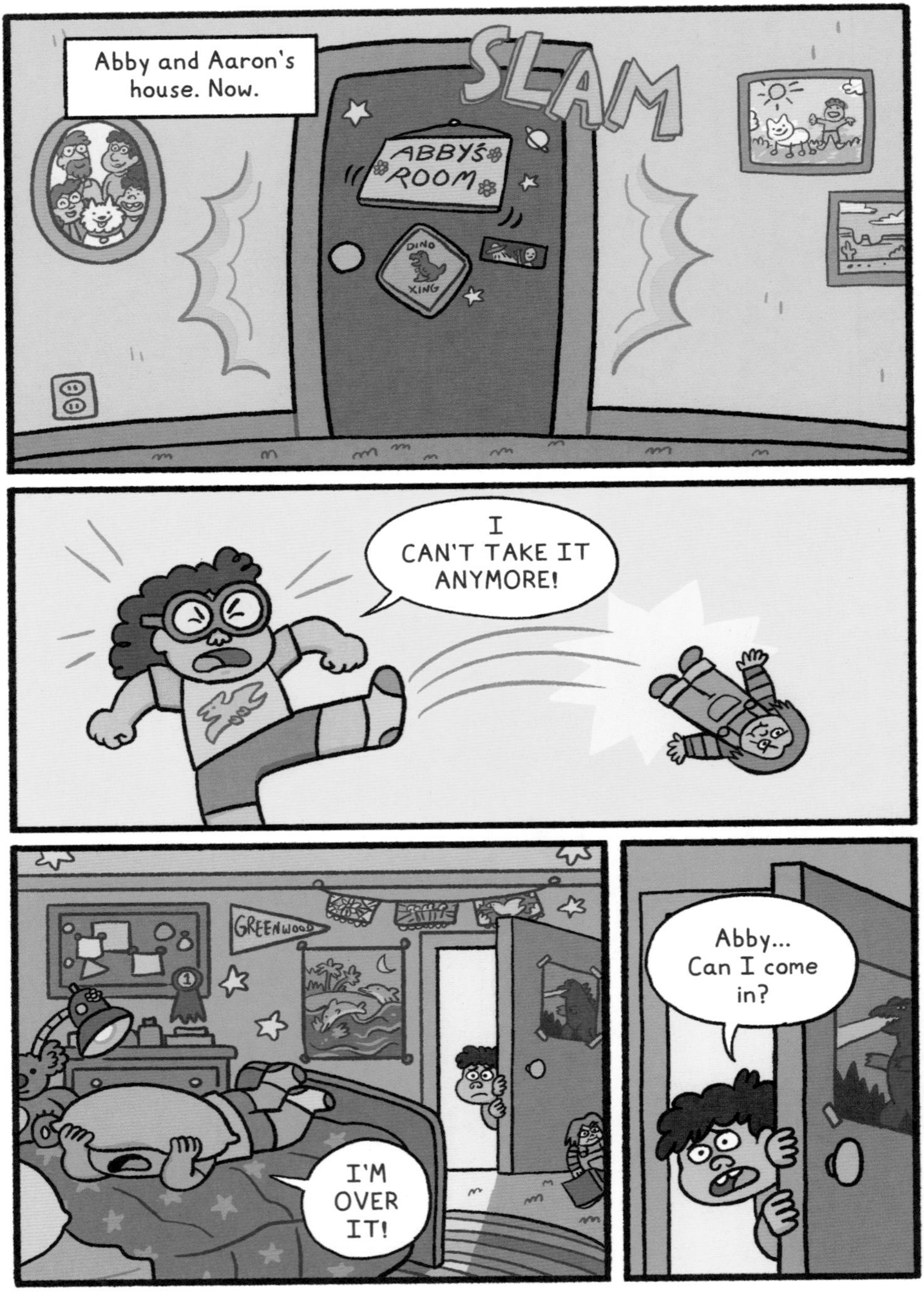
Abby and Aaron's house. Now.
SLAM
ABBY'S ROOM
DINO XING
I CAN'T TAKE IT ANYMORE!
GREENWOOD
I'M OVER IT!
Abby... Can I come in?

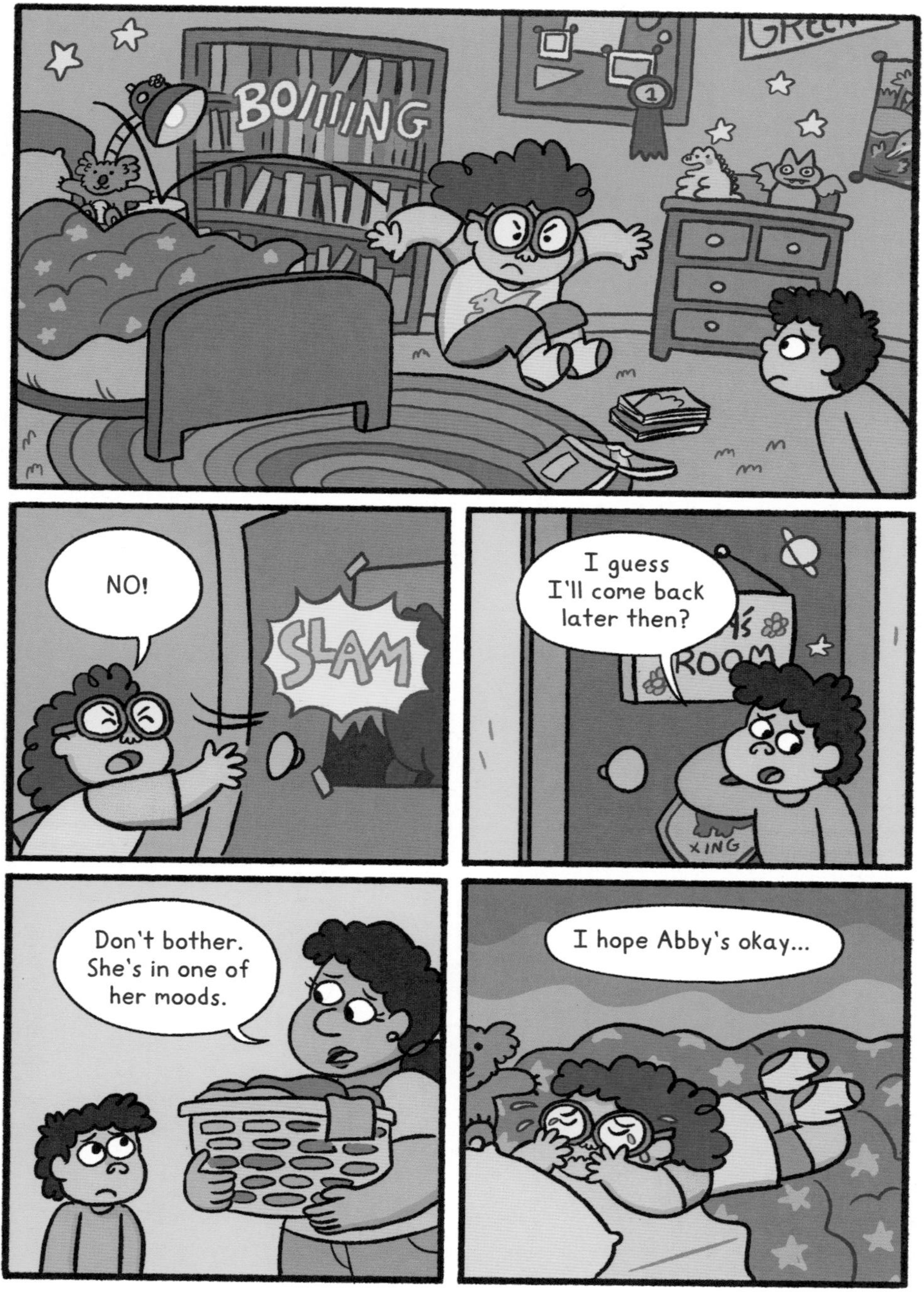
BOIIIING
GREEN
NO!
SLAM
I guess I'll come back later then?
ROOM
XING
Don't bother. She's in one of her moods.
I hope Abby's okay...

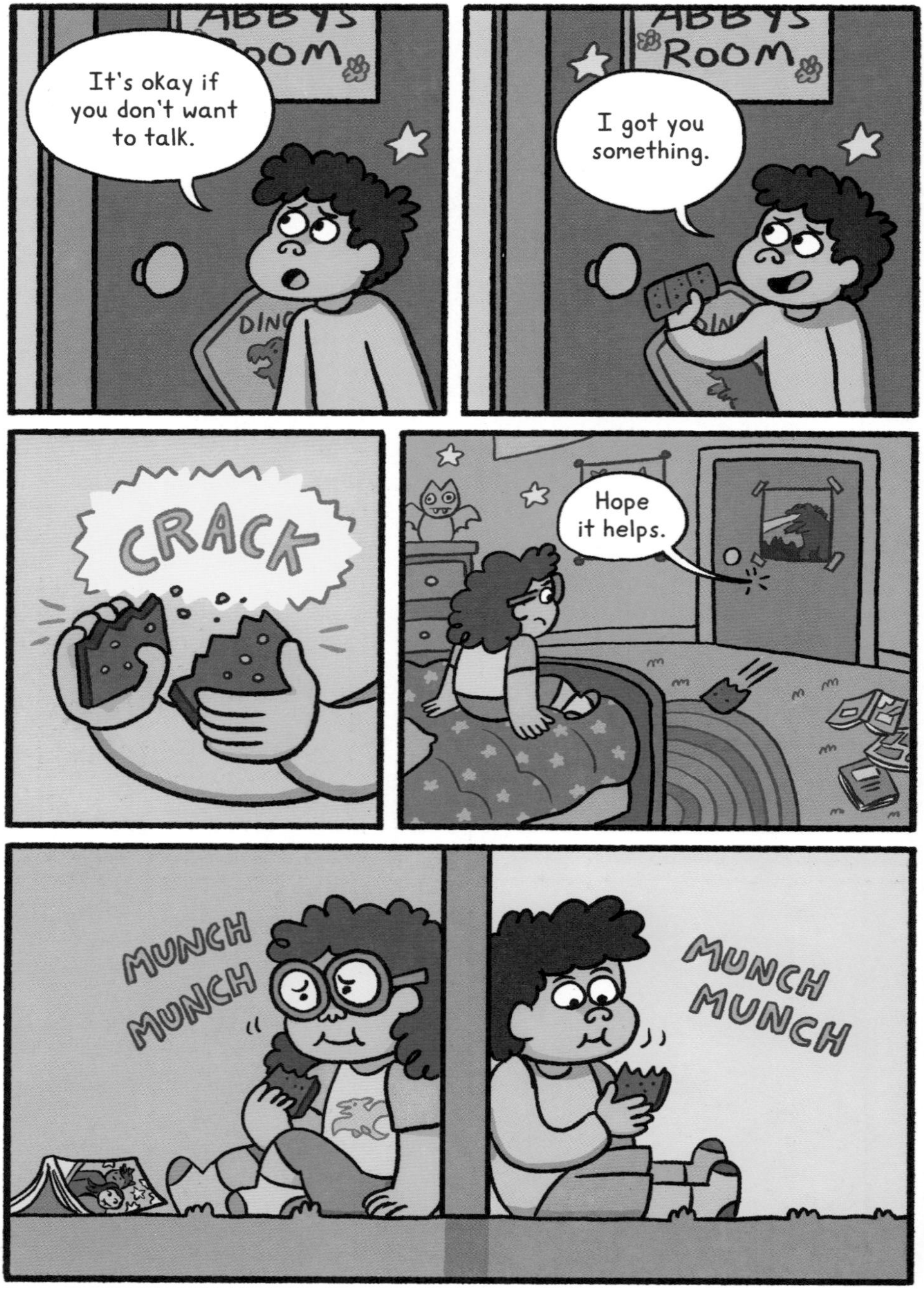
ABBYS ROOM
It's okay if you don't want to talk.
ABBYS ROOM
I got you something.
DINO
CRACK
Hope it helps.
MUNCH MUNCH
MUNCH MUNCH

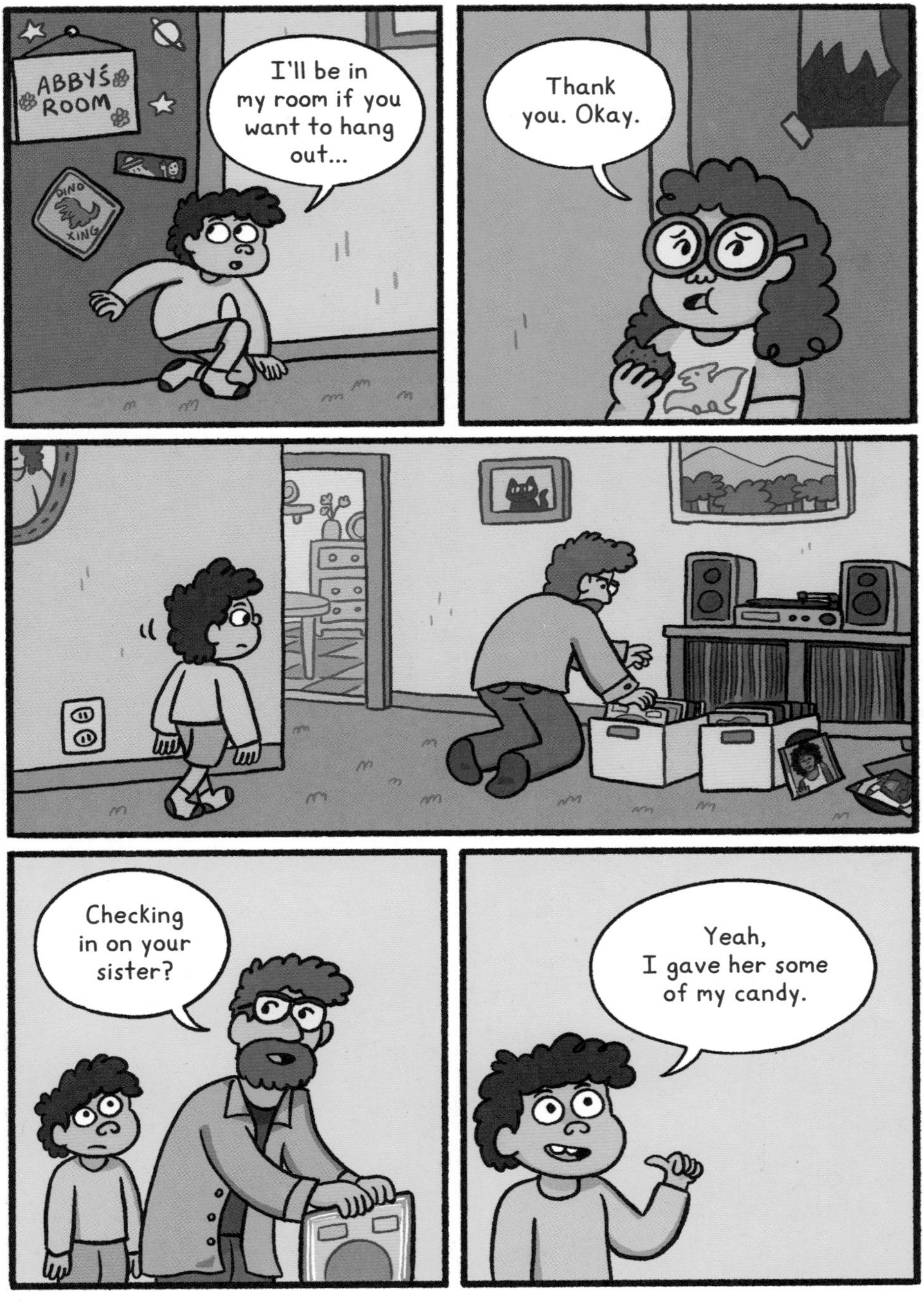
ABBY'S ROOM
DINO XING
I'll be in my room if you want to hang out...
Thank you. Okay.
Checking in on your sister?
Yeah, I gave her some of my candy.

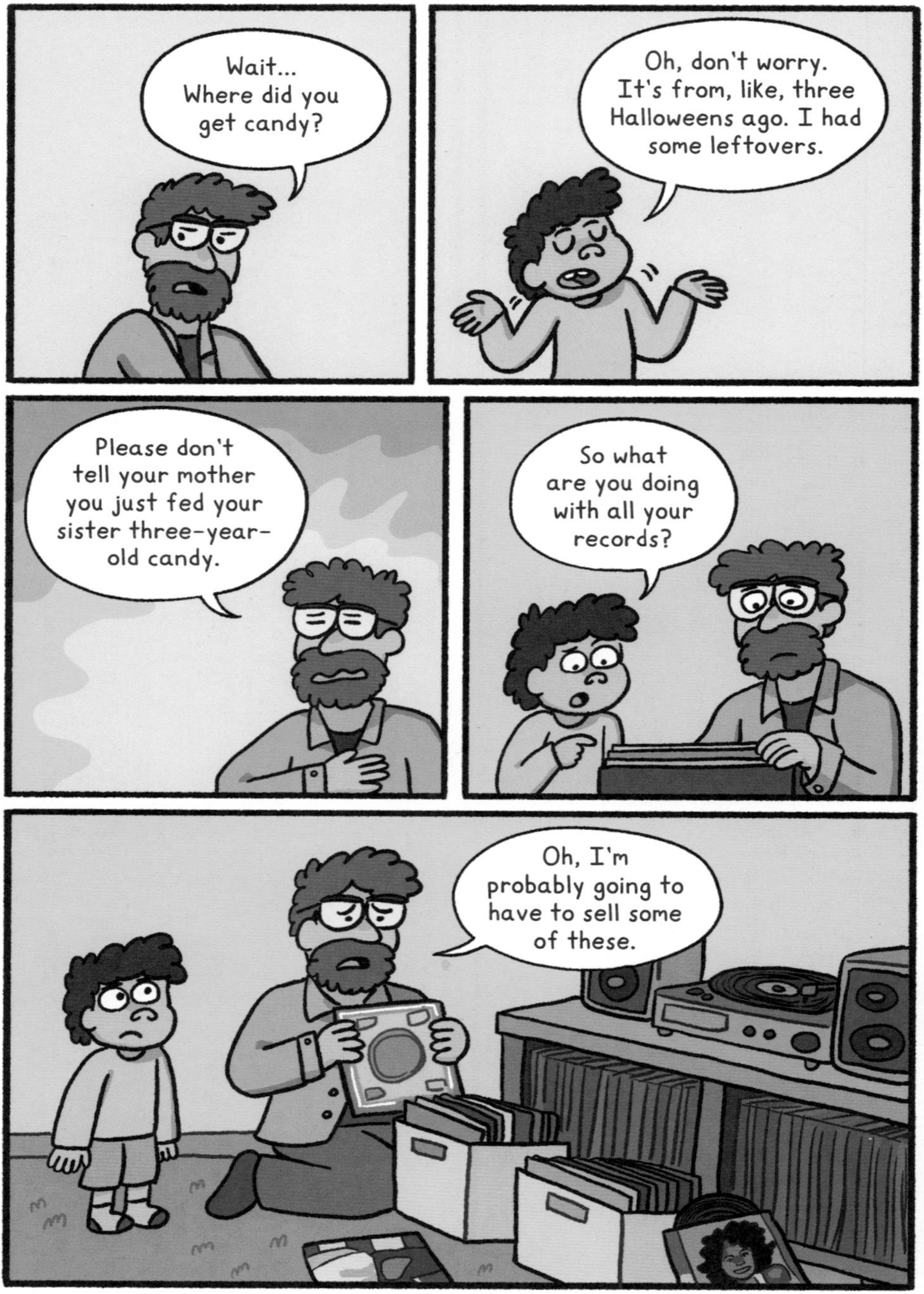
Wait... Where did you get candy?
Oh, don't worry. It's from, like, three Halloweens ago. I had some leftovers.
Please don't tell your mother you just fed your sister three-year-old candy.
So what are you doing with all your records?
Oh, I'm probably going to have to sell some of these.

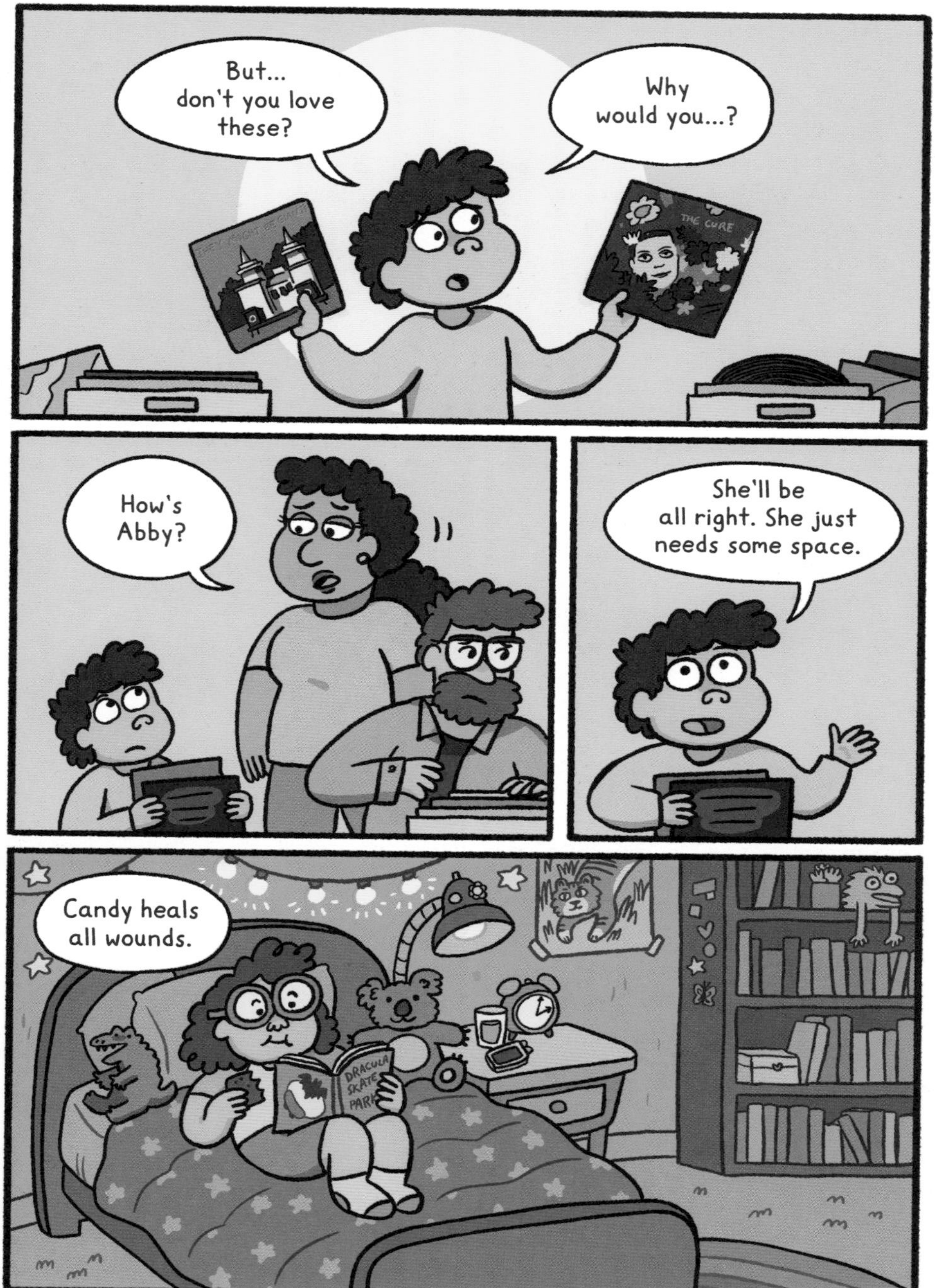
But... don't you love these?
Why would you...?
THE CURE
How's Abby?
She'll be all right. She just needs some space.
Candy heals all wounds.
DRACULA SKATE PARK

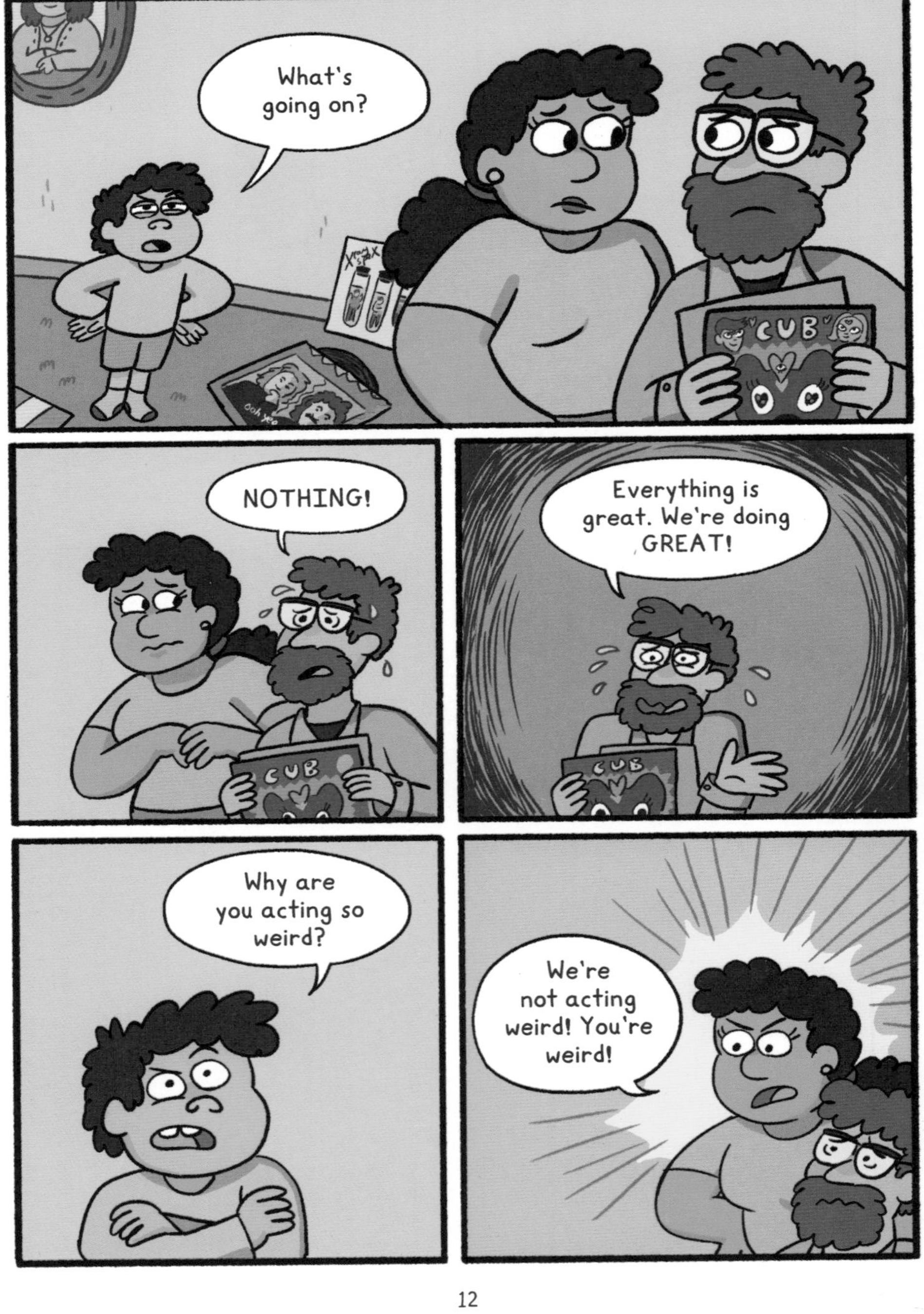
What's going on?
CUB
NOTHING!
CUB
Everything is great. We're doing GREAT!
CUB
Why are you acting so weird?
We're not acting weird! You're weird!

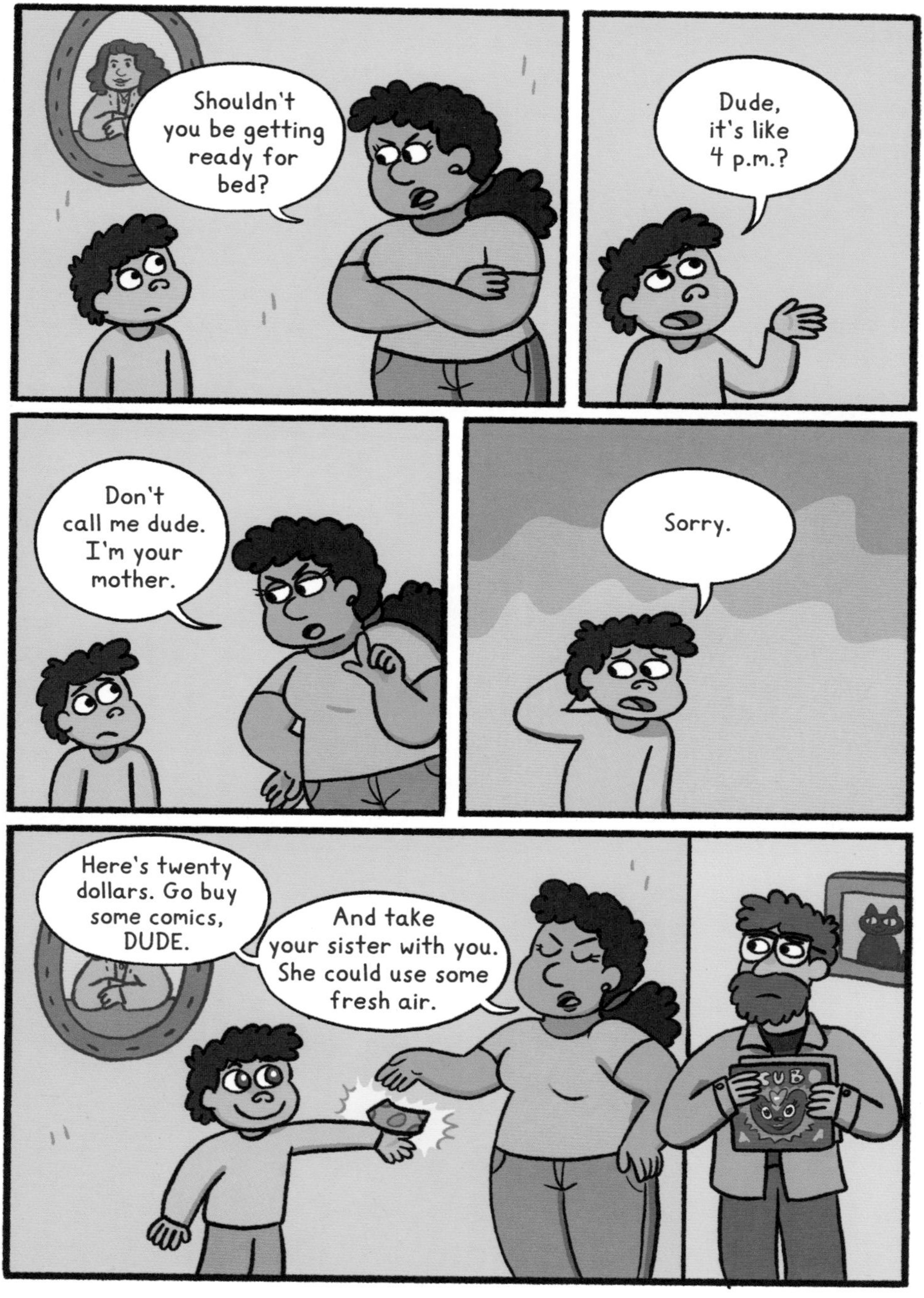

Shouldn't you be getting ready for bed?
Dude, it's like 4 p.m.?
Don't call me dude. I'm your mother.
Sorry.
Here's twenty dollars. Go buy some comics, DUDE.
And take your sister with you. She could use some fresh air.
CUB

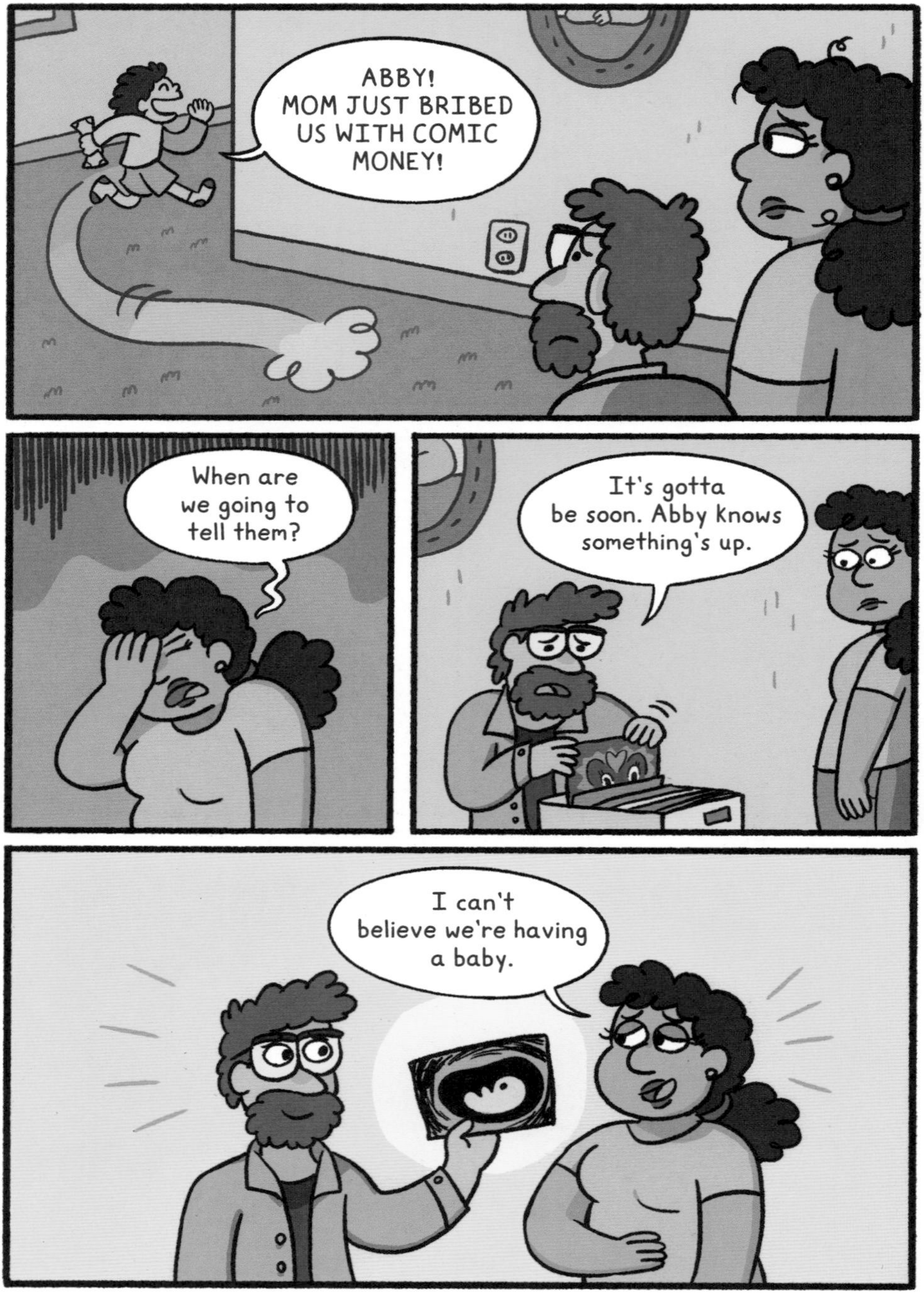
ABBY! MOM JUST BRIBED US WITH COMIC MONEY!
When are we going to tell them?
It's gotta be soon. Abby knows something's up.
I can't believe we're having a baby.

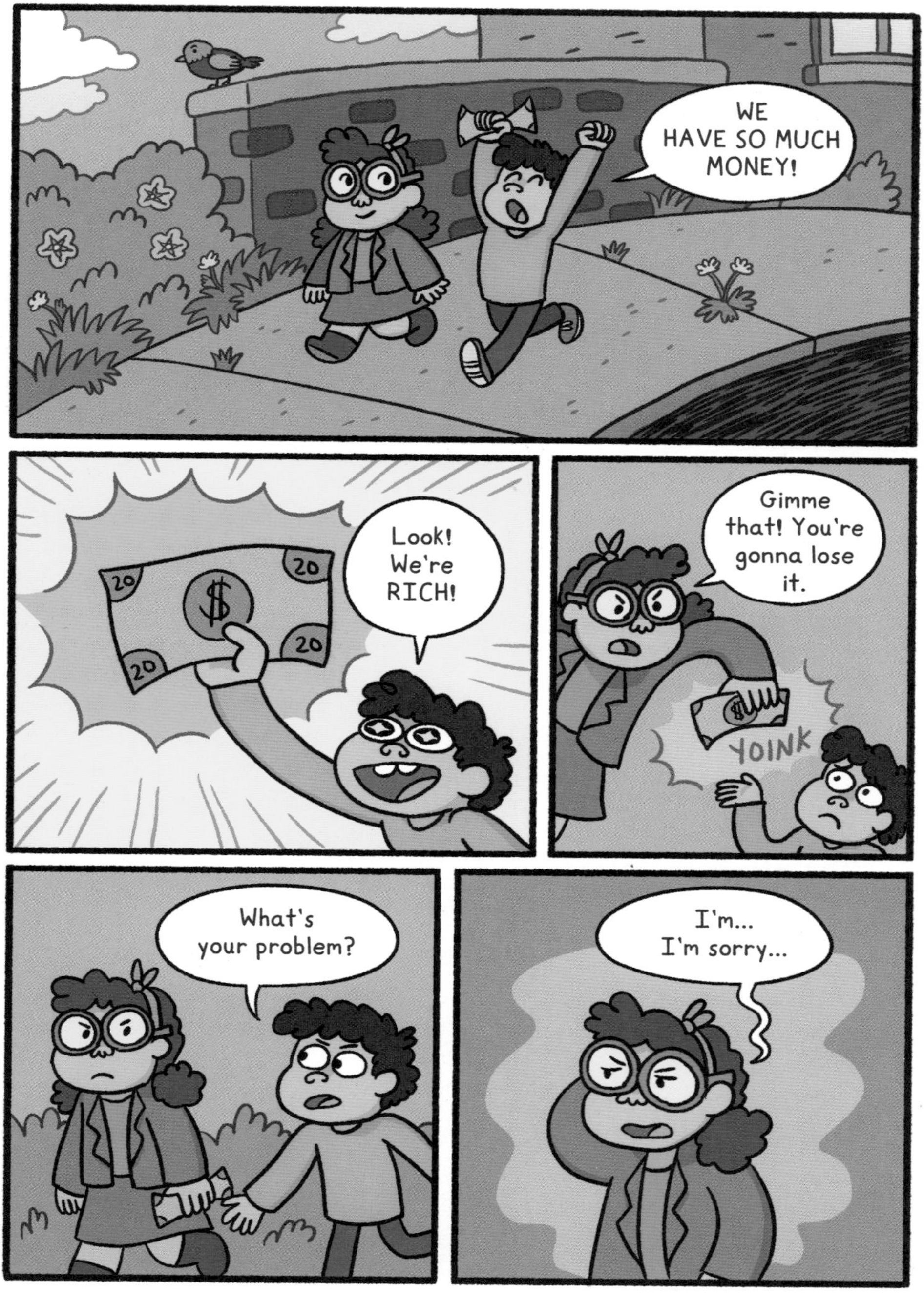
WE HAVE SO MUCH MONEY!
Look! We're RICH!
Gimme that! You're gonna lose it.
YOINK
What's your problem?
I'm... I'm sorry...

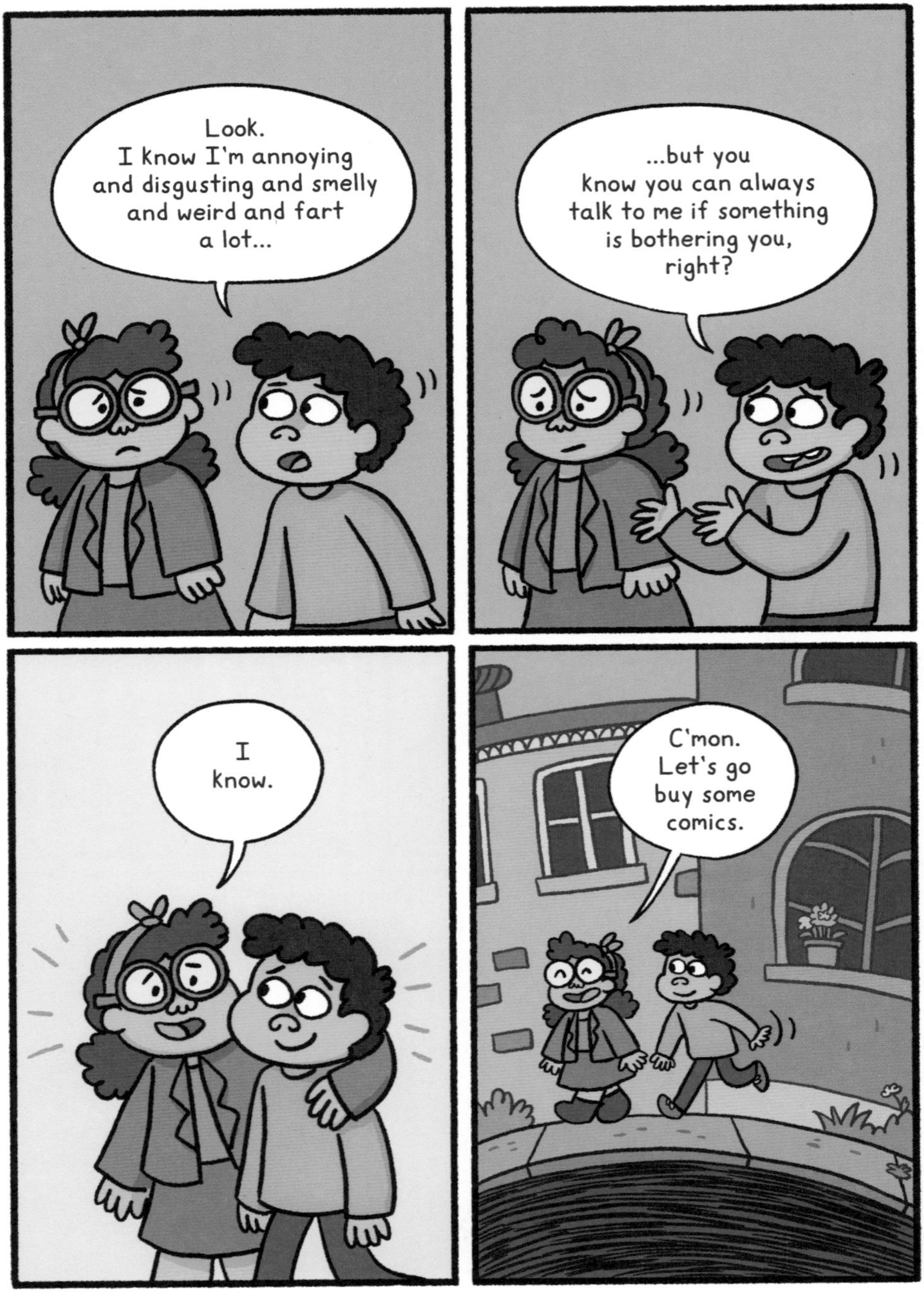
Look.
I know I'm annoying and disgusting and smelly and weird and fart a lot...
...but you know you can always talk to me if something is bothering you, right?
I know.
C'mon. Let's go buy some comics.

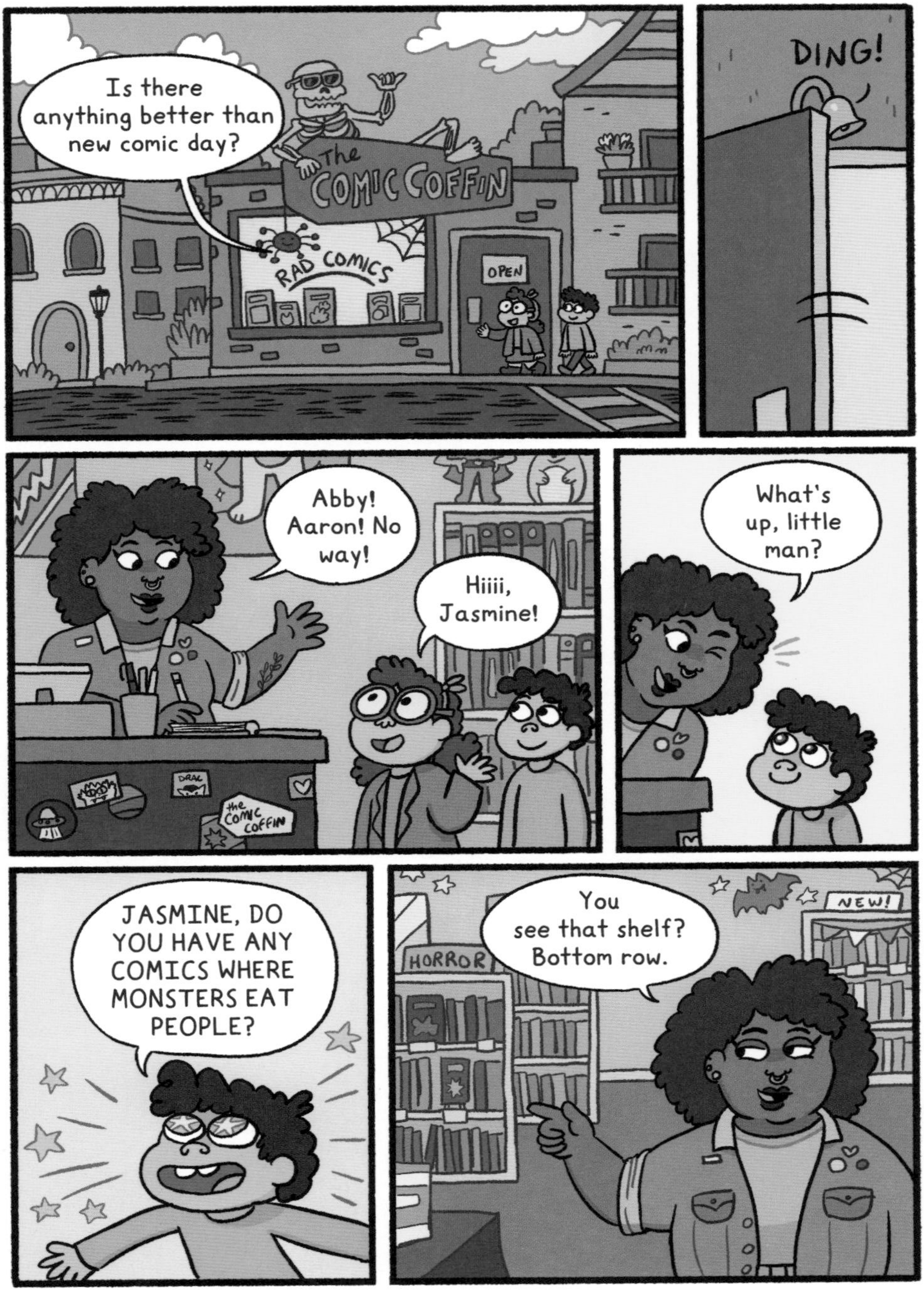

Is there anything better than new comic day?
The COMIC COFFIN
RAD COMICS
OPEN
DING!
Abby! Aaron! No way!
Hiiii, Jasmine!
the COMIC COFFIN
What's up, little man?
JASMINE, DO YOU HAVE ANY COMICS WHERE MONSTERS EAT PEOPLE?
HORROR
NEW!
You see that shelf? Bottom row.

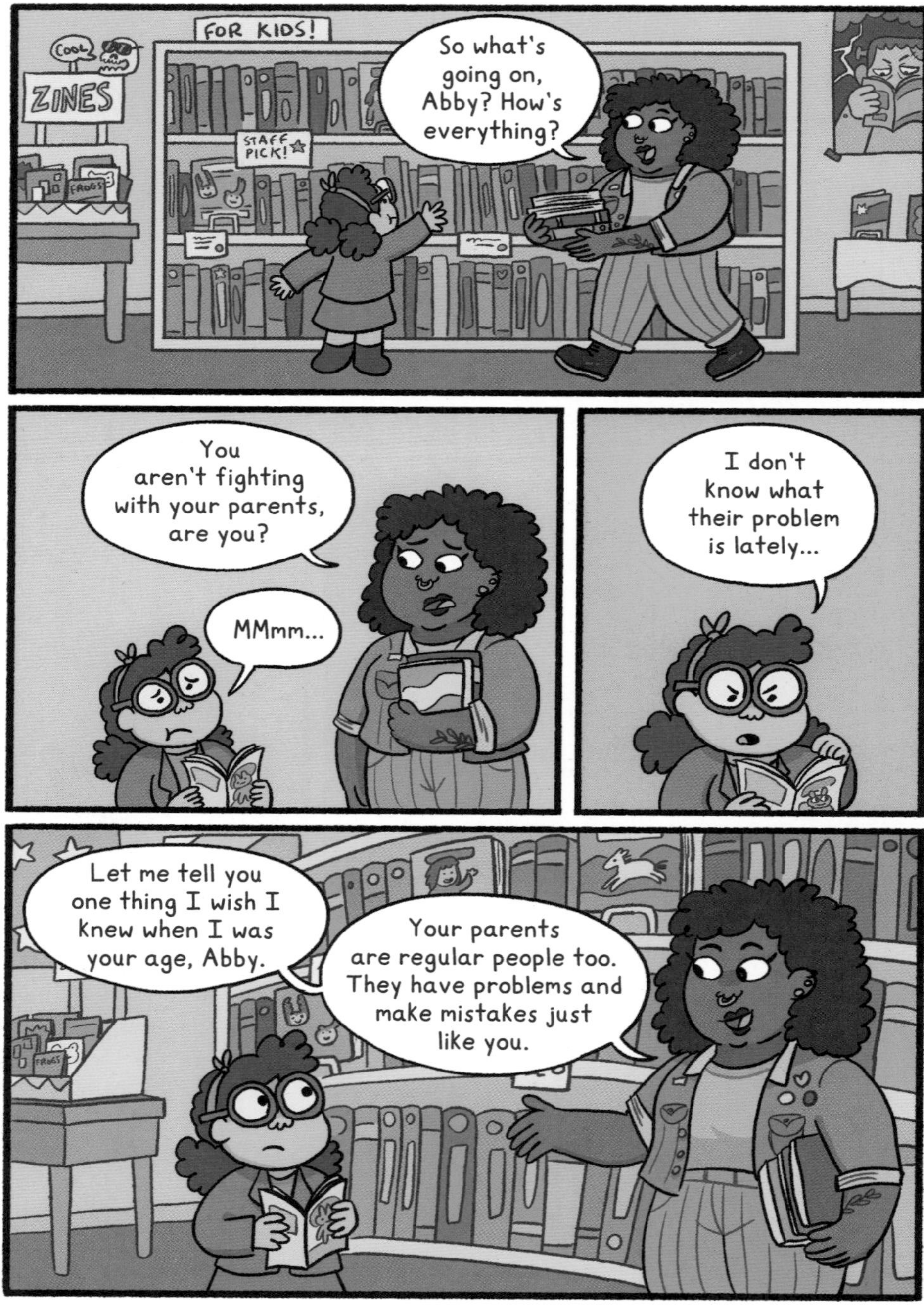
FOR KIDS!
ZINES
COOL
STAFF PICK!
FROGS
So what's going on, Abby? How's everything?
You aren't fighting with your parents, are you?
MMmm...
I don't know what their problem is lately...
Let me tell you one thing I wish I knew when I was your age, Abby.
Your parents are regular people too. They have problems and make mistakes just like you.

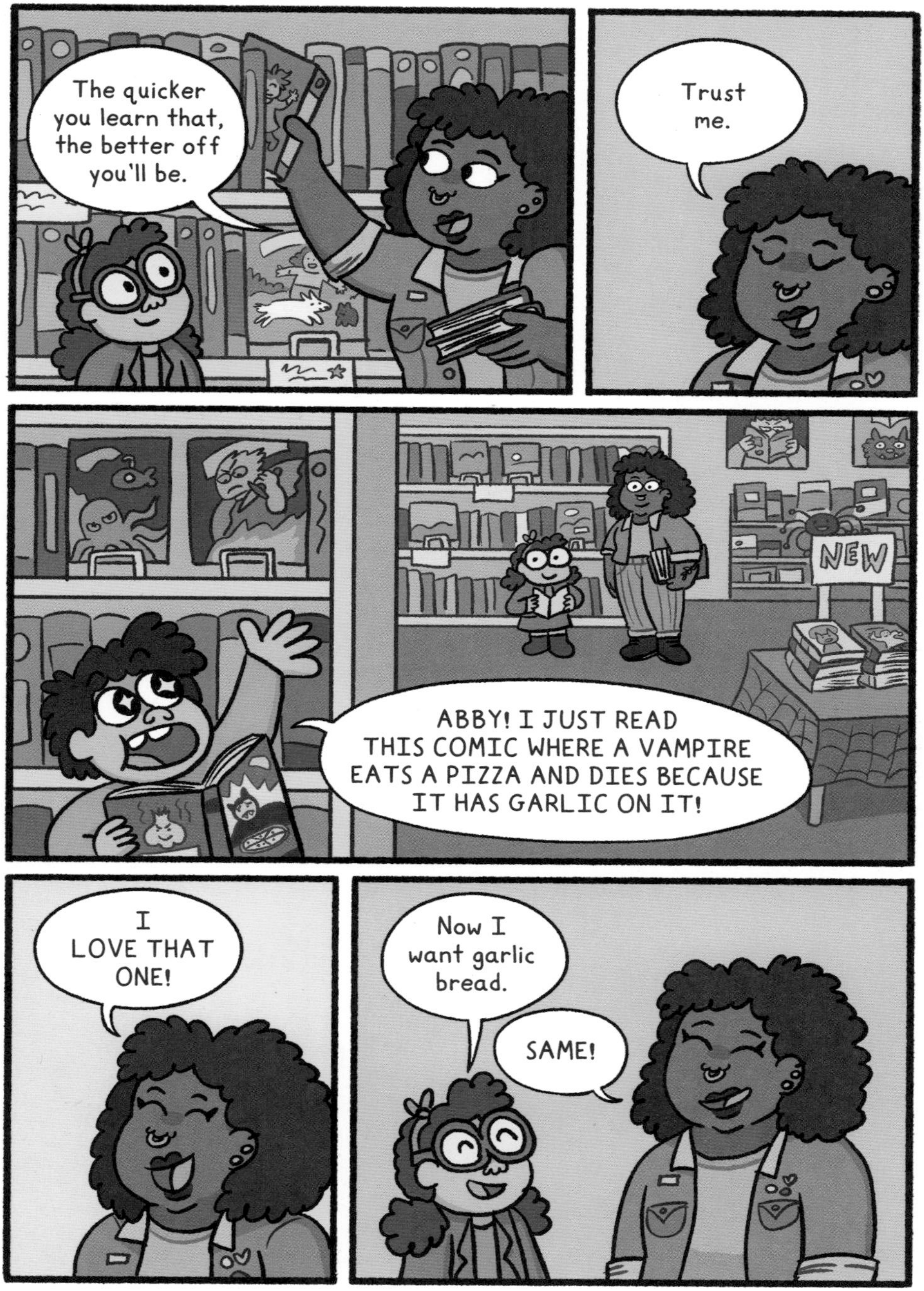
The quicker you learn that, the better off you'll be.
Trust me.
NEW
ABBY! I JUST READ THIS COMIC WHERE A VAMPIRE EATS A PIZZA AND DIES BECAUSE IT HAS GARLIC ON IT!
I LOVE THAT ONE!
Now I want garlic bread.
SAME!

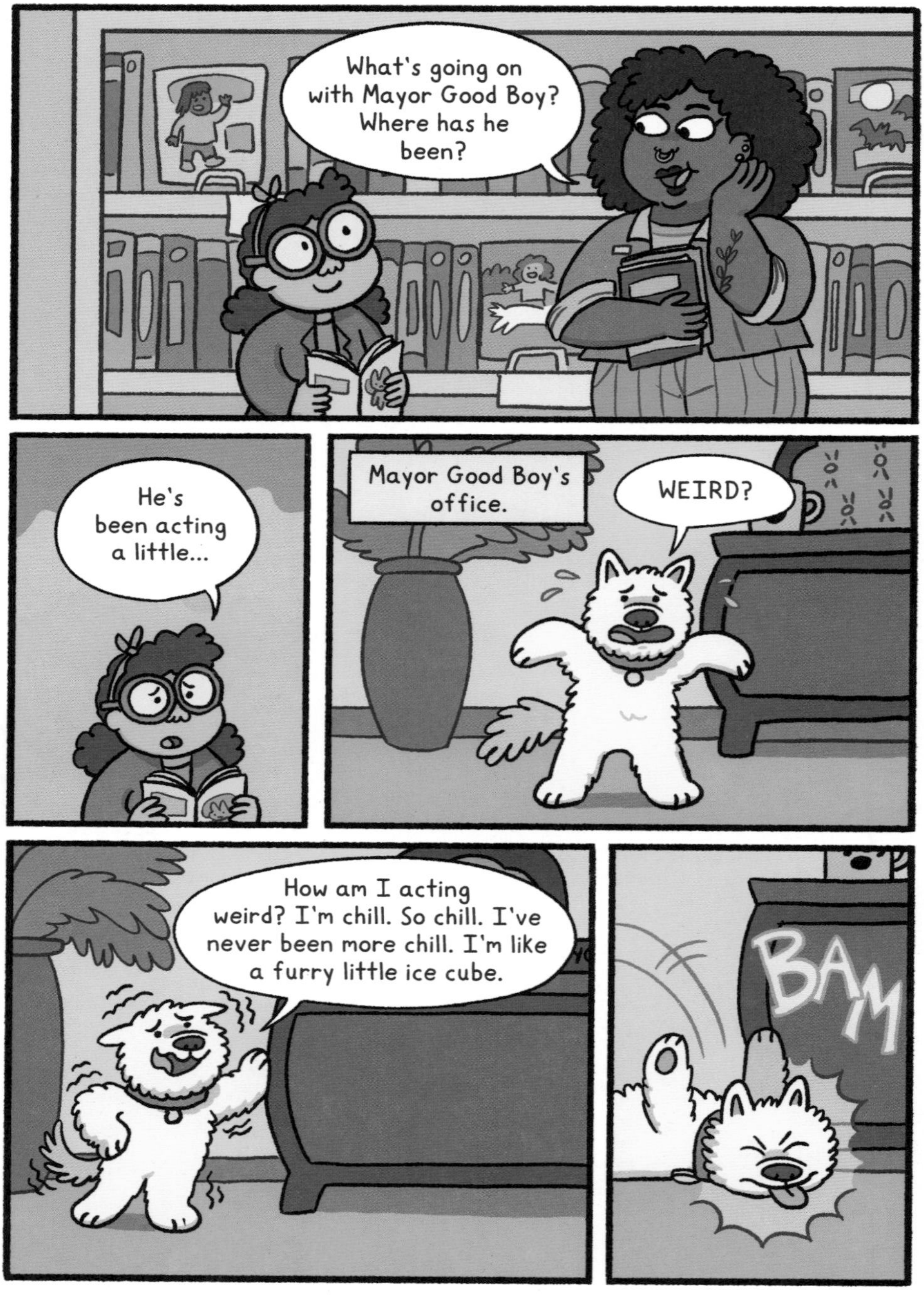
What's going on with Mayor Good Boy? Where has he been?
He's been acting a little...
Mayor Good Boy's office.
WEIRD?
How am I acting weird? I'm chill. So chill. I've never been more chill. I'm like a furry little ice cube.
BAM

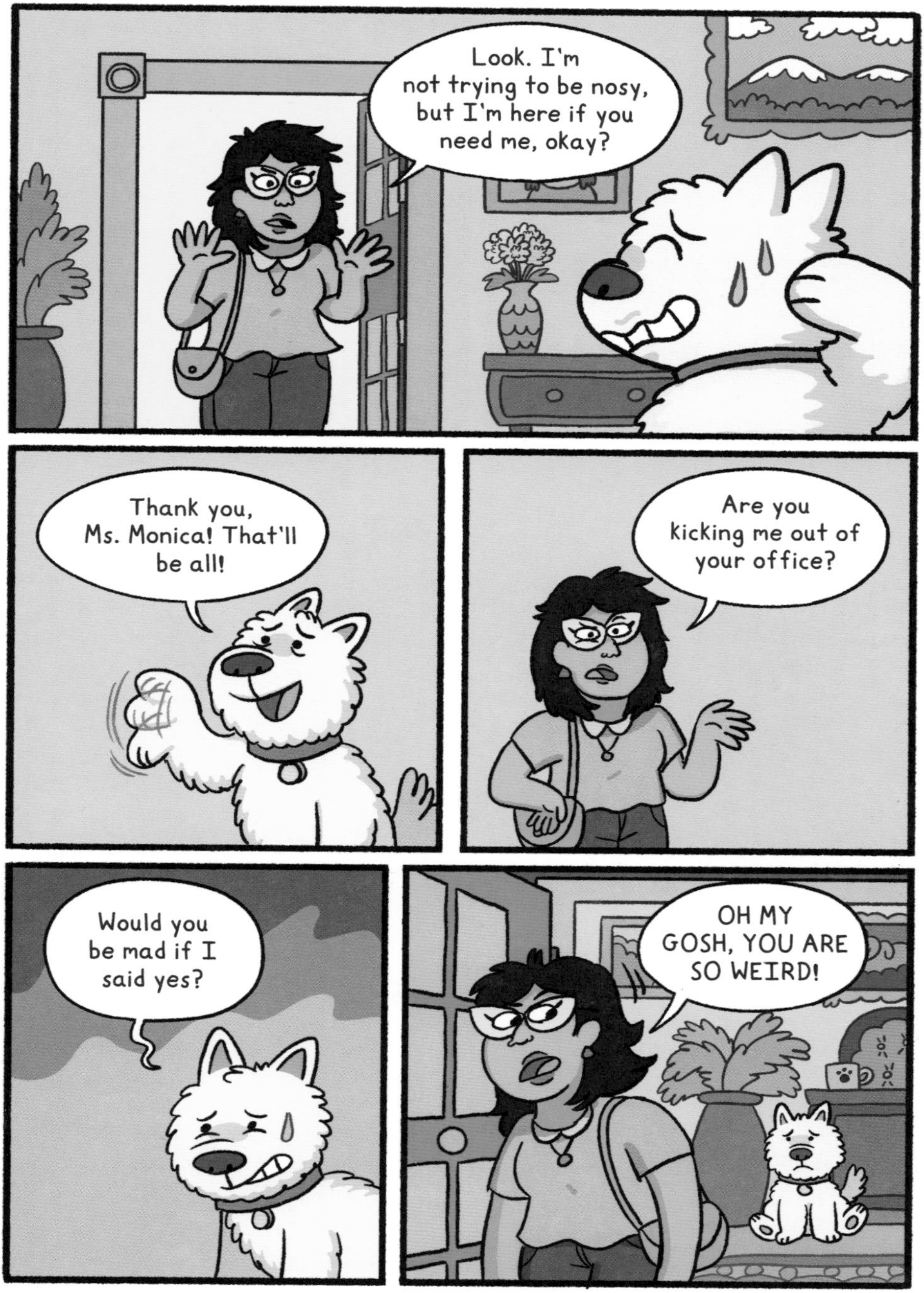

Look. I'm not trying to be nosy, but I'm here if you need me, okay?
Thank you, Ms. Monica! That'll be all!
Are you kicking me out of your office?
Would you be mad if I said yes?
OH MY GOSH, YOU ARE SO WEIRD!

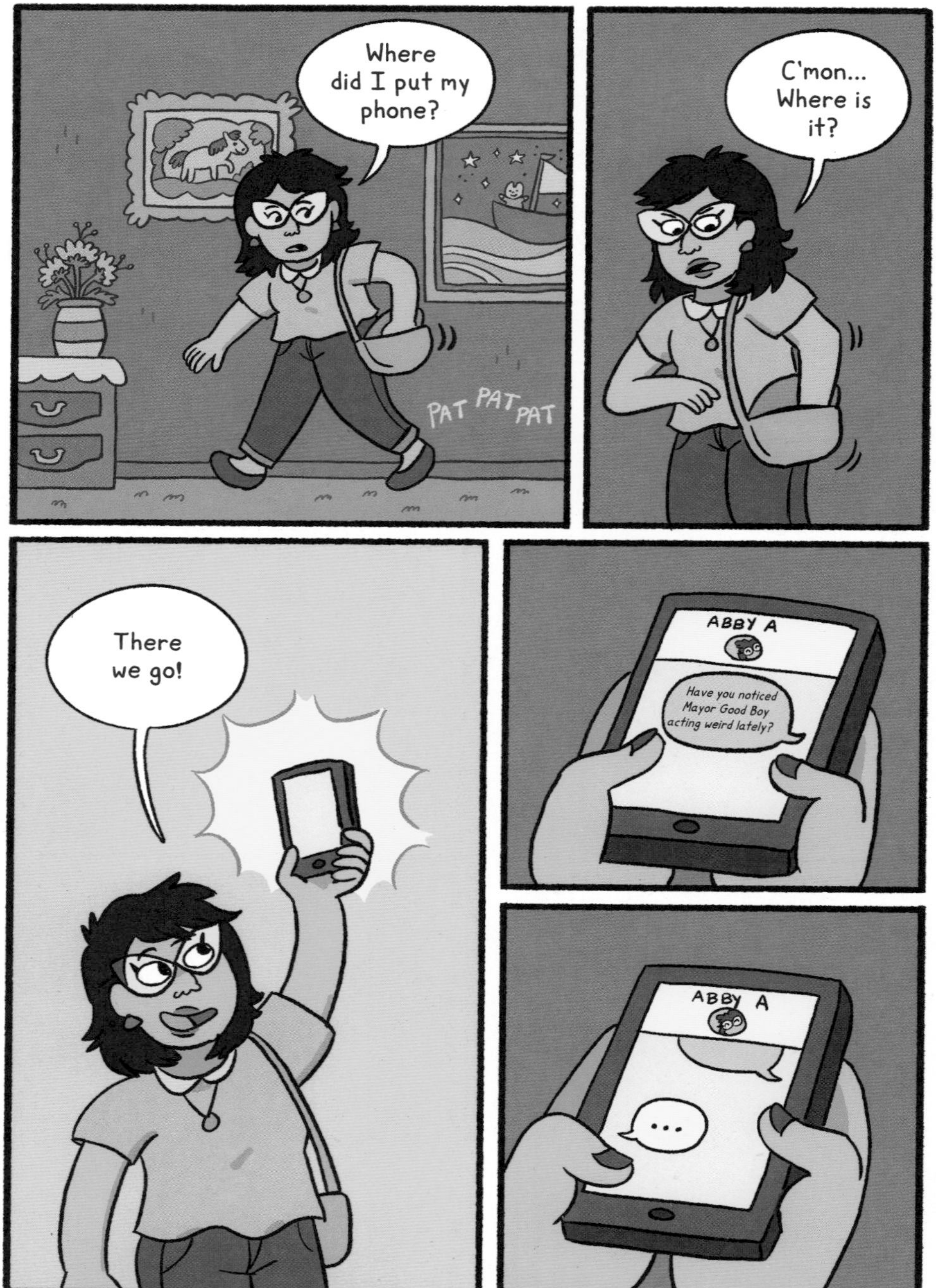
Where did I put my phone?
PAT PAT PAT
C'mon... Where is it?
There we go!
ABBY A
Have you noticed Mayor Good Boy acting weird lately?
ABBY A
...

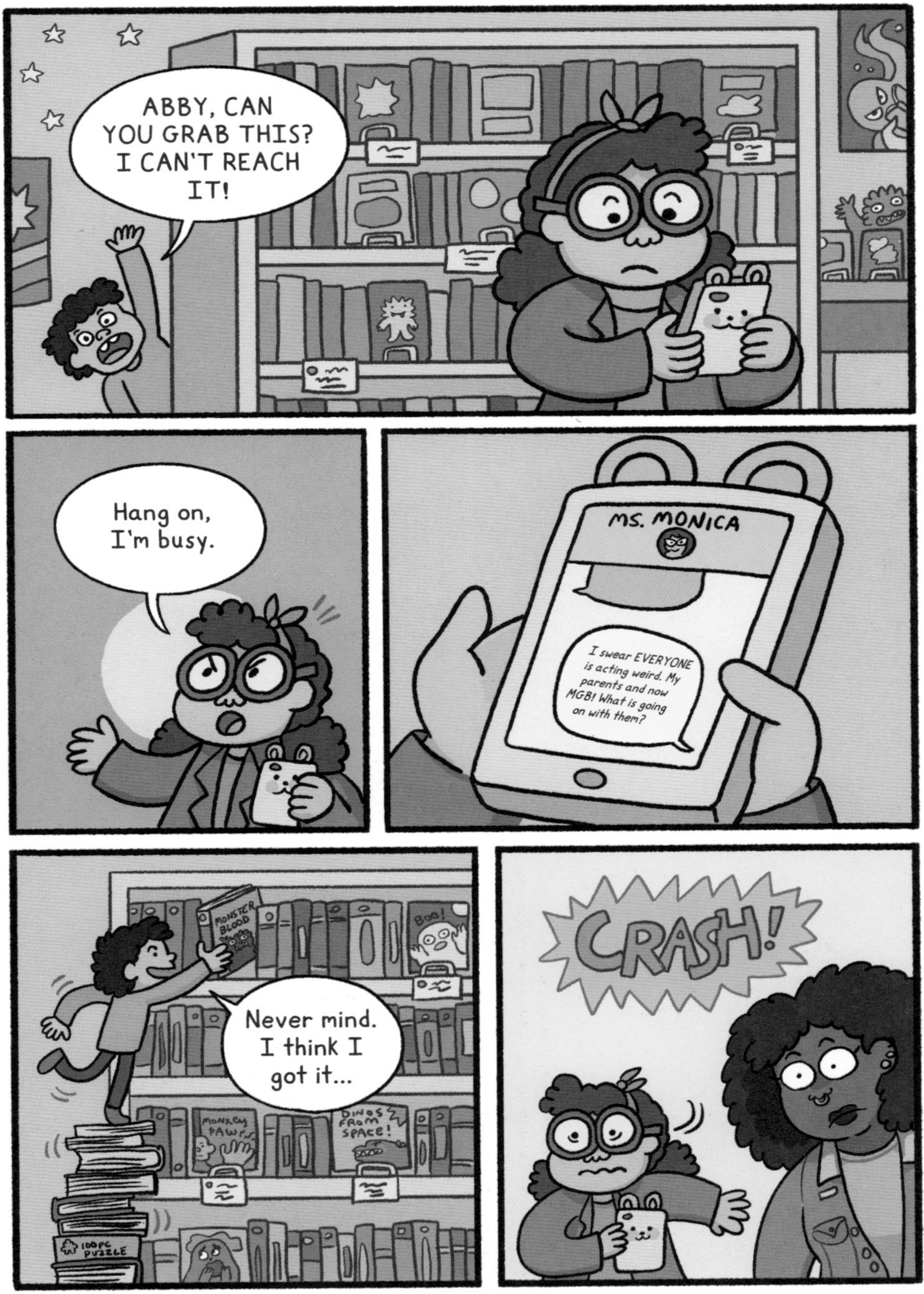
ABBY, CAN YOU GRAB THIS? I CAN'T REACH IT!
Hang on, I'm busy.
MS. MONICA
I swear EVERYONE is acting weird. My parents and now MGB! What is going on with them?
MONSTER BLOOD
BOO!
Never mind. I think I got it...
MONKEY PAW
DINOS FROM SPACE!
100 PC PUZZLE
CRASH!

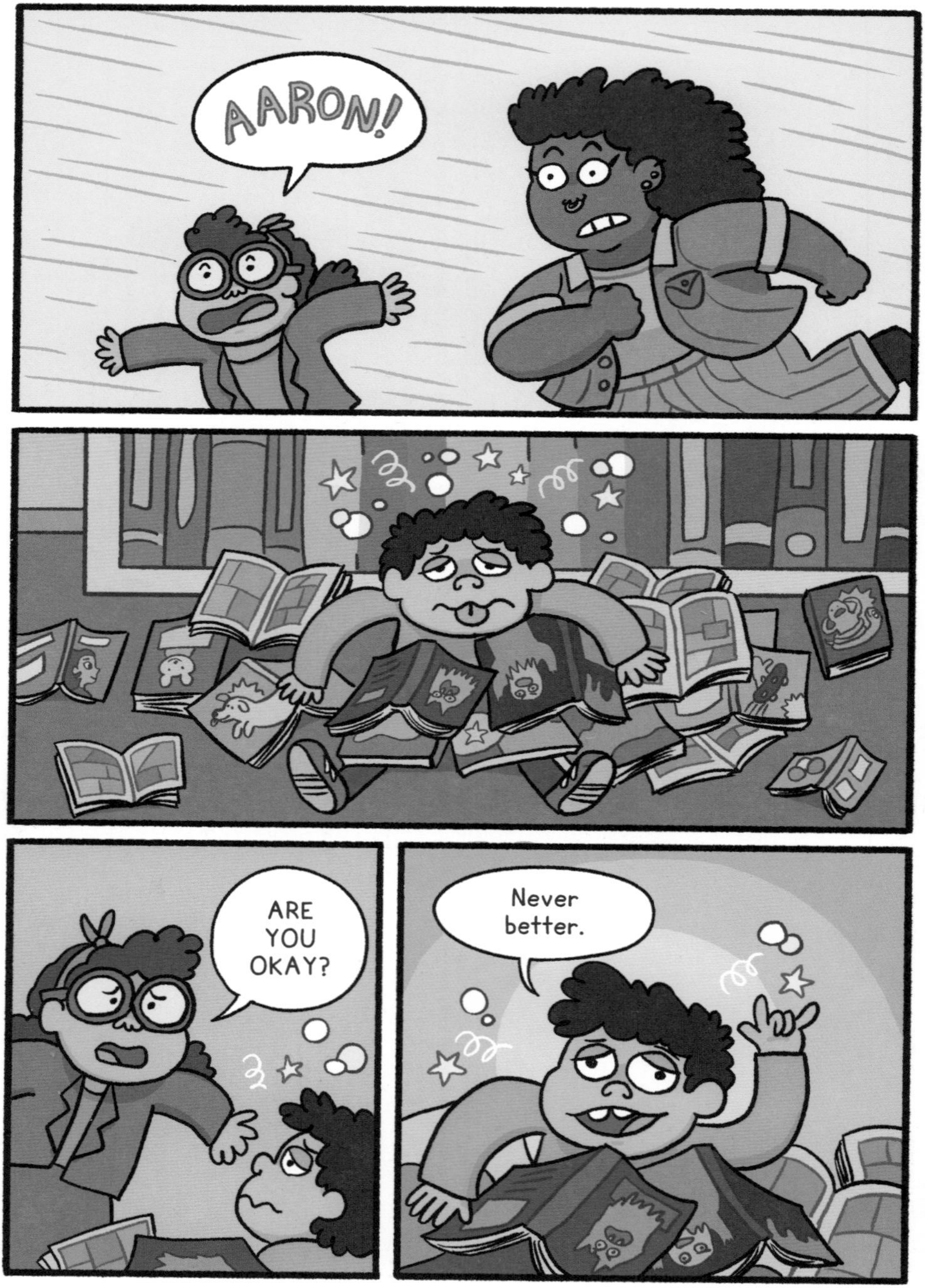
AARON!
ARE YOU OKAY?
Never better.

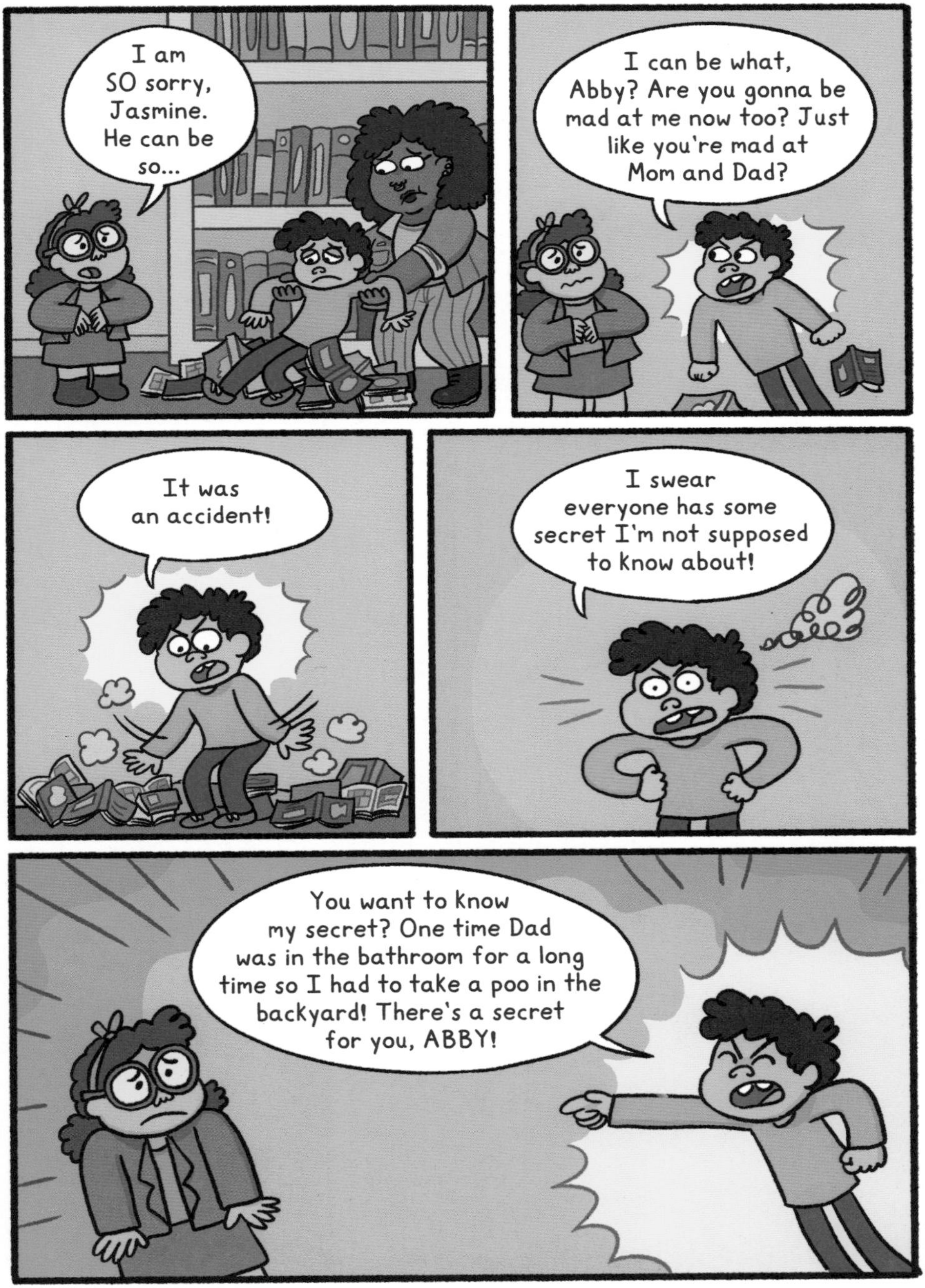
I am SO sorry, Jasmine. He can be so...
I can be what, Abby? Are you gonna be mad at me now too? Just like you're mad at Mom and Dad?
It was an accident!
I swear everyone has some secret I'm not supposed to know about!
You want to know my secret? One time Dad was in the bathroom for a long time so I had to take a poo in the backyard! There's a secret for you, ABBY!

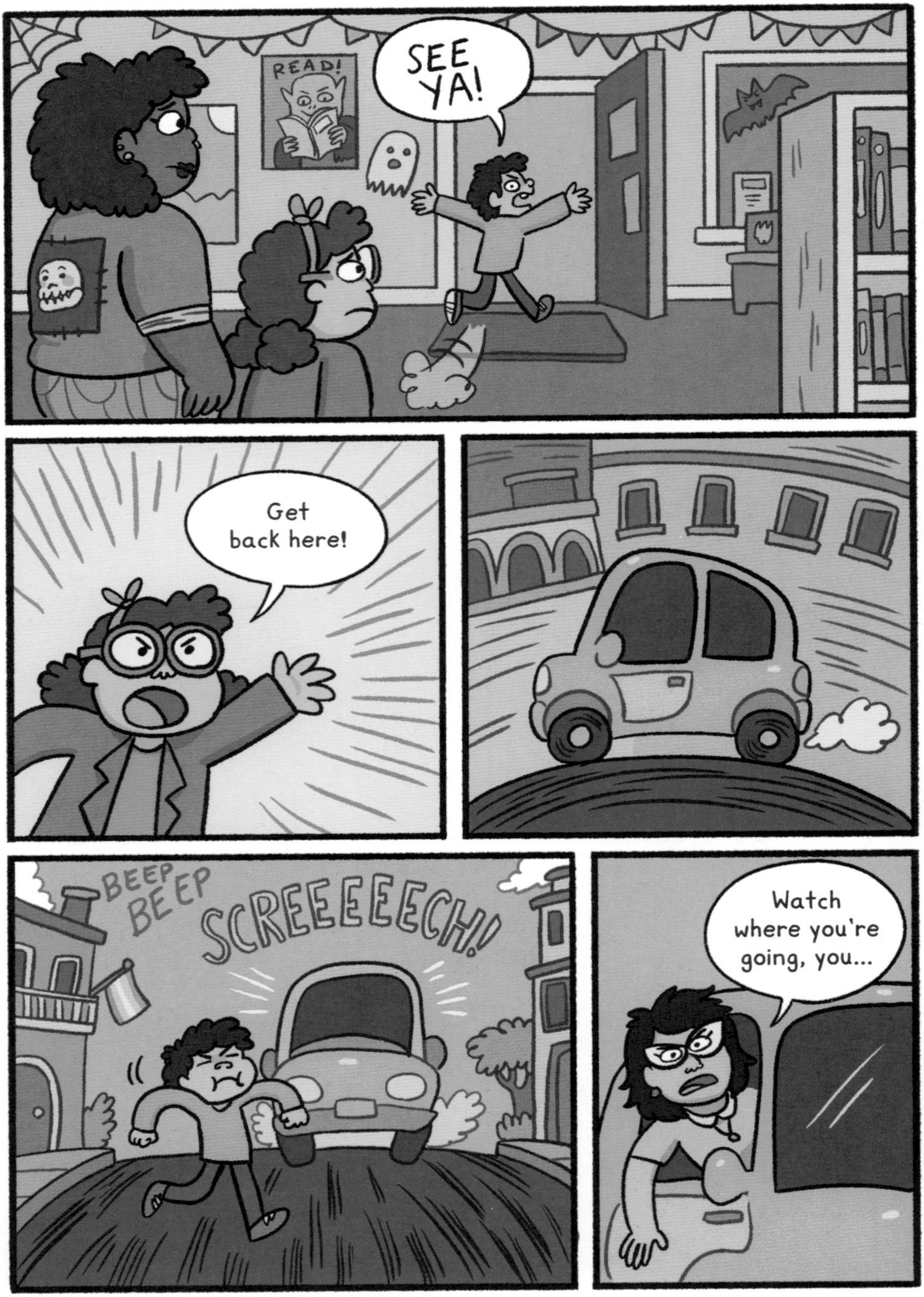
READ!
SEE YA!
Get back here!
BEEP BEEP
SCREEEEEECH!
Watch where you're going, you...

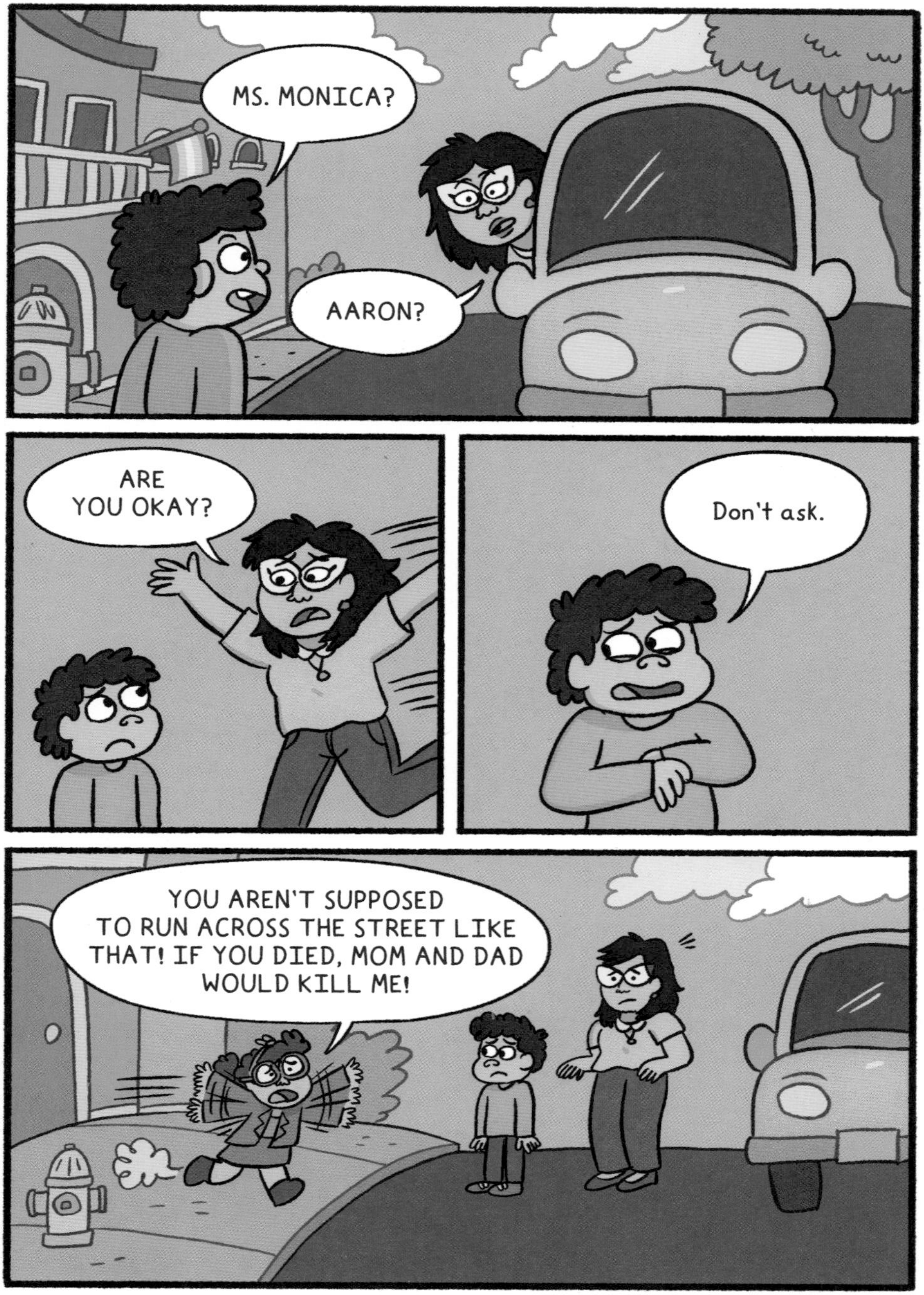
MS. MONICA?
AARON?
ARE YOU OKAY?
Don't ask.
YOU AREN'T SUPPOSED TO RUN ACROSS THE STREET LIKE THAT! IF YOU DIED, MOM AND DAD WOULD KILL ME!

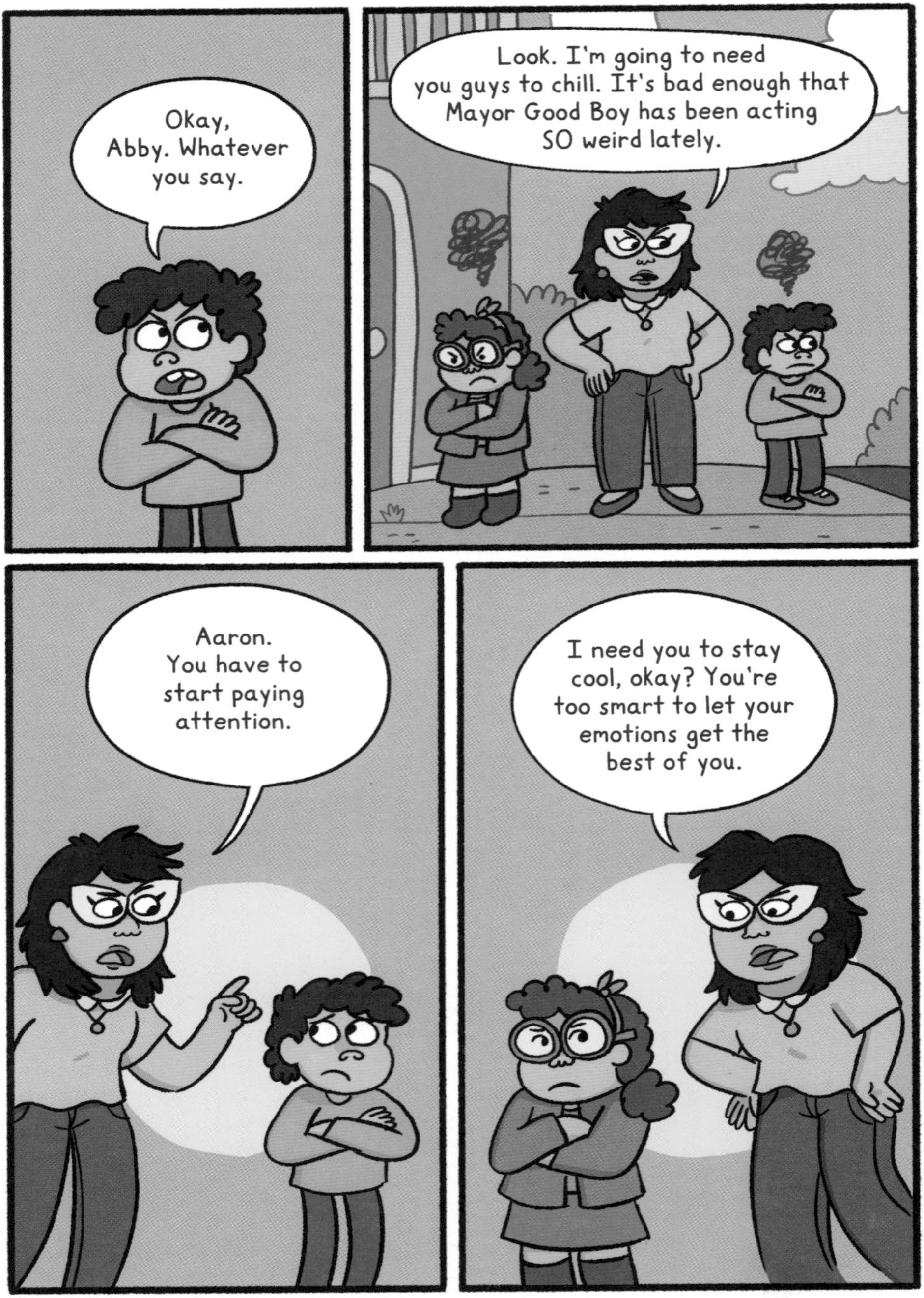
Okay, Abby. Whatever you say.
Look. I'm going to need you guys to chill. It's bad enough that Mayor Good Boy has been acting SO weird lately.
Aaron. You have to start paying attention.
I need you to stay cool, okay? You're too smart to let your emotions get the best of you.

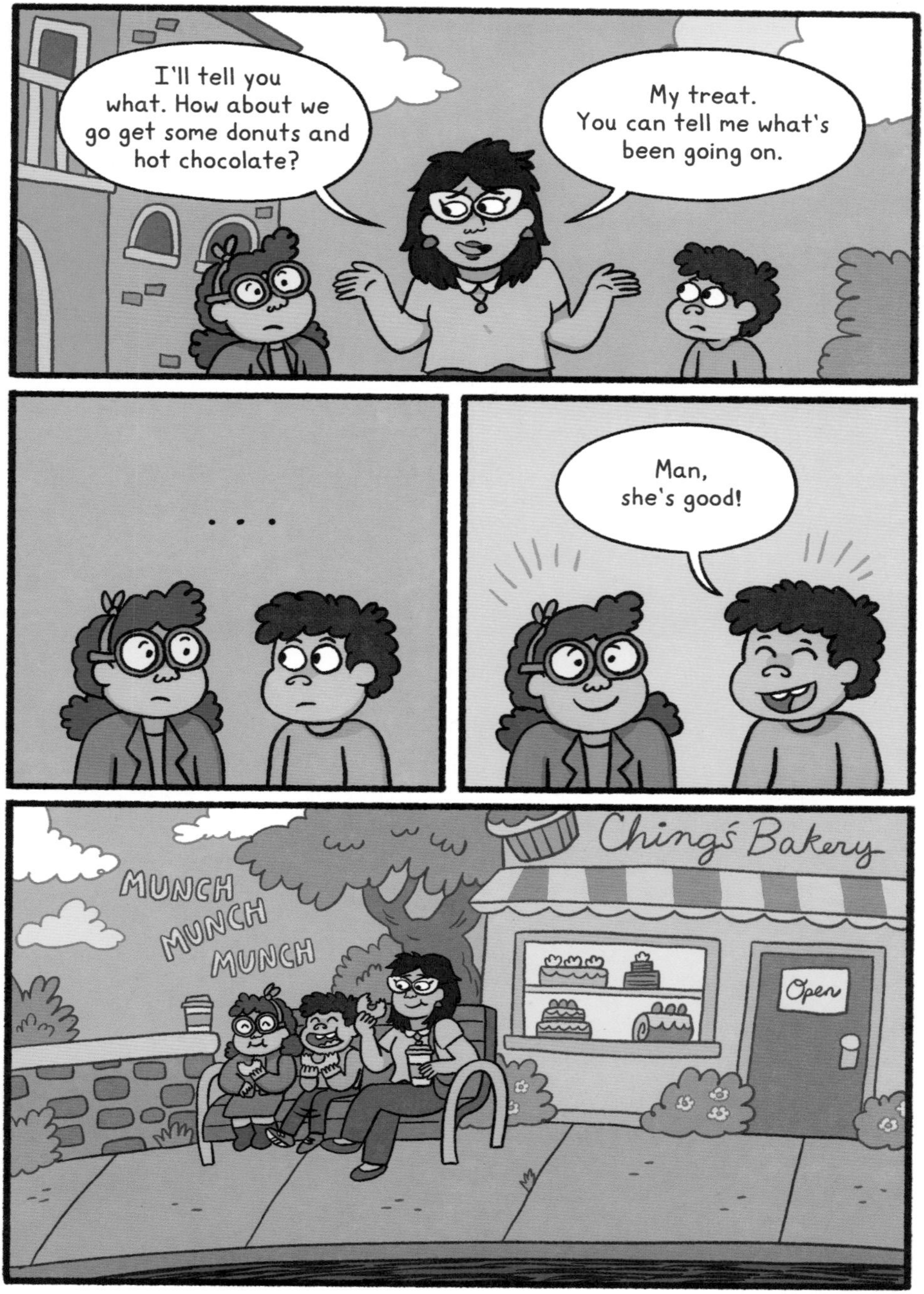
I'll tell you what. How about we go get some donuts and hot chocolate?
My treat. You can tell me what's been going on.
. . .
Man, she's good!
Ching's Bakery
MUNCH
MUNCH
MUNCH
Open

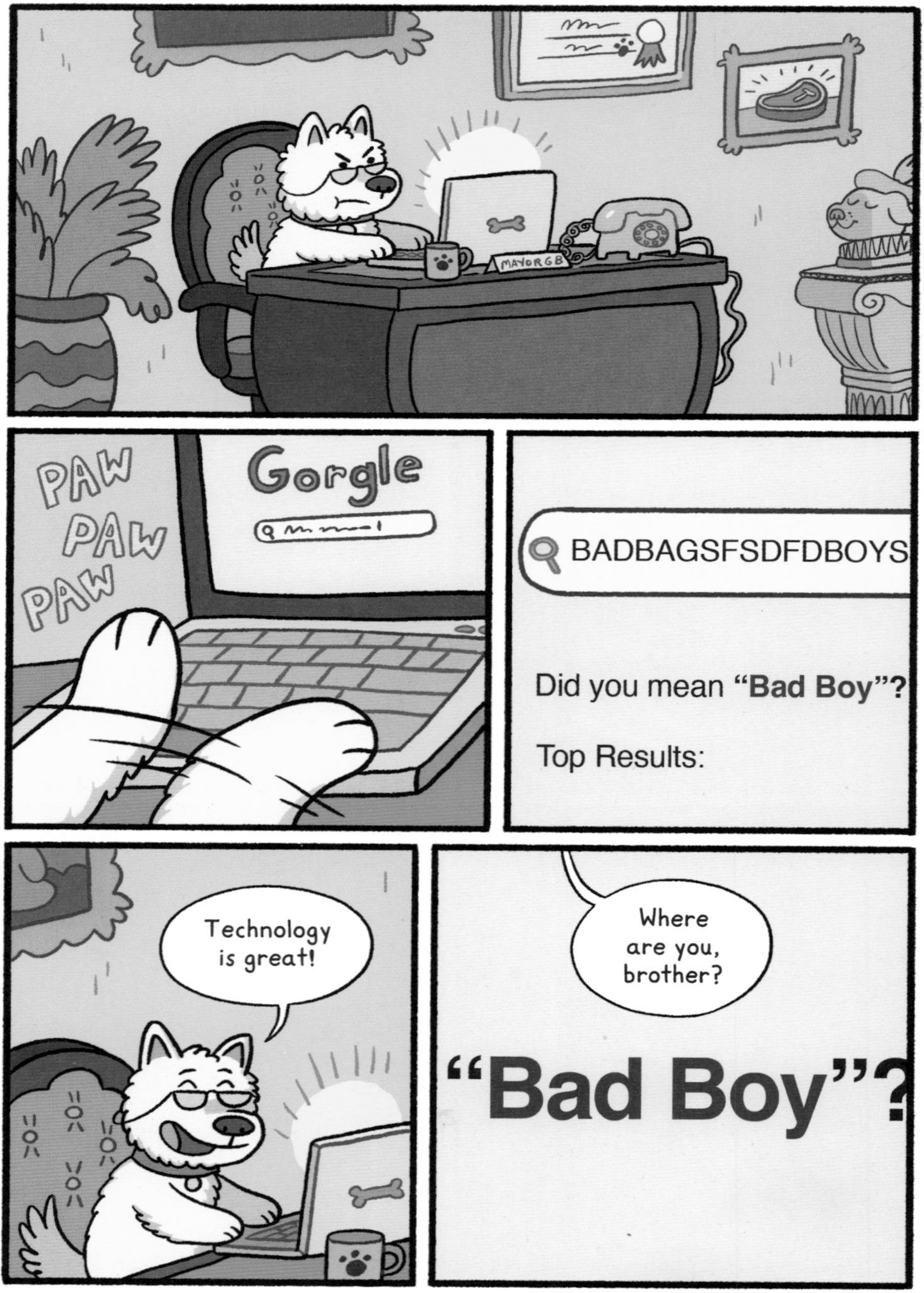
MAYOR GB
PAW
PAW
PAW
Gorgle
BADBAGSFSDFDBOYS
Did you mean "**Bad Boy**"?
Top Results:
Technology is great!
Where are you, brother?
"Bad Boy"?

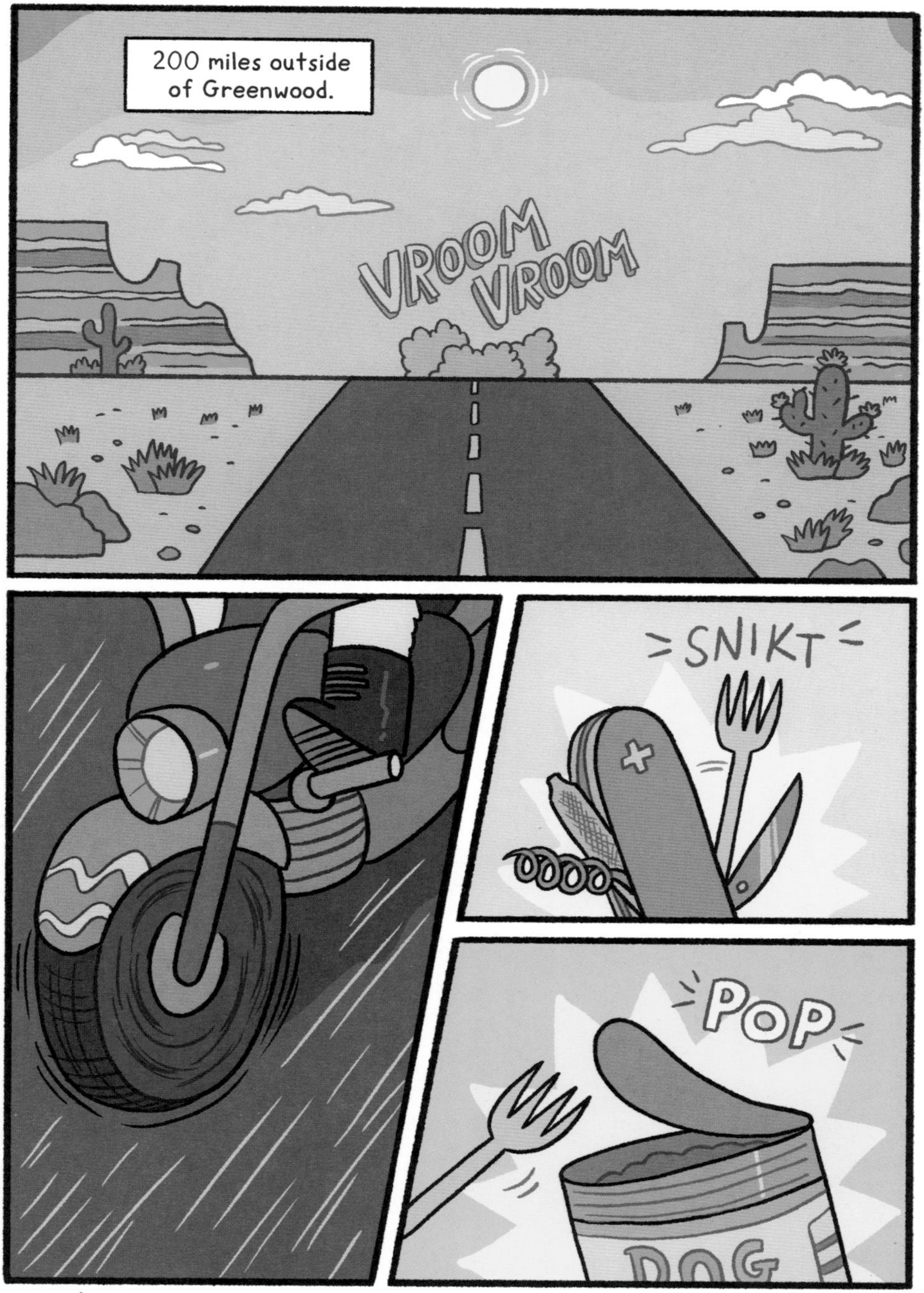

200 miles outside of Greenwood.
VROOM VROOM
SNIKT
POP
DOG

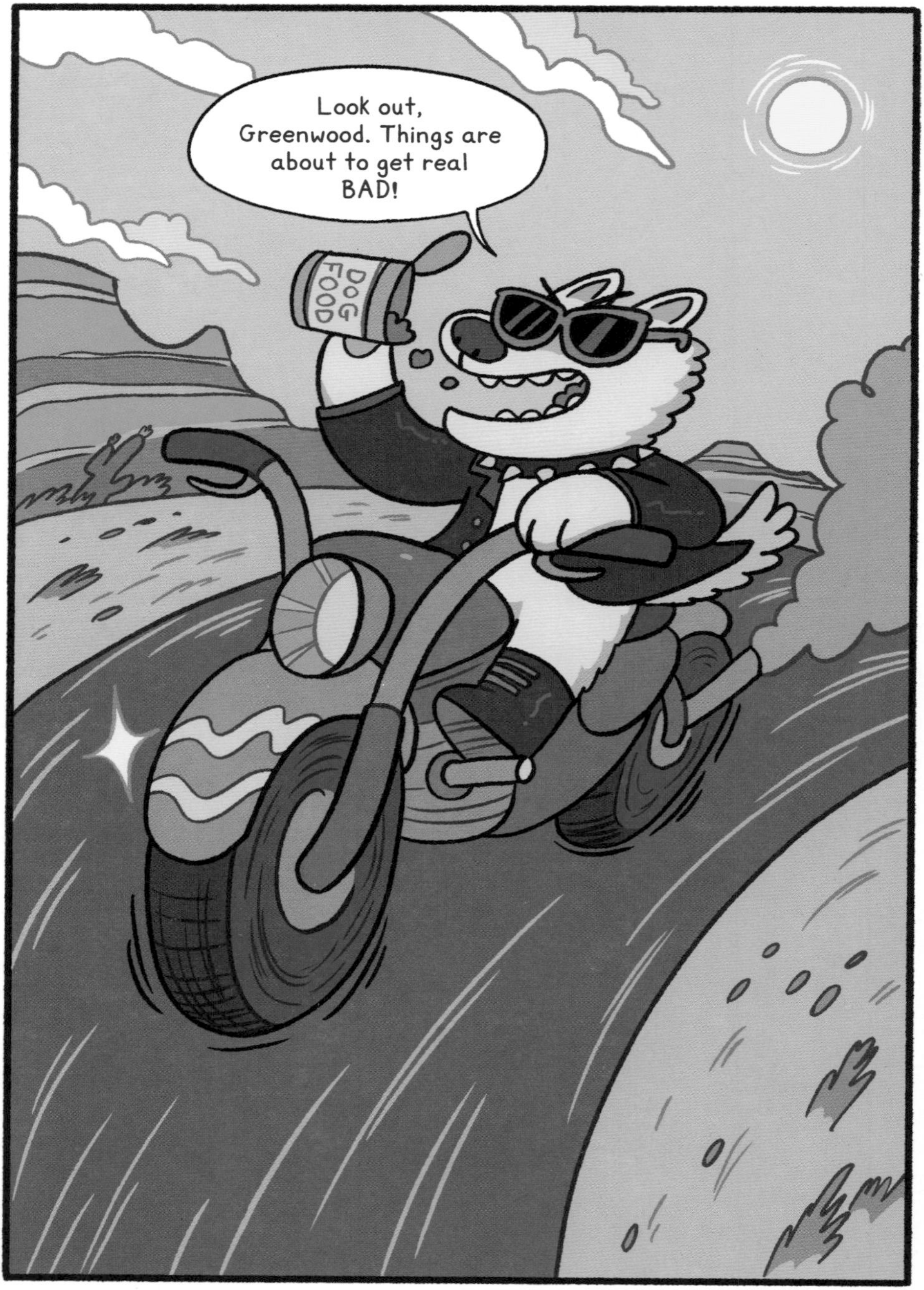
Look out, Greenwood. Things are about to get real BAD!
DOG FOOD

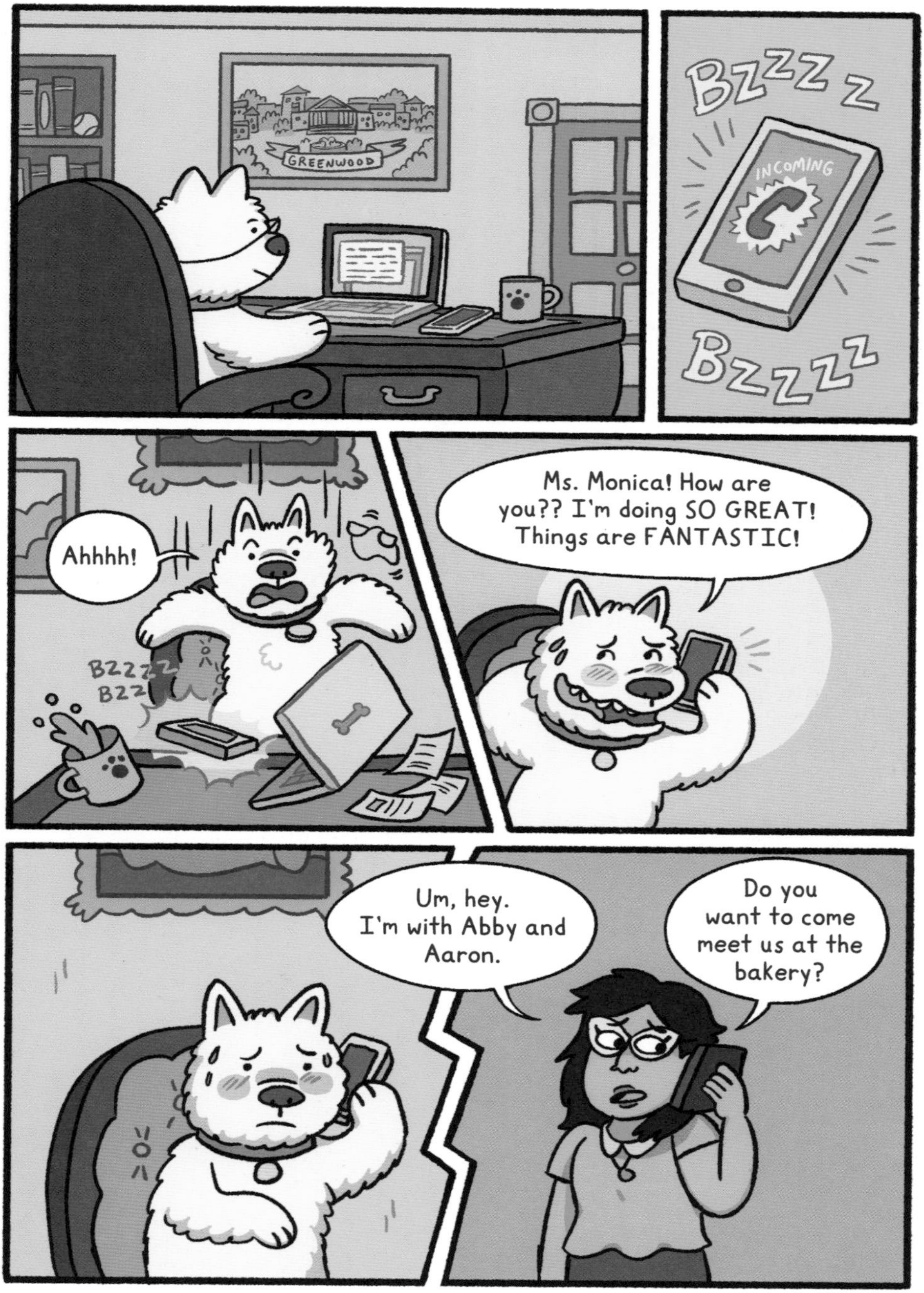
GREENWOOD
BZZZ Z
INCOMING
BZZZZZ
Ahhhh!
BZZZZ
BZZ
Ms. Monica! How are you?? I'm doing SO GREAT! Things are FANTASTIC!
Um, hey. I'm with Abby and Aaron.
Do you want to come meet us at the bakery?

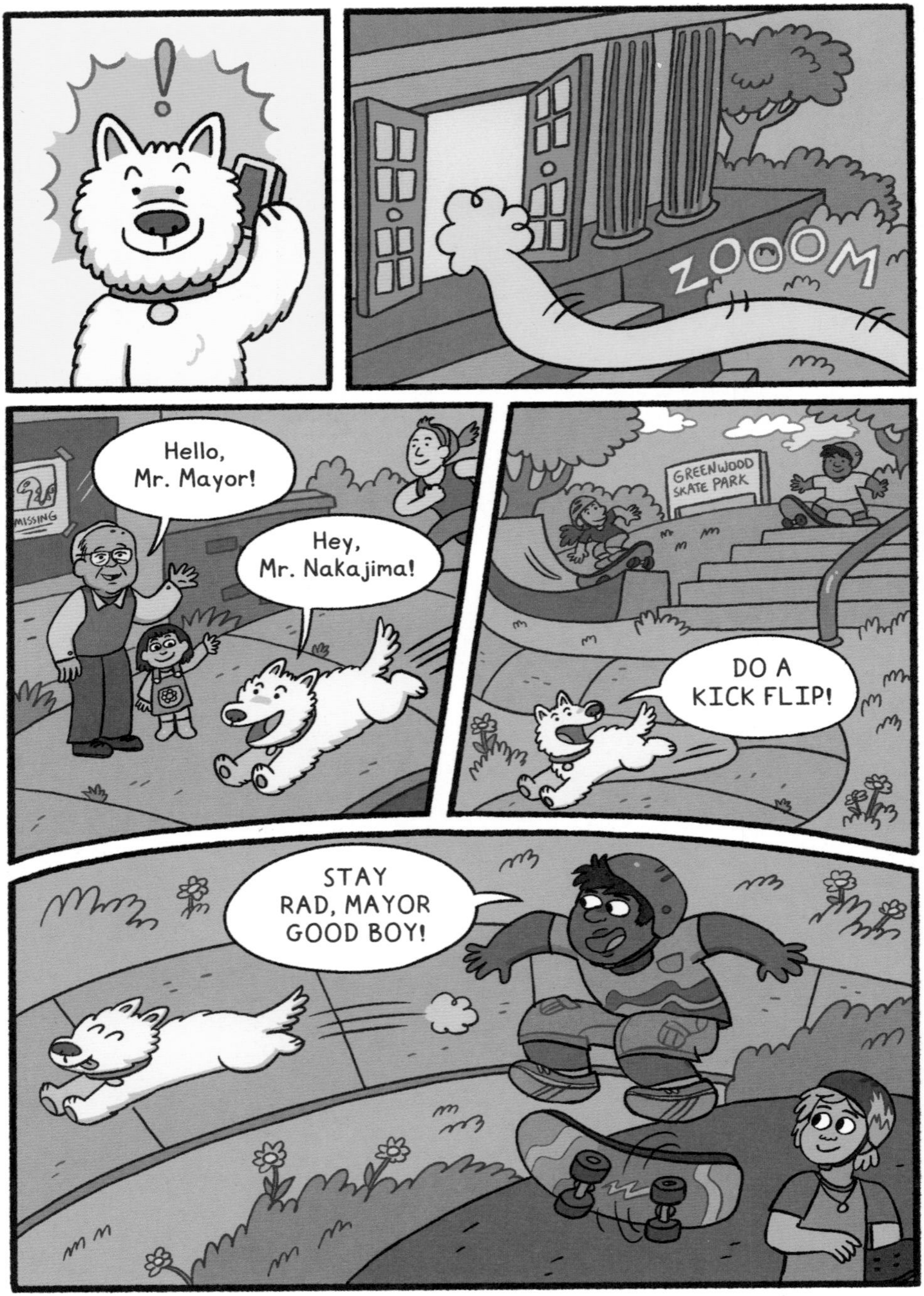
!
ZOOOM
Hello, Mr. Mayor!
MISSING
Hey, Mr. Nakajima!
GREENWOOD SKATE PARK
DO A KICK FLIP!
STAY RAD, MAYOR GOOD BOY!

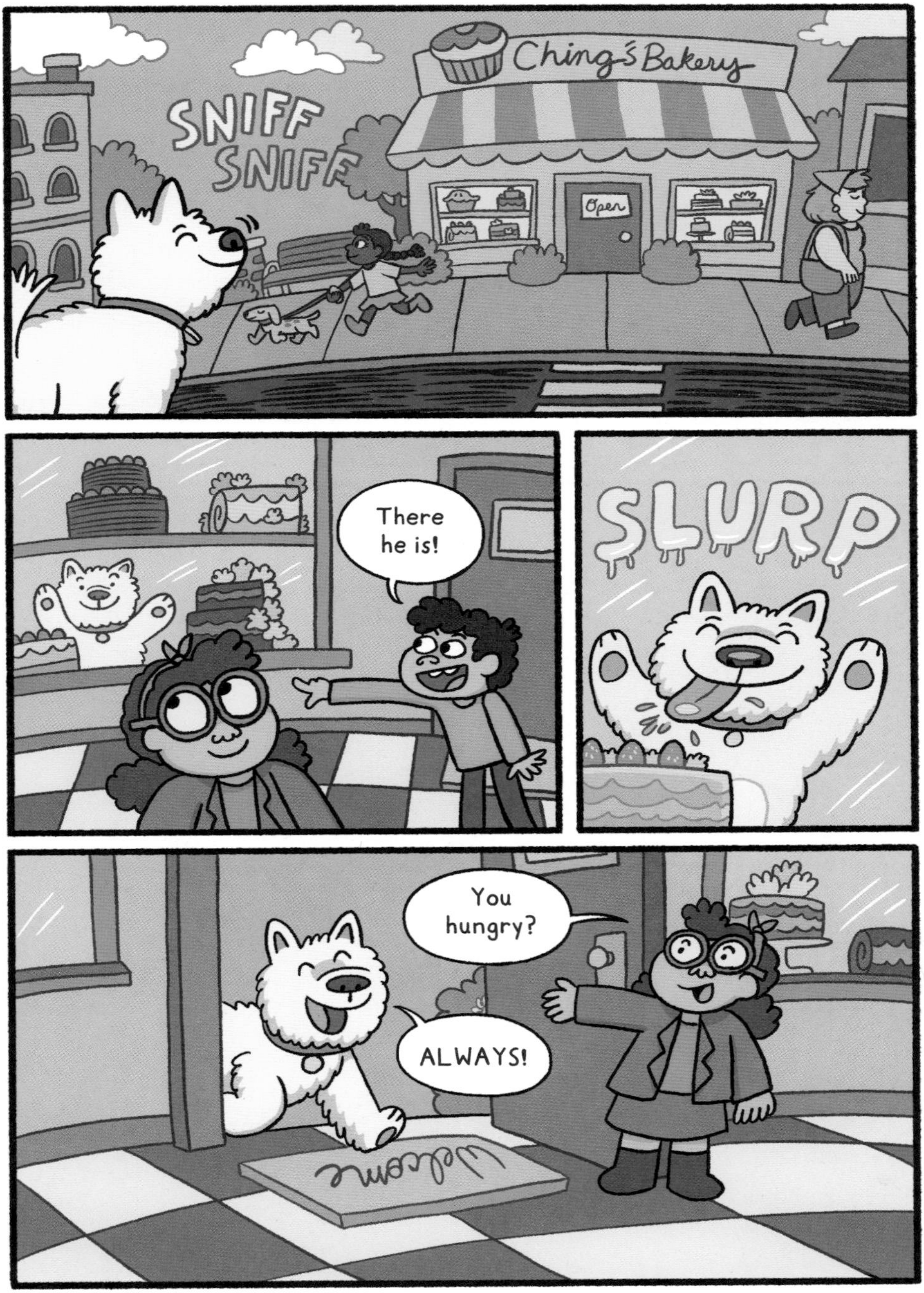
Ching's Bakery
SNIFF
SNIFF
Open
There he is!
SLURP
You hungry?
ALWAYS!

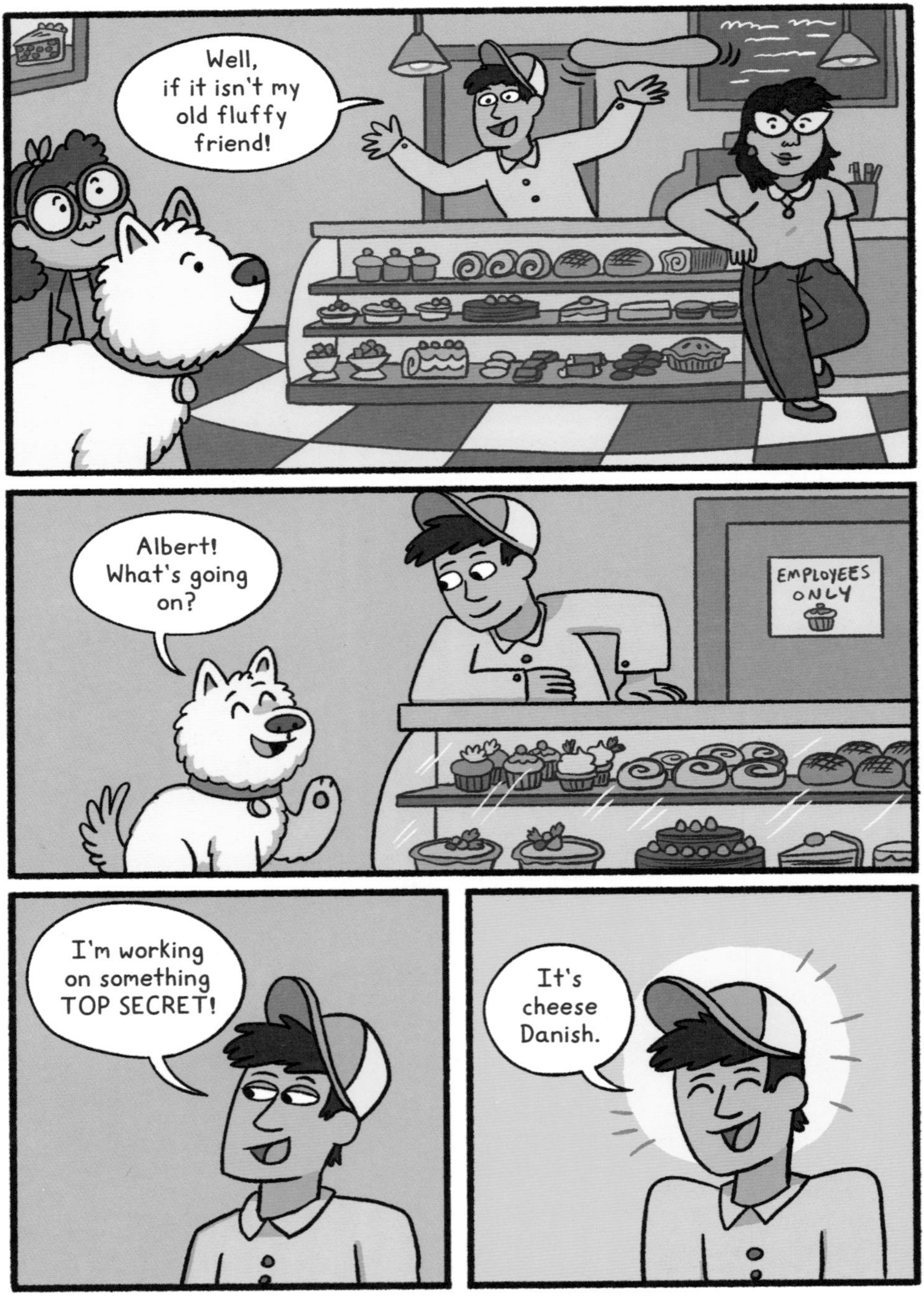
Well, if it isn't my old fluffy friend!
Albert! What's going on?
EMPLOYEES ONLY
I'm working on something TOP SECRET!
It's cheese Danish.

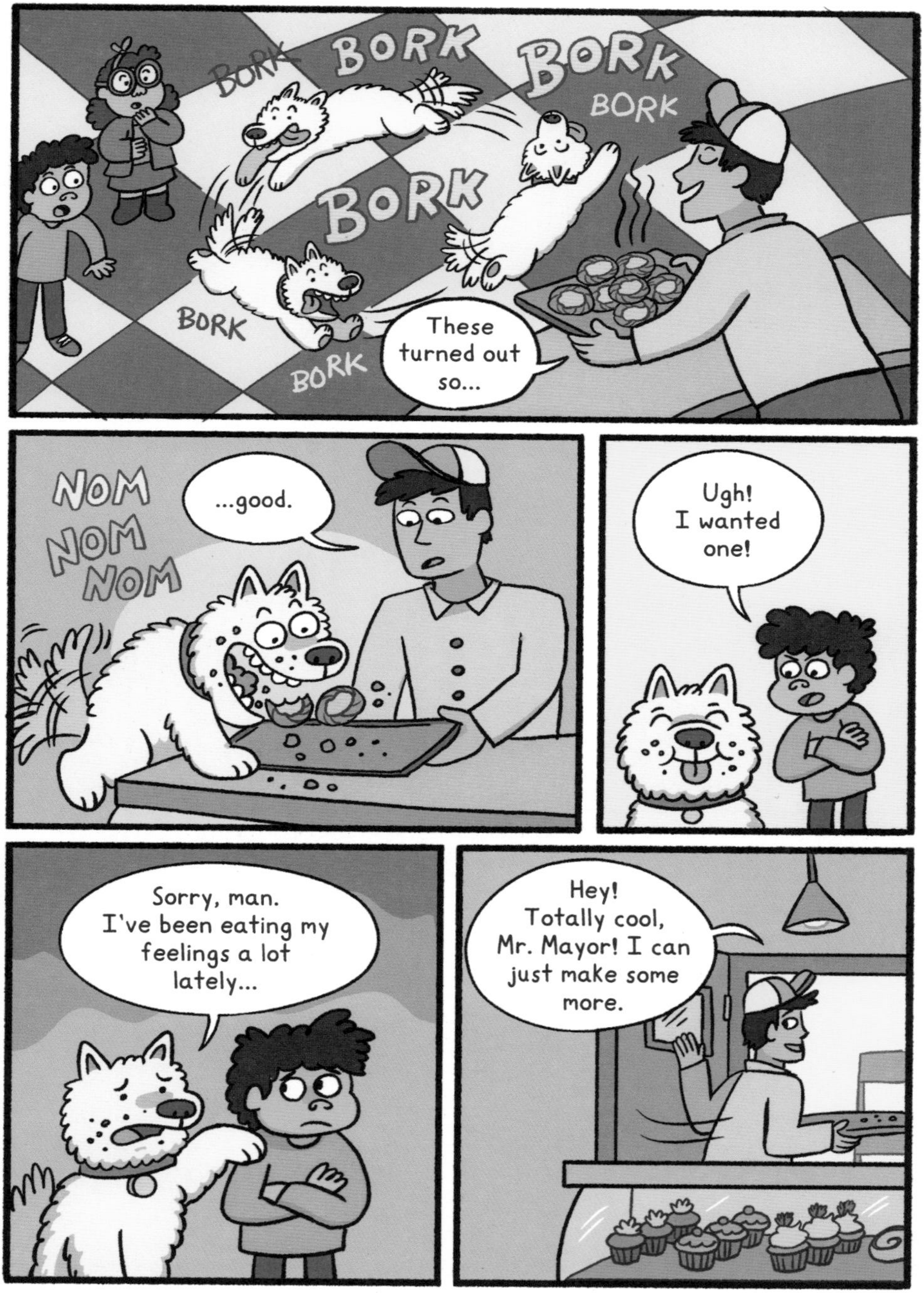
BORK
BORK
BORK
BORK
BORK
BORK
BORK
These turned out so...
NOM NOM NOM
...good.
Ugh! I wanted one!
Sorry, man. I've been eating my feelings a lot lately...
Hey! Totally cool, Mr. Mayor! I can just make some more.

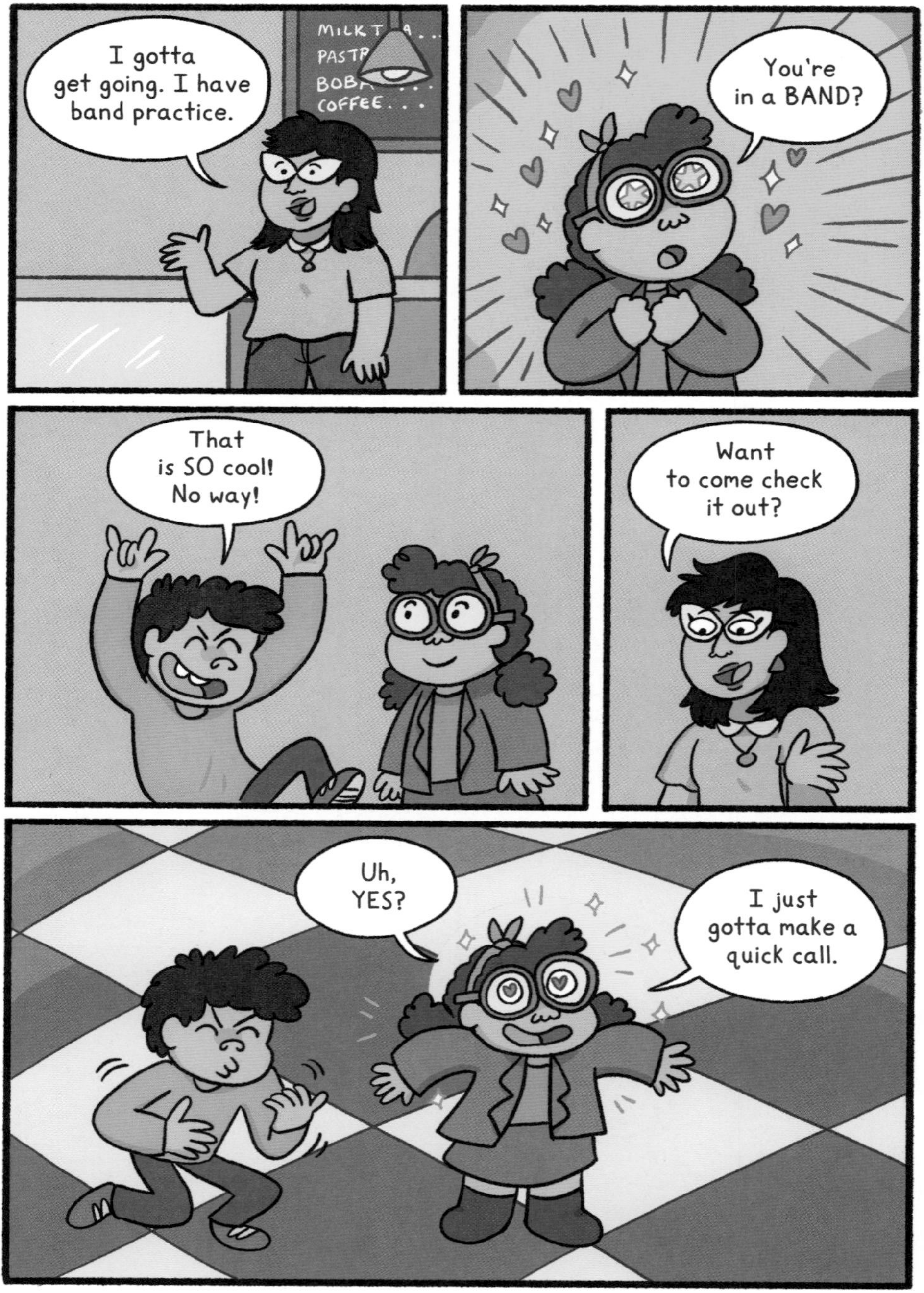
COFFEE. . .
I gotta get going. I have band practice.
You're in a BAND?
That is SO cool! No way!
Want to come check it out?
Uh, YES?
I just gotta make a quick call.

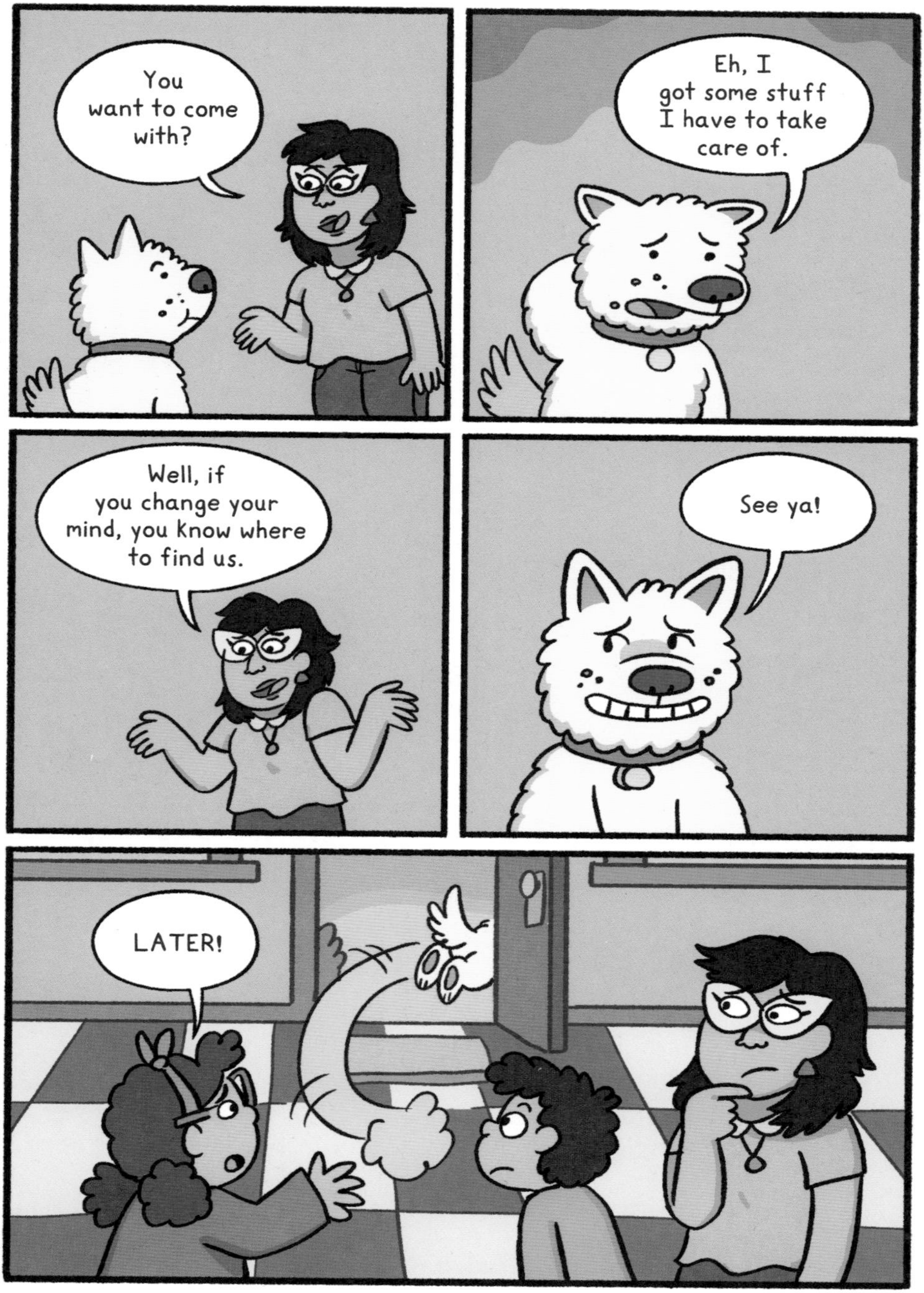
You want to come with?
Eh, I got some stuff I have to take care of.
Well, if you change your mind, you know where to find us.
See ya!
LATER!

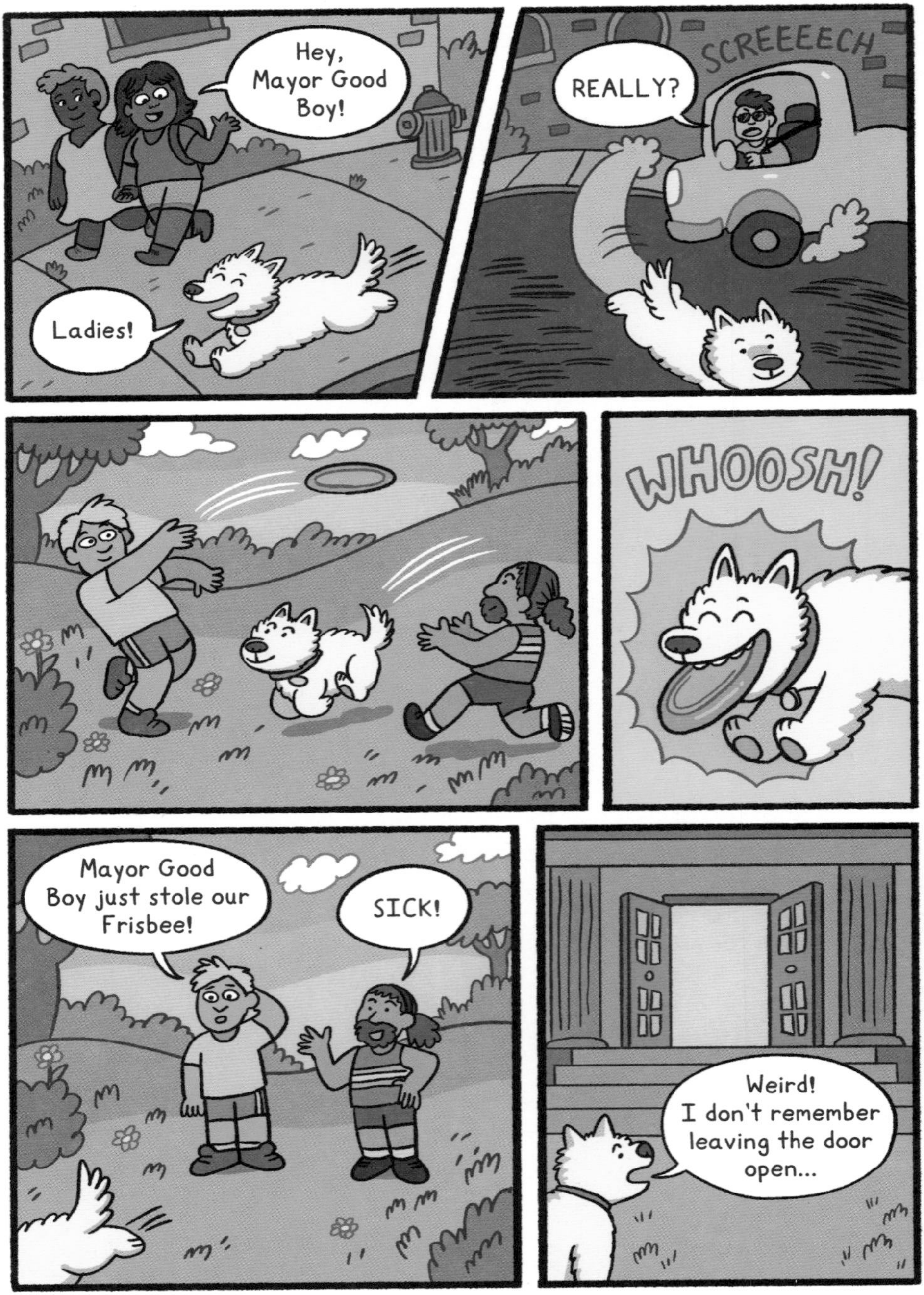
Hey, Mayor Good Boy!
Ladies!
SCREEEECH
REALLY?
WHOOSH!
Mayor Good Boy just stole our Frisbee!
SICK!
Weird! I don't remember leaving the door open...

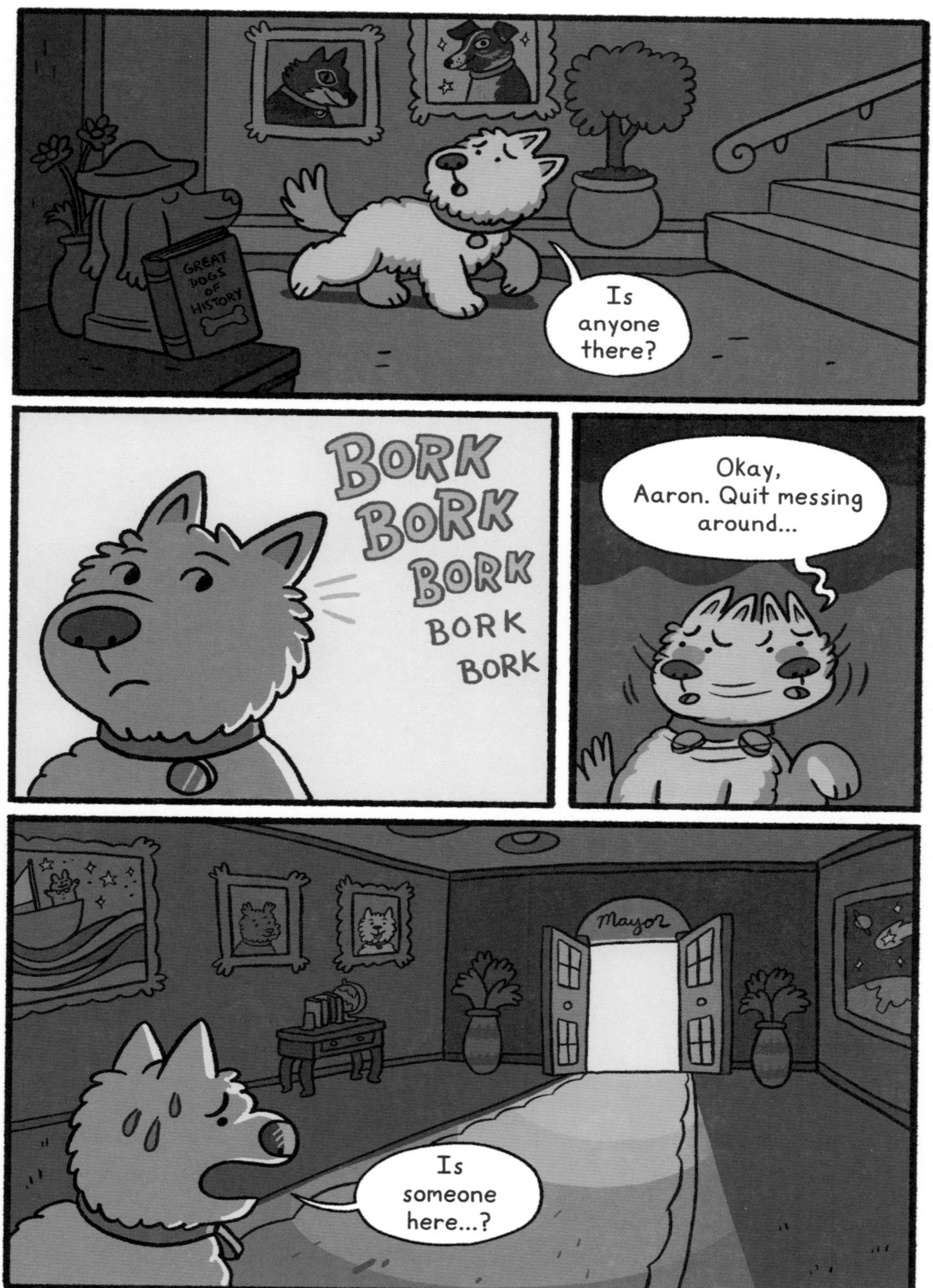
GREAT DOGS OF HISTORY
Is anyone there?
BORK BORK BORK BORK BORK
Okay, Aaron. Quit messing around...
Mayor
Is someone here...?

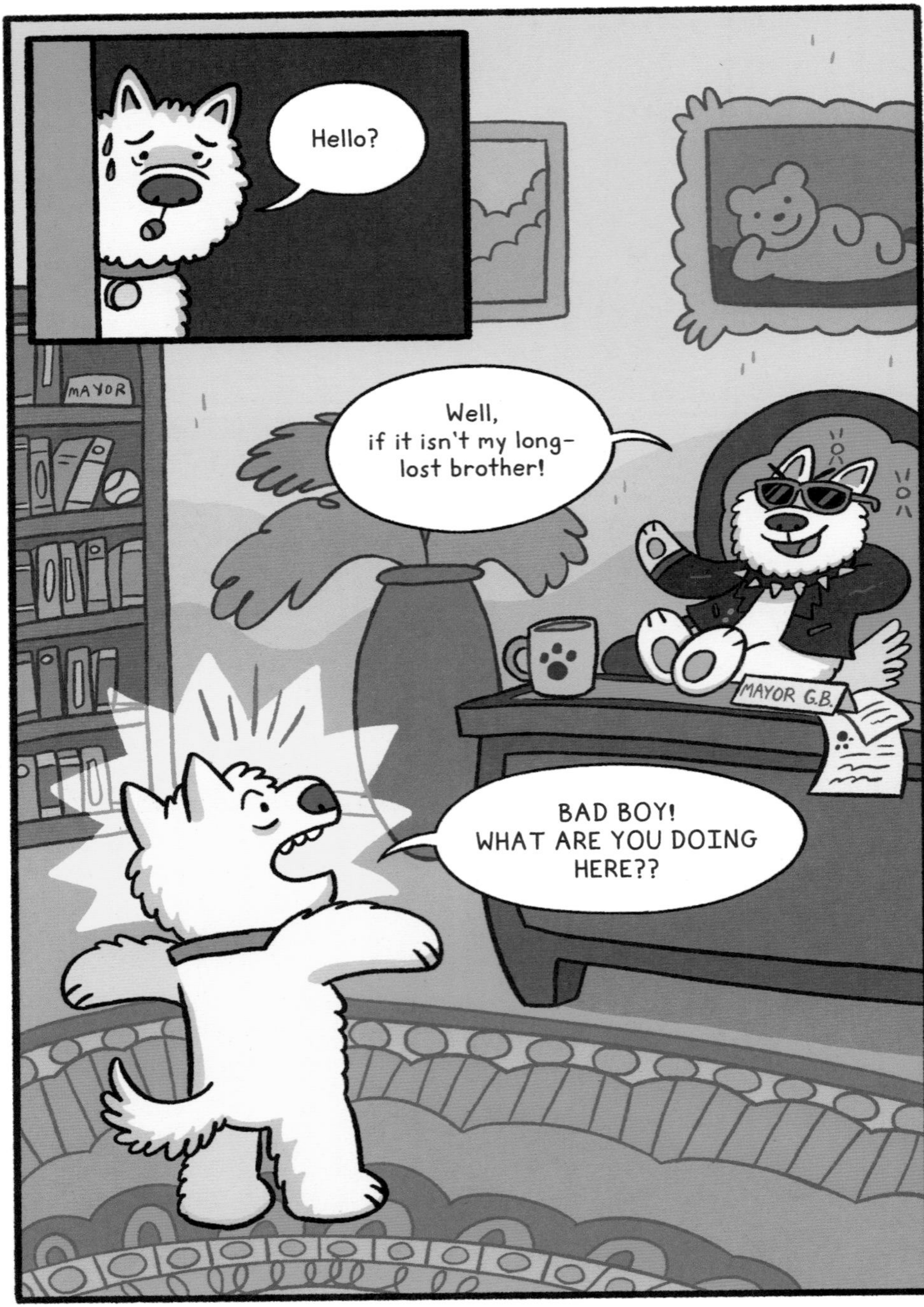
Hello?
Well, if it isn't my long-lost brother!
MAYOR
MAYOR G.B.
BAD BOY! WHAT ARE YOU DOING HERE??

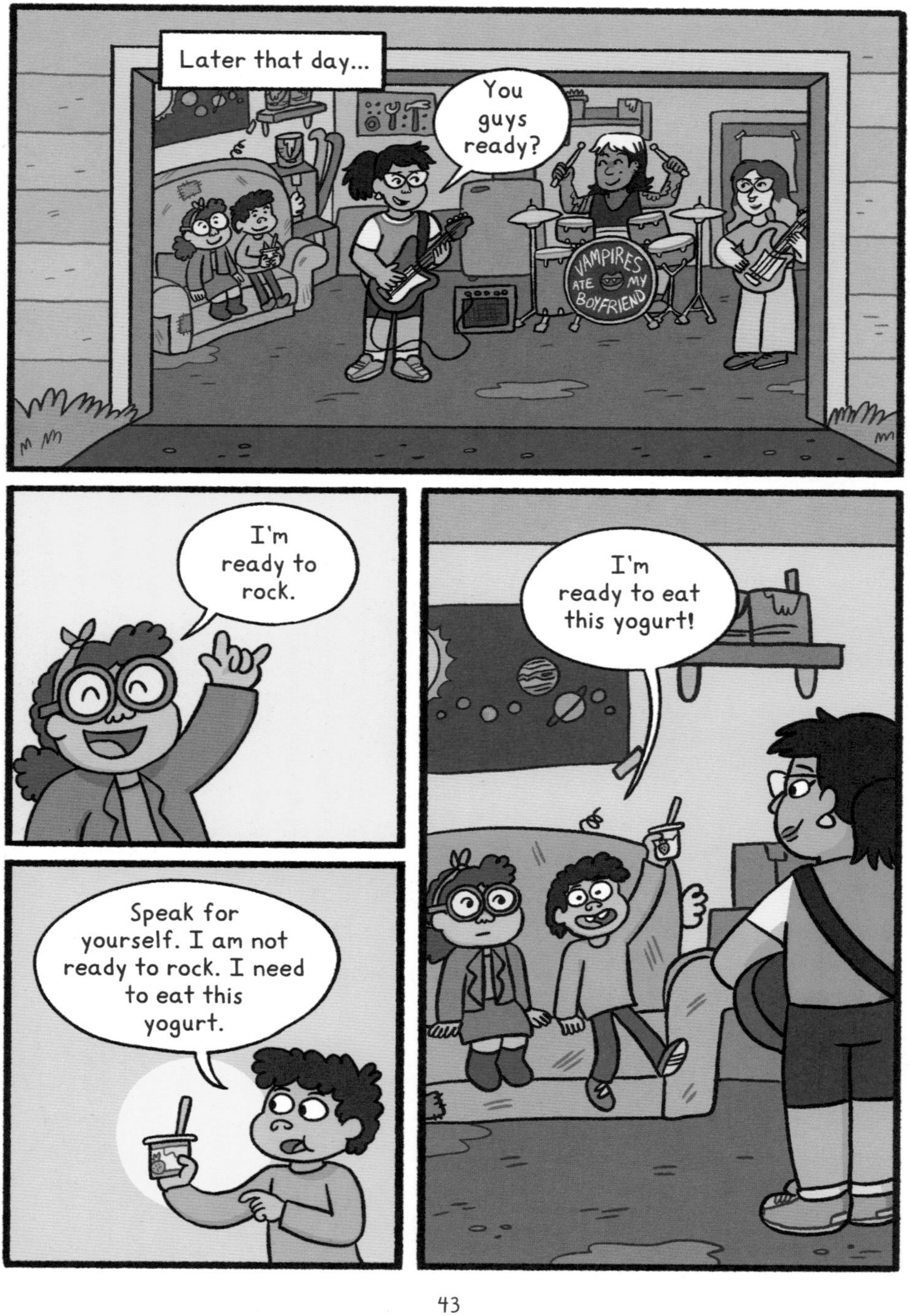
Later that day...
You guys ready?
VAMPIRES ATE MY BOYFRIEND
I'm ready to rock.
Speak for yourself. I am not ready to rock. I need to eat this yogurt.
I'm ready to eat this yogurt!

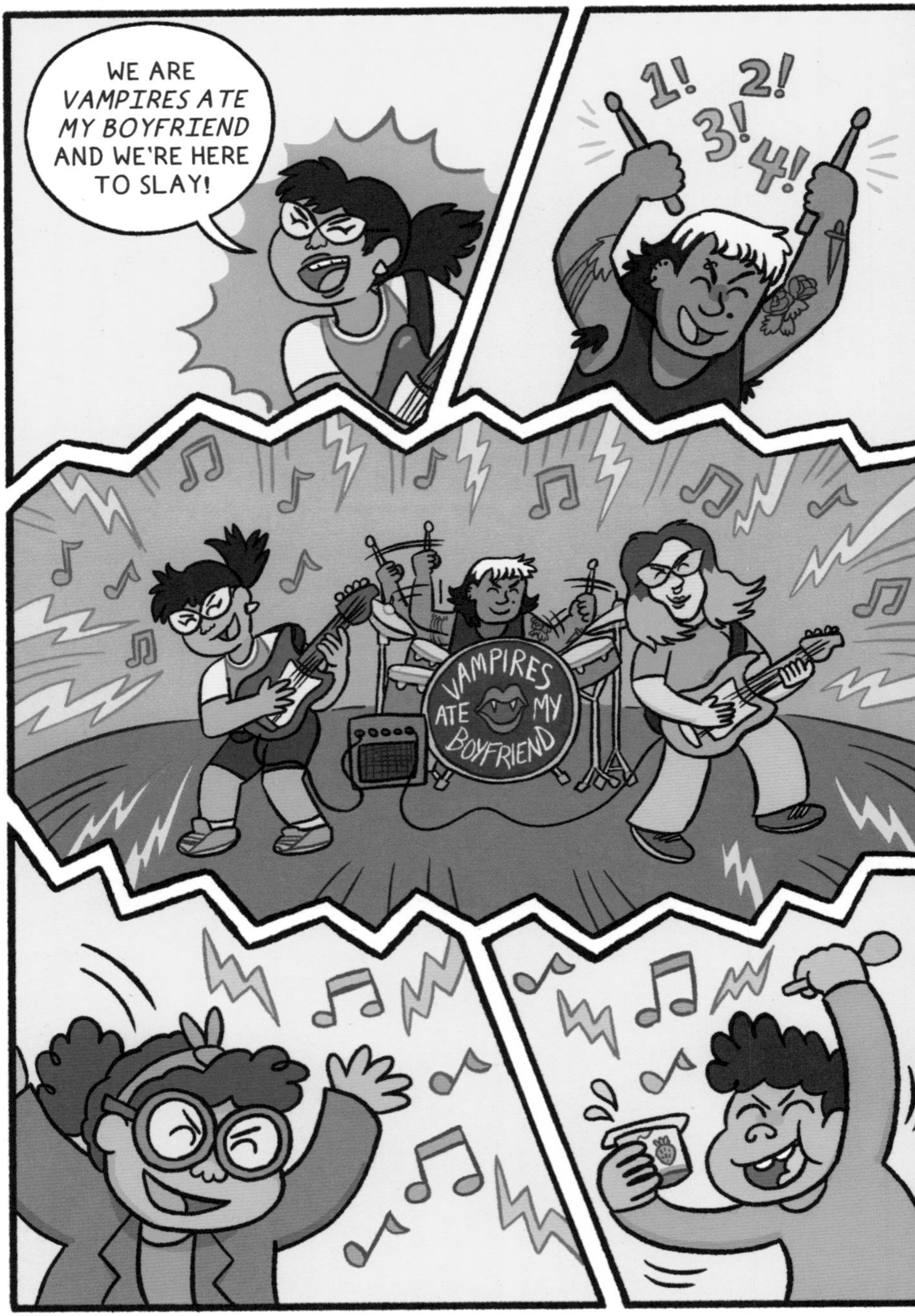
WE ARE VAMPIRES ATE MY BOYFRIEND AND WE'RE HERE TO SLAY!
1! 2! 3! 4!
VAMPIRES ATE MY BOYFRIEND

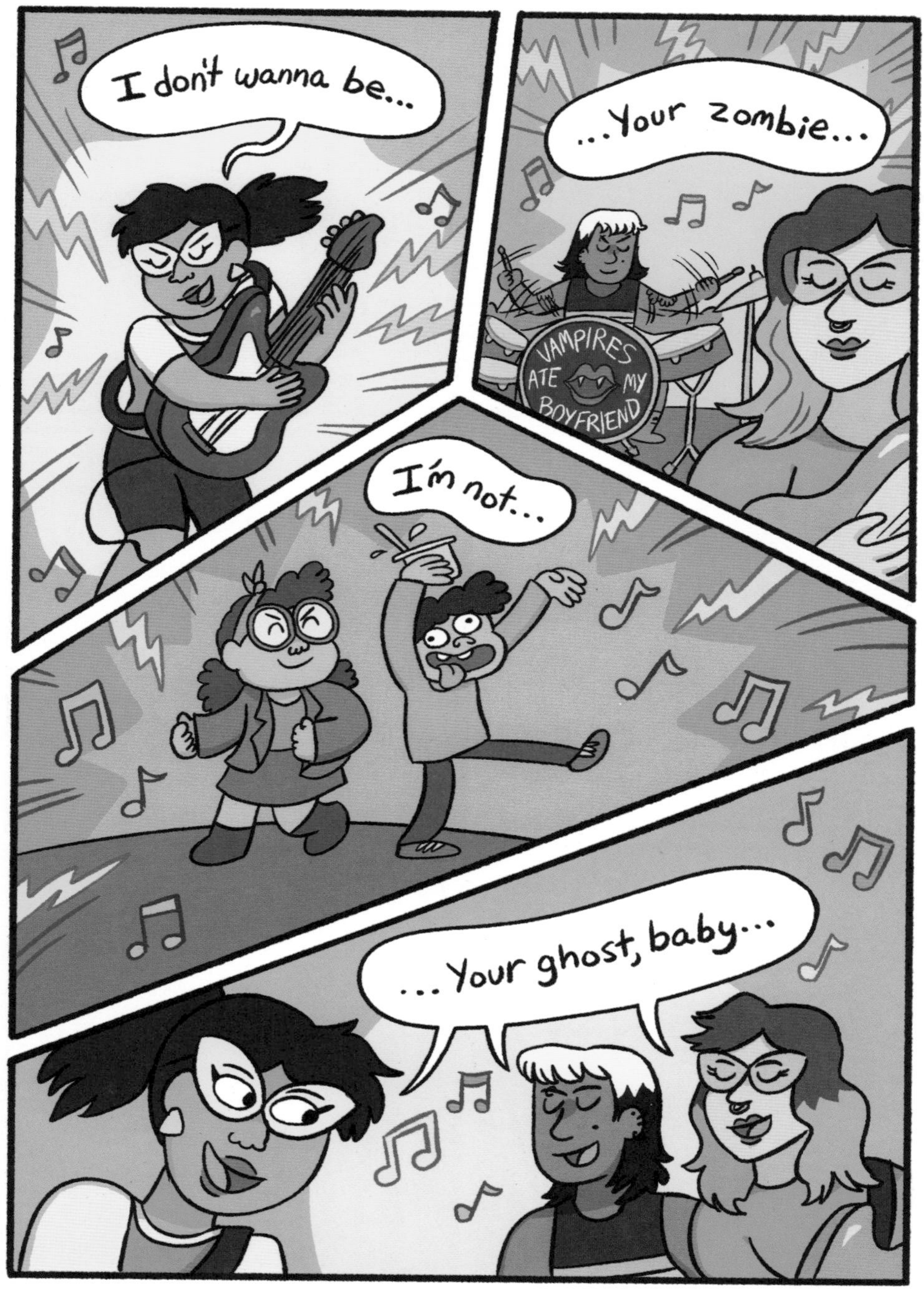
I don't wanna be...
...Your zombie...
VAMPIRES ATE MY BOYFRIEND
I'm not...
...Your ghost, baby...

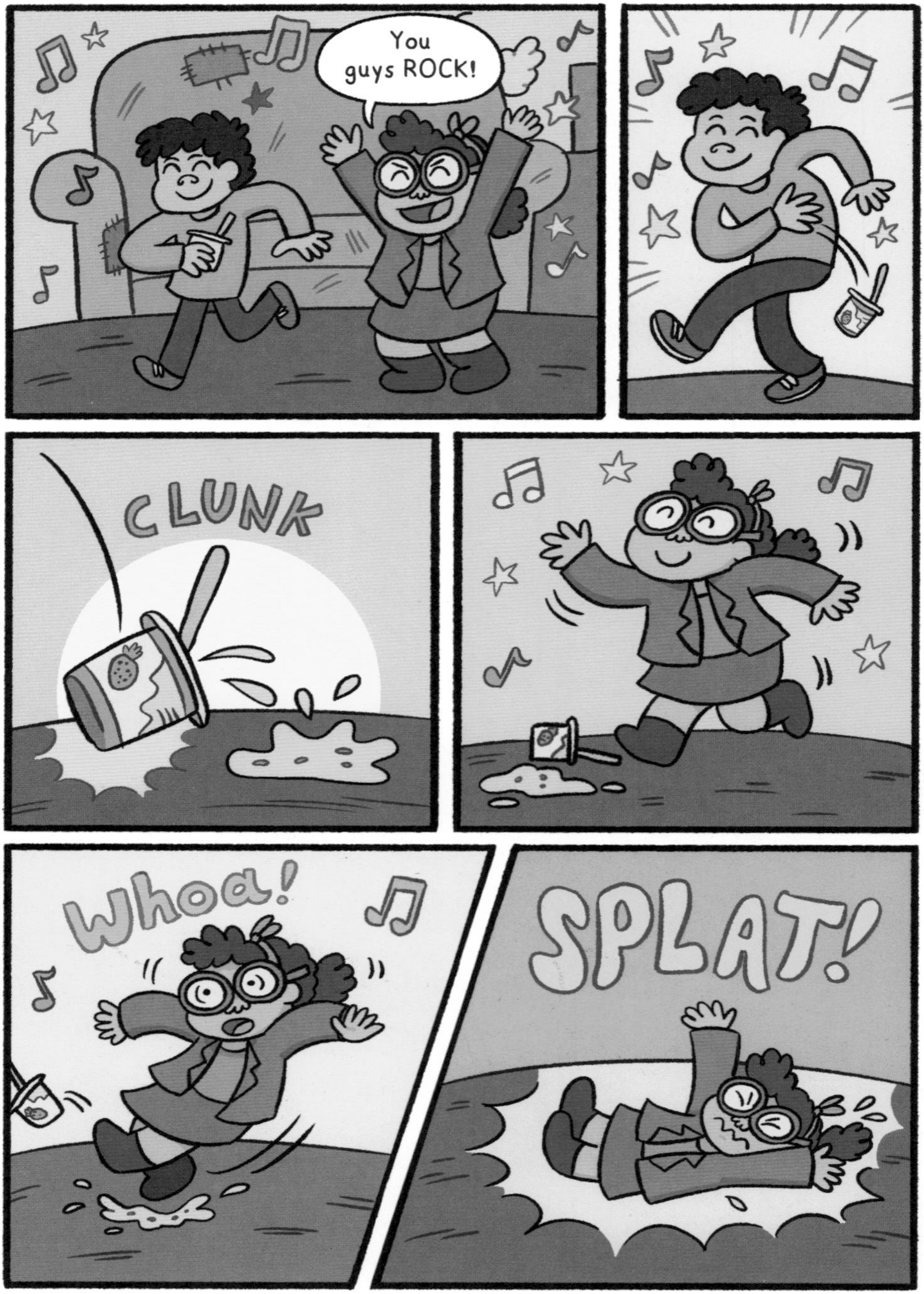
You guys ROCK!
CLUNK
Whoa!
SPLAT!

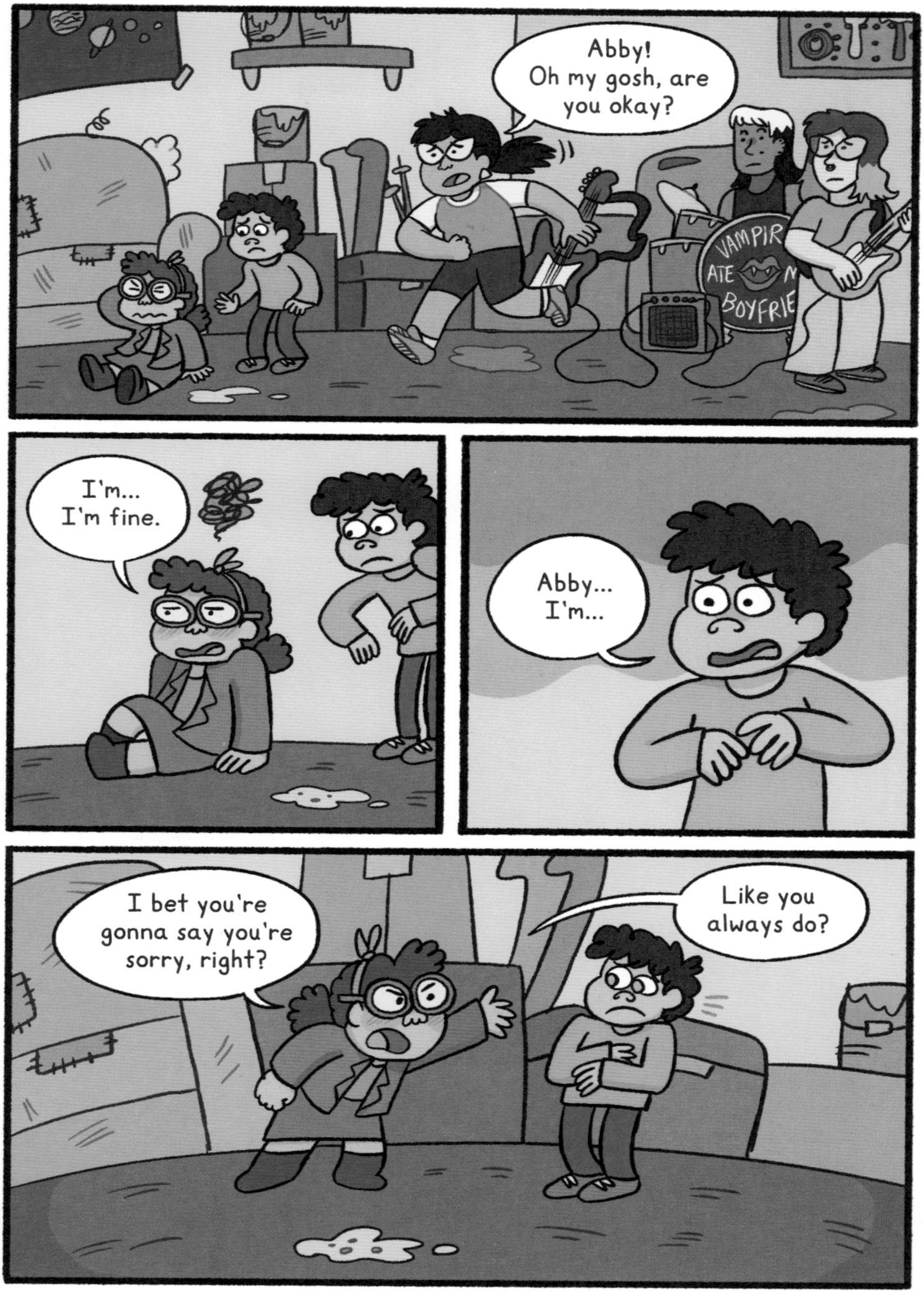
Abby!
Oh my gosh, are you okay?
VAMPIR ATE M BOYFRIE
I'm...
I'm fine.
Abby...
I'm...
I bet you're gonna say you're sorry, right?
Like you always do?

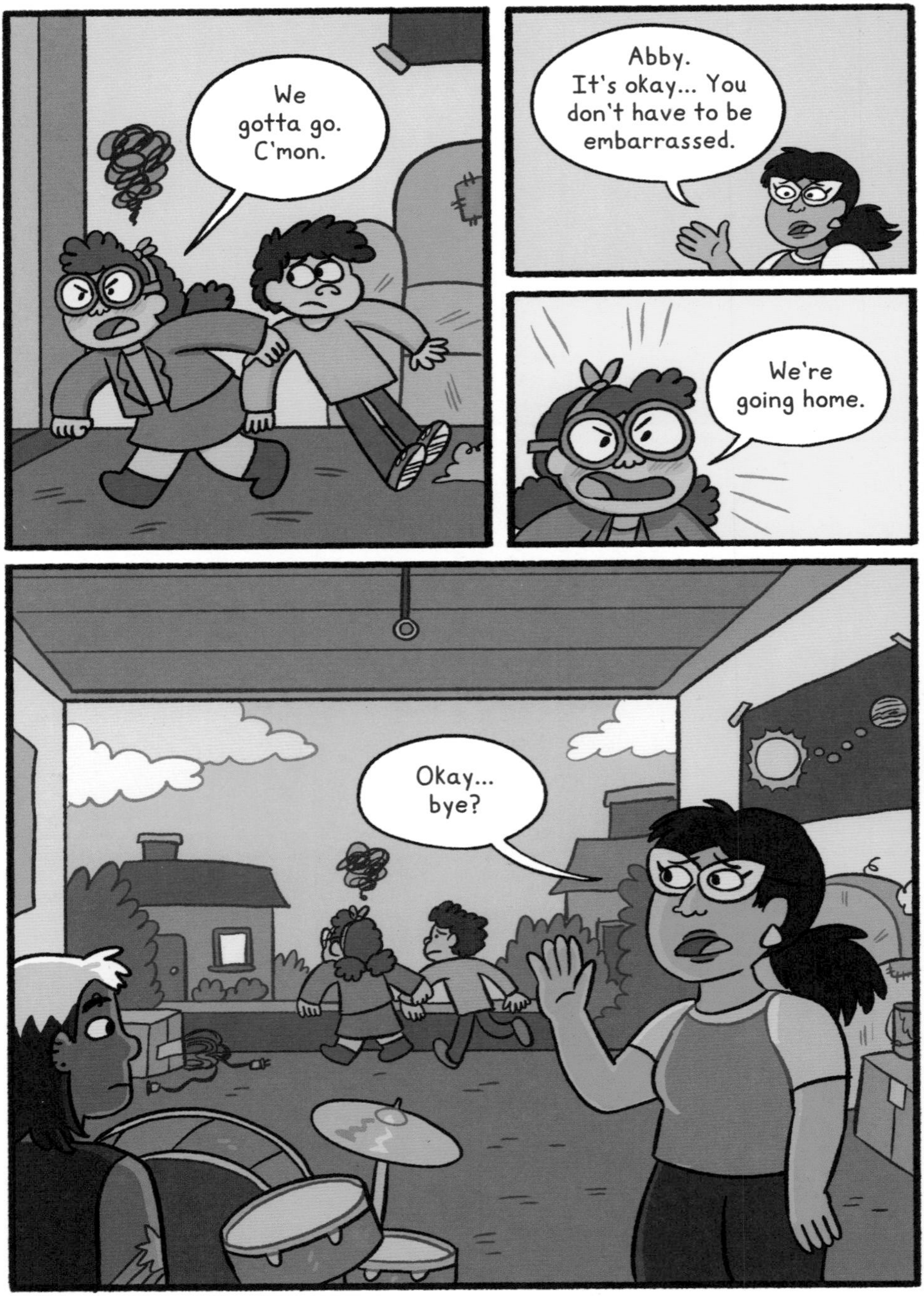
We gotta go. C'mon.
Abby. It's okay... You don't have to be embarrassed.
We're going home.
Okay... bye?

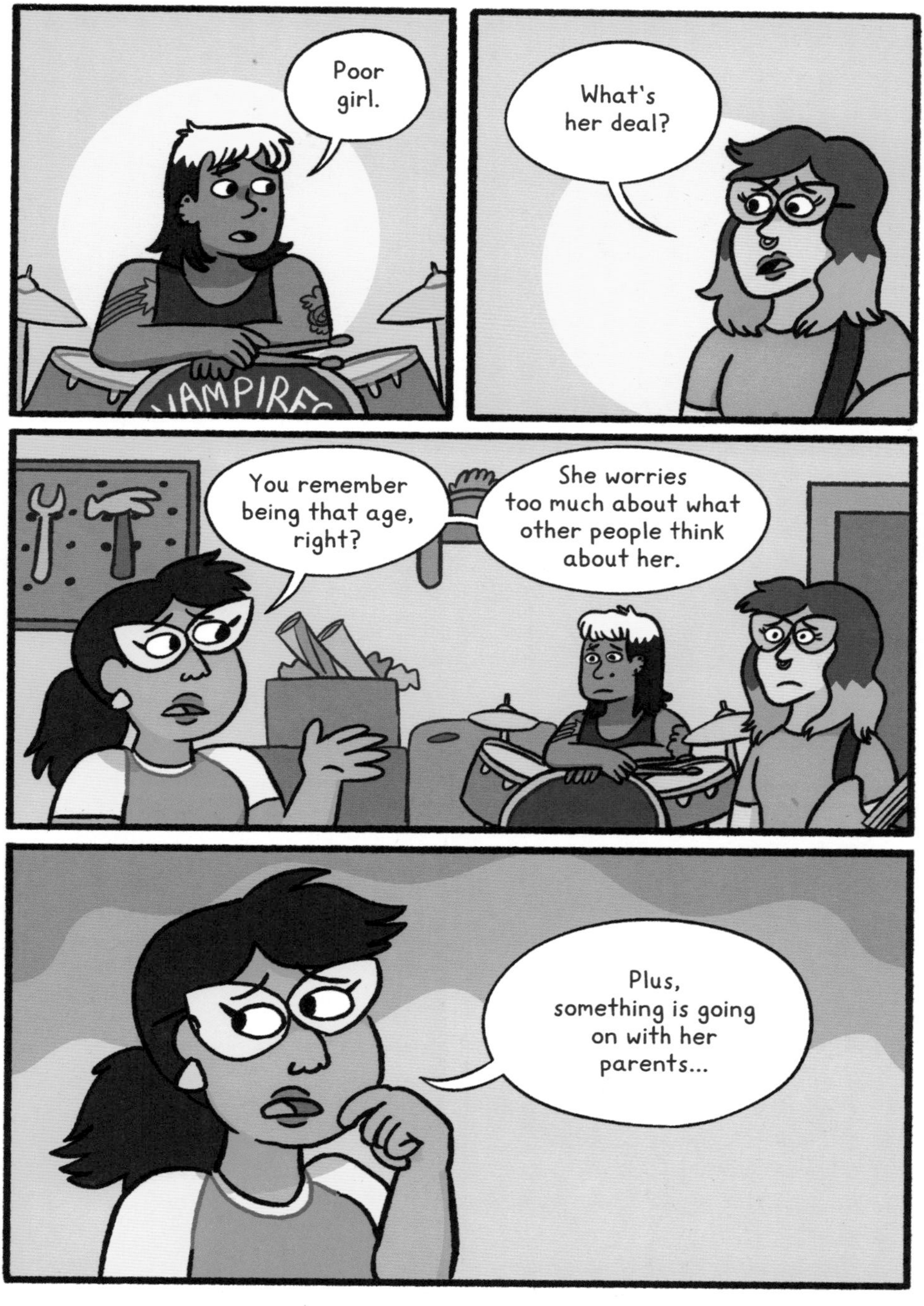
Poor girl.
What's her deal?
You remember being that age, right?
She worries too much about what other people think about her.
VAMPIRES
Plus, something is going on with her parents...

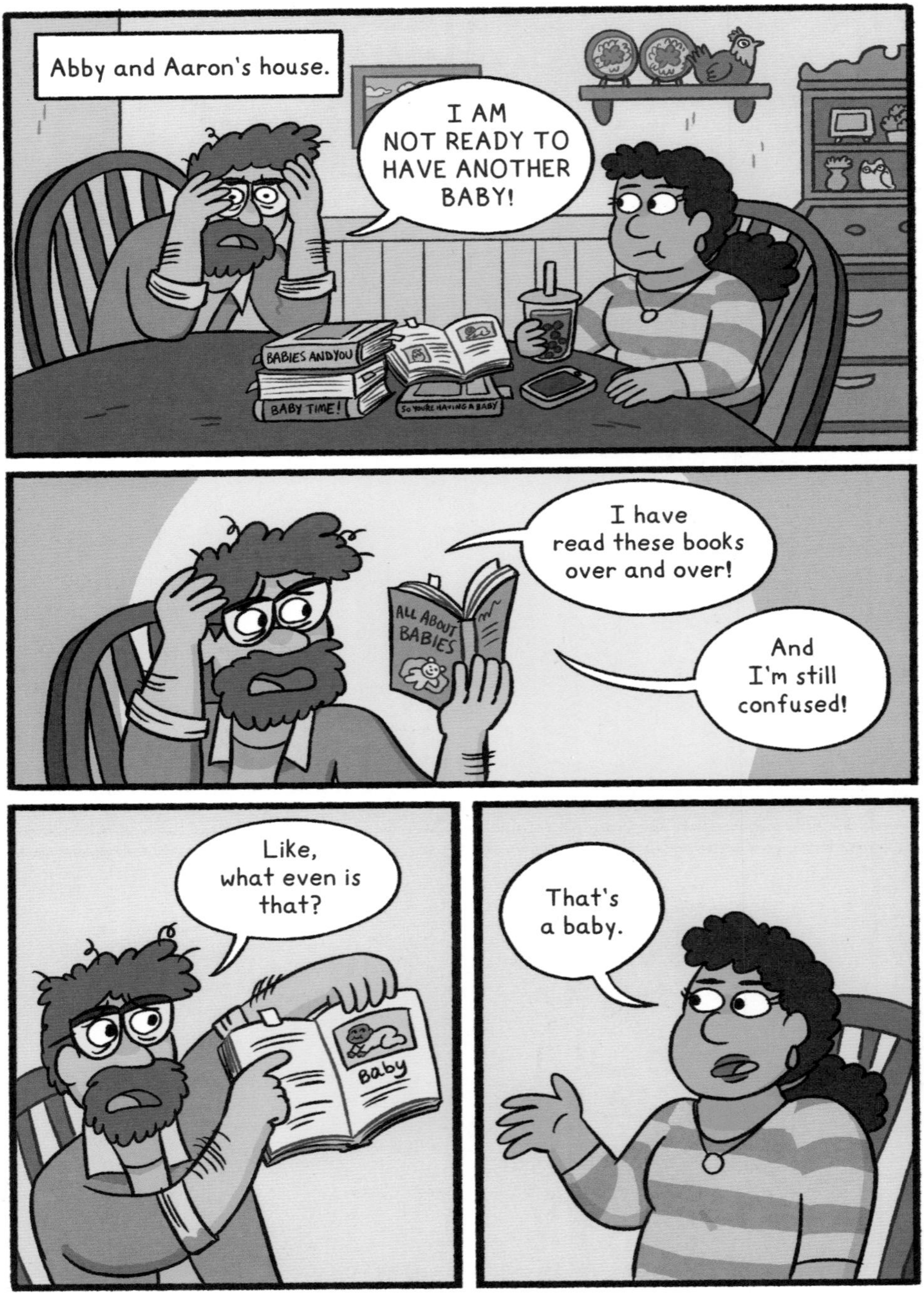

Abby and Aaron's house.
I AM NOT READY TO HAVE ANOTHER BABY!
BABIES AND YOU
BABY TIME!
SO YOU'RE HAVING A BABY
I have read these books over and over!
ALL ABOUT BABIES
And I'm still confused!
Like, what even is that?
Baby
That's a baby.

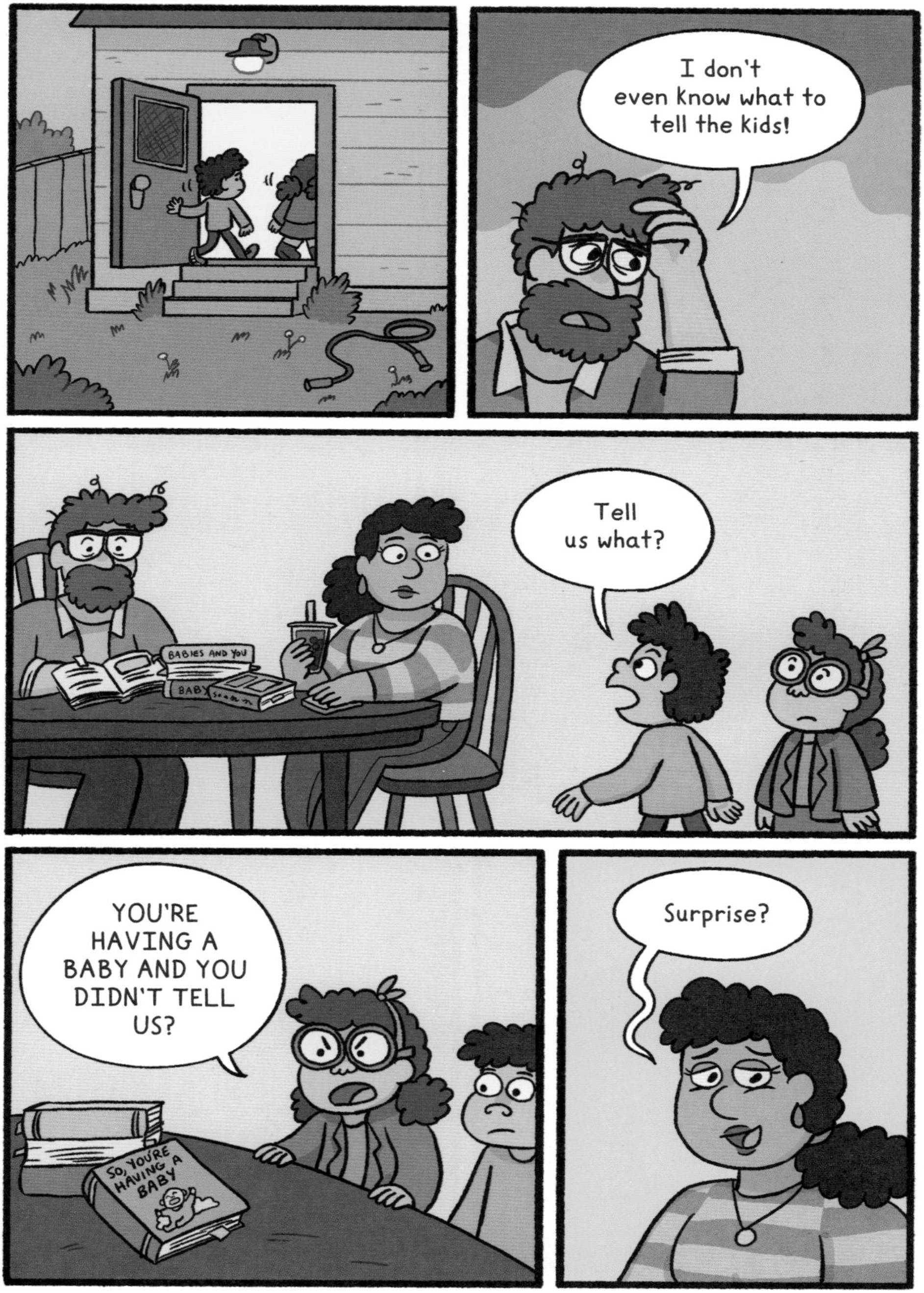
I don't even know what to tell the kids!
BABIES AND YOU
BABY
Tell us what?
YOU'RE HAVING A BABY AND YOU DIDN'T TELL US?
SO, YOU'RE HAVING A BABY
Surprise?

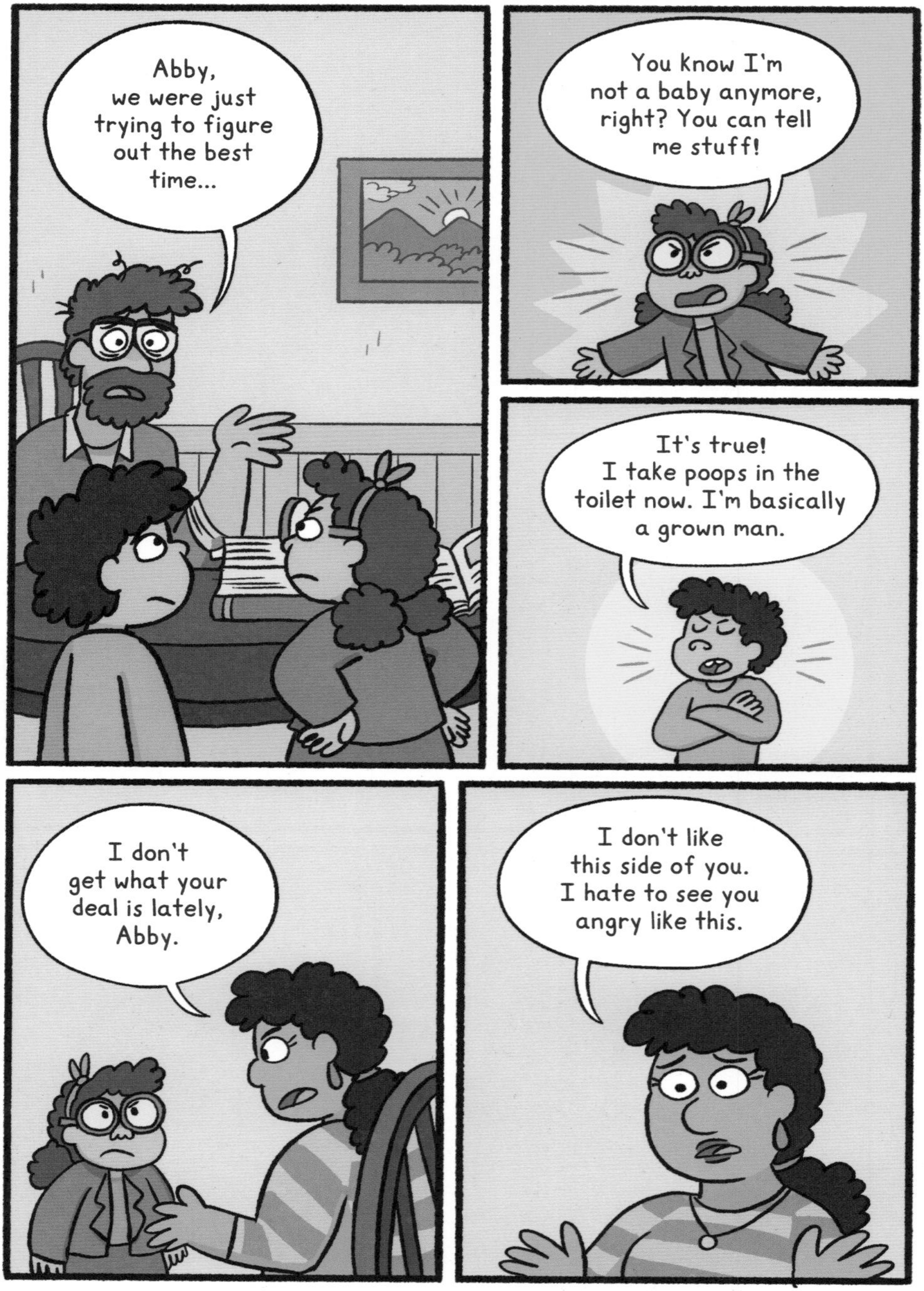
Abby, we were just trying to figure out the best time...
You know I'm not a baby anymore, right? You can tell me stuff!
It's true! I take poops in the toilet now. I'm basically a grown man.
I don't get what your deal is lately, Abby.
I don't like this side of you. I hate to see you angry like this.

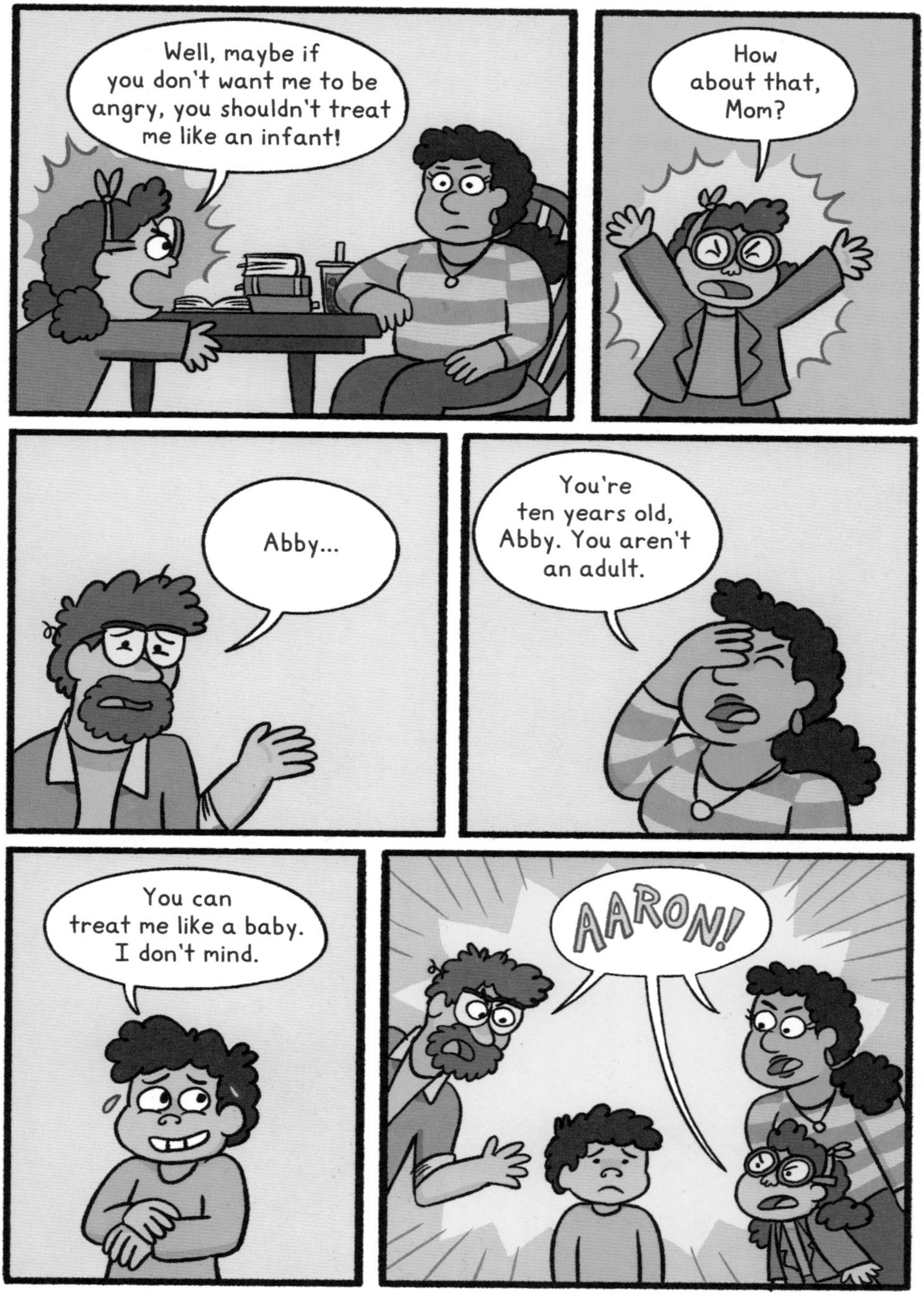
Well, maybe if you don't want me to be angry, you shouldn't treat me like an infant!
How about that, Mom?
Abby...
You're ten years old, Abby. You aren't an adult.
You can treat me like a baby. I don't mind.
AARON!

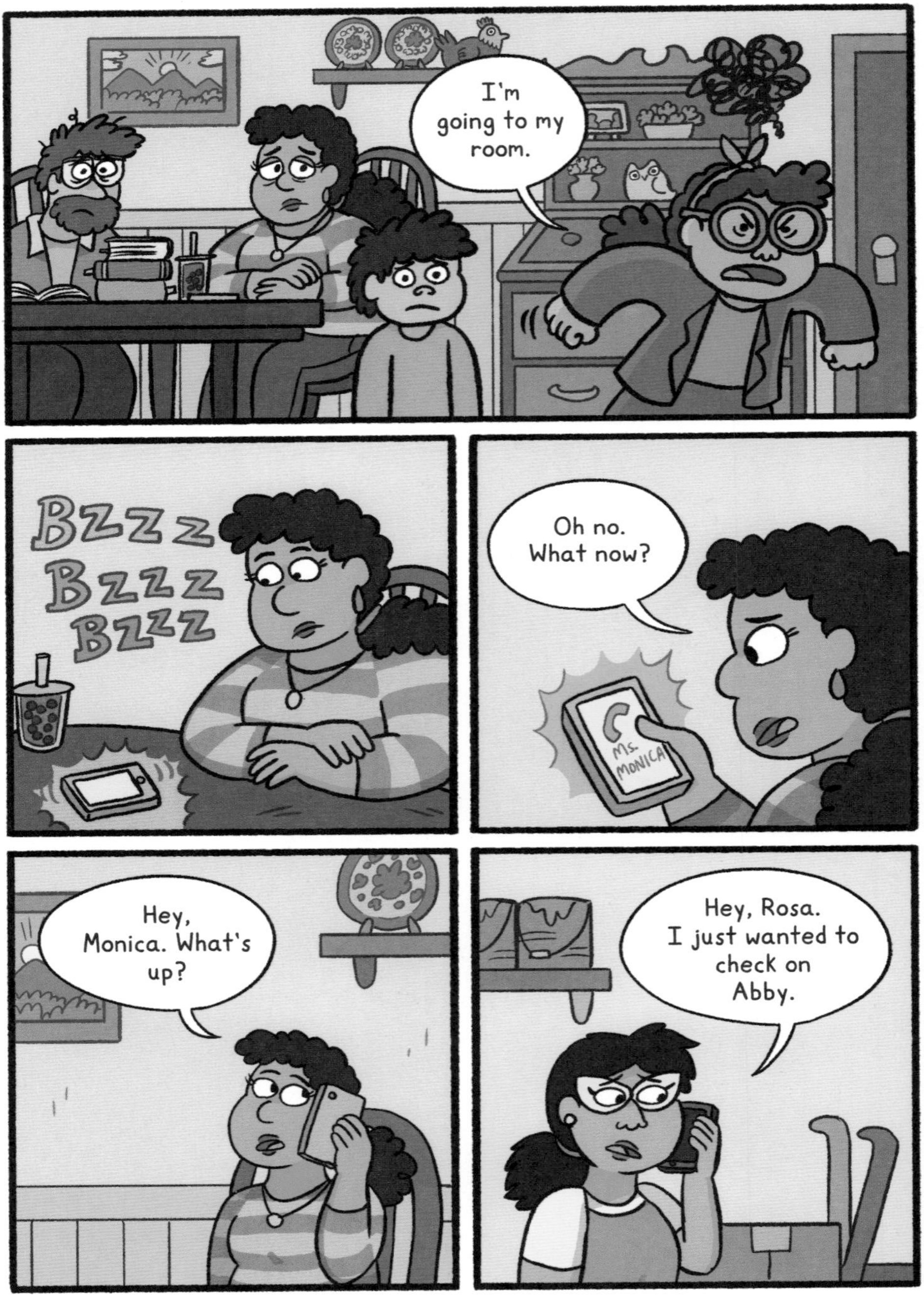
I'm going to my room.
BZZZ BZZZ BZZZ
Oh no. What now?
MS. MONICA
Hey, Monica. What's up?
Hey, Rosa. I just wanted to check on Abby.

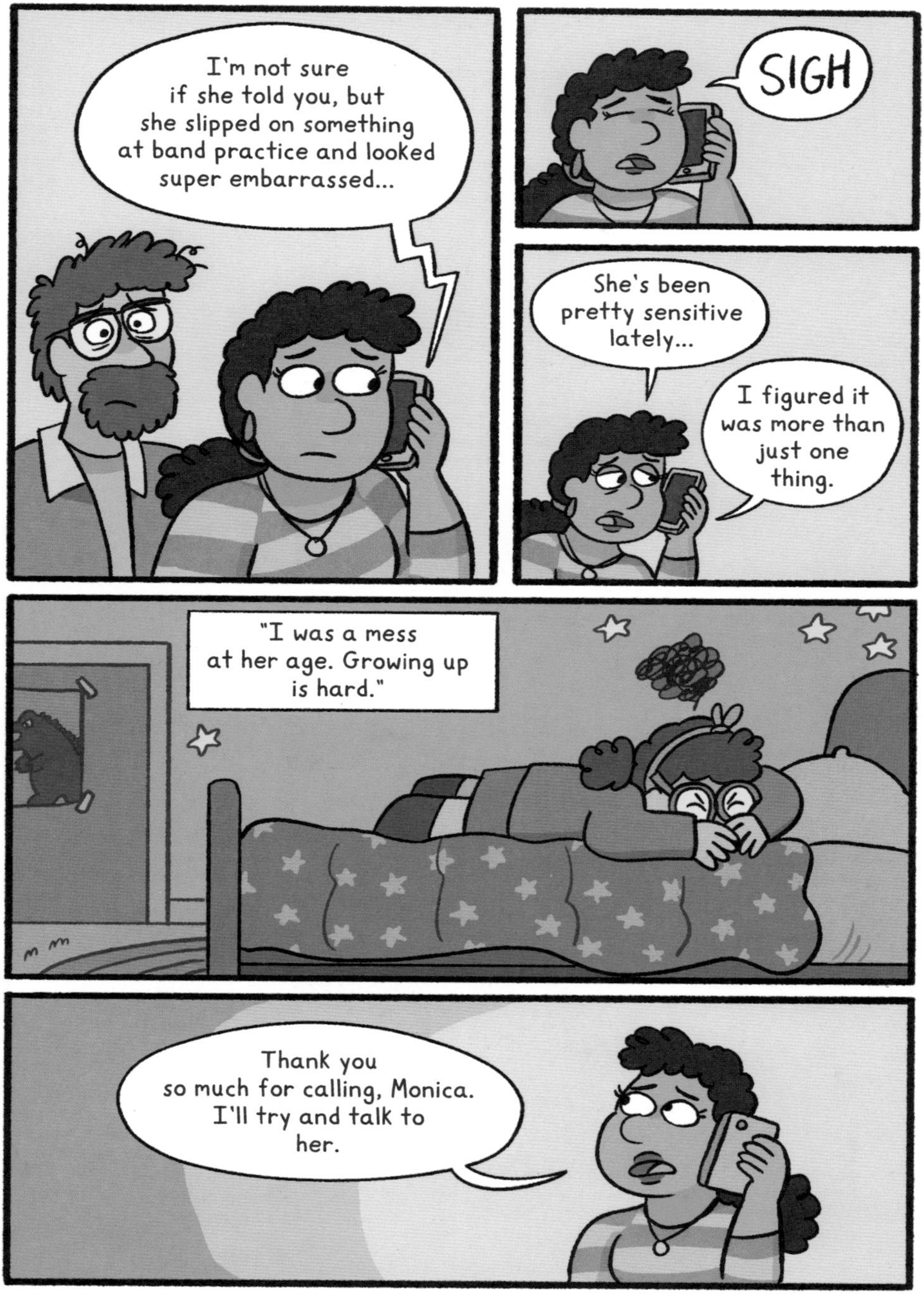
I'm not sure if she told you, but she slipped on something at band practice and looked super embarrassed...
SIGH
She's been pretty sensitive lately...
I figured it was more than just one thing.
"I was a mess at her age. Growing up is hard."
Thank you so much for calling, Monica. I'll try and talk to her.

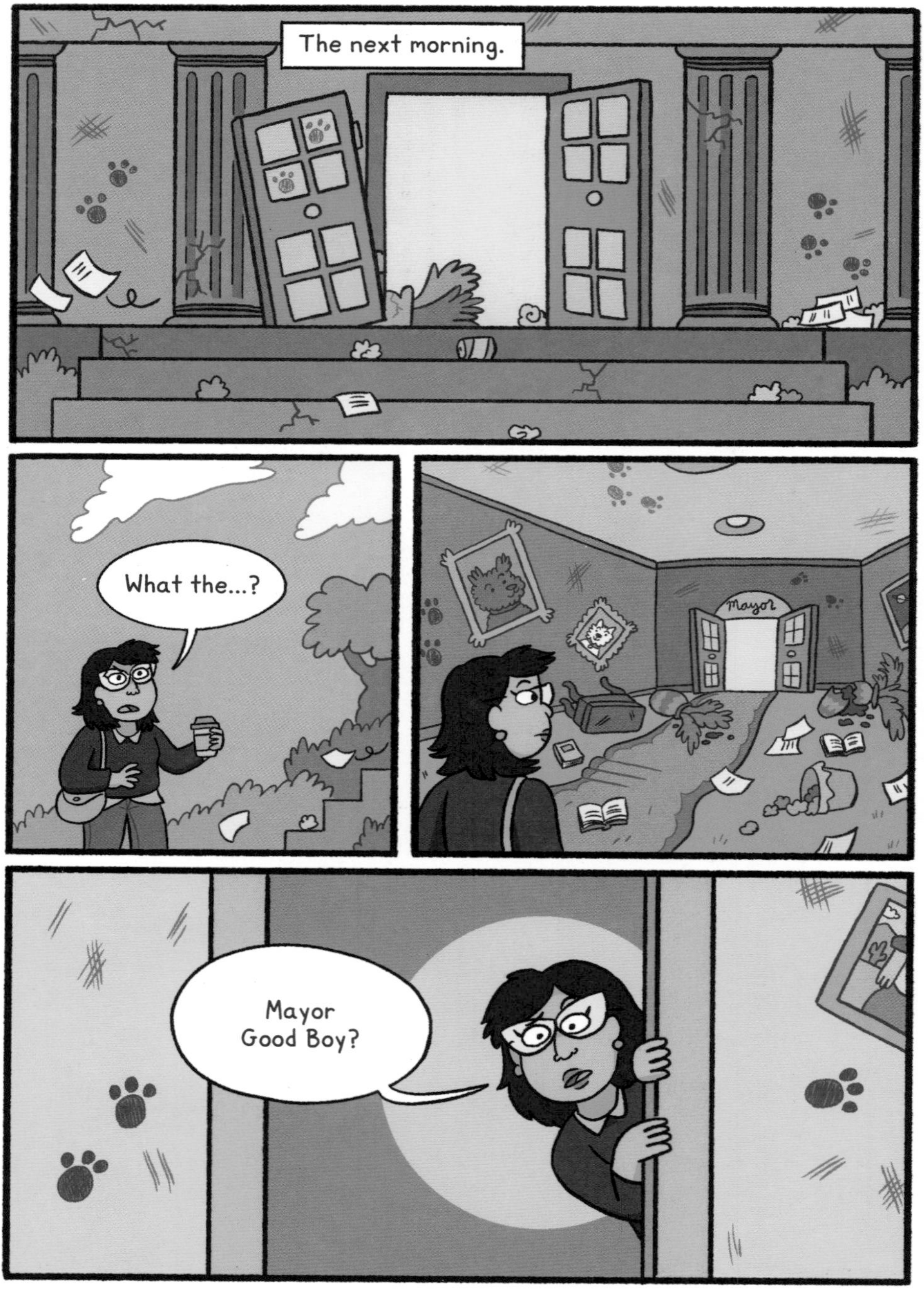
The next morning.
What the...?
Mayor
Mayor Good Boy?

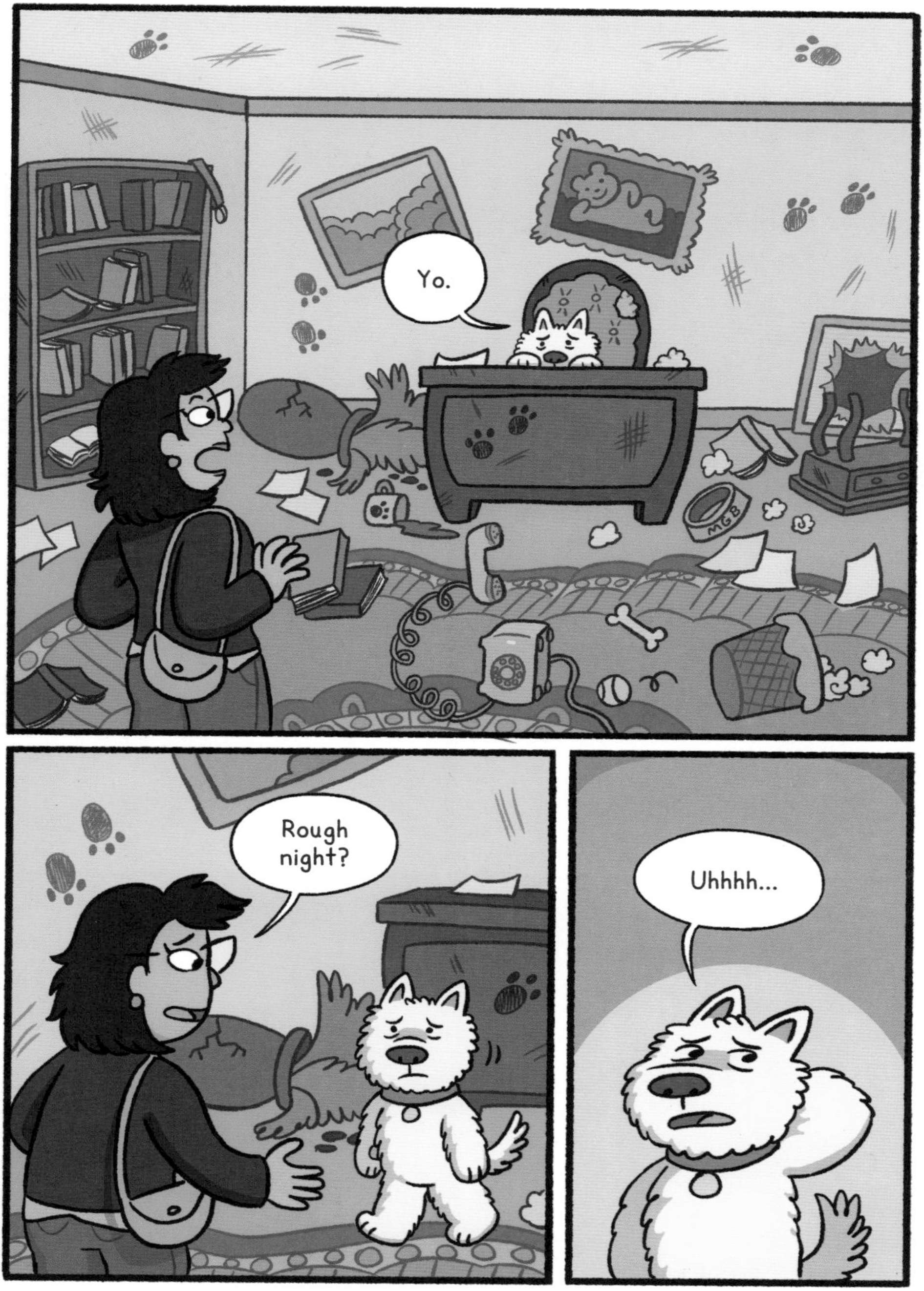
Yo.
MGB
Rough night?
Uhhhh...

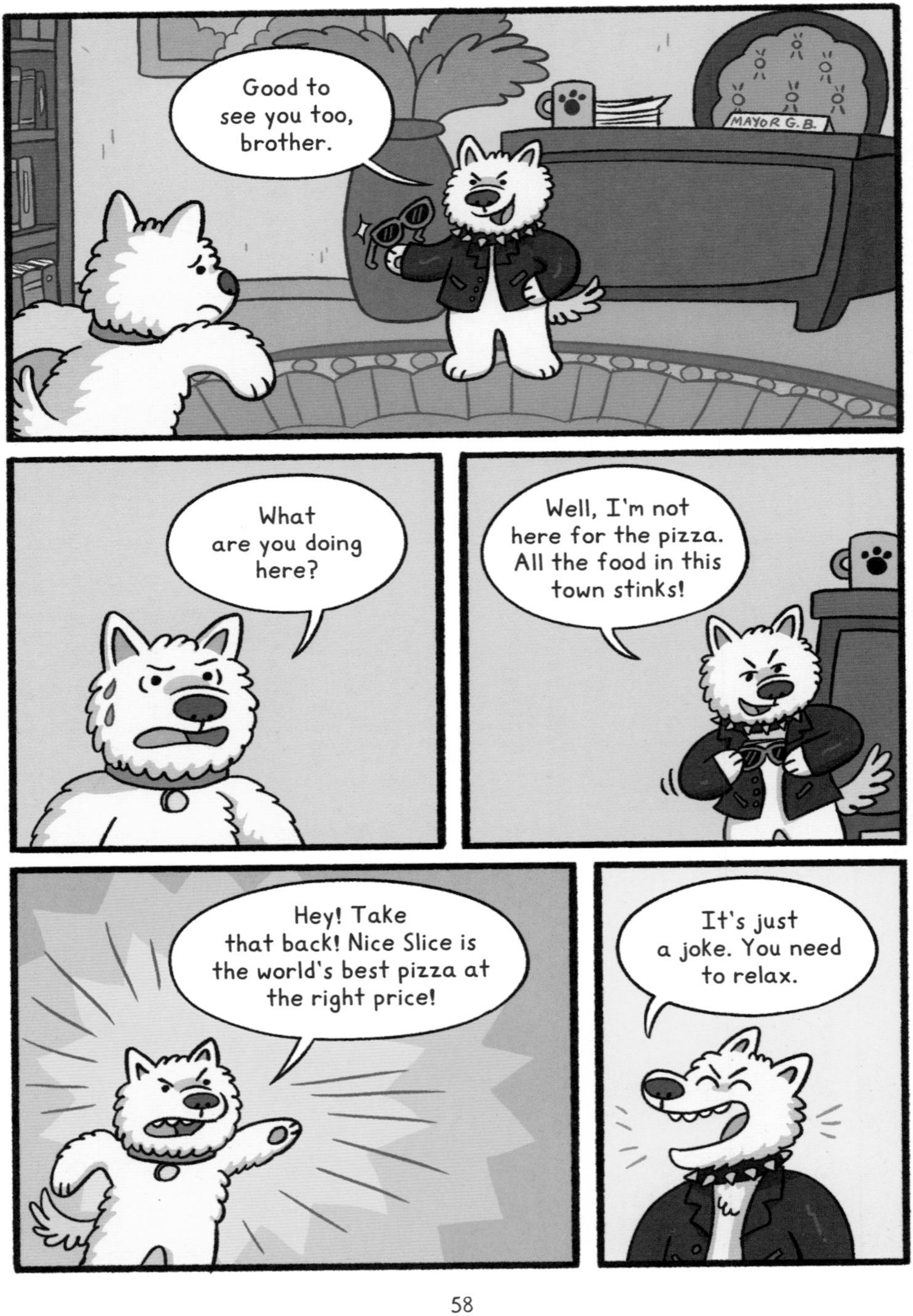
Good to see you too, brother.
MAYOR G.B.
What are you doing here?
Well, I'm not here for the pizza. All the food in this town stinks!
Hey! Take that back! Nice Slice is the world's best pizza at the right price!
It's just a joke. You need to relax.

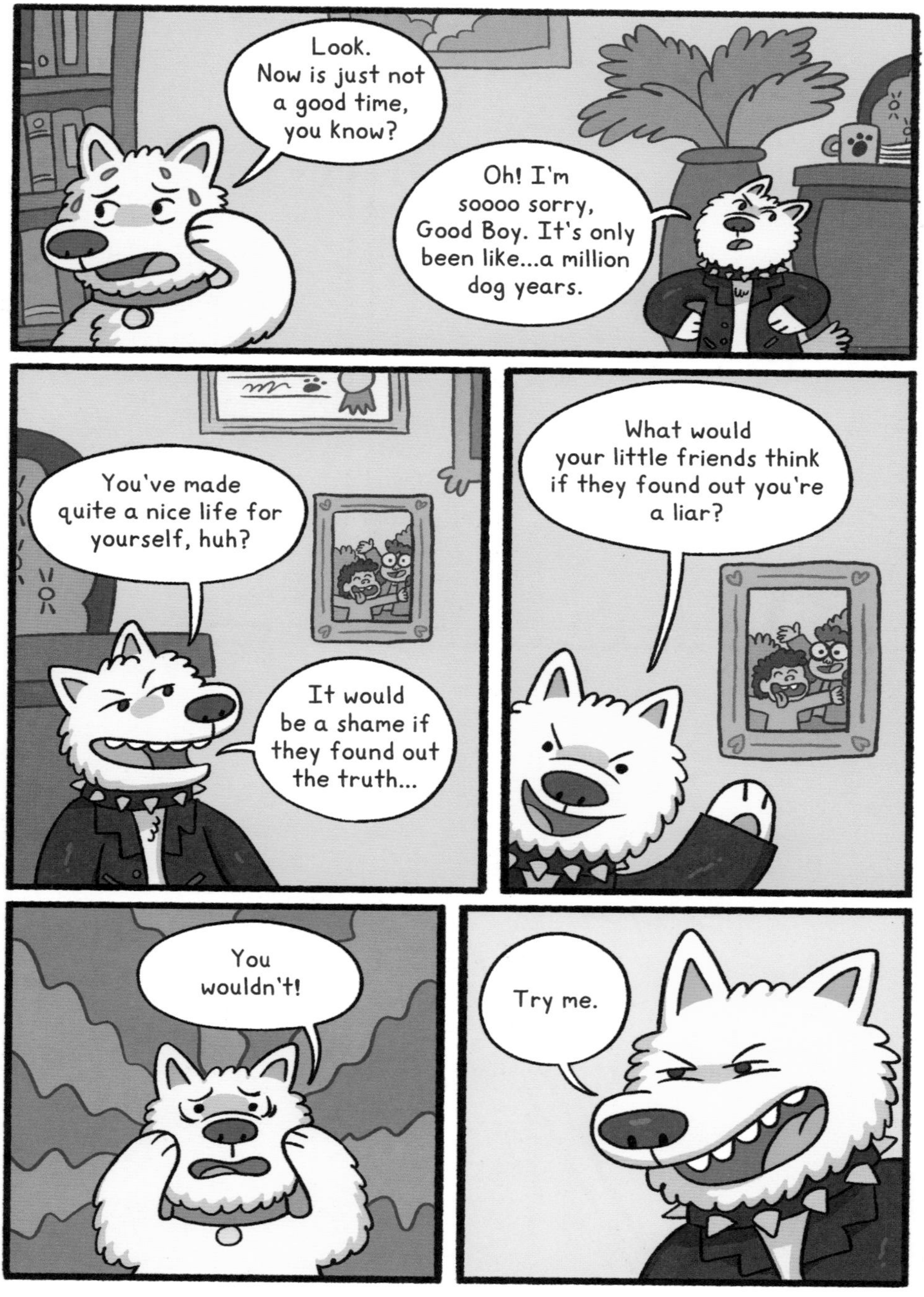
Look. Now is just not a good time, you know?
Oh! I'm soooo sorry, Good Boy. It's only been like...a million dog years.
You've made quite a nice life for yourself, huh?
It would be a shame if they found out the truth...
What would your little friends think if they found out you're a liar?
You wouldn't!
Try me.

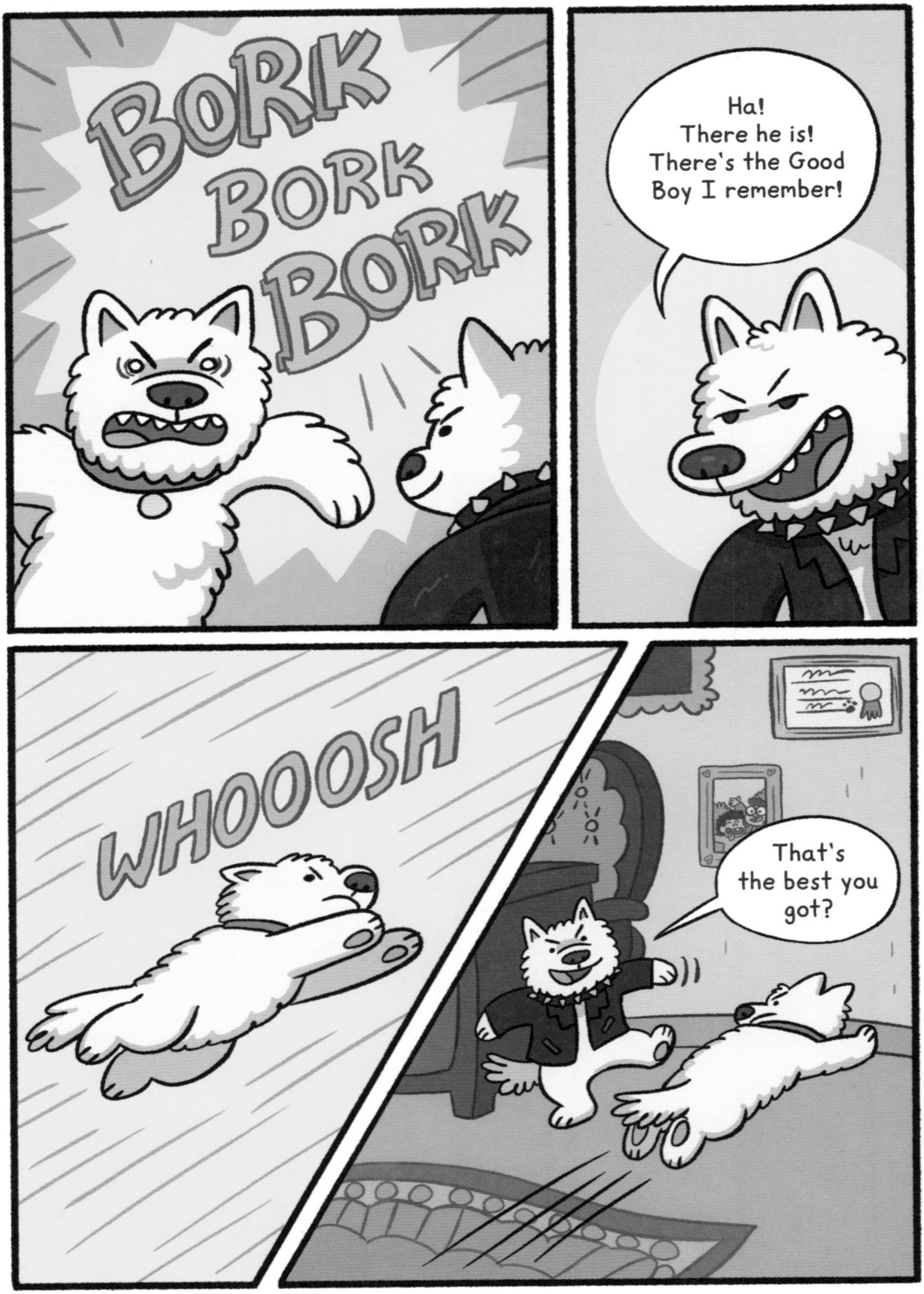
BORK BORK BORK
Ha! There he is! There's the Good Boy I remember!
WHOOOSH
That's the best you got?

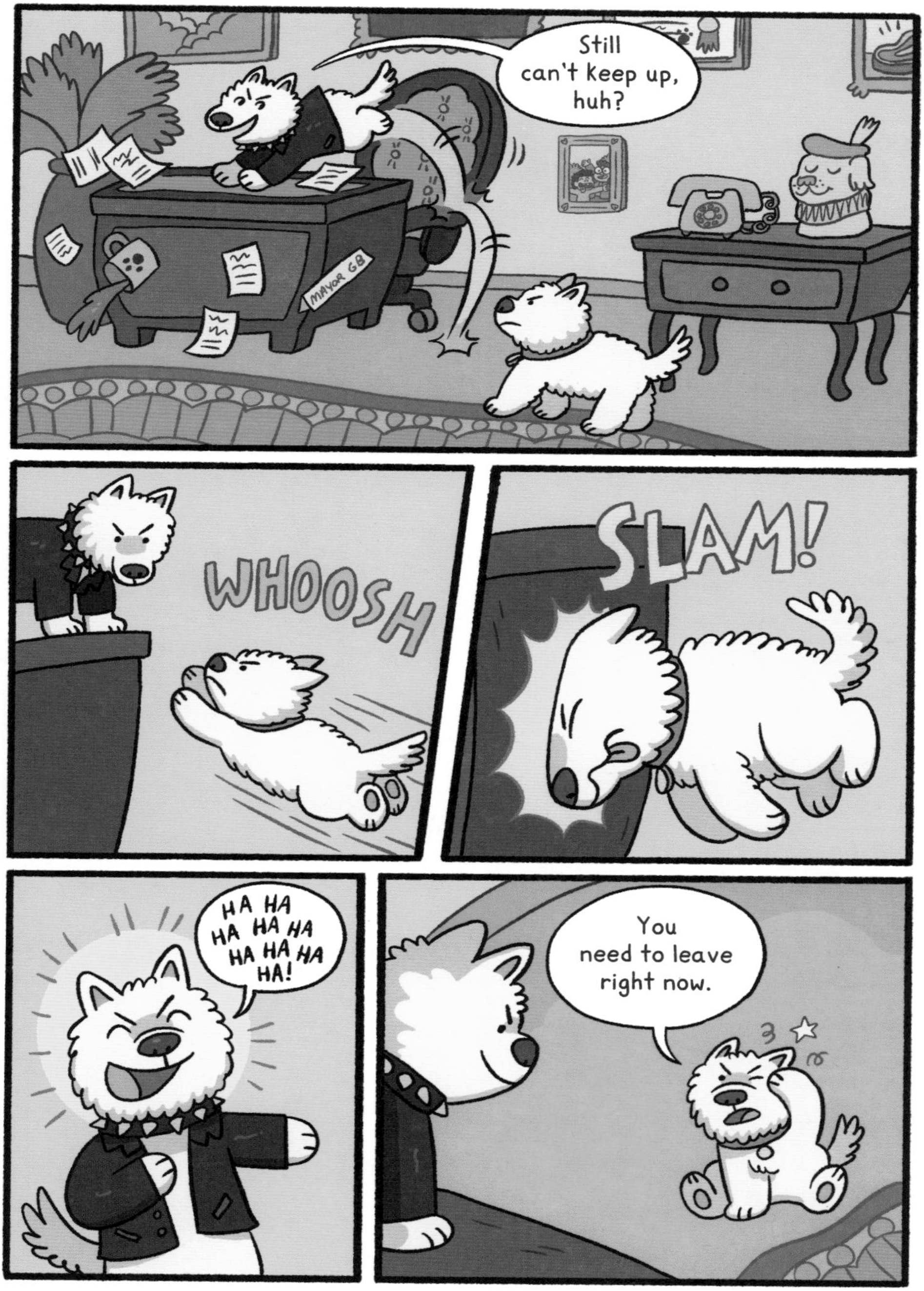
Still can't keep up, huh?
MAYOR GB
WHOOSH
SLAM!
HA HA HA HA HA HA HA HA HA!
You need to leave right now.

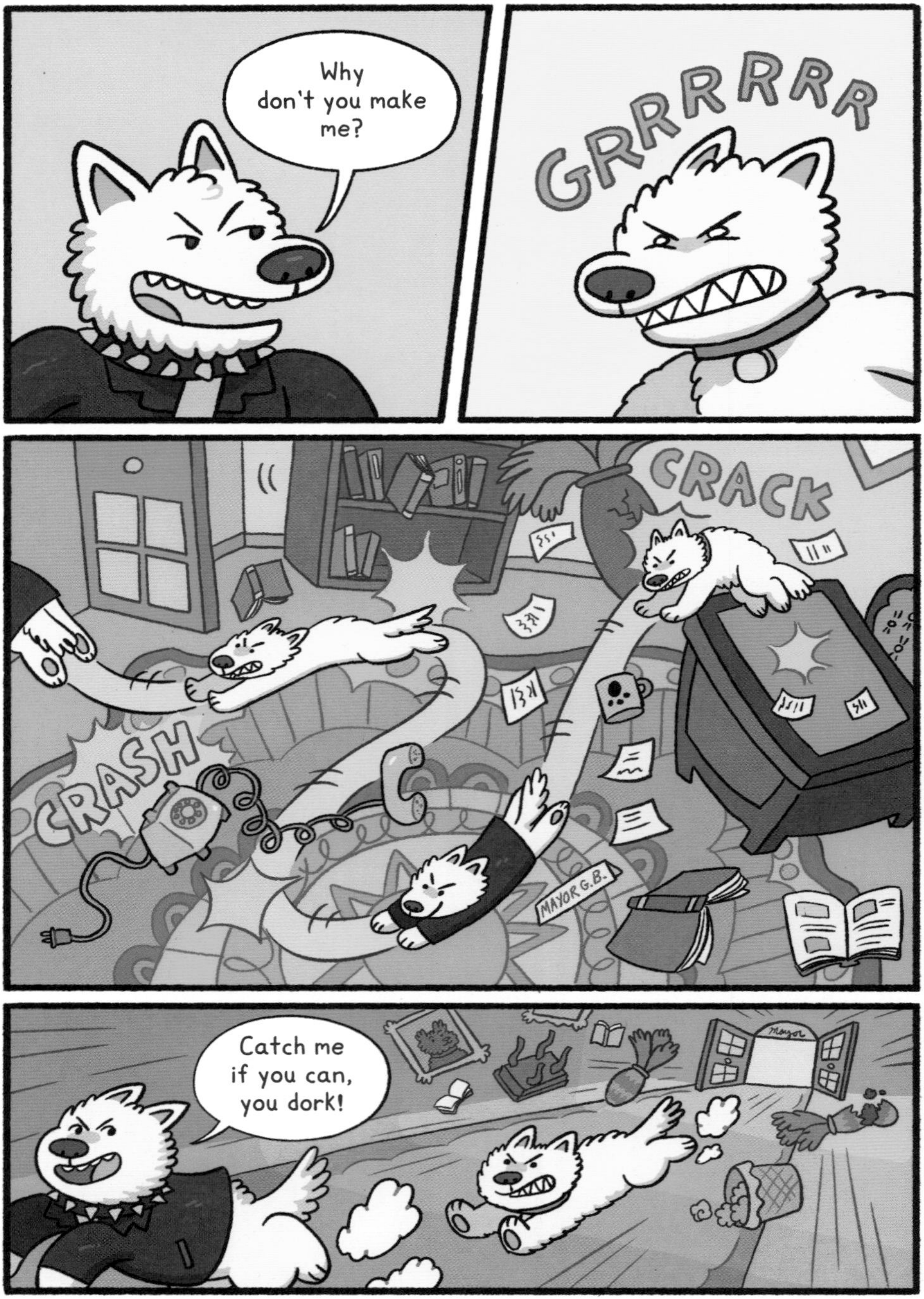
Why don't you make me?
GRRRRRRR
CRACK
CRASH
MAYOR G.B.
Catch me if you can, you dork!

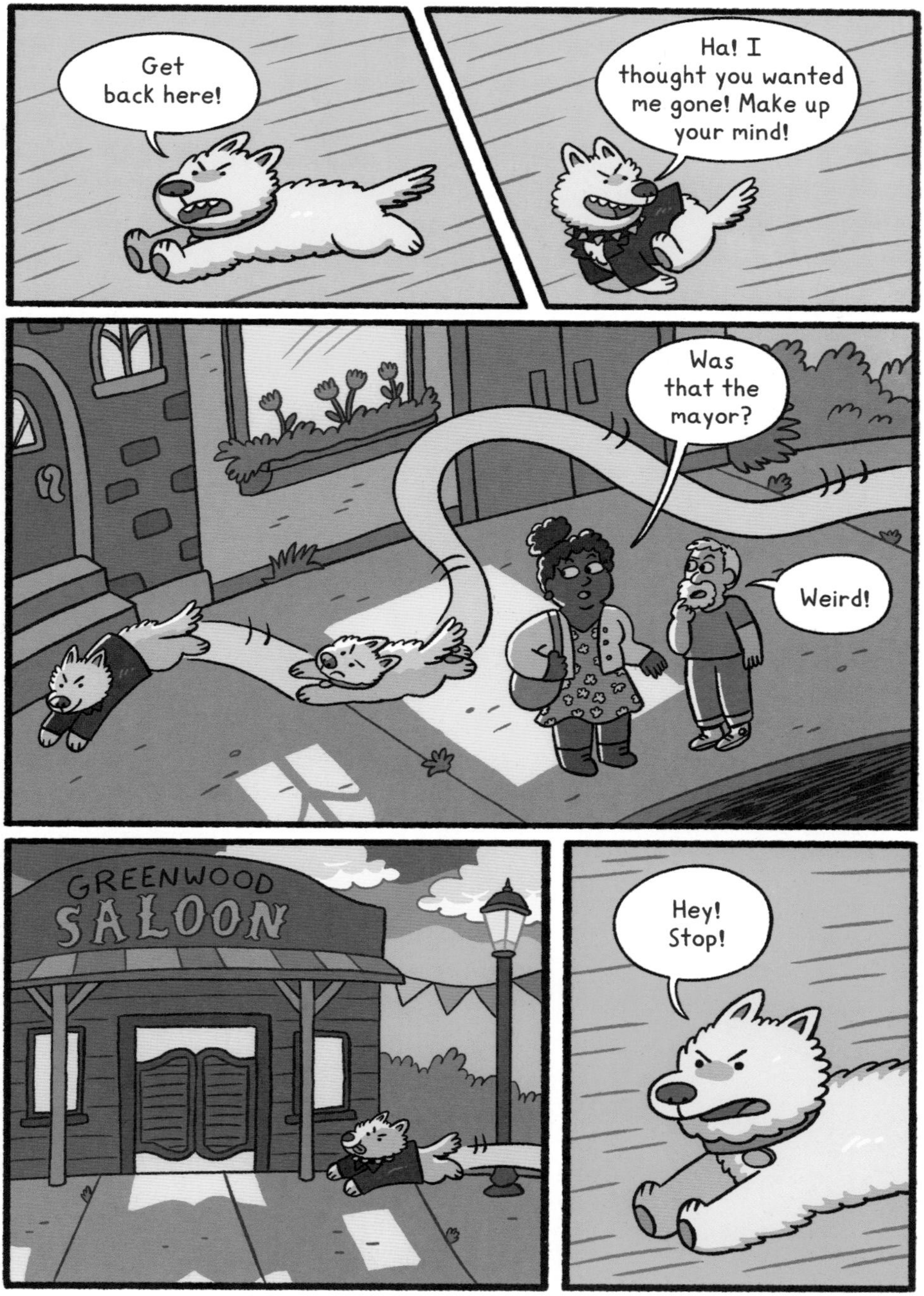
Get back here!
Ha! I thought you wanted me gone! Make up your mind!
Was that the mayor?
Weird!
GREENWOOD SALOON
Hey! Stop!

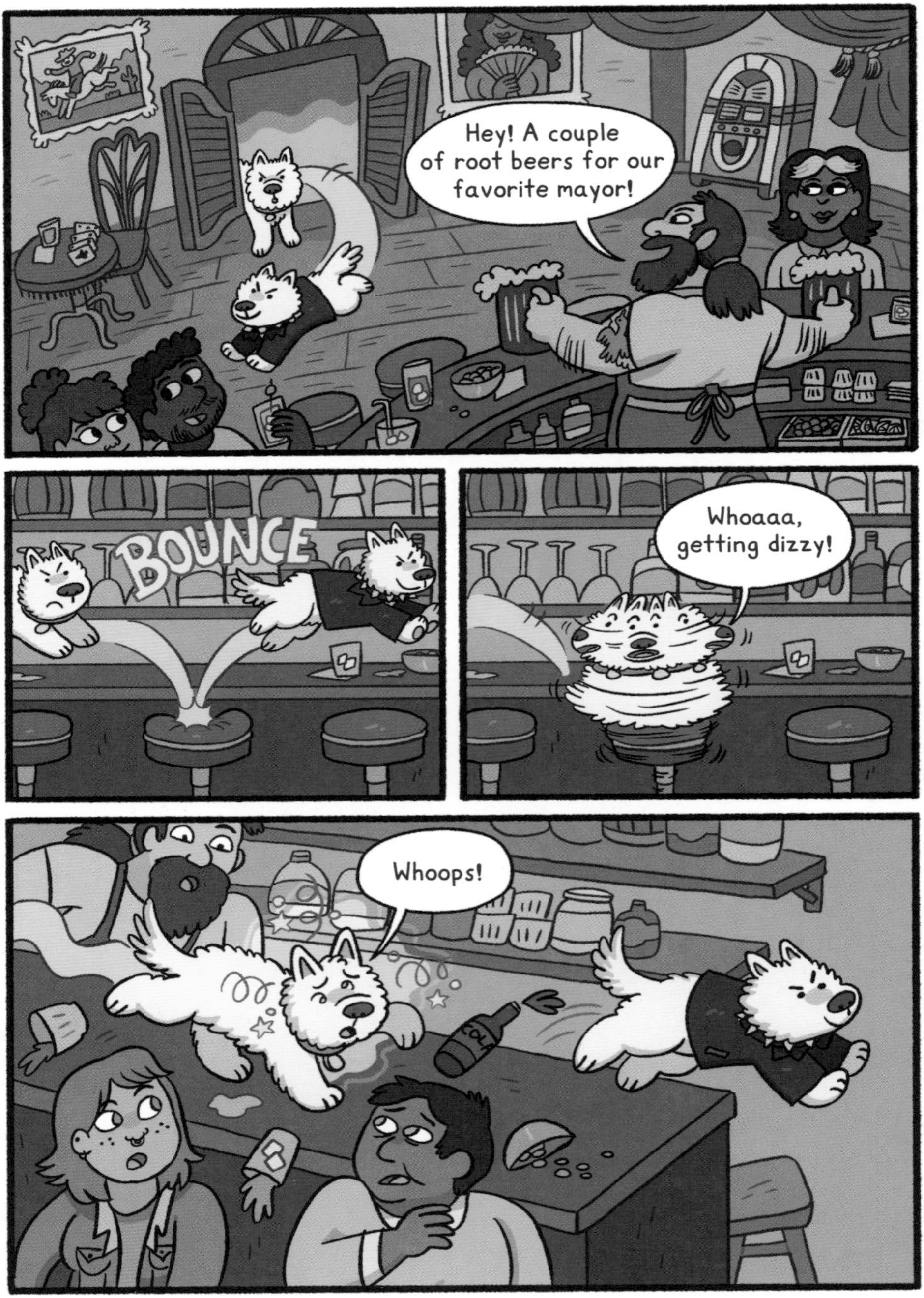
Hey! A couple of root beers for our favorite mayor!
BOUNCE
Whoaaa, getting dizzy!
COLA
Whoops!

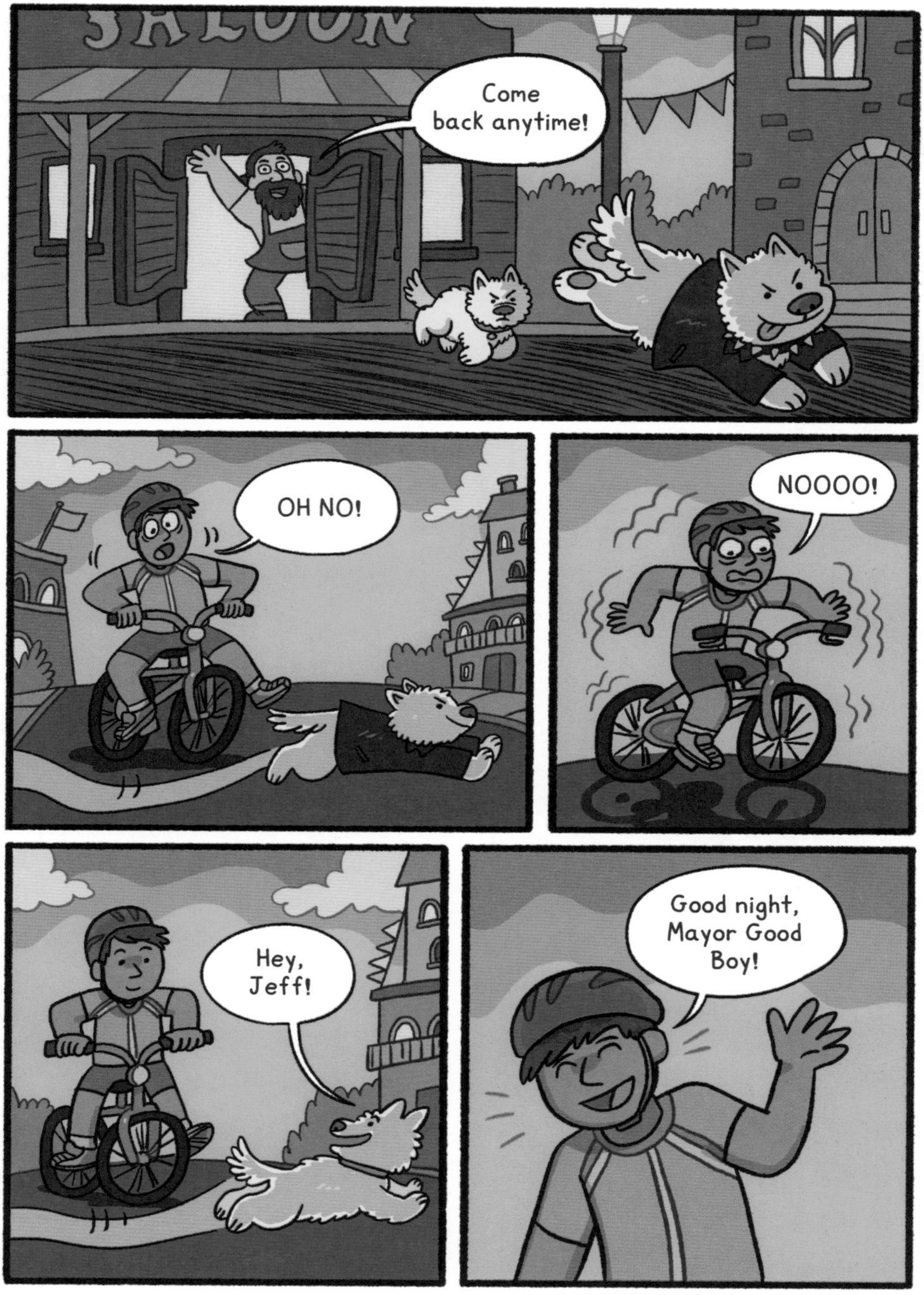
SALOON
Come back anytime!
OH NO!
NOOOO!
Hey, Jeff!
Good night, Mayor Good Boy!

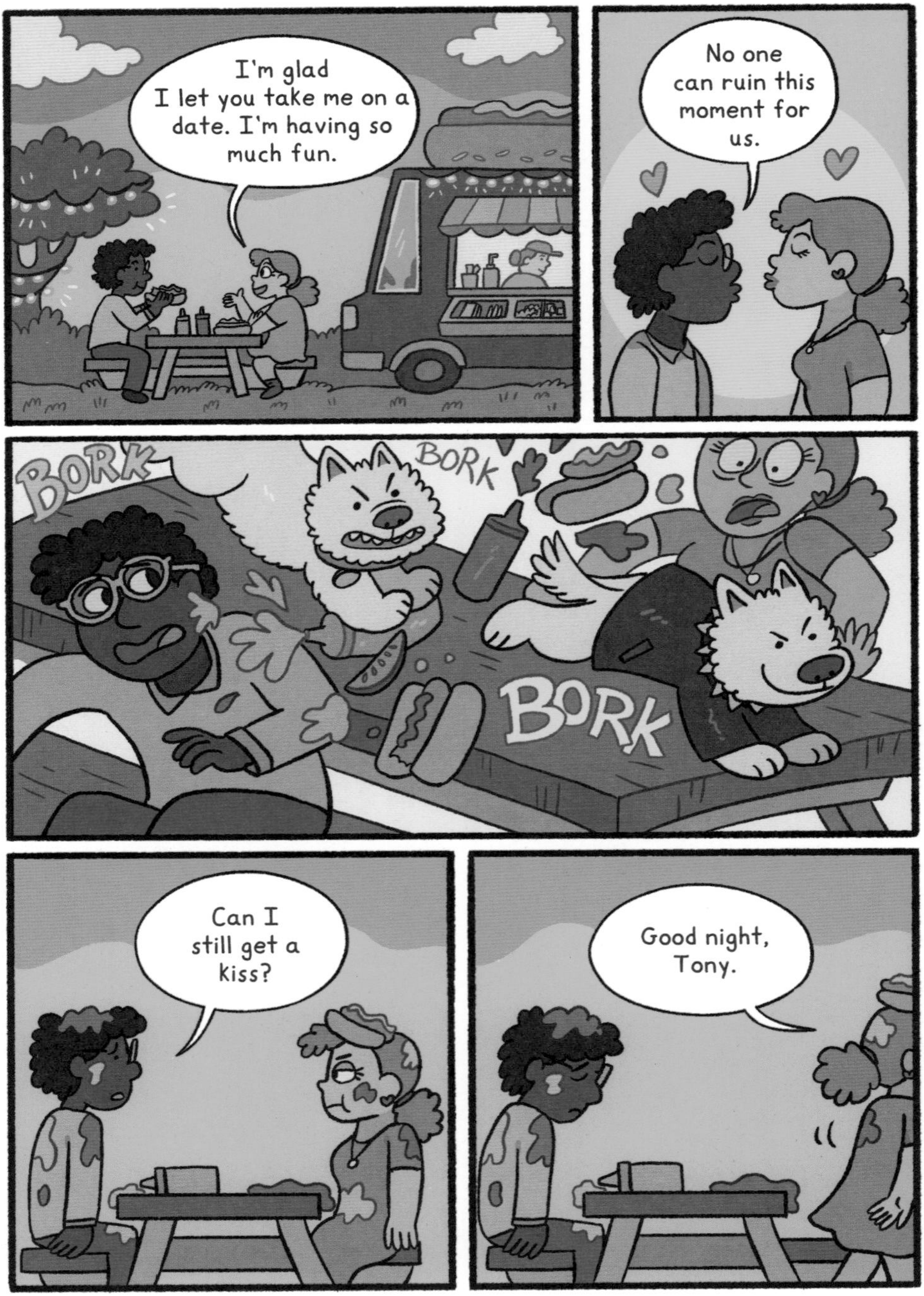
I'm glad I let you take me on a date. I'm having so much fun.
No one can ruin this moment for us.
BORK
BORK
BORK
Can I still get a kiss?
Good night, Tony.

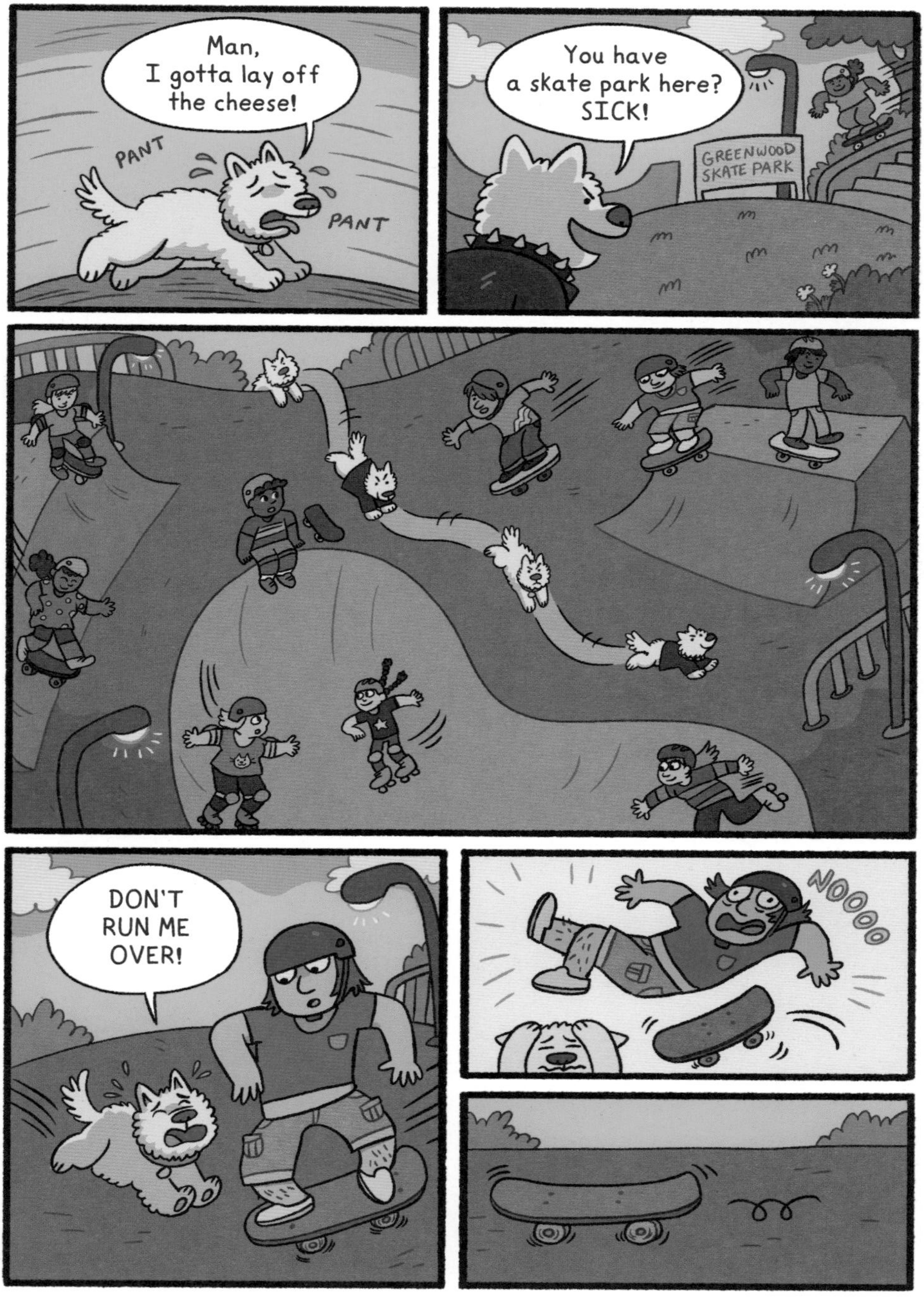

Man, I gotta lay off the cheese!
PANT
PANT
You have a skate park here? SICK!
GREENWOOD SKATE PARK
DON'T RUN ME OVER!
NOOOO

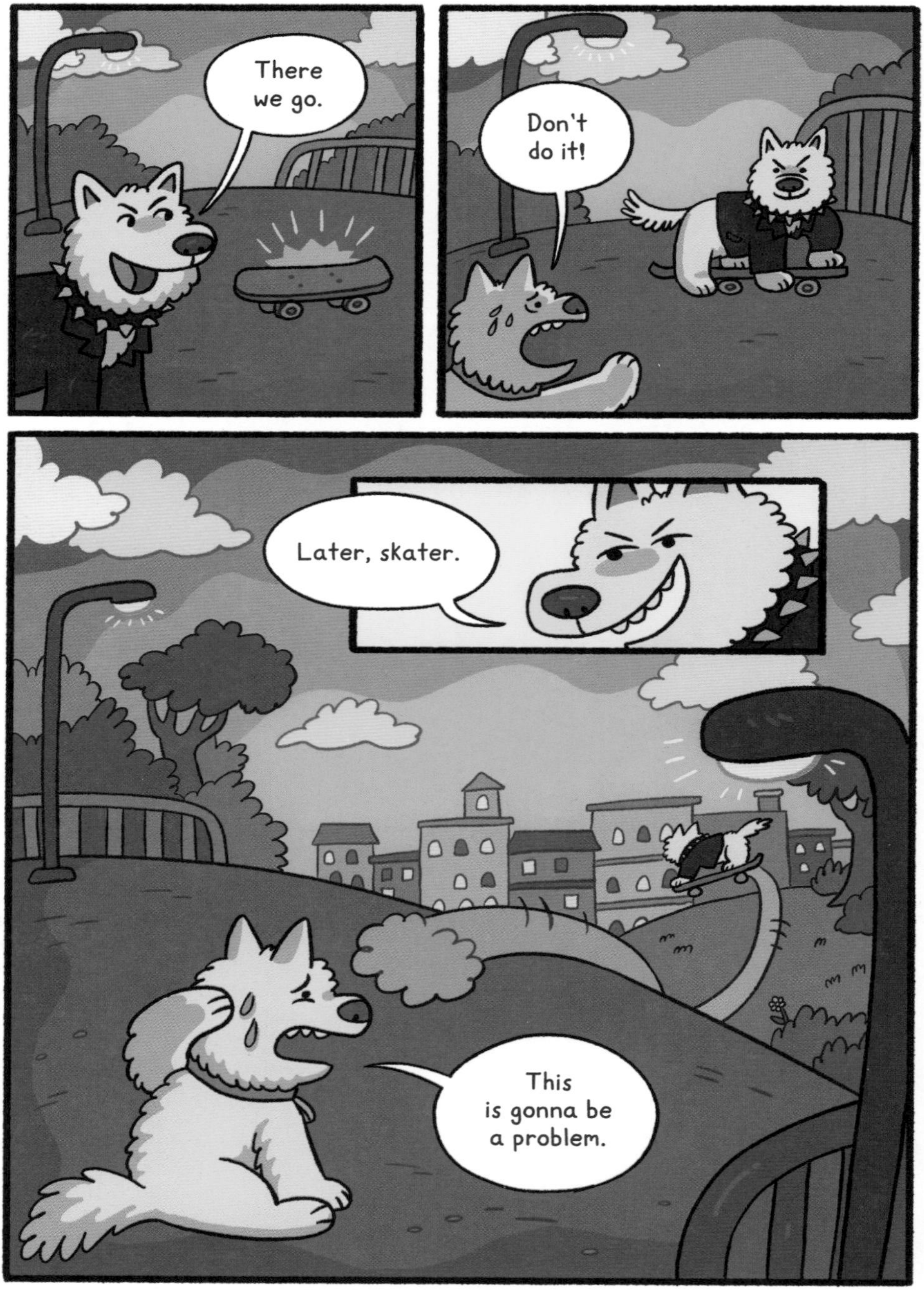
There we go.
Don't do it!
Later, skater.
This is gonna be a problem.

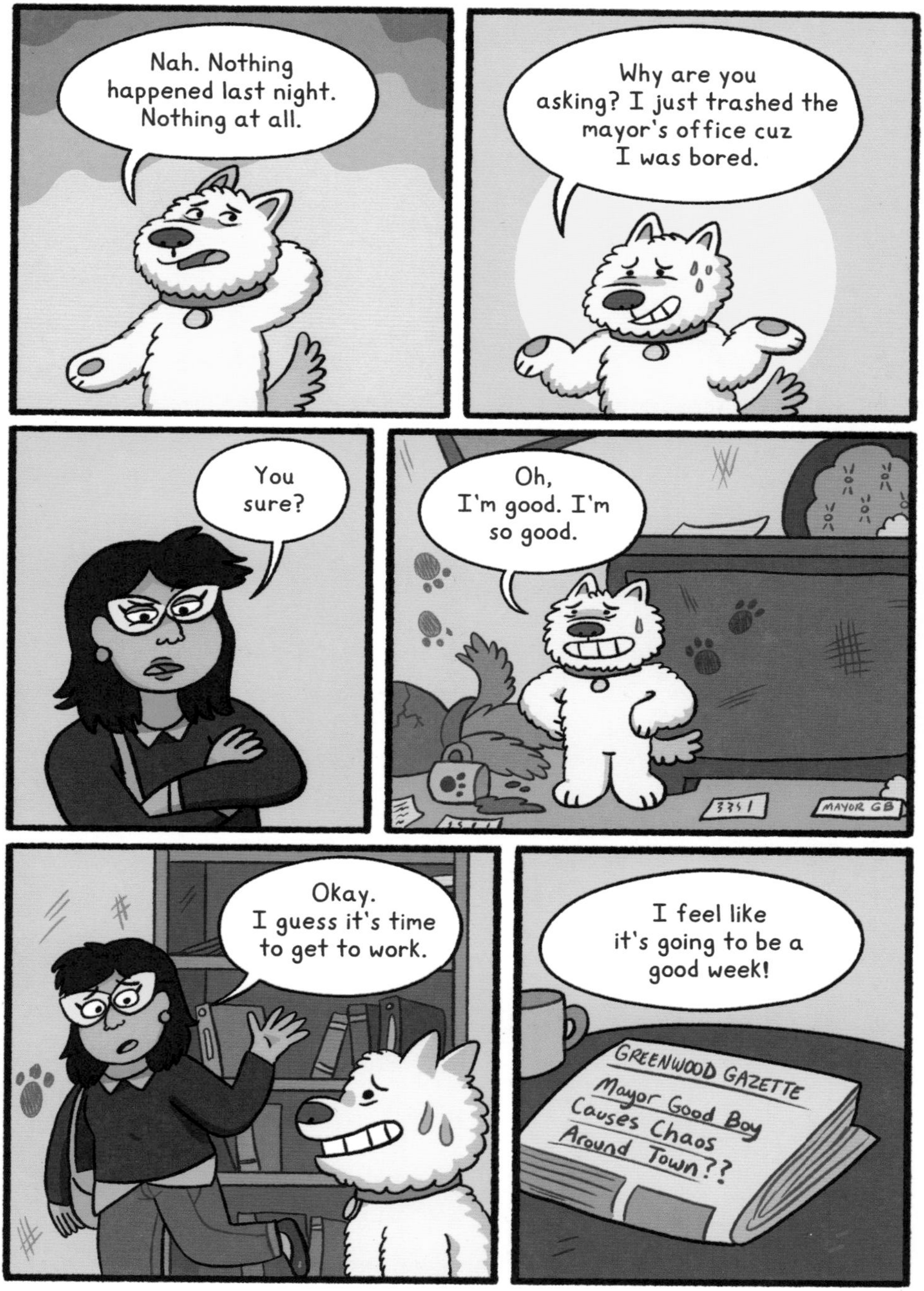
Nah. Nothing happened last night. Nothing at all.
Why are you asking? I just trashed the mayor's office cuz I was bored.
You sure?
Oh, I'm good. I'm so good.
MAYOR GB
Okay. I guess it's time to get to work.
I feel like it's going to be a good week!
GREENWOOD GAZETTE
Mayor Good Boy Causes Chaos Around Town??

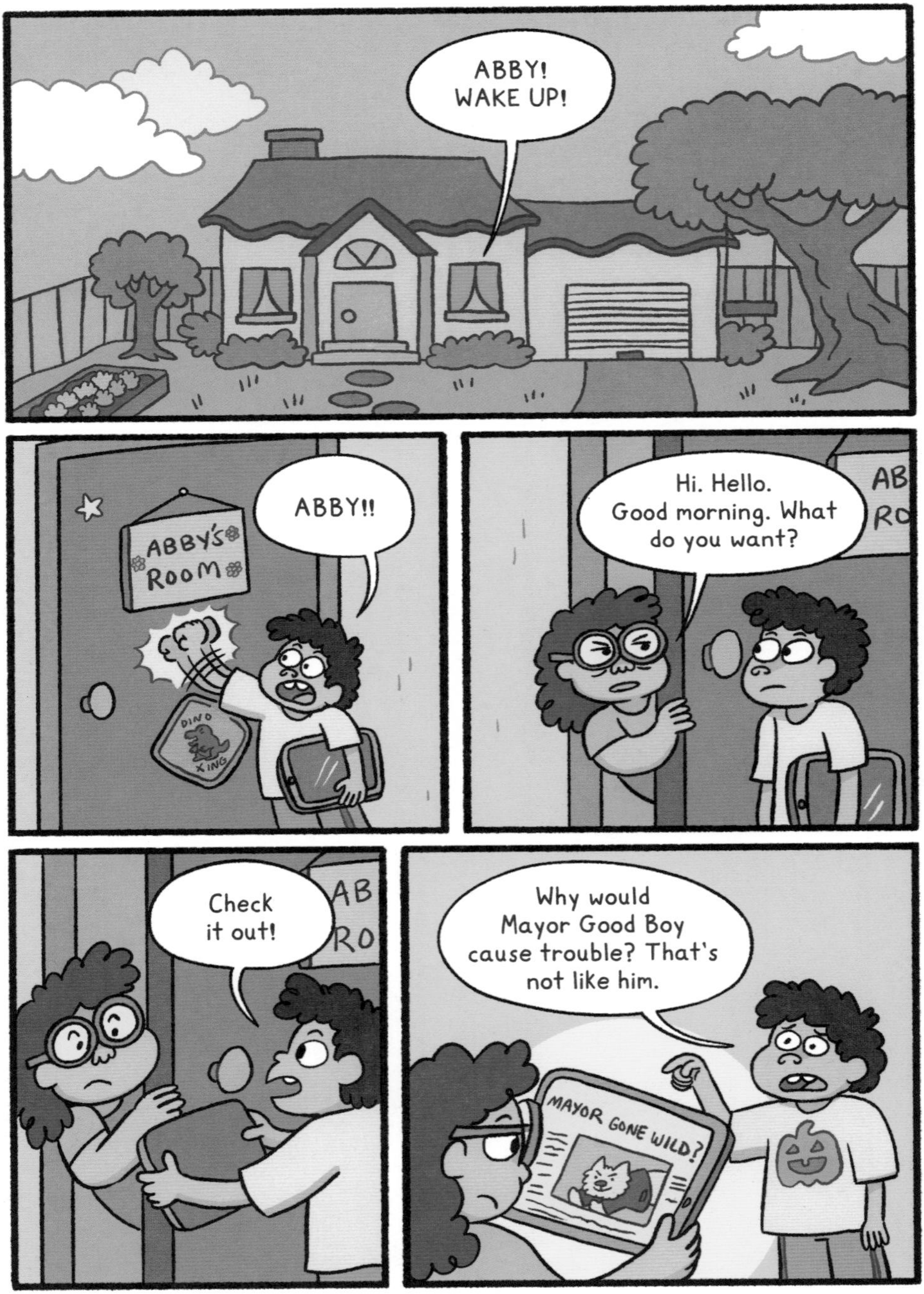
ABBY!
WAKE UP!
ABBY'S ROOM
ABBY!!
DINO XING
Hi. Hello.
Good morning. What
do you want?
Check
it out!
Why would
Mayor Good Boy
cause trouble? That's
not like him.
MAYOR GONE WILD?

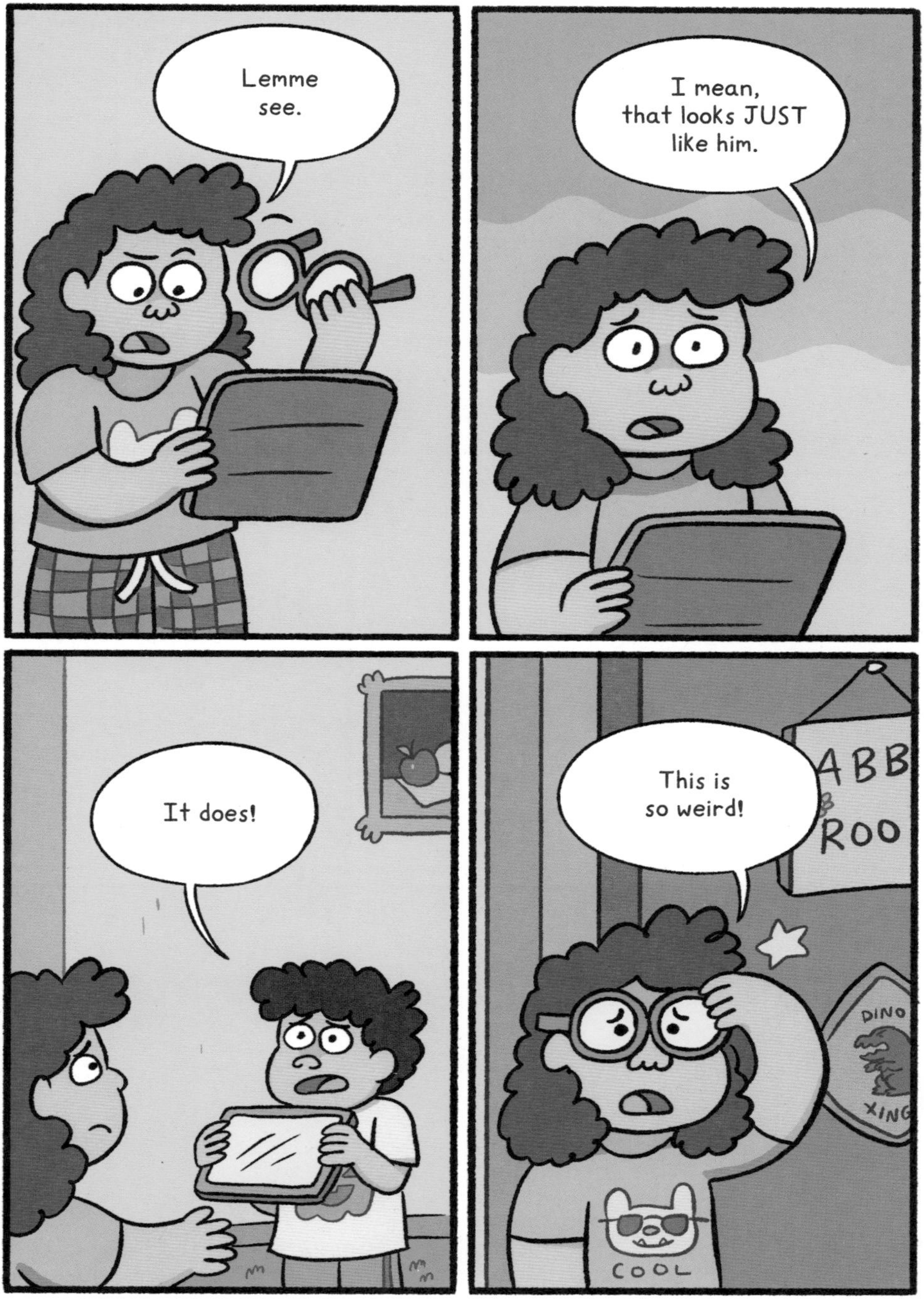
Lemme see.
I mean, that looks JUST like him.
It does!
This is so weird!
ABB
ROO
DINO
XING
COOL

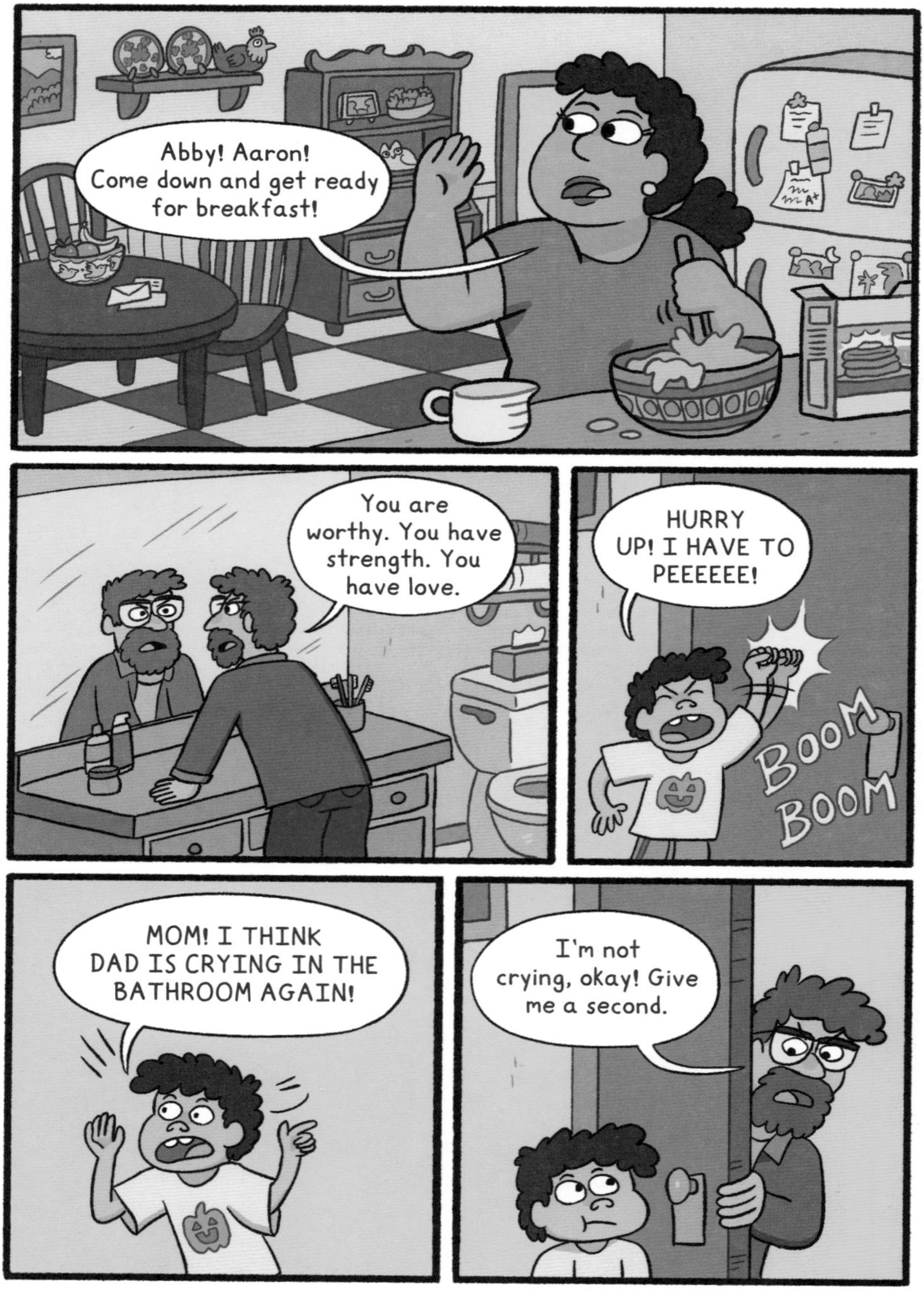
Abby! Aaron! Come down and get ready for breakfast!
You are worthy. You have strength. You have love.
HURRY UP! I HAVE TO PEEEEEE!
BOOM BOOM
MOM! I THINK DAD IS CRYING IN THE BATHROOM AGAIN!
I'm not crying, okay! Give me a second.

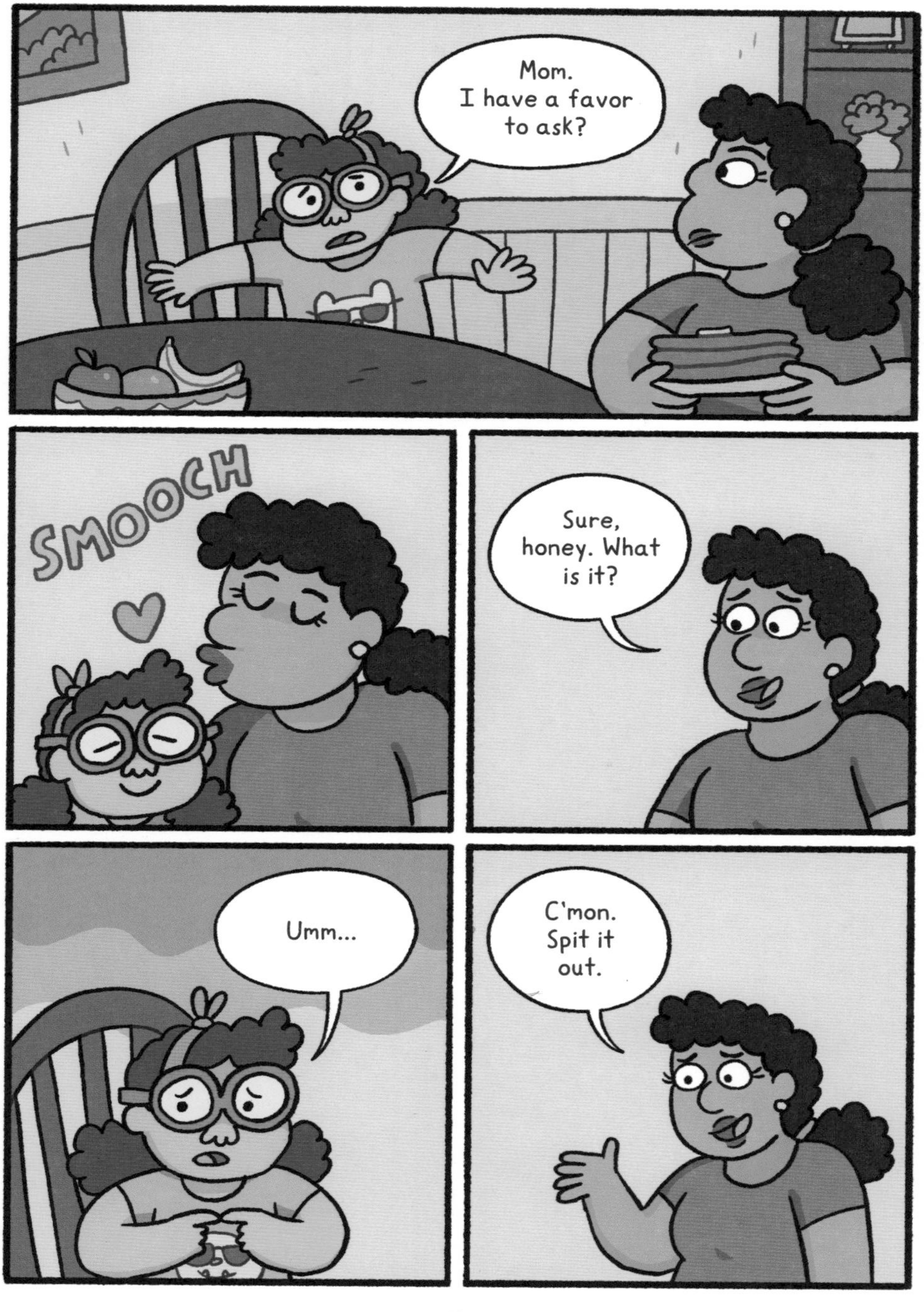
Mom.
I have a favor to ask?
SMOOCH
Sure, honey. What is it?
Umm...
C'mon. Spit it out.

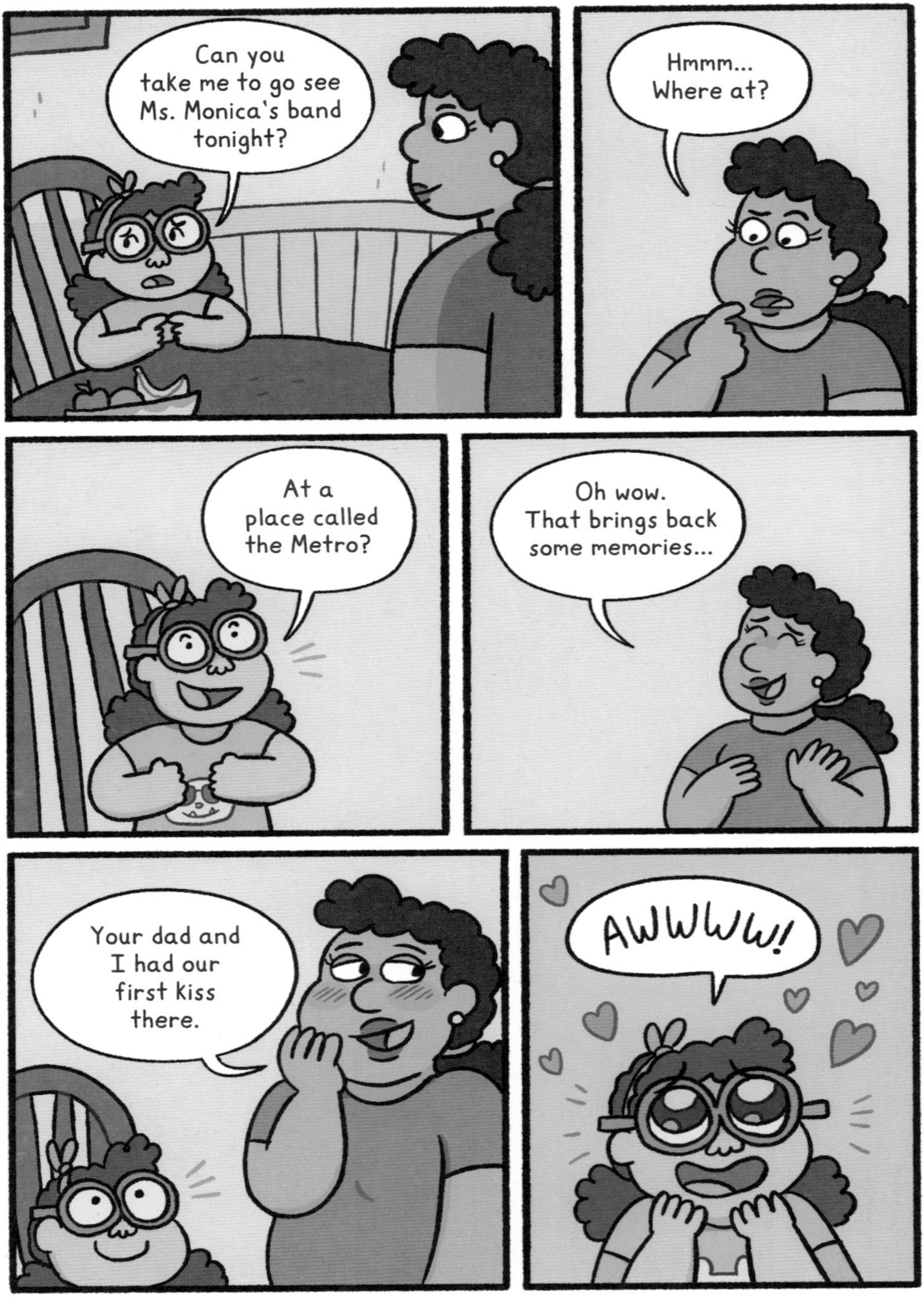

Can you take me to go see Ms. Monica's band tonight?
Hmmm... Where at?
At a place called the Metro?
Oh wow. That brings back some memories...
Your dad and I had our first kiss there.
AWWWW!

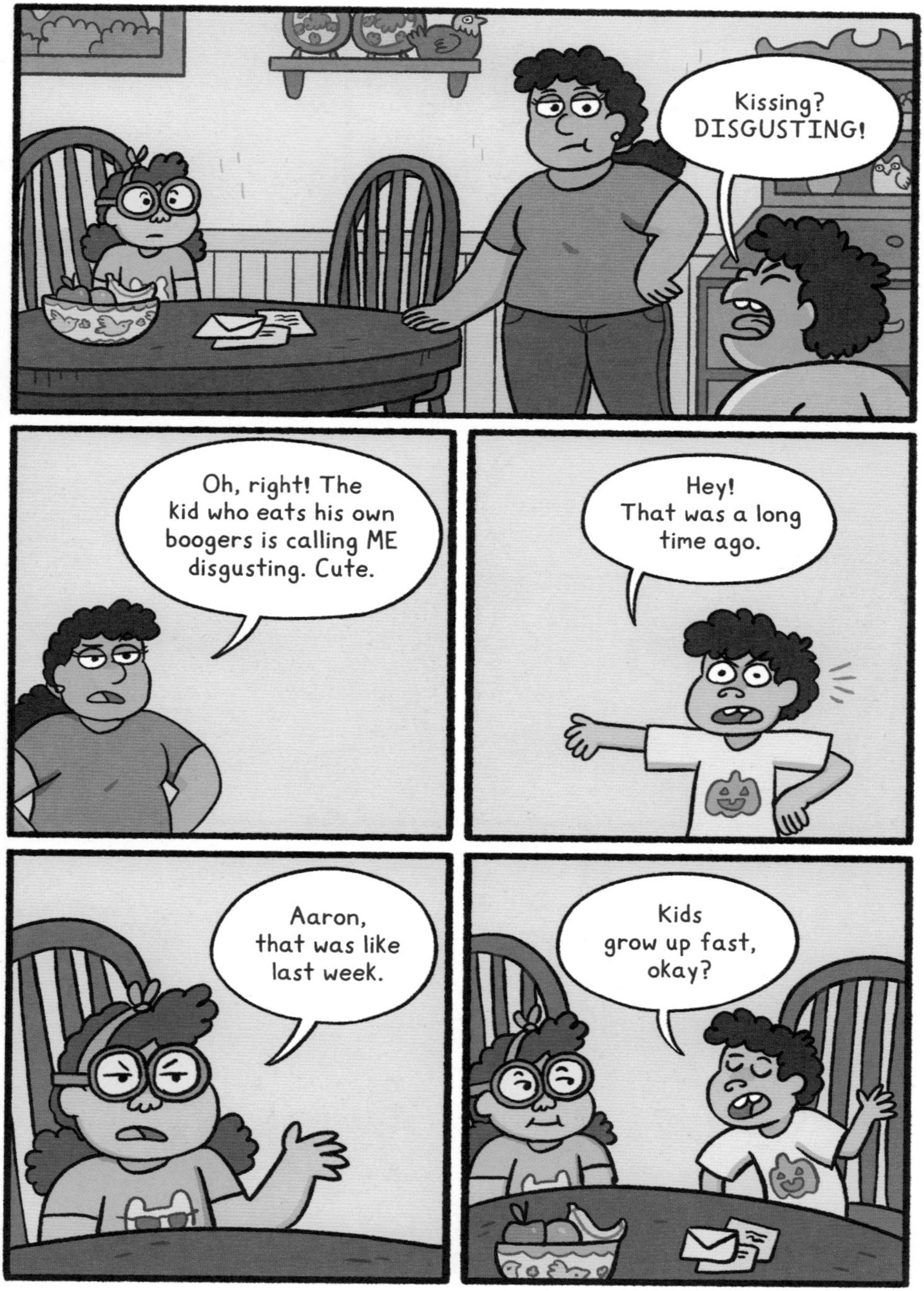
Kissing? DISGUSTING!
Oh, right! The kid who eats his own boogers is calling ME disgusting. Cute.
Hey! That was a long time ago.
Aaron, that was like last week.
Kids grow up fast, okay?

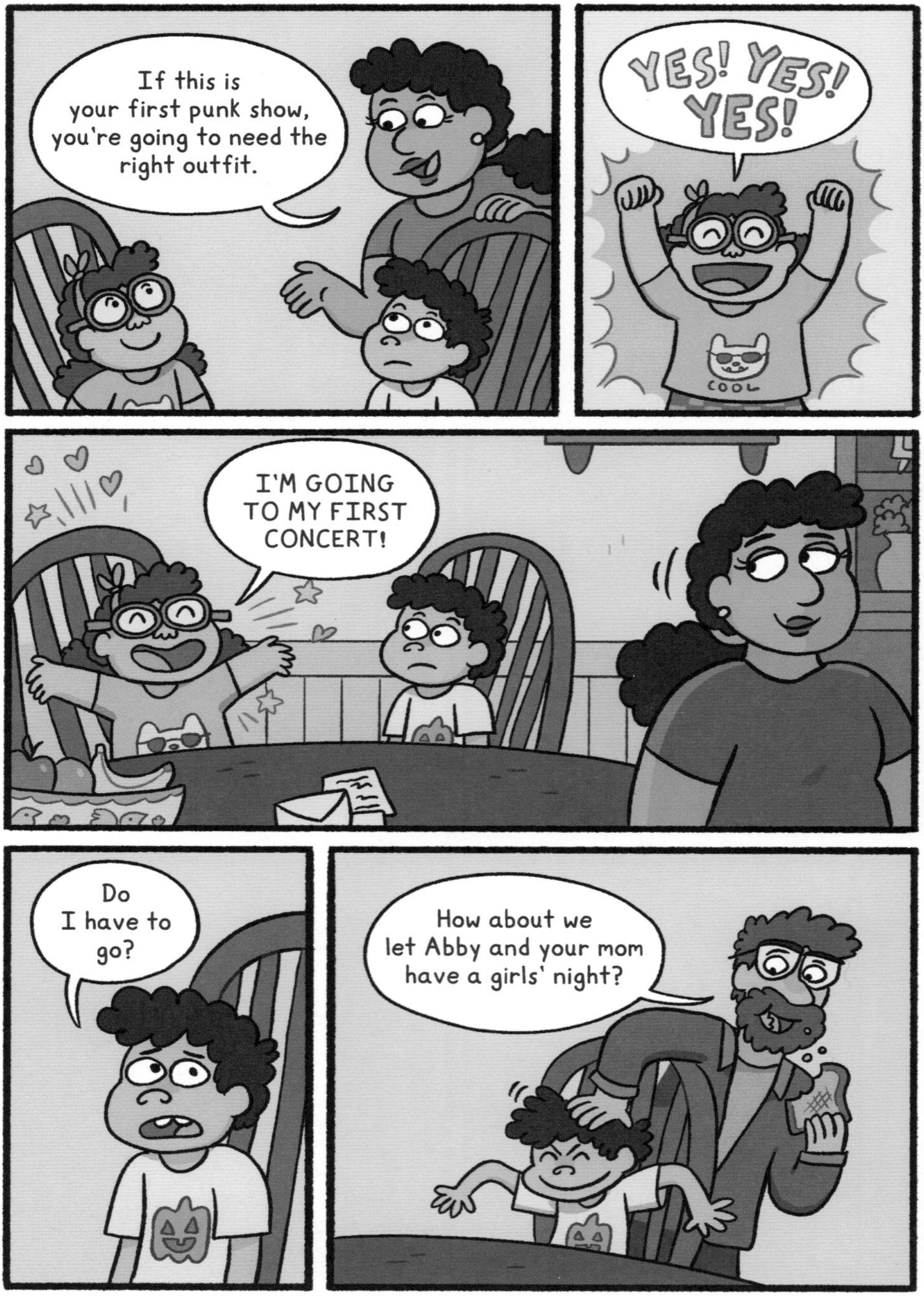
If this is your first punk show, you're going to need the right outfit.
YES! YES! YES!
COOL
I'M GOING TO MY FIRST CONCERT!
Do I have to go?
How about we let Abby and your mom have a girls' night?

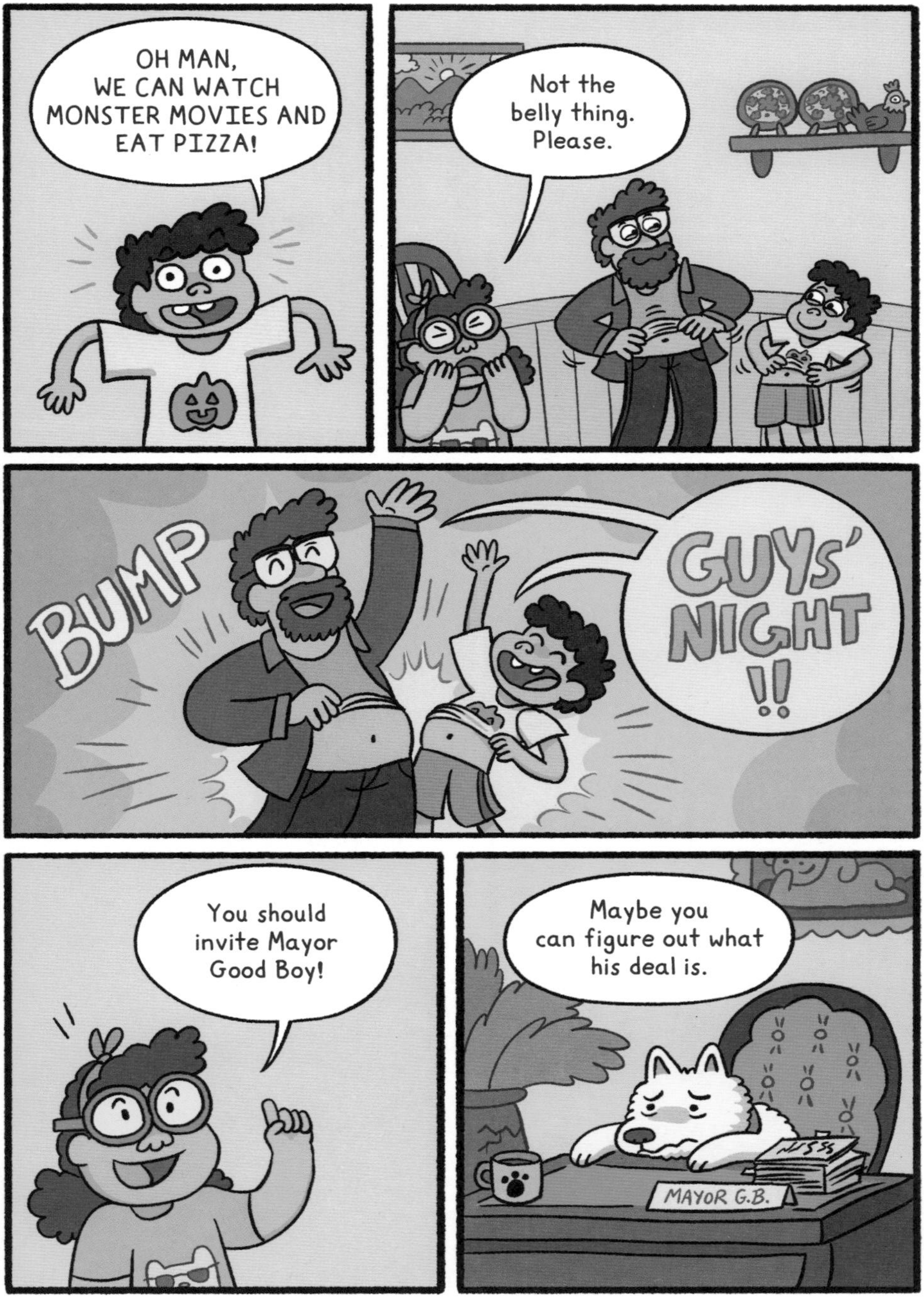
OH MAN, WE CAN WATCH MONSTER MOVIES AND EAT PIZZA!
Not the belly thing. Please.
BUMP
GUYS' NIGHT!!
You should invite Mayor Good Boy!
Maybe you can figure out what his deal is.
MAYOR G.B.

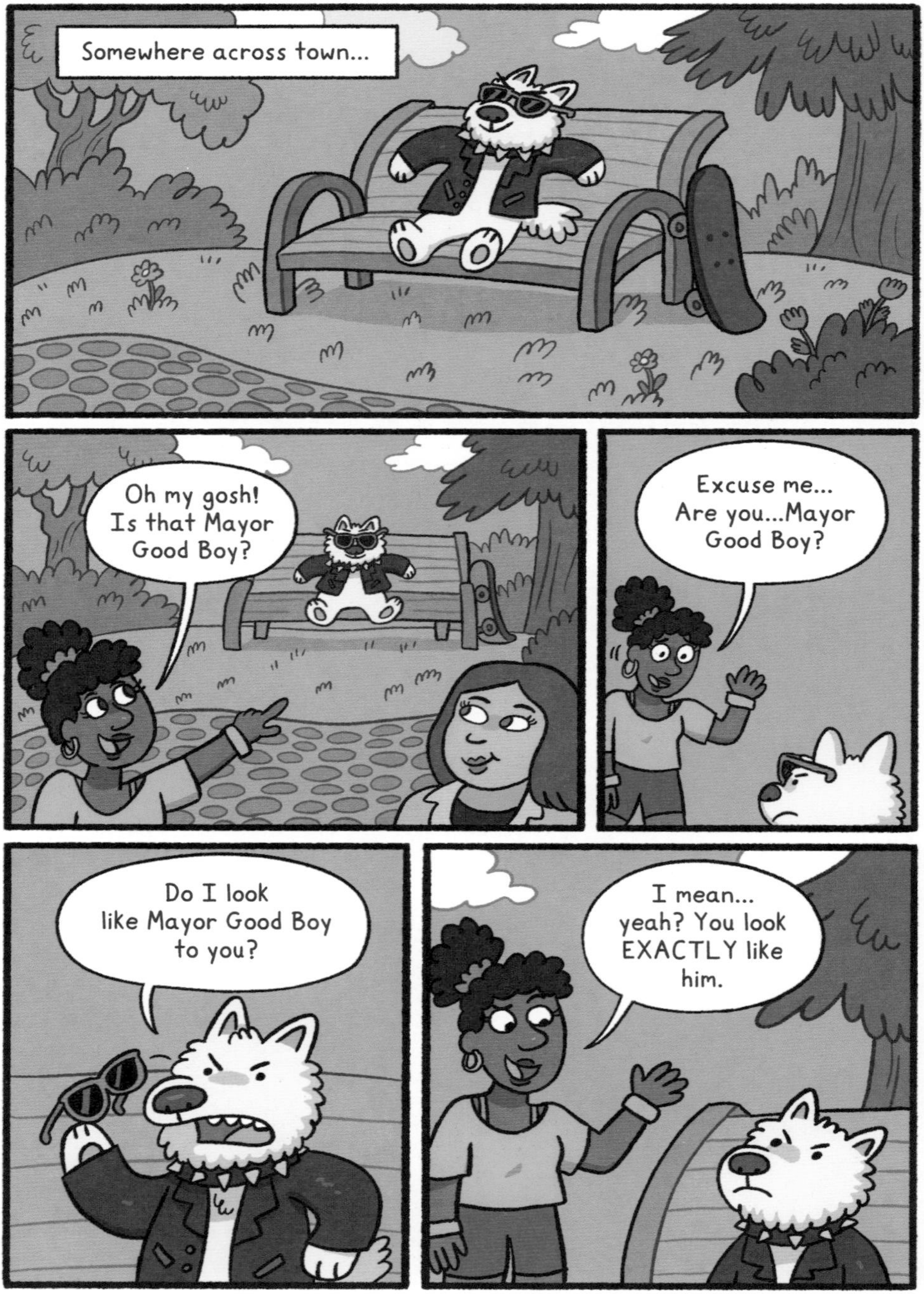

Somewhere across town...
Oh my gosh! Is that Mayor Good Boy?
Excuse me... Are you...Mayor Good Boy?
Do I look like Mayor Good Boy to you?
I mean... yeah? You look EXACTLY like him.

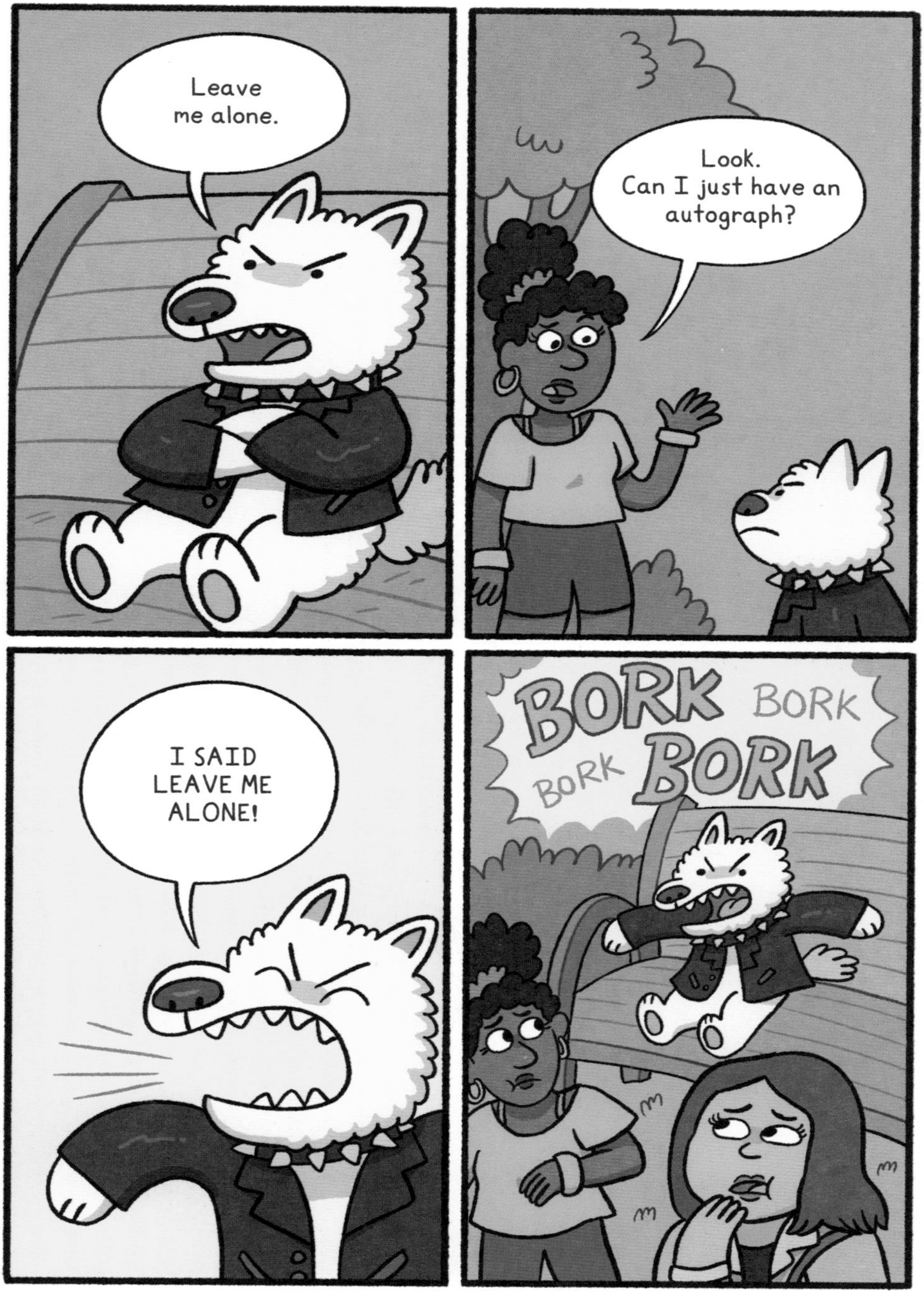
Leave me alone.
Look. Can I just have an autograph?
I SAID LEAVE ME ALONE!
BORK BORK BORK BORK

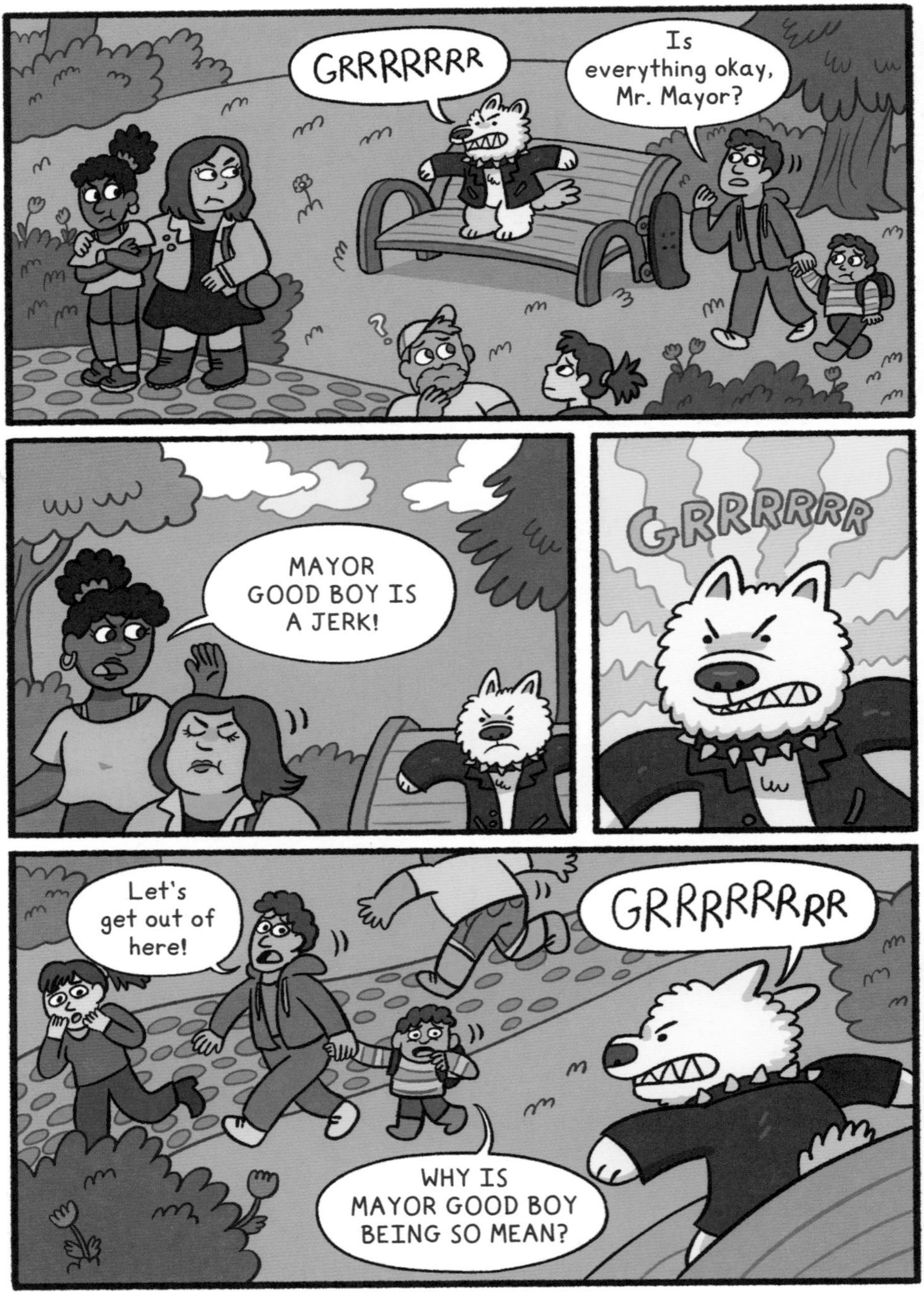
GRRRRRRR
Is everything okay, Mr. Mayor?
MAYOR GOOD BOY IS A JERK!
GRRRRRRR
Let's get out of here!
GRRRRRRRR
WHY IS MAYOR GOOD BOY BEING SO MEAN?

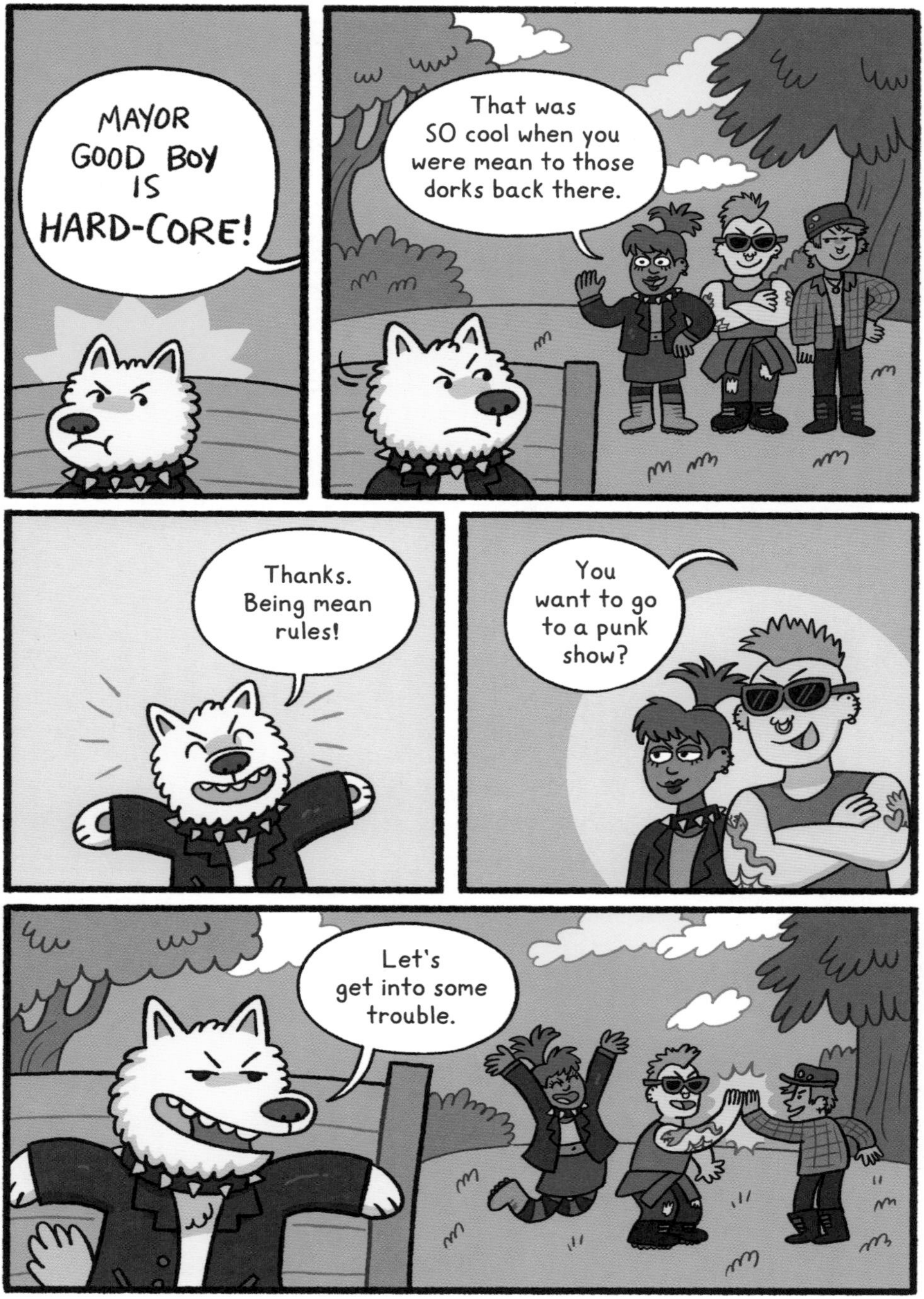
MAYOR GOOD BOY IS HARD-CORE!
That was SO cool when you were mean to those dorks back there.
Thanks. Being mean rules!
You want to go to a punk show?
Let's get into some trouble.

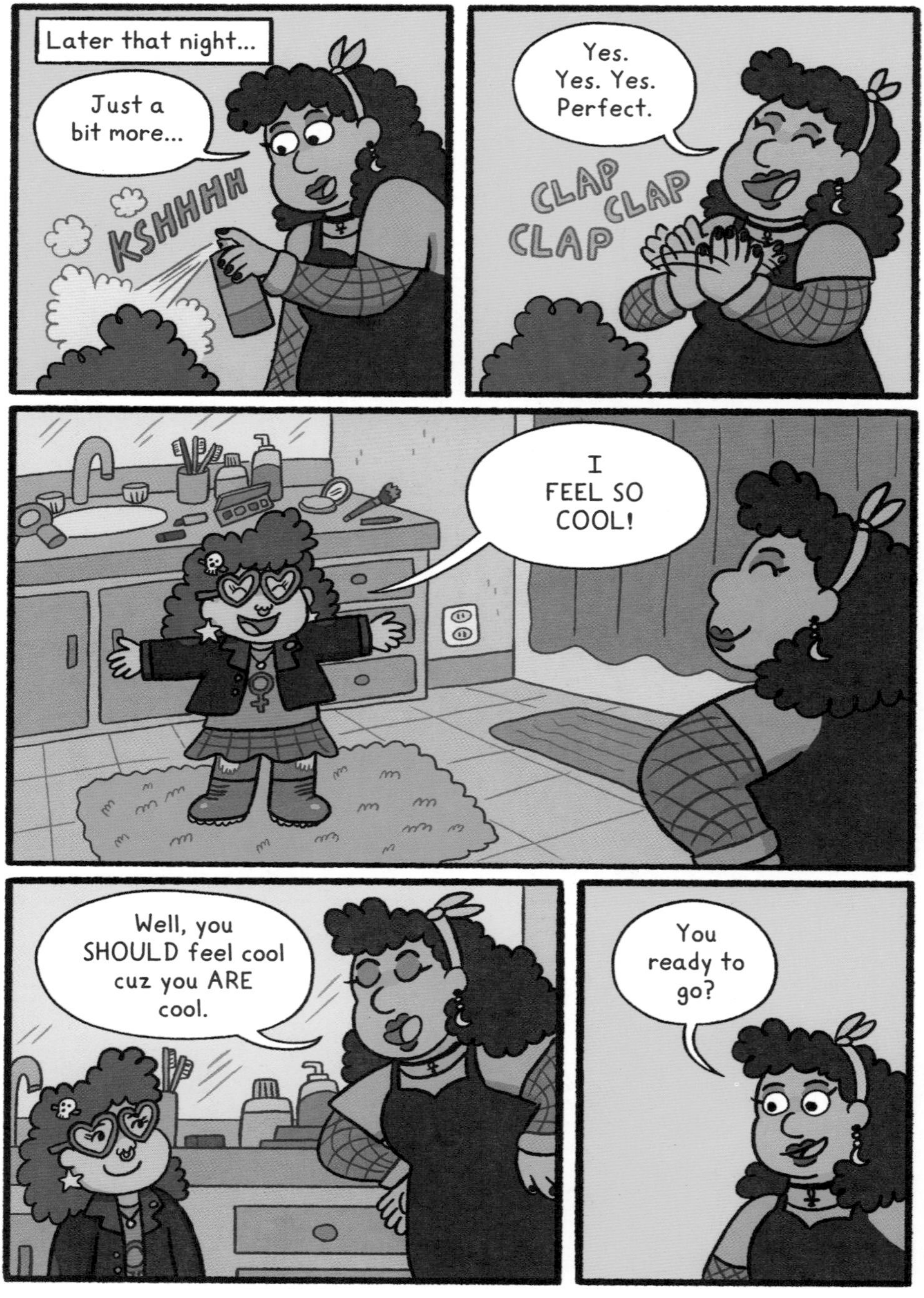
Later that night...
Just a bit more...
KSHHHH
Yes. Yes. Yes. Perfect.
CLAP CLAP CLAP
I FEEL SO COOL!
Well, you SHOULD feel cool cuz you ARE cool.
You ready to go?

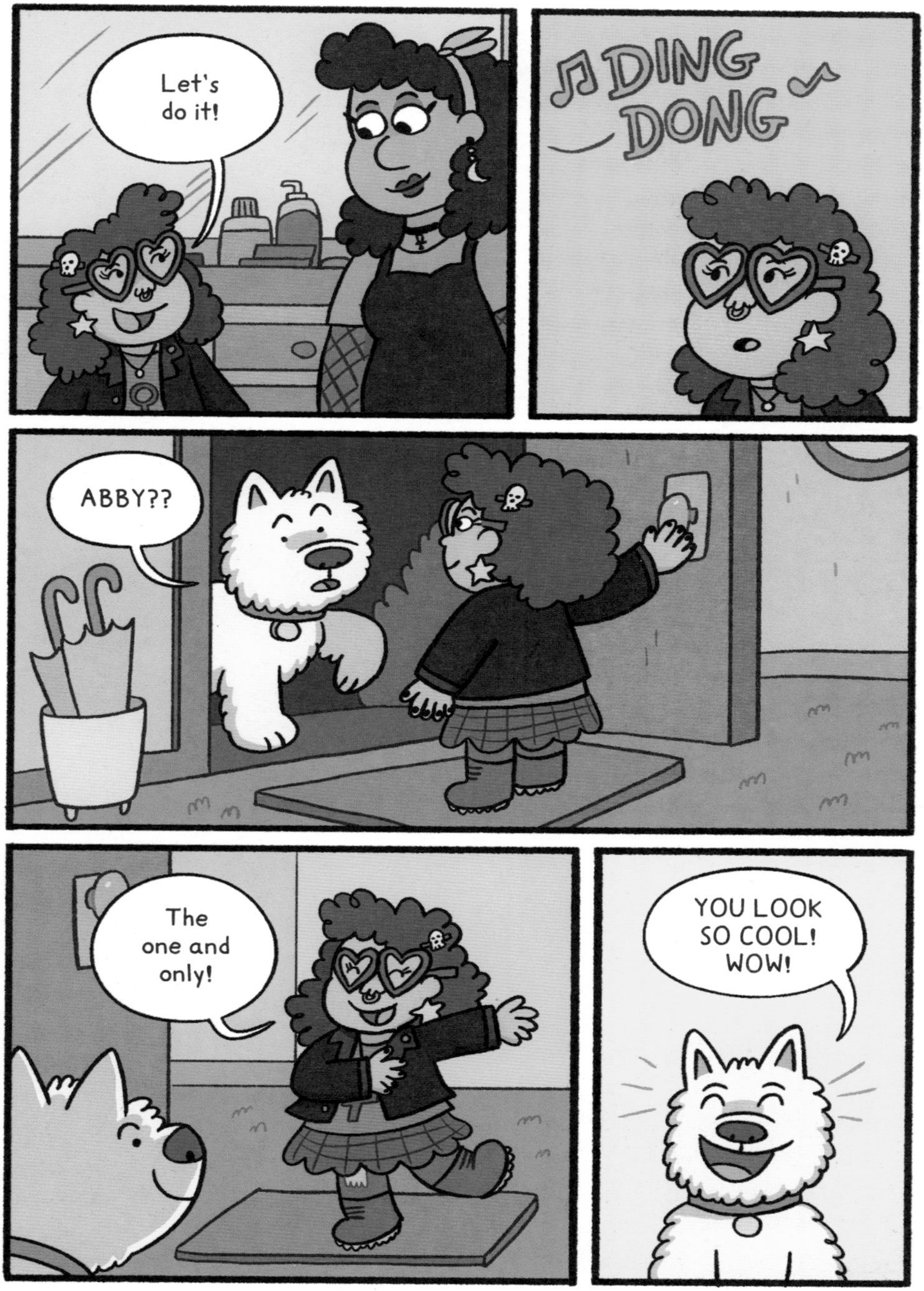
Let's do it!
DING DONG
ABBY??
The one and only!
YOU LOOK SO COOL! WOW!

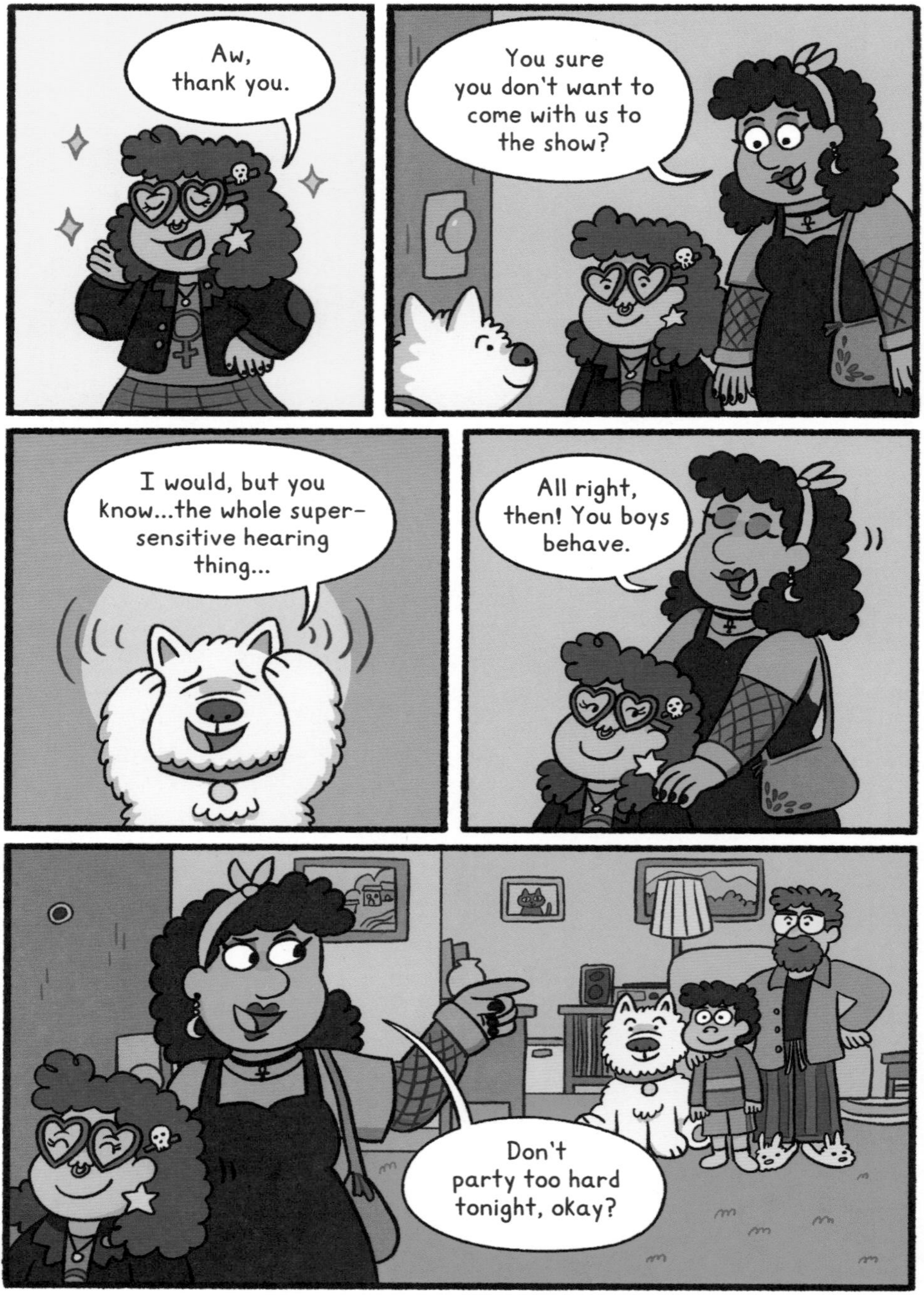
Aw, thank you.
You sure you don't want to come with us to the show?
I would, but you know...the whole super-sensitive hearing thing...
All right, then! You boys behave.
Don't party too hard tonight, okay?

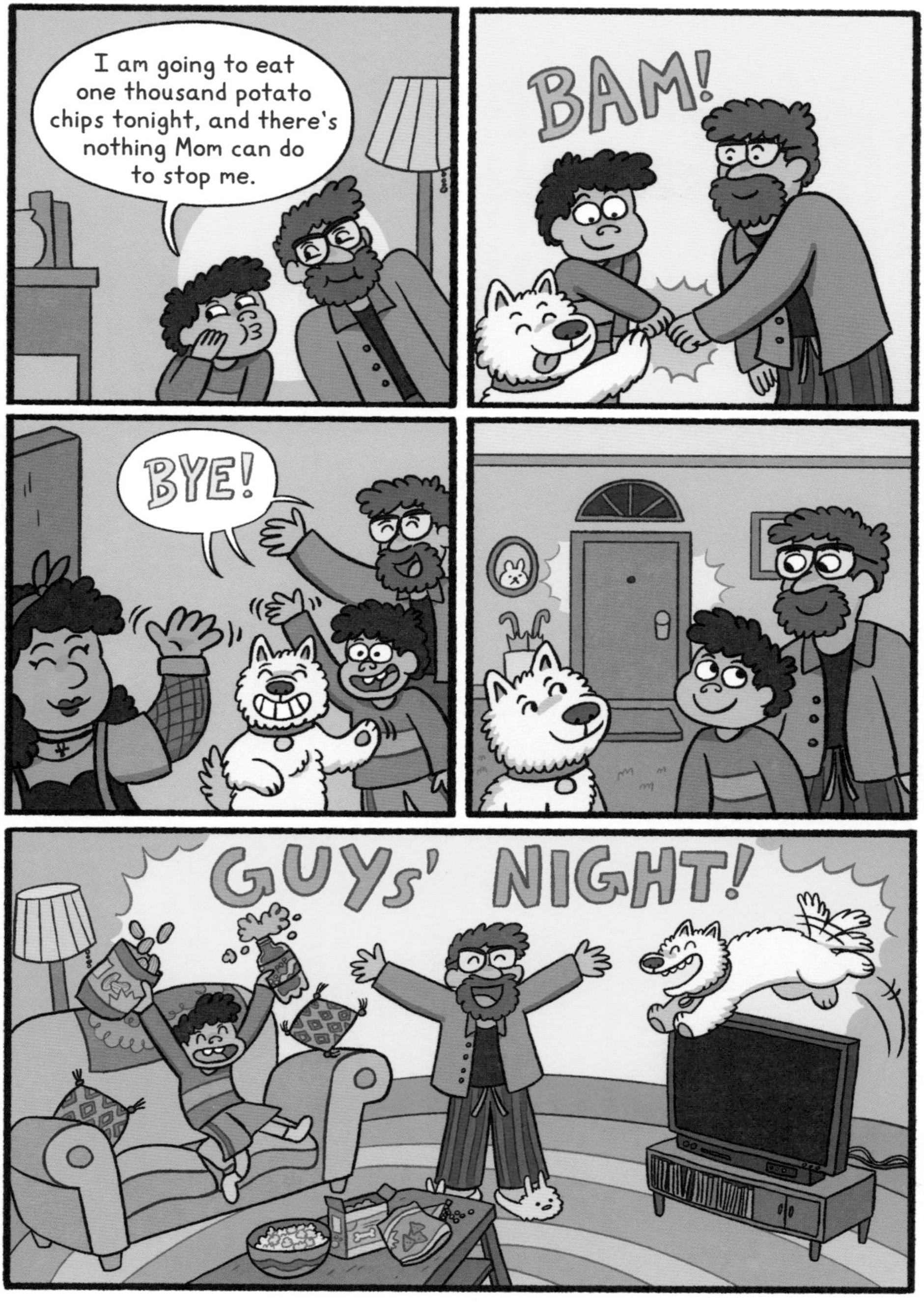
I am going to eat one thousand potato chips tonight, and there's nothing Mom can do to stop me.
BAM!
BYE!
GUYs' NIGHT!

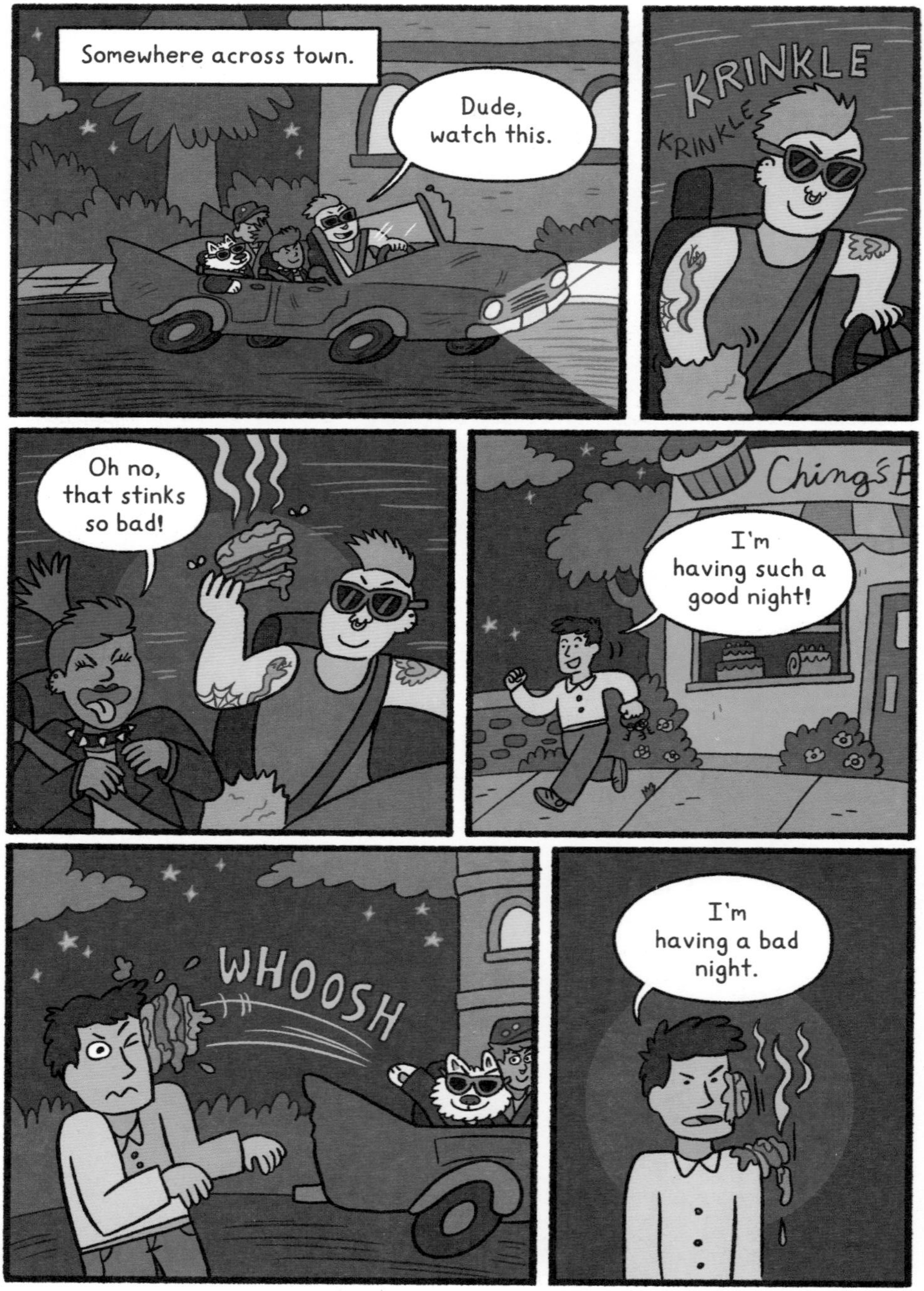
Somewhere across town.
Dude, watch this.
KRINKLE
KRINKLE
Oh no, that stinks so bad!
Ching's B
I'm having such a good night!
WHOOSH
I'm having a bad night.

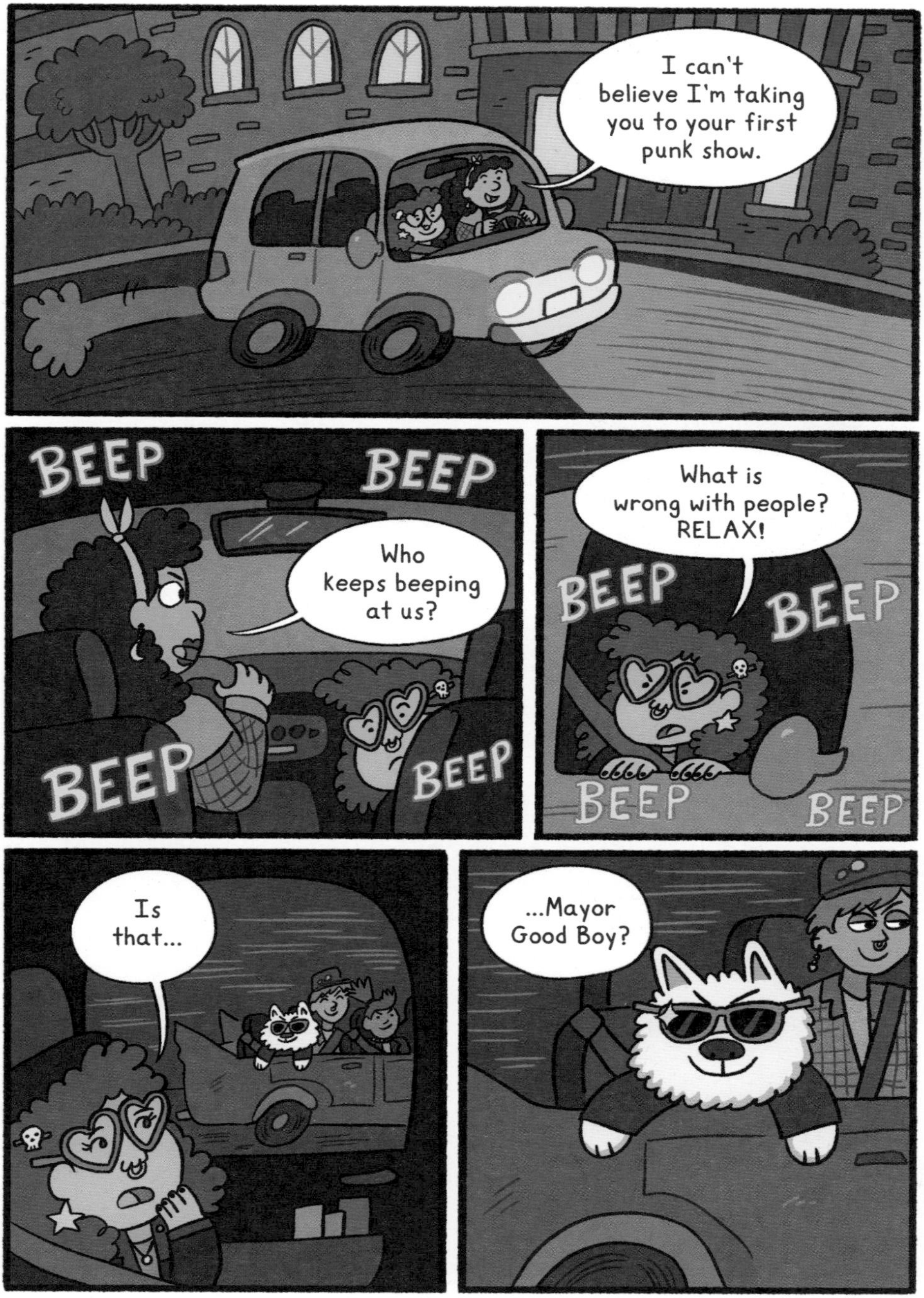
I can't believe I'm taking you to your first punk show.
BEEP
BEEP
Who keeps beeping at us?
BEEP
BEEP
What is wrong with people? RELAX!
BEEP
BEEP
BEEP
BEEP
Is that...
...Mayor Good Boy?

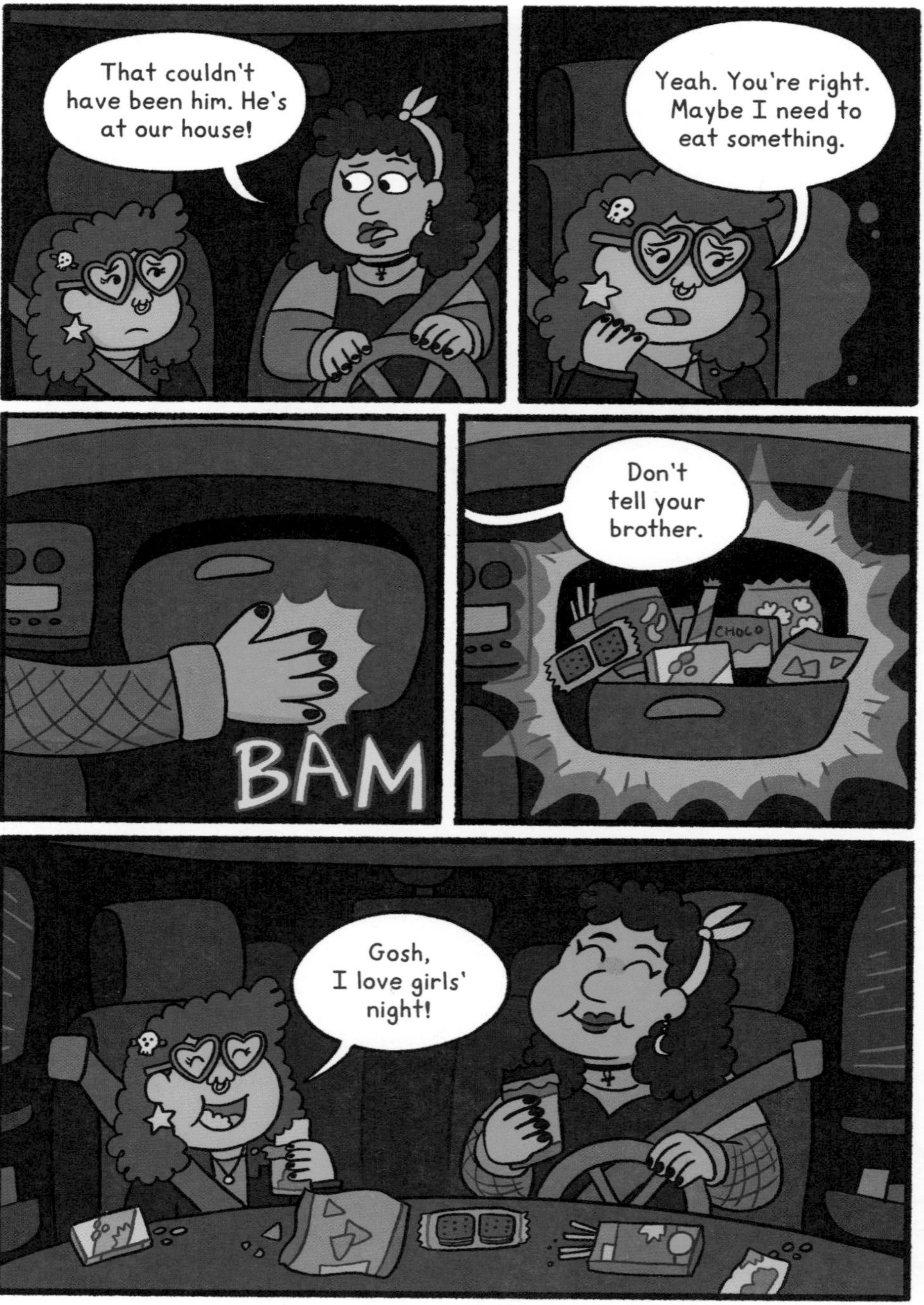
That couldn't have been him. He's at our house!
Yeah. You're right. Maybe I need to eat something.
BAM
Don't tell your brother.
CHOCO
Gosh, I love girls' night!

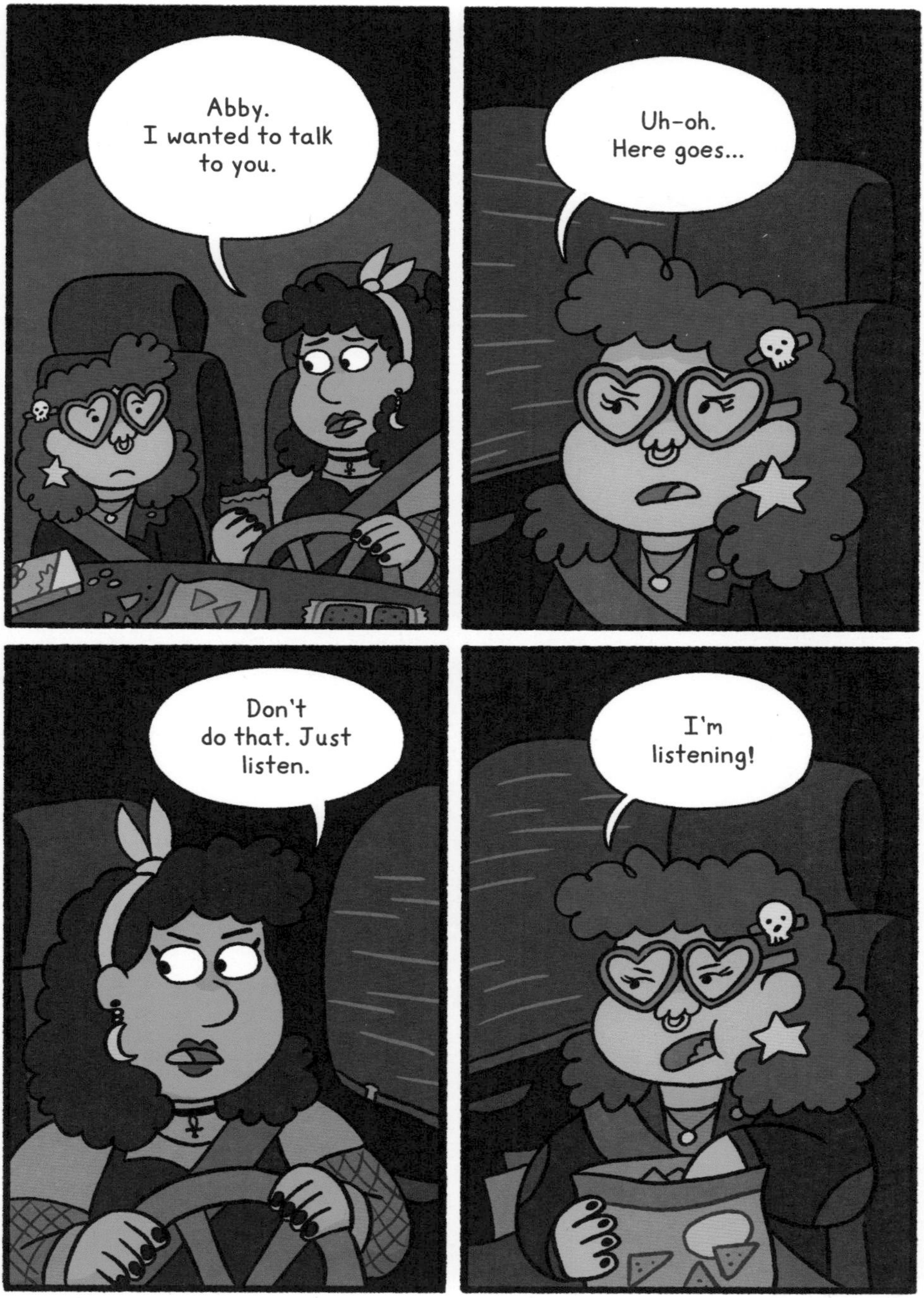
Abby.
I wanted to talk to you.
Uh-oh.
Here goes...
Don't do that. Just listen.
I'm listening!

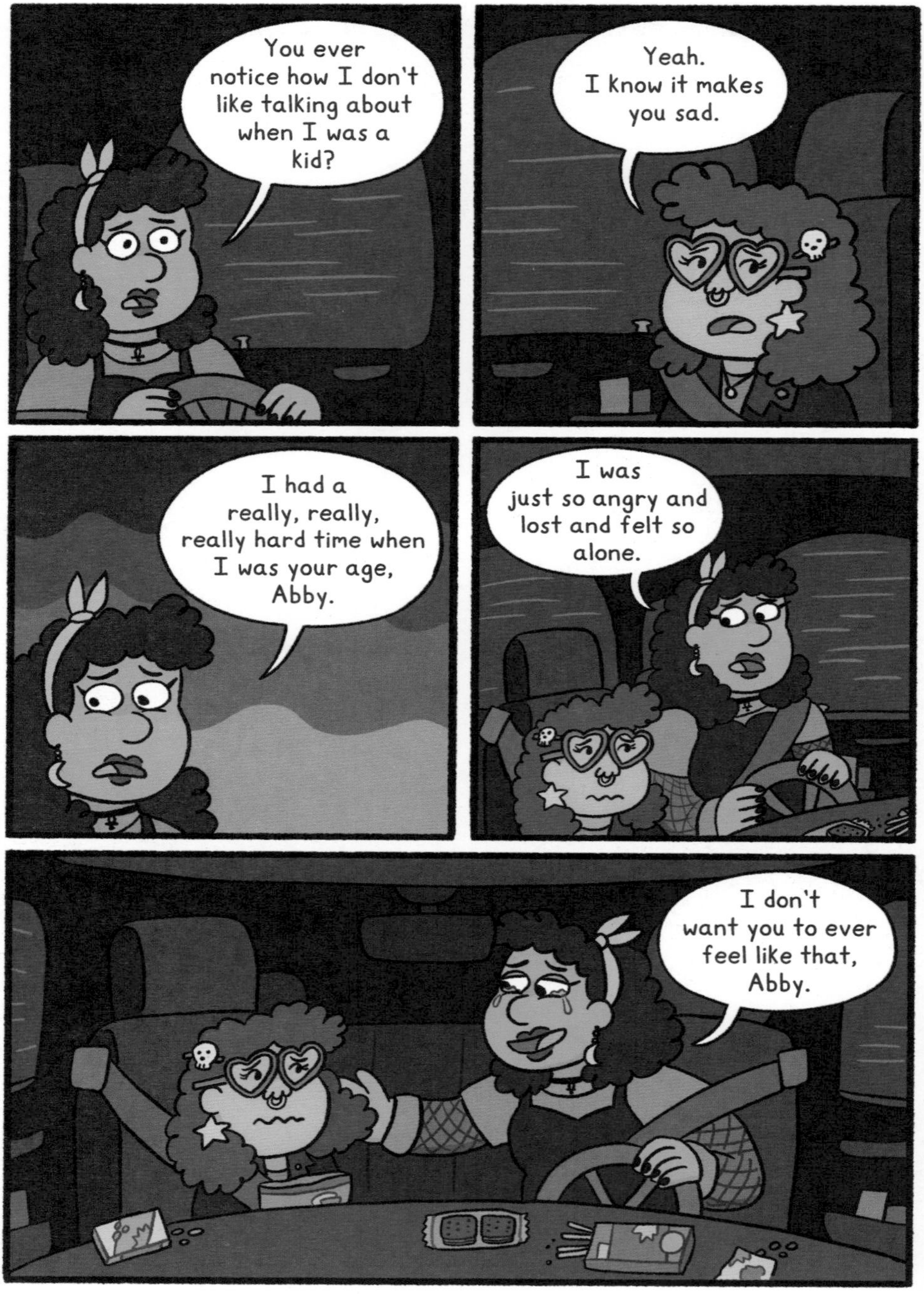
You ever notice how I don't like talking about when I was a kid?
Yeah. I know it makes you sad.
I had a really, really, really hard time when I was your age, Abby.
I was just so angry and lost and felt so alone.
I don't want you to ever feel like that, Abby.

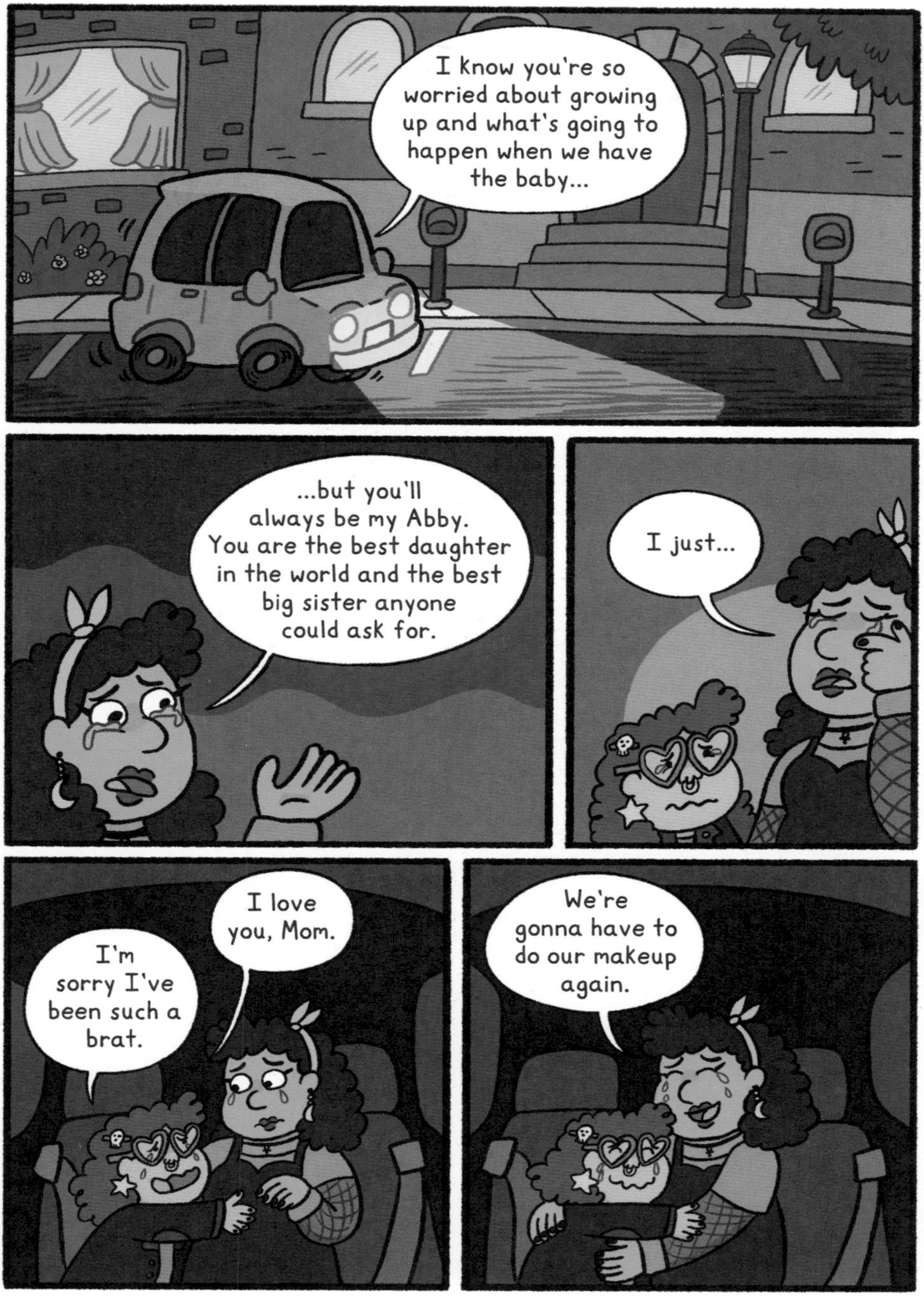
I know you're so worried about growing up and what's going to happen when we have the baby...
...but you'll always be my Abby. You are the best daughter in the world and the best big sister anyone could ask for.
I just...
I'm sorry I've been such a brat.
I love you, Mom.
We're gonna have to do our makeup again.

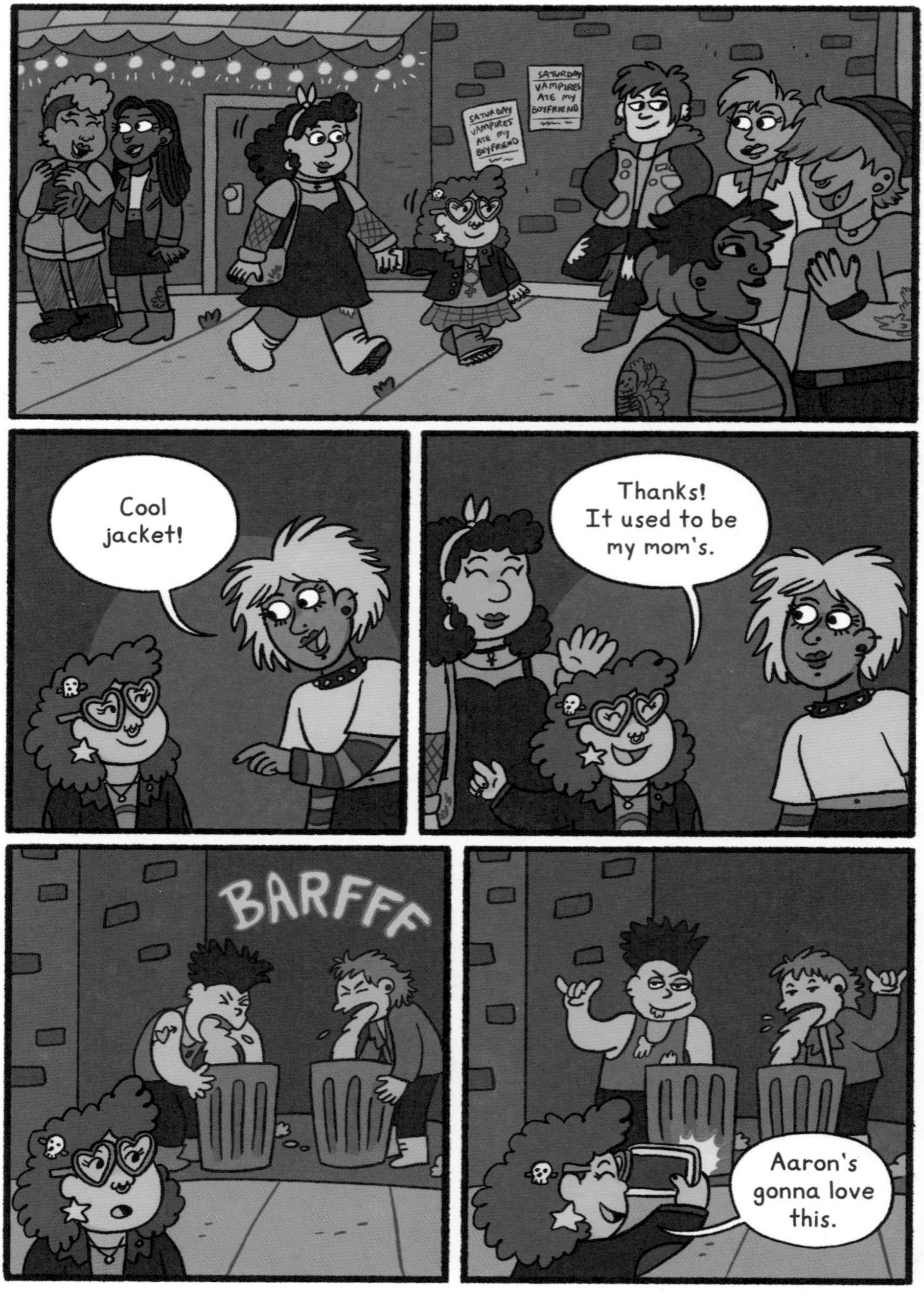
SATURDAY VAMPIRES ATE MY BOYFRIEND
SATURDAY VAMPIRES ATE MY BOYFRIEND
Cool jacket!
Thanks! It used to be my mom's.
BARFFF
Aaron's gonna love this.

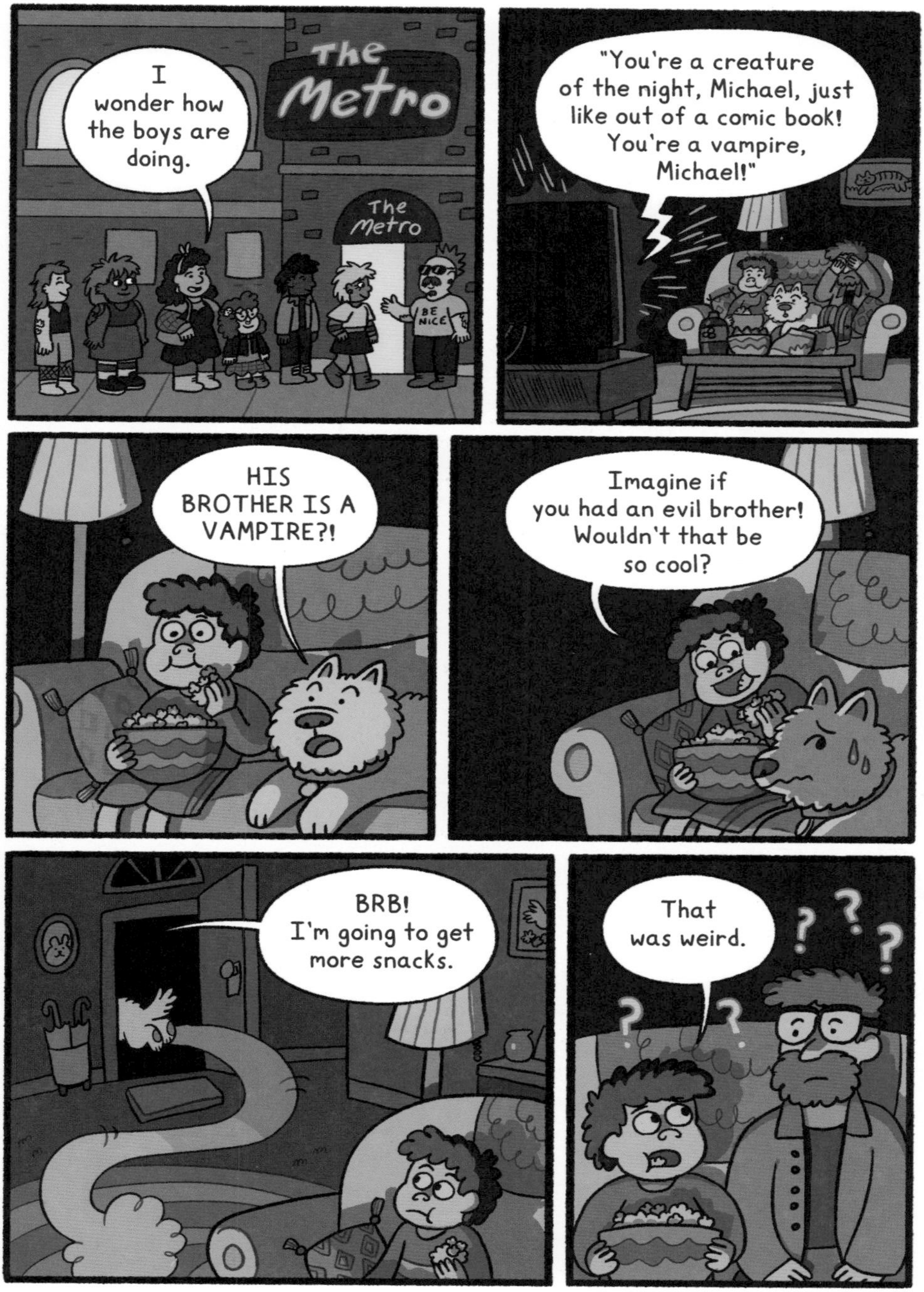

The Metro
I wonder how the boys are doing.
The Metro
BE NICE
"You're a creature of the night, Michael, just like out of a comic book! You're a vampire, Michael!"
HIS BROTHER IS A VAMPIRE?!
Imagine if you had an evil brother! Wouldn't that be so cool?
BRB! I'm going to get more snacks.
That was weird.

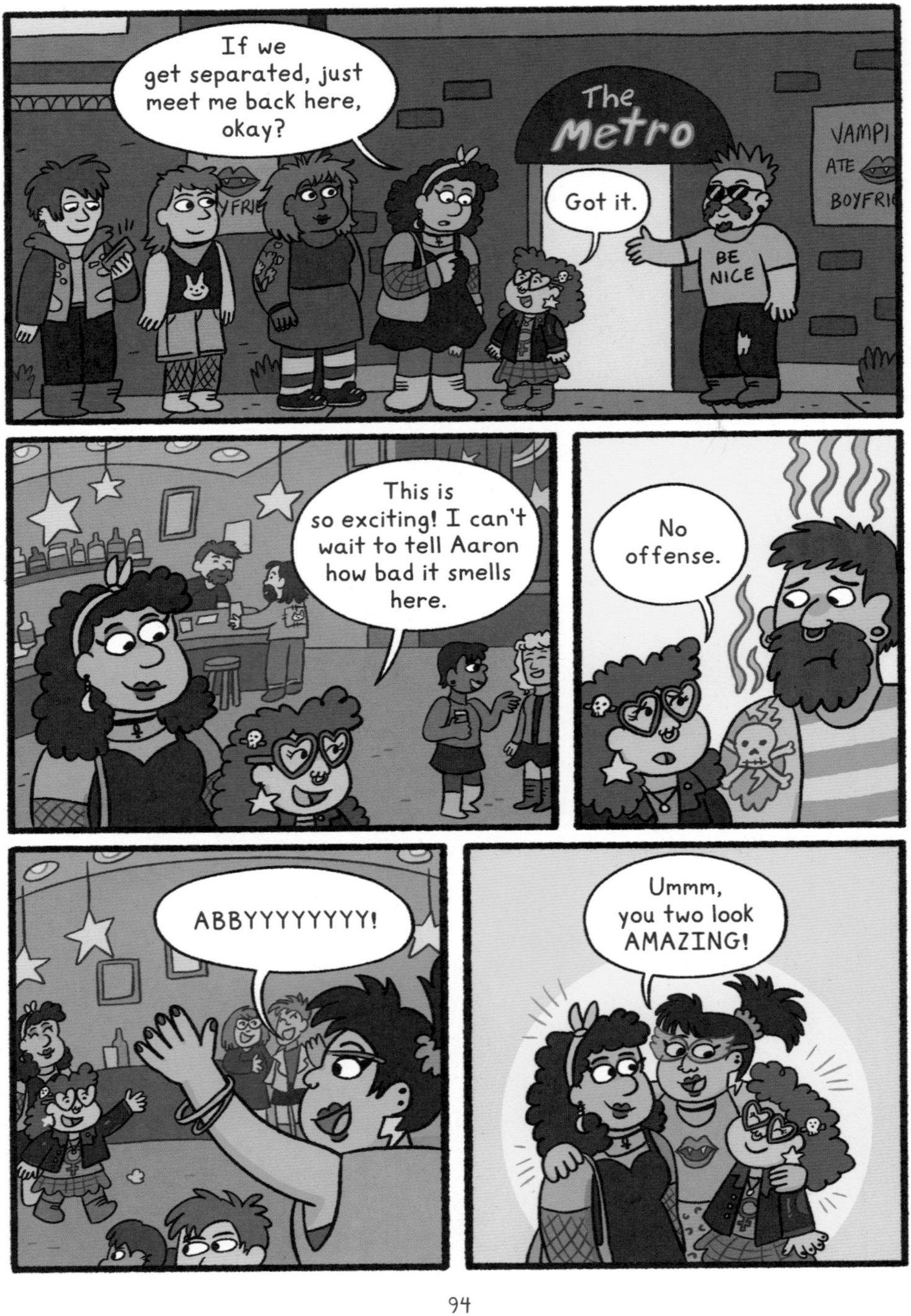
If we get separated, just meet me back here, okay?
The Metro
VAMPI ATE BOYFRI
Got it.
BE NICE
This is so exciting! I can't wait to tell Aaron how bad it smells here.
No offense.
ABBYYYYYYYYY!
Ummm, you two look AMAZING!

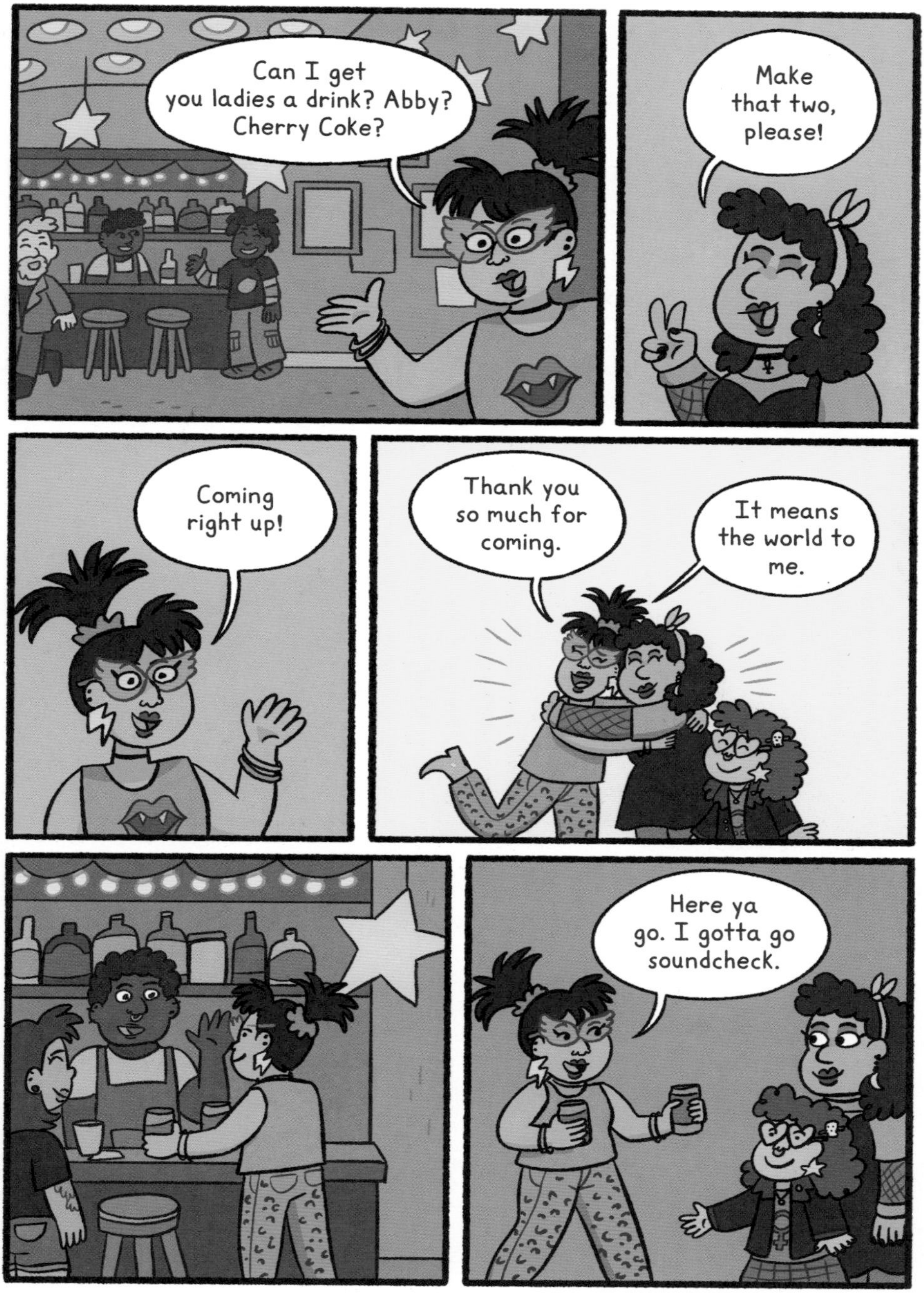
Can I get you ladies a drink? Abby? Cherry Coke?
Make that two, please!
Coming right up!
Thank you so much for coming.
It means the world to me.
Here ya go. I gotta go soundcheck.

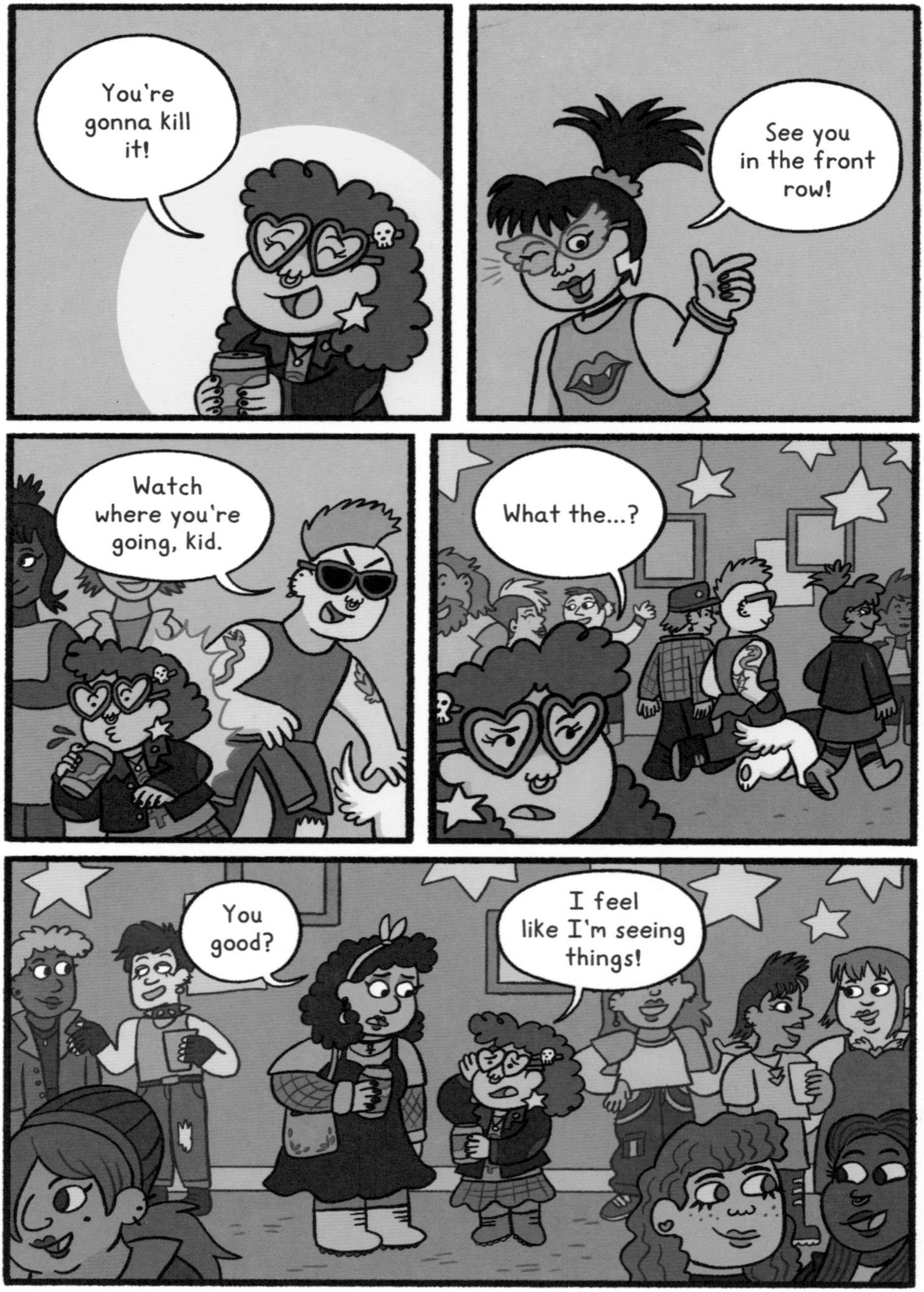
You're gonna kill it!
See you in the front row!
Watch where you're going, kid.
What the...?
You good?
I feel like I'm seeing things!

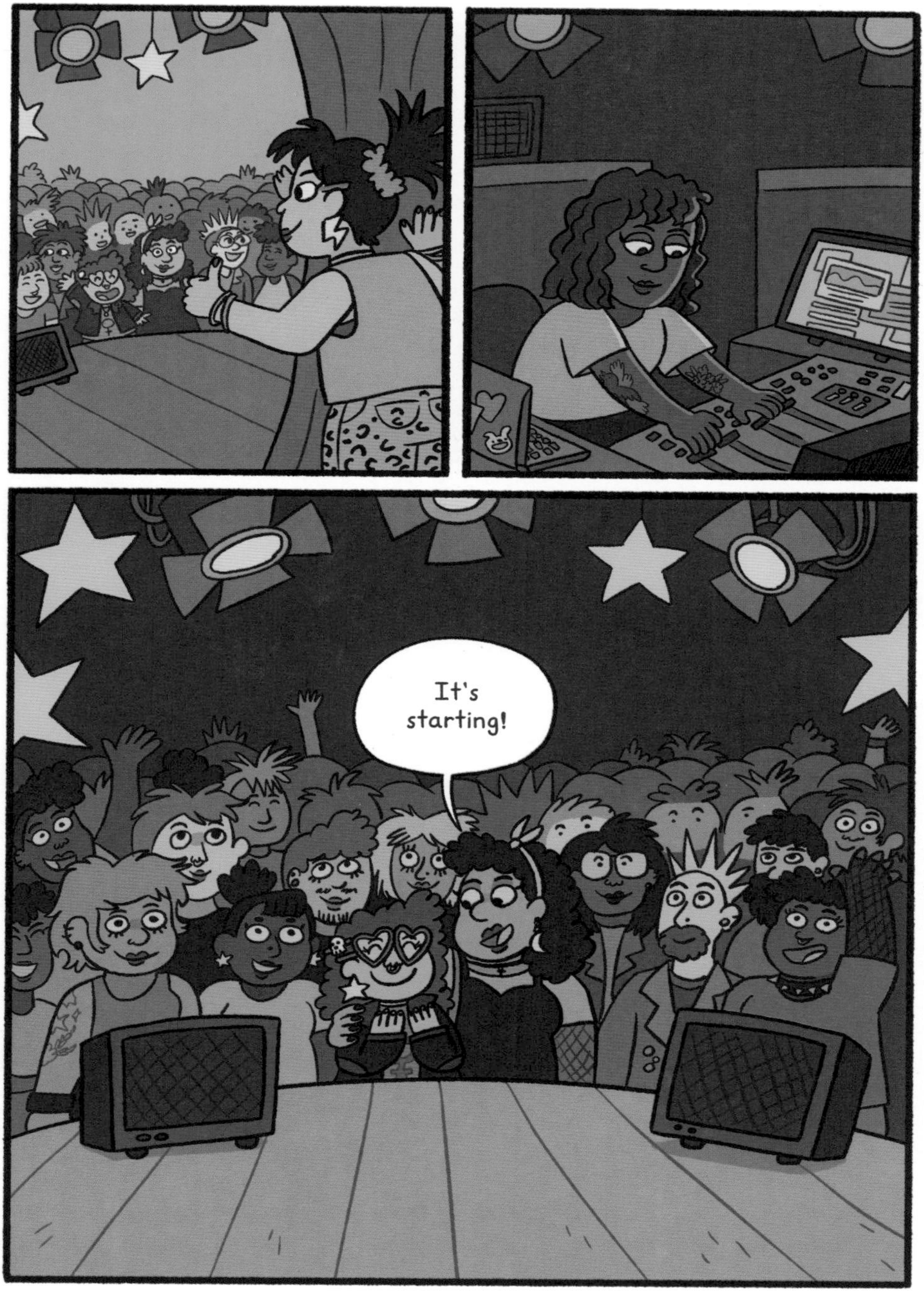
It's starting!

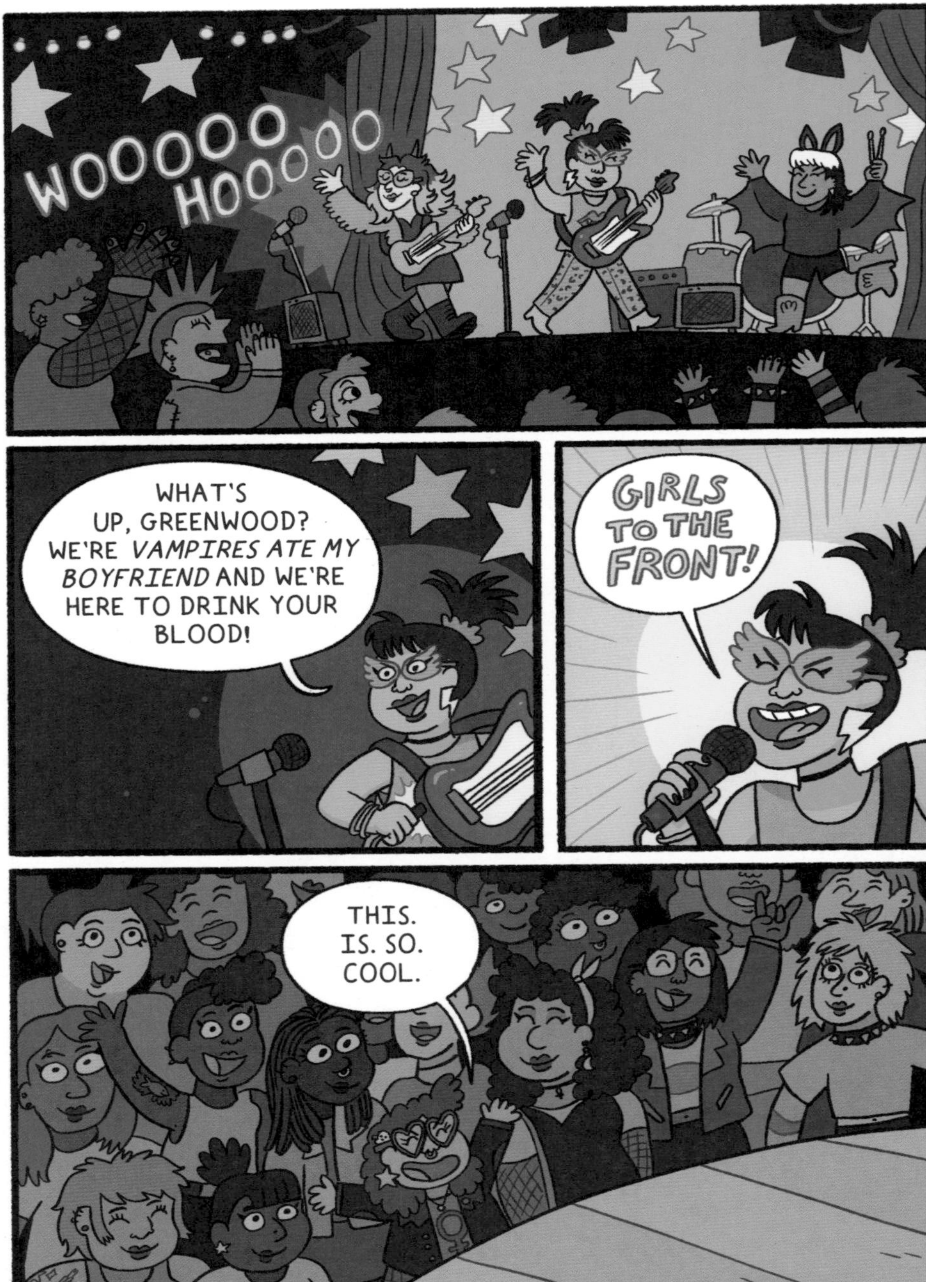
WOOOOO HOOOOOO
WHAT'S UP, GREENWOOD? WE'RE *VAMPIRES ATE MY BOYFRIEND* AND WE'RE HERE TO DRINK YOUR BLOOD!
GIRLS TO THE FRONT!
THIS. IS. SO. COOL.

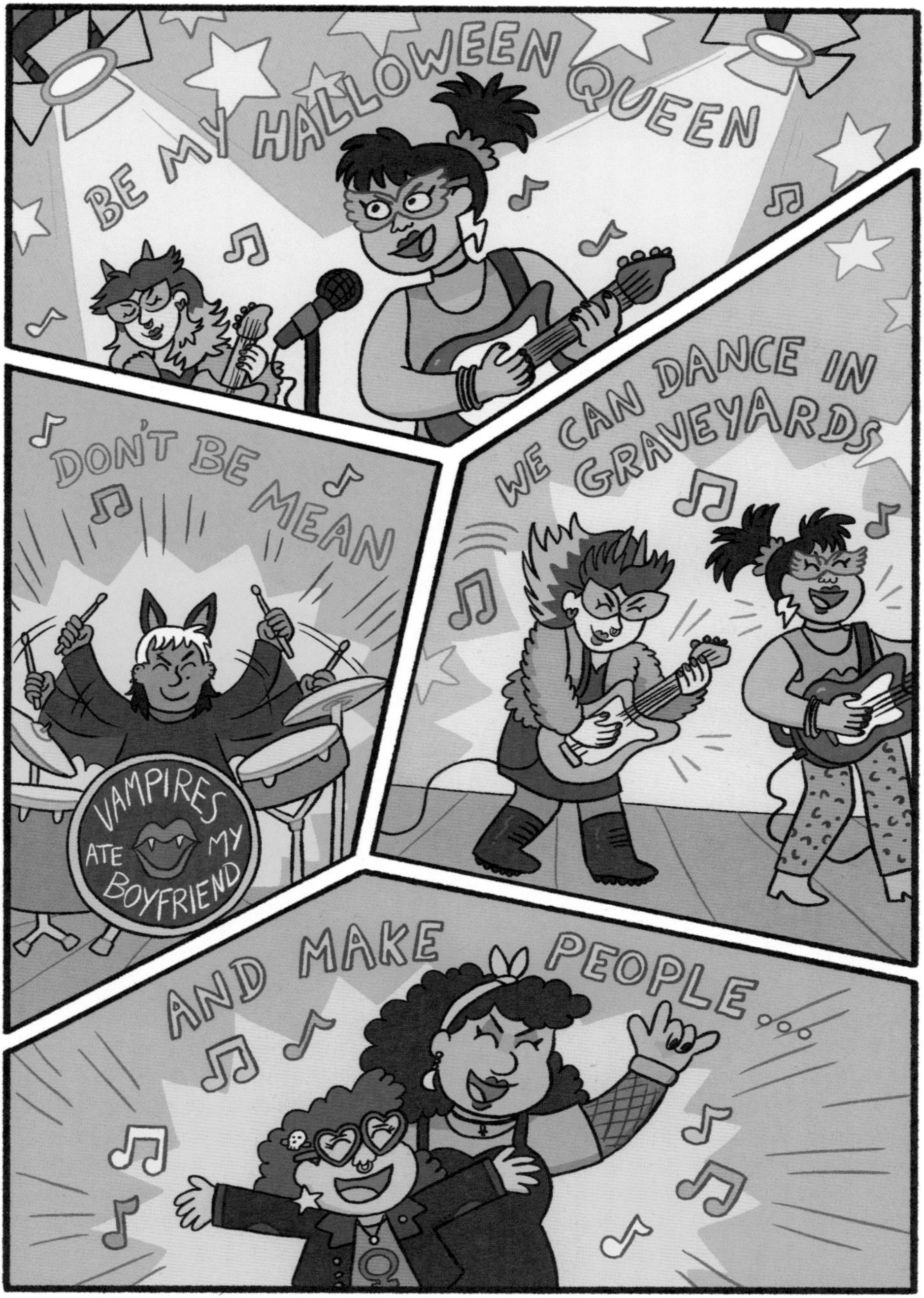
BE MY HALLOWEEN QUEEN
DON'T BE MEAN
VAMPIRES ATE MY BOYFRIEND
WE CAN DANCE IN GRAVEYARDS
AND MAKE PEOPLE...

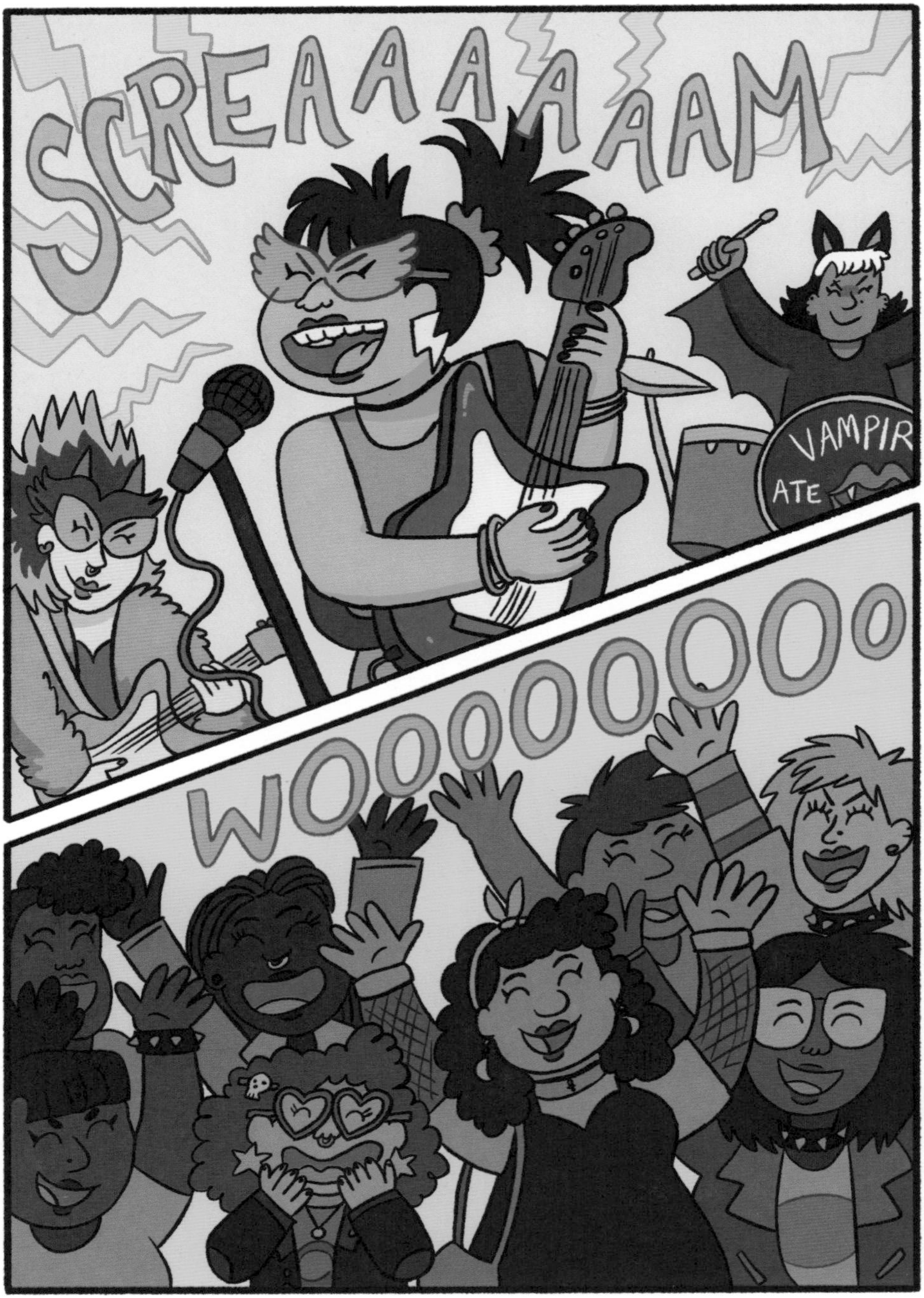
SCREAAAAAAAM
VAMPIR
ATE
WOOOOOOOOOO

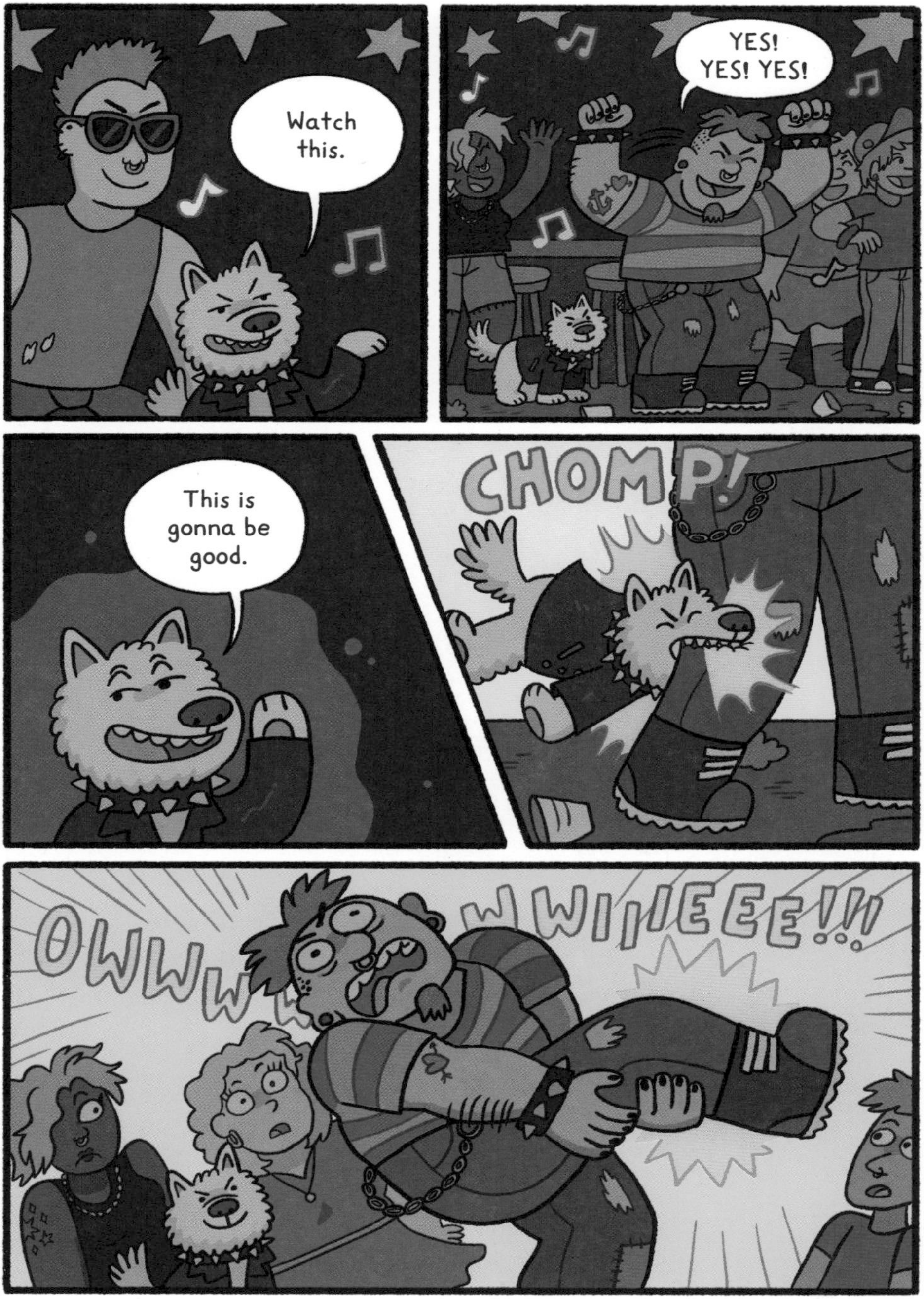

Watch this.
YES! YES! YES!
This is gonna be good.
CHOMP!
OWWW WWIIIEEE!!!

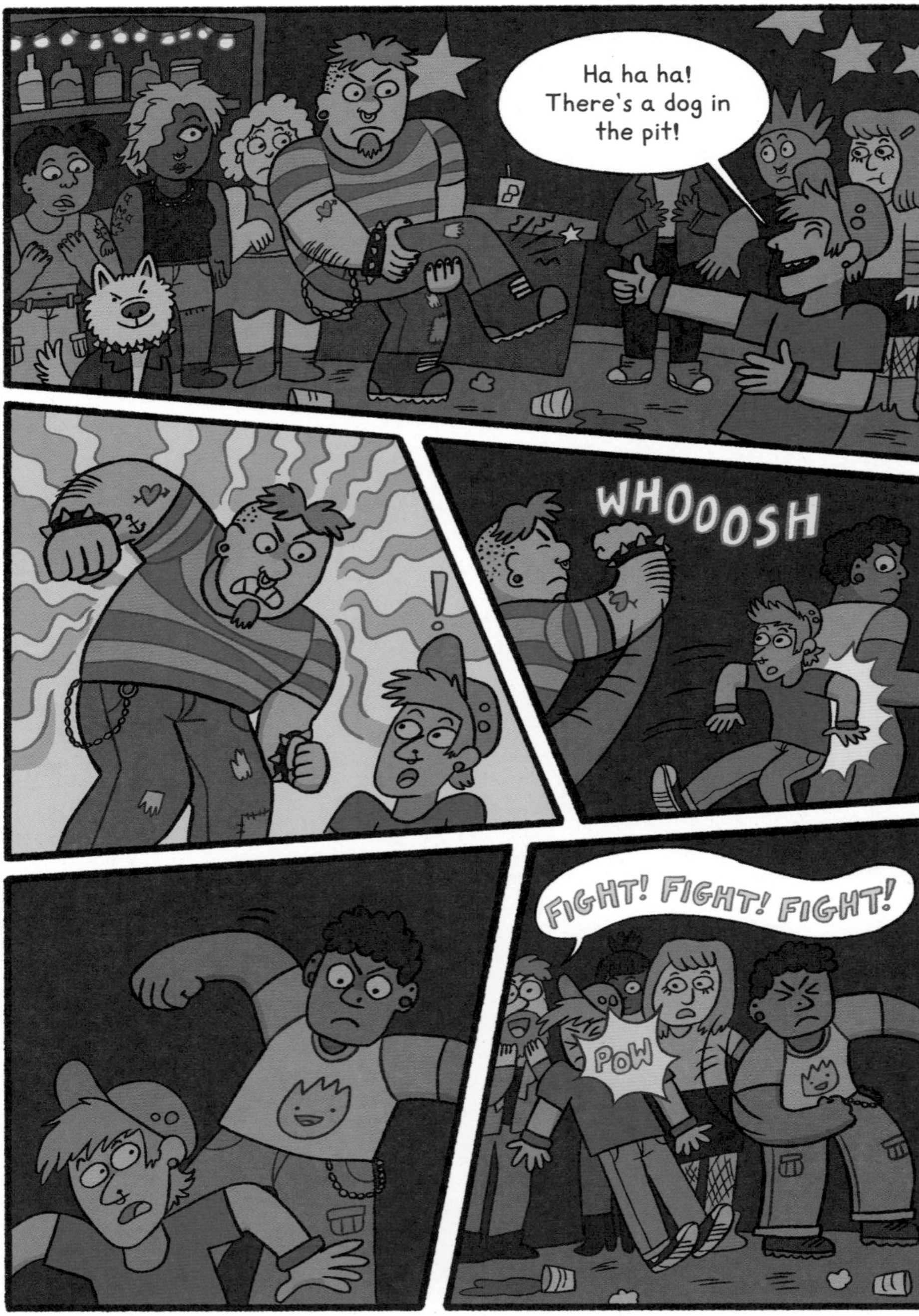

Ha ha ha! There's a dog in the pit!
!
WHOOOSH
FIGHT! FIGHT! FIGHT!
POW

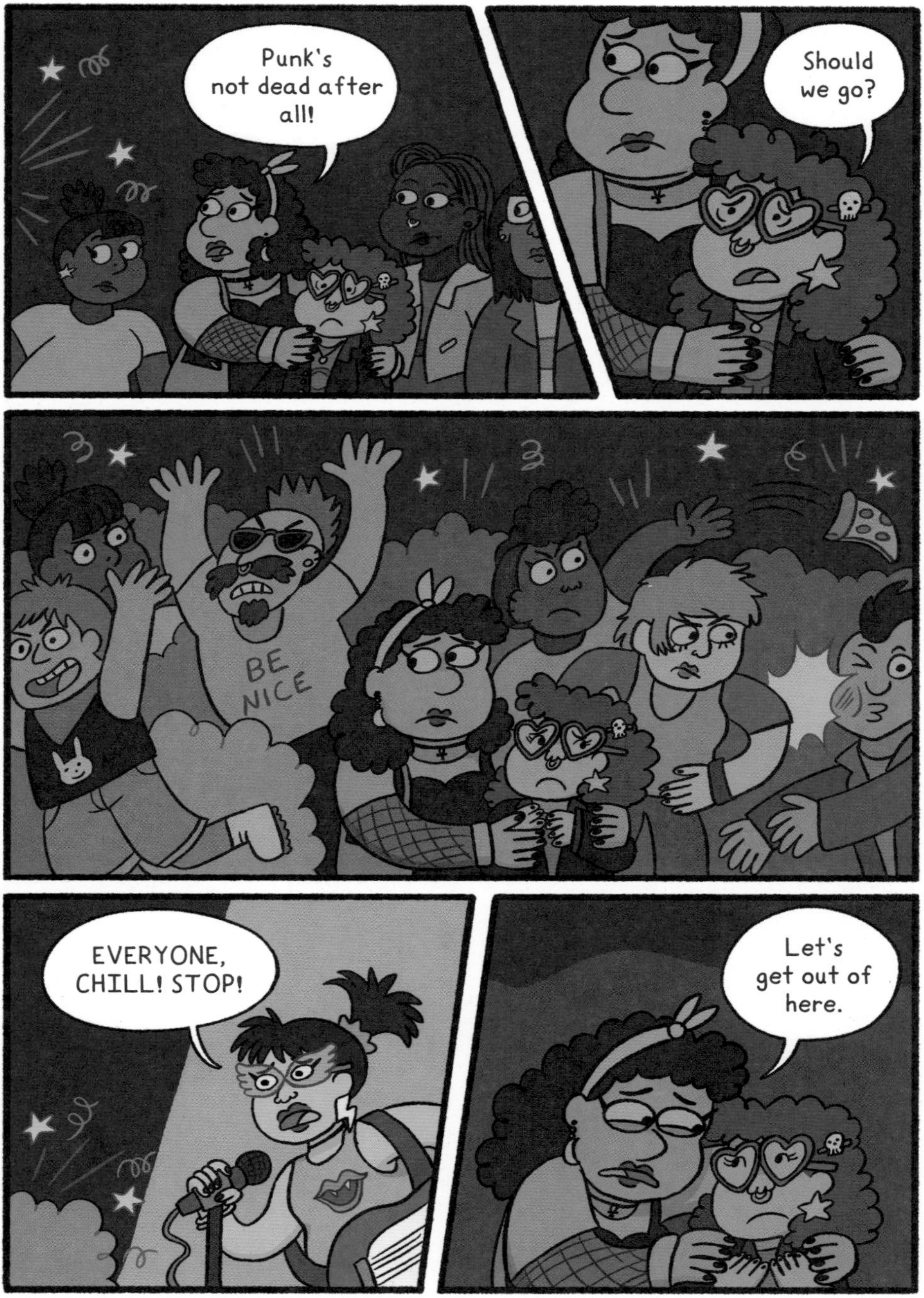

Punk's not dead after all!
Should we go?
BE NICE
EVERYONE, CHILL! STOP!
Let's get out of here.

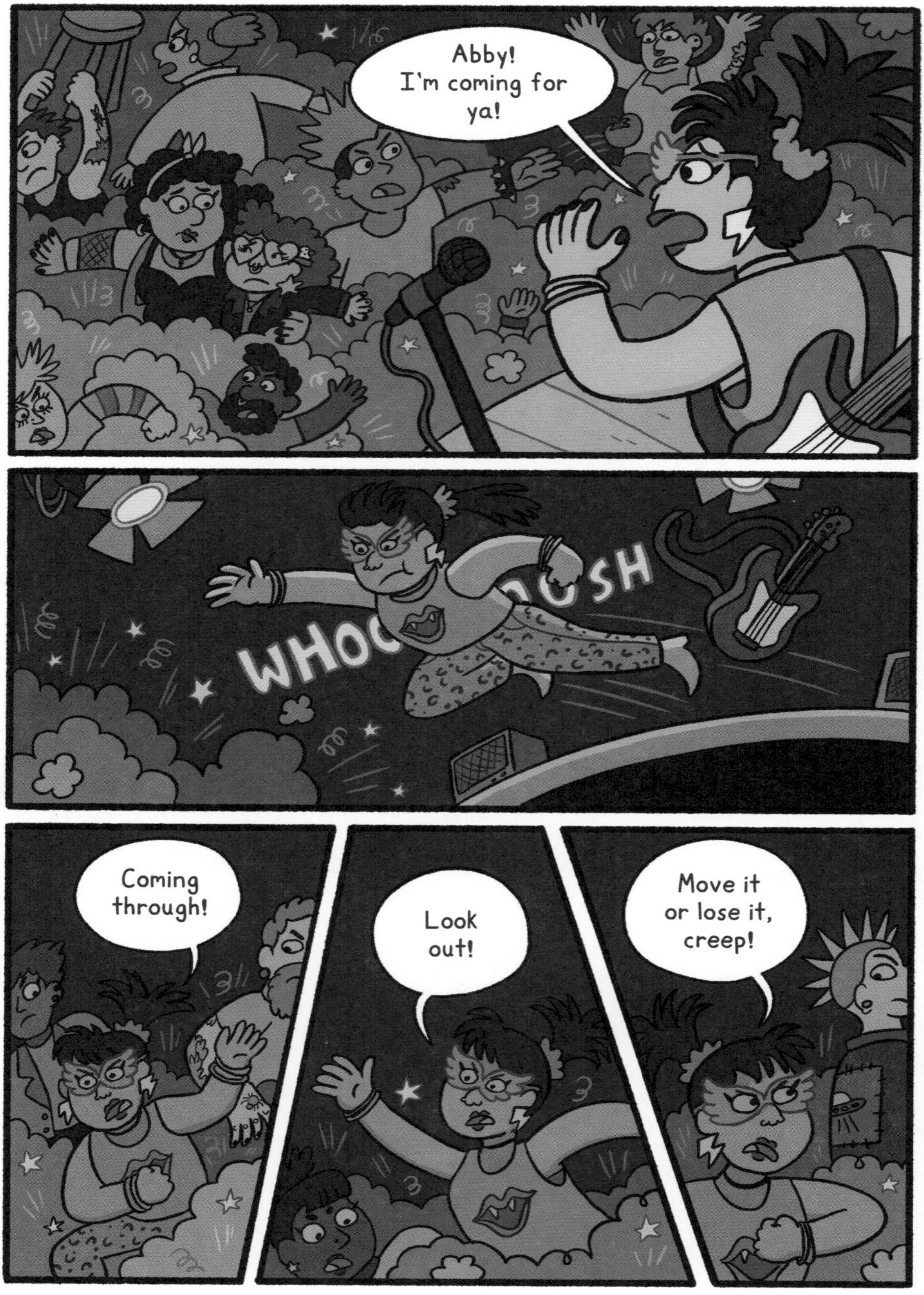

Abby! I'm coming for ya!
WHOOOOSH
Coming through!
Look out!
Move it or lose it, creep!

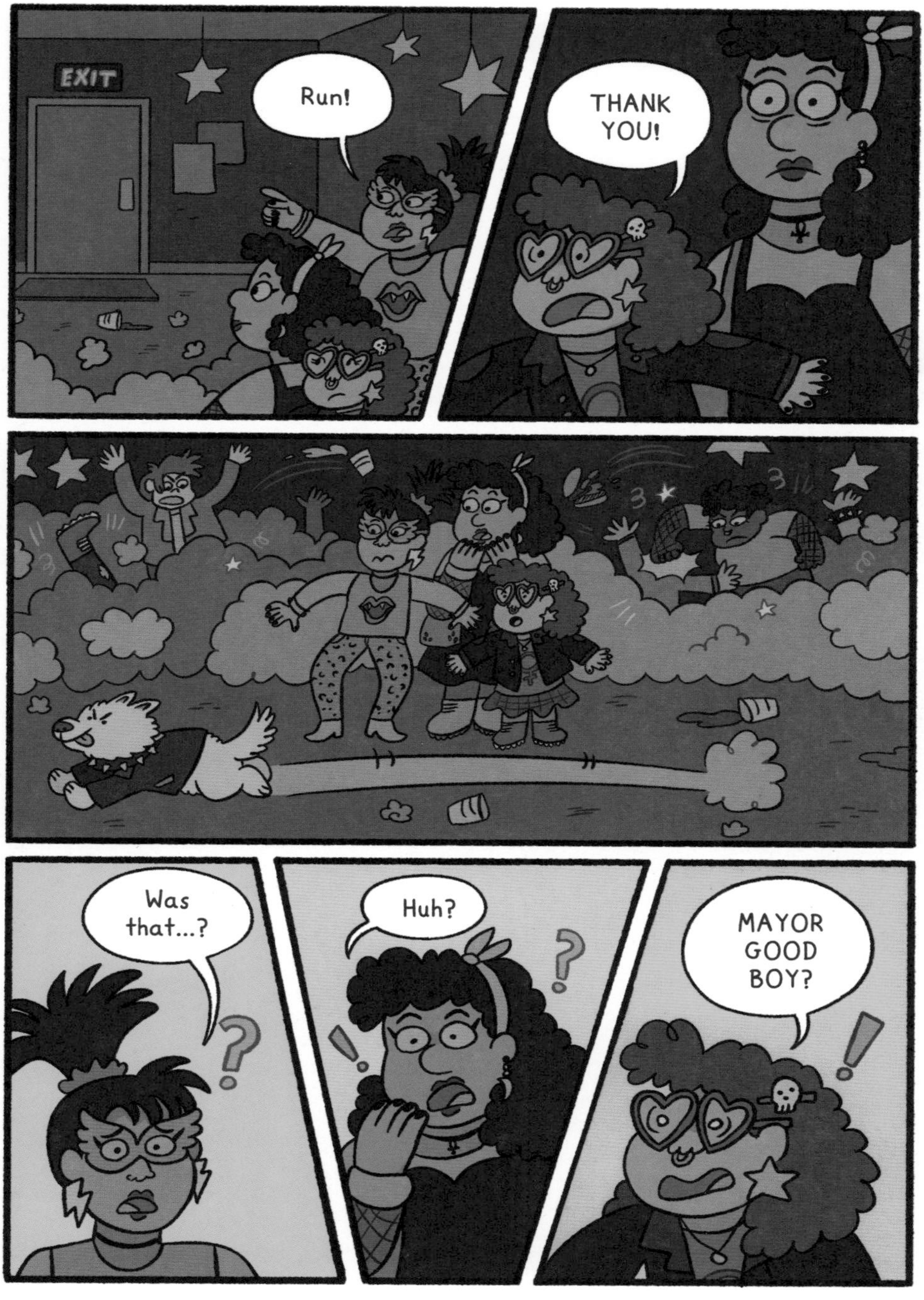

EXIT
Run!
THANK YOU!
Was that...?
Huh?
MAYOR GOOD BOY?

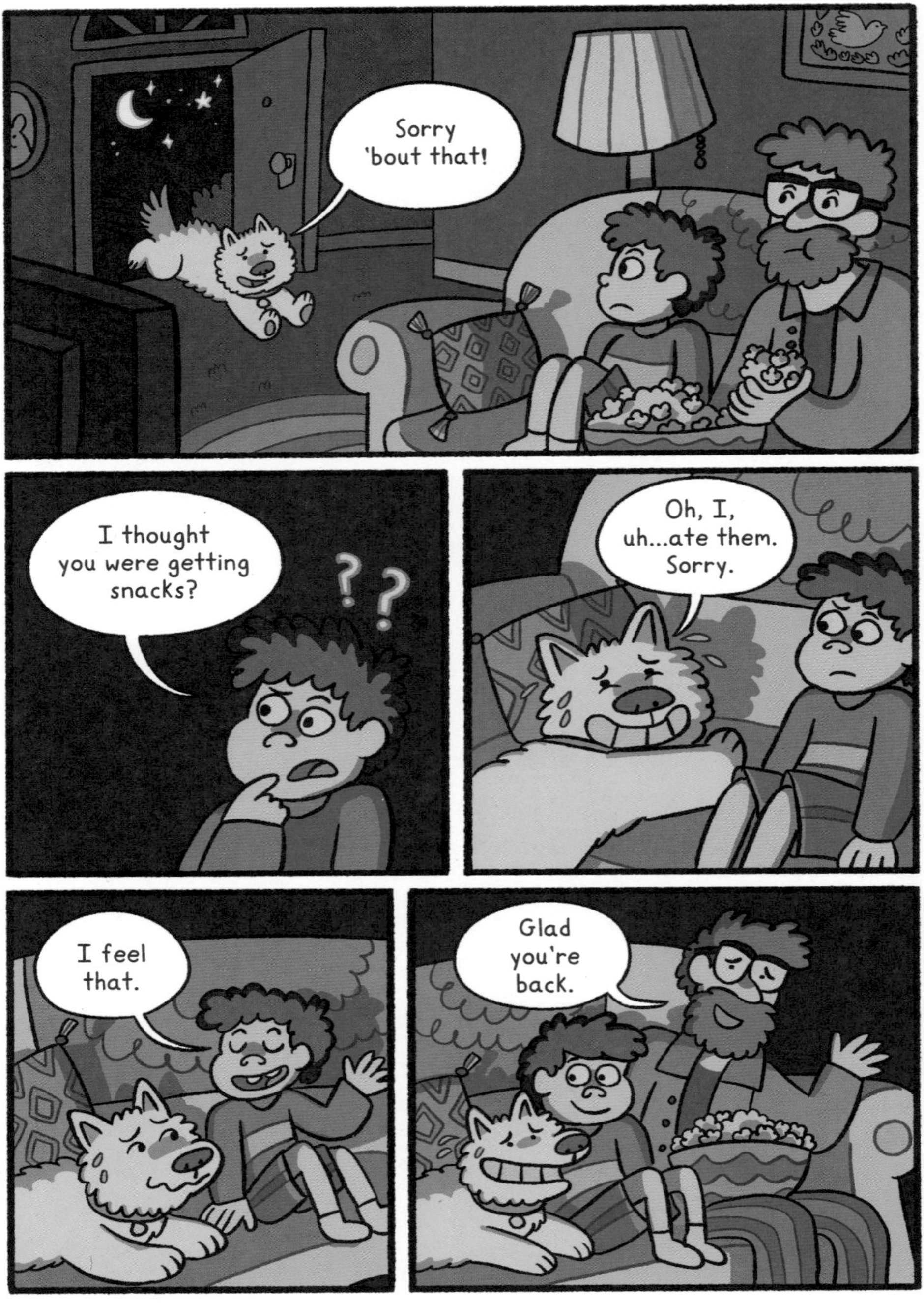
Sorry 'bout that!
I thought you were getting snacks?
??
Oh, I, uh...ate them. Sorry.
I feel that.
Glad you're back.

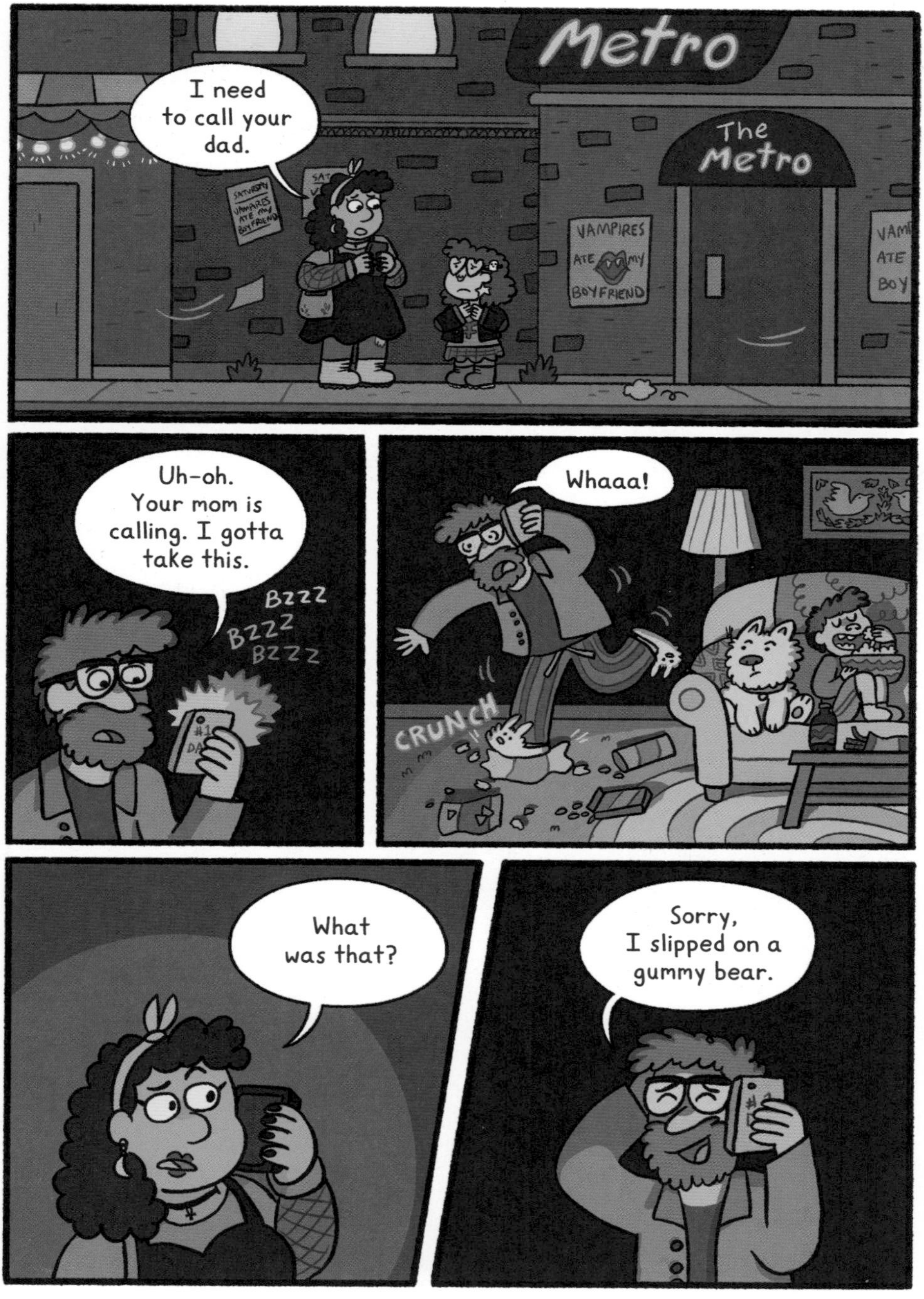
Metro
I need to call your dad.
SATURDAY VAMPIRES ATE MY BOYFRIEND
The Metro
VAMPIRES ATE MY BOYFRIEND
VAMP ATE BOY
Uh-oh. Your mom is calling. I gotta take this.
BZZZ
BZZZ
BZZZ
Whaaa!
CRUNCH
What was that?
Sorry, I slipped on a gummy bear.

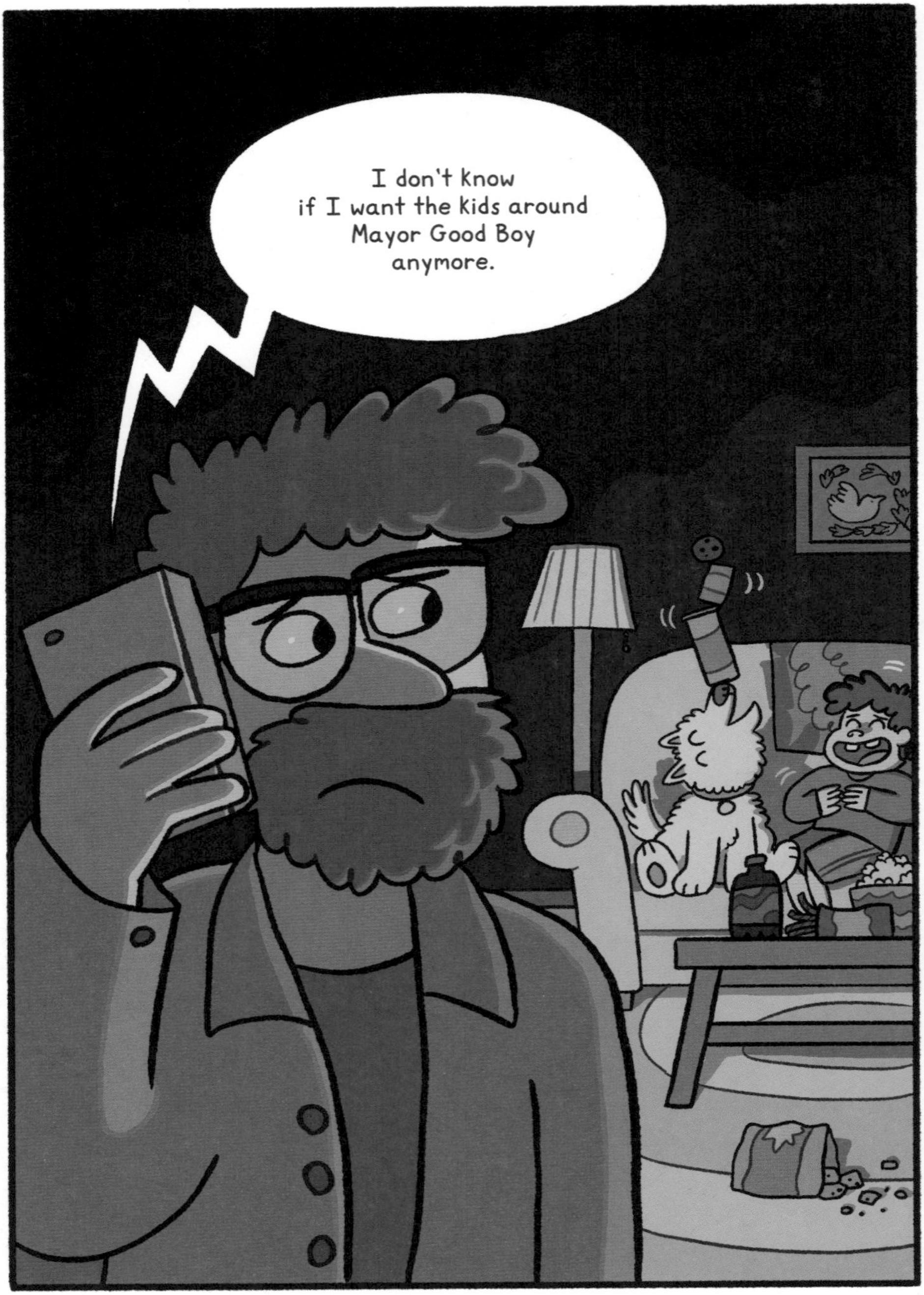
I don't know
if I want the kids around
Mayor Good Boy
anymore.

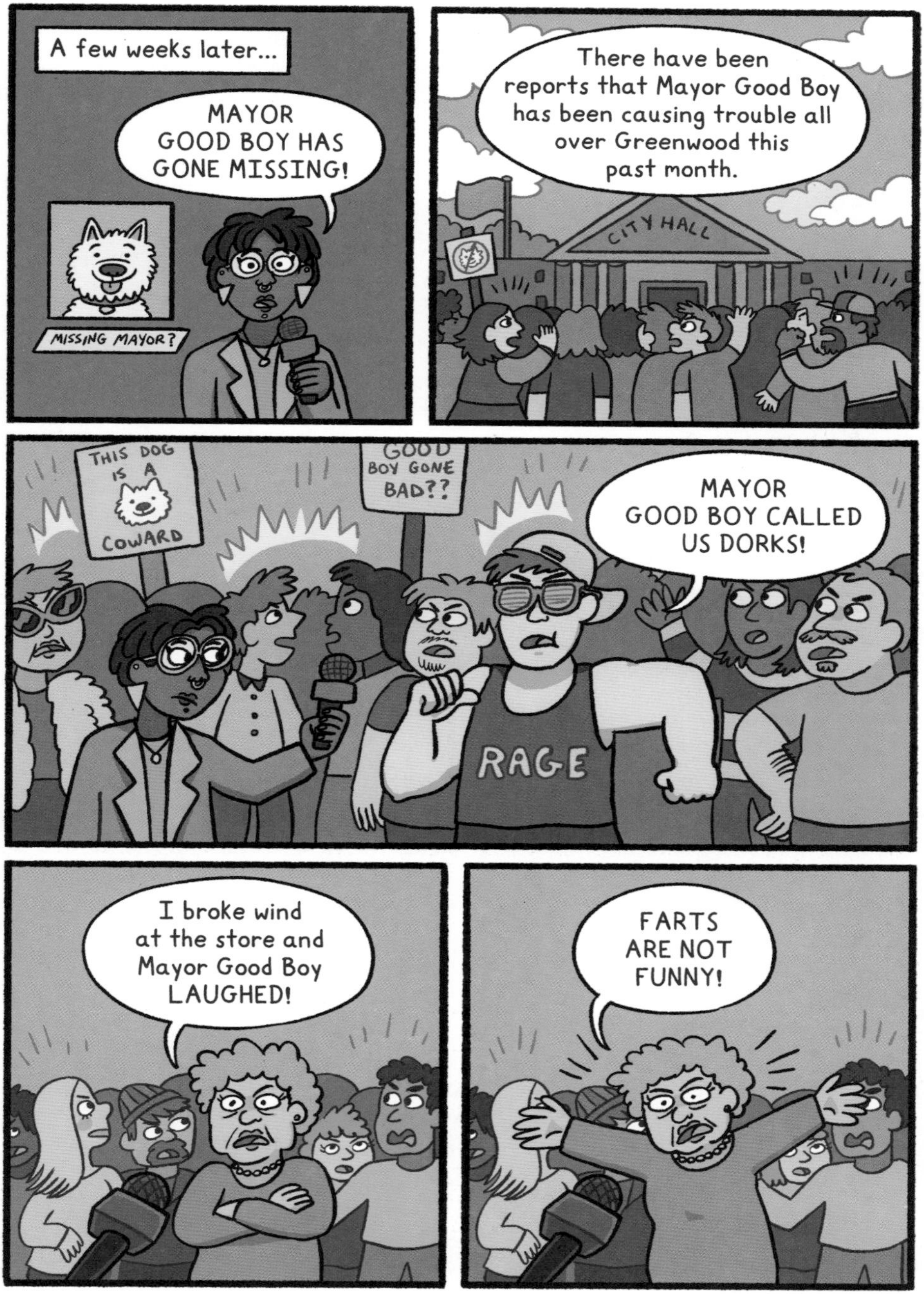
A few weeks later...
MAYOR GOOD BOY HAS GONE MISSING!
MISSING MAYOR?
There have been reports that Mayor Good Boy has been causing trouble all over Greenwood this past month.
CITY HALL
THIS DOG IS A COWARD
GOOD BOY GONE BAD??
MAYOR GOOD BOY CALLED US DORKS!
RAGE
I broke wind at the store and Mayor Good Boy LAUGHED!
FARTS ARE NOT FUNNY!

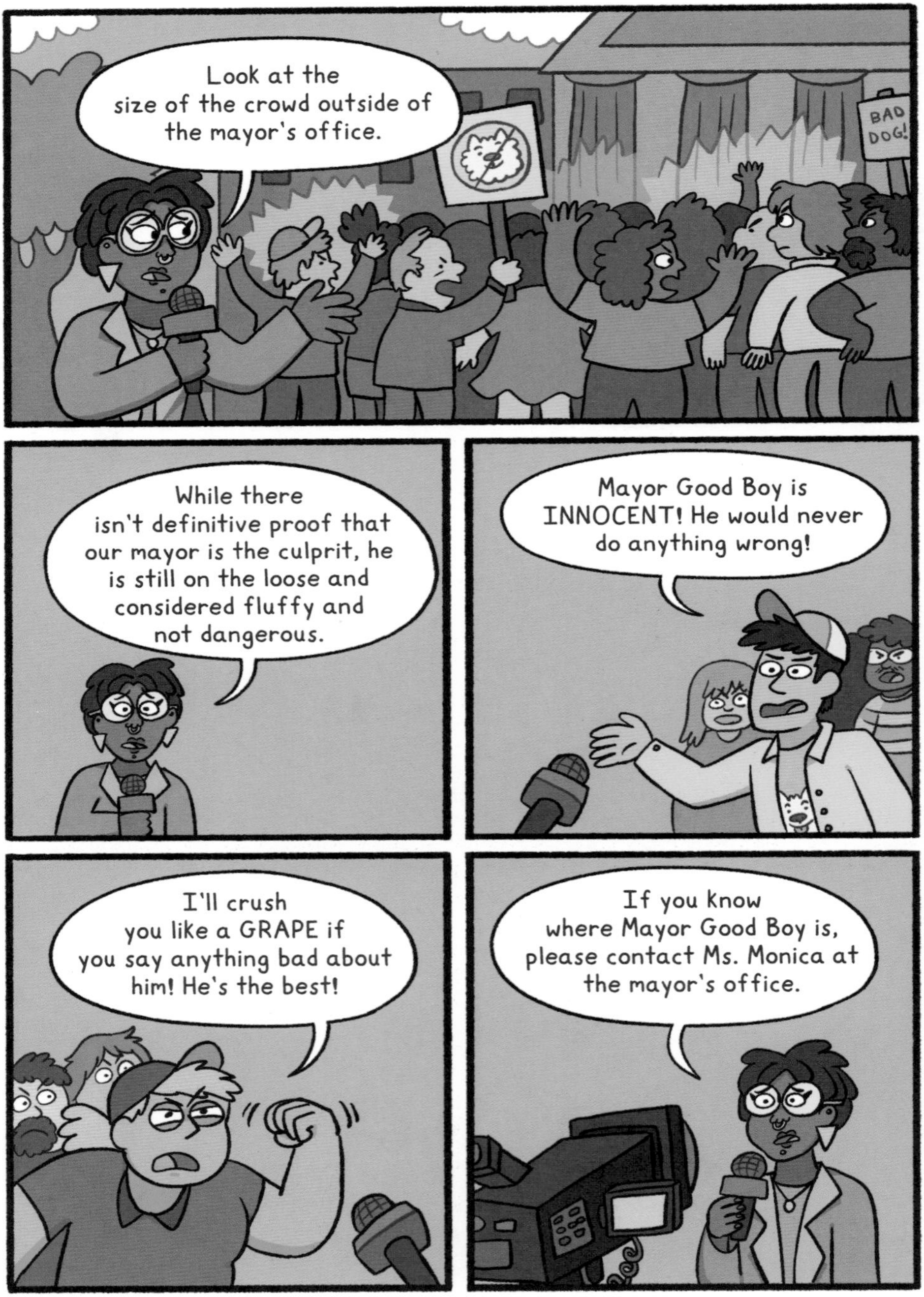
Look at the size of the crowd outside of the mayor's office.
BAD DOG!
While there isn't definitive proof that our mayor is the culprit, he is still on the loose and considered fluffy and not dangerous.
Mayor Good Boy is INNOCENT! He would never do anything wrong!
I'll crush you like a GRAPE if you say anything bad about him! He's the best!
If you know where Mayor Good Boy is, please contact Ms. Monica at the mayor's office.

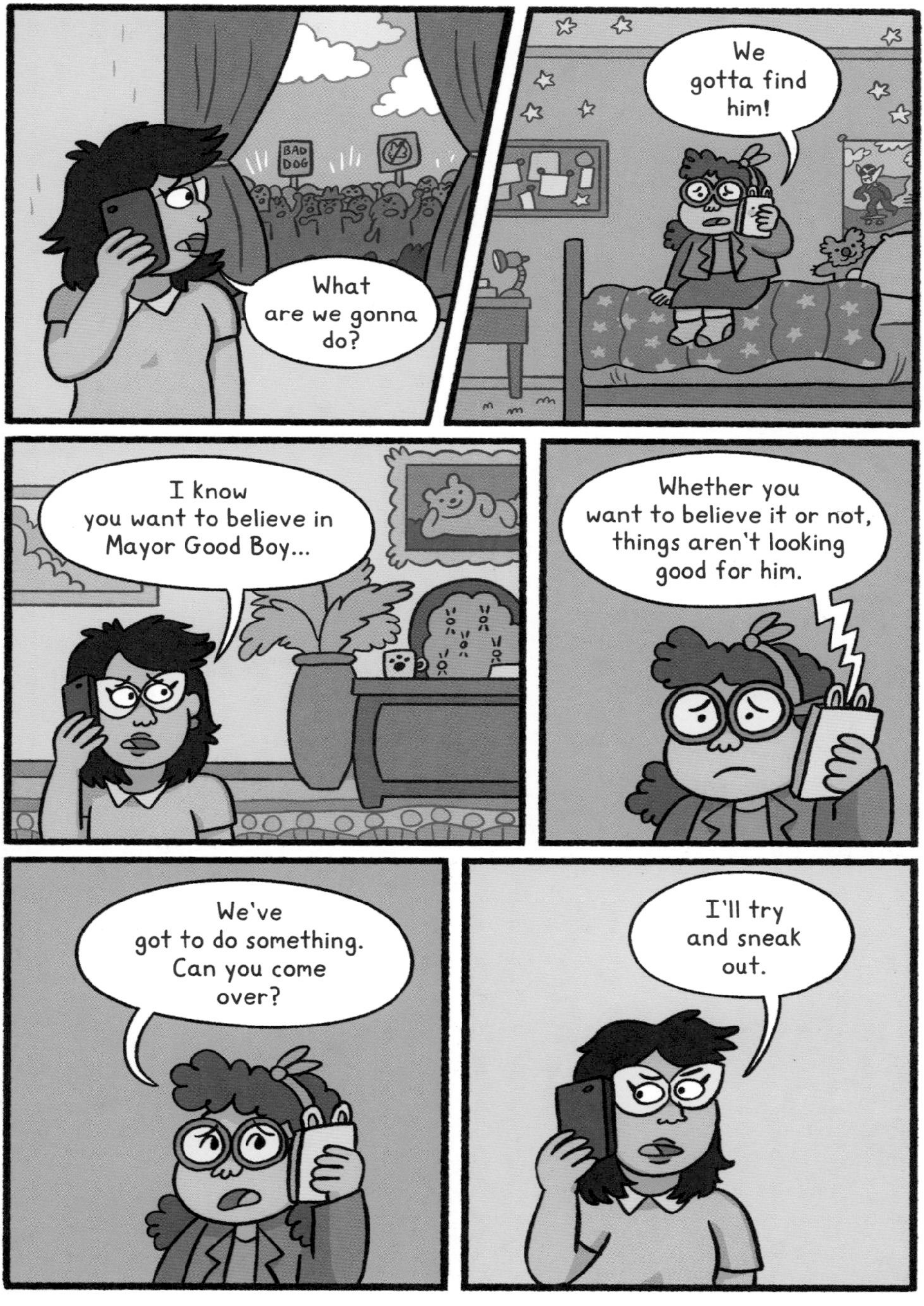
BAD DOG
What are we gonna do?
We gotta find him!
I know you want to believe in Mayor Good Boy...
Whether you want to believe it or not, things aren't looking good for him.
We've got to do something. Can you come over?
I'll try and sneak out.

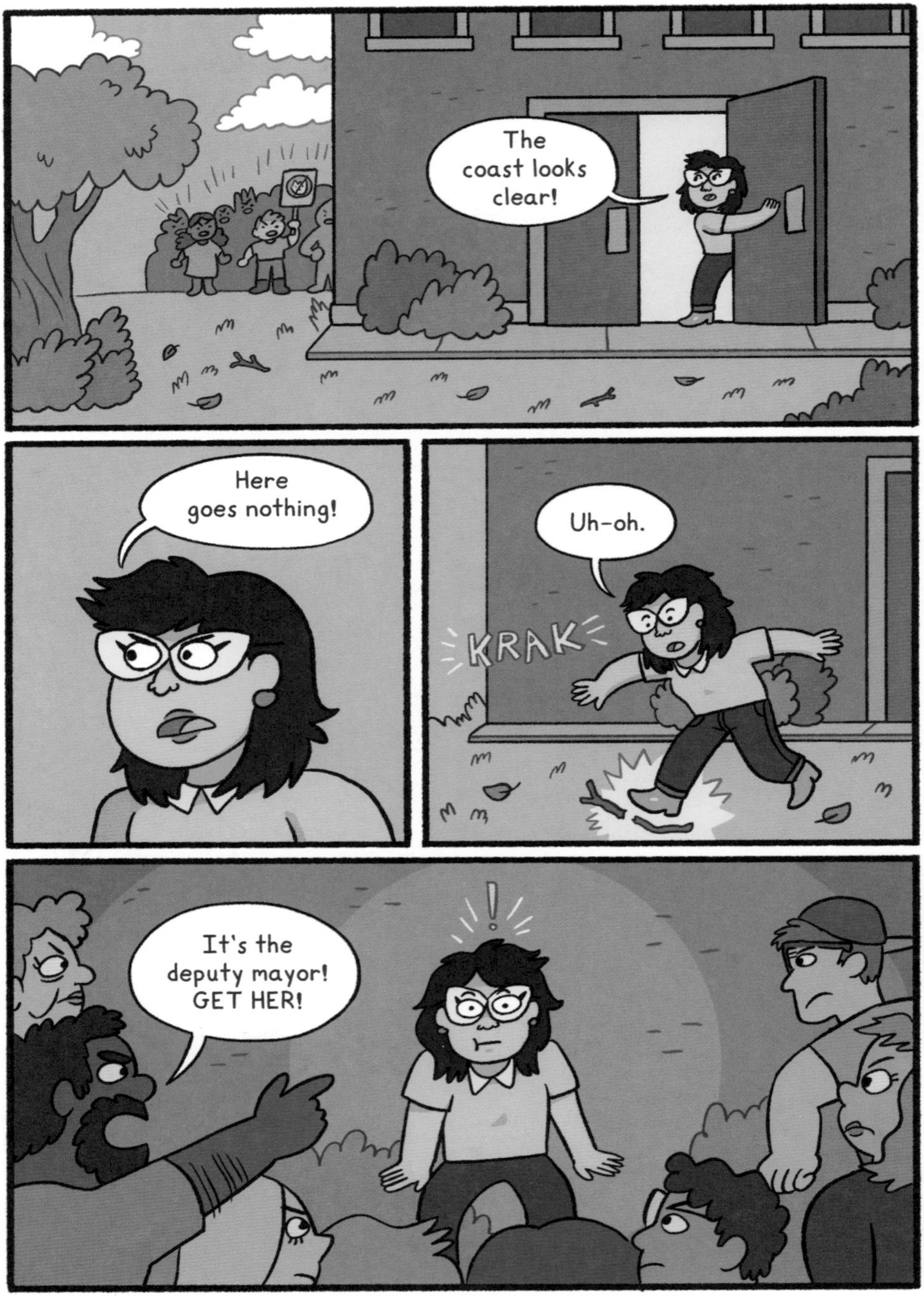
The coast looks clear!
Here goes nothing!
Uh-oh.
KRAK
!
It's the deputy mayor! GET HER!

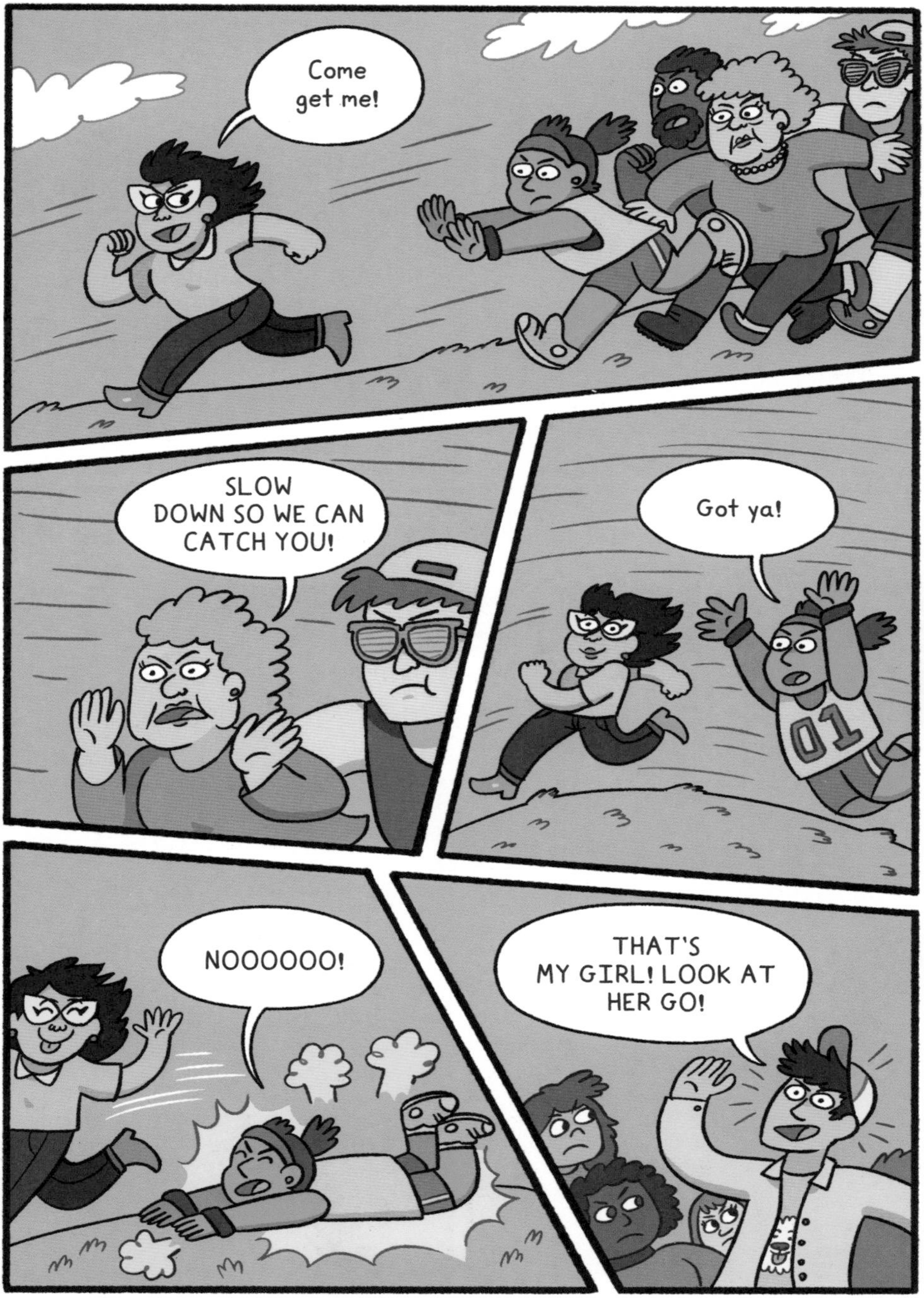
Come get me!
SLOW DOWN SO WE CAN CATCH YOU!
Got ya!
01
NOOOOOO!
THAT'S MY GIRL! LOOK AT HER GO!

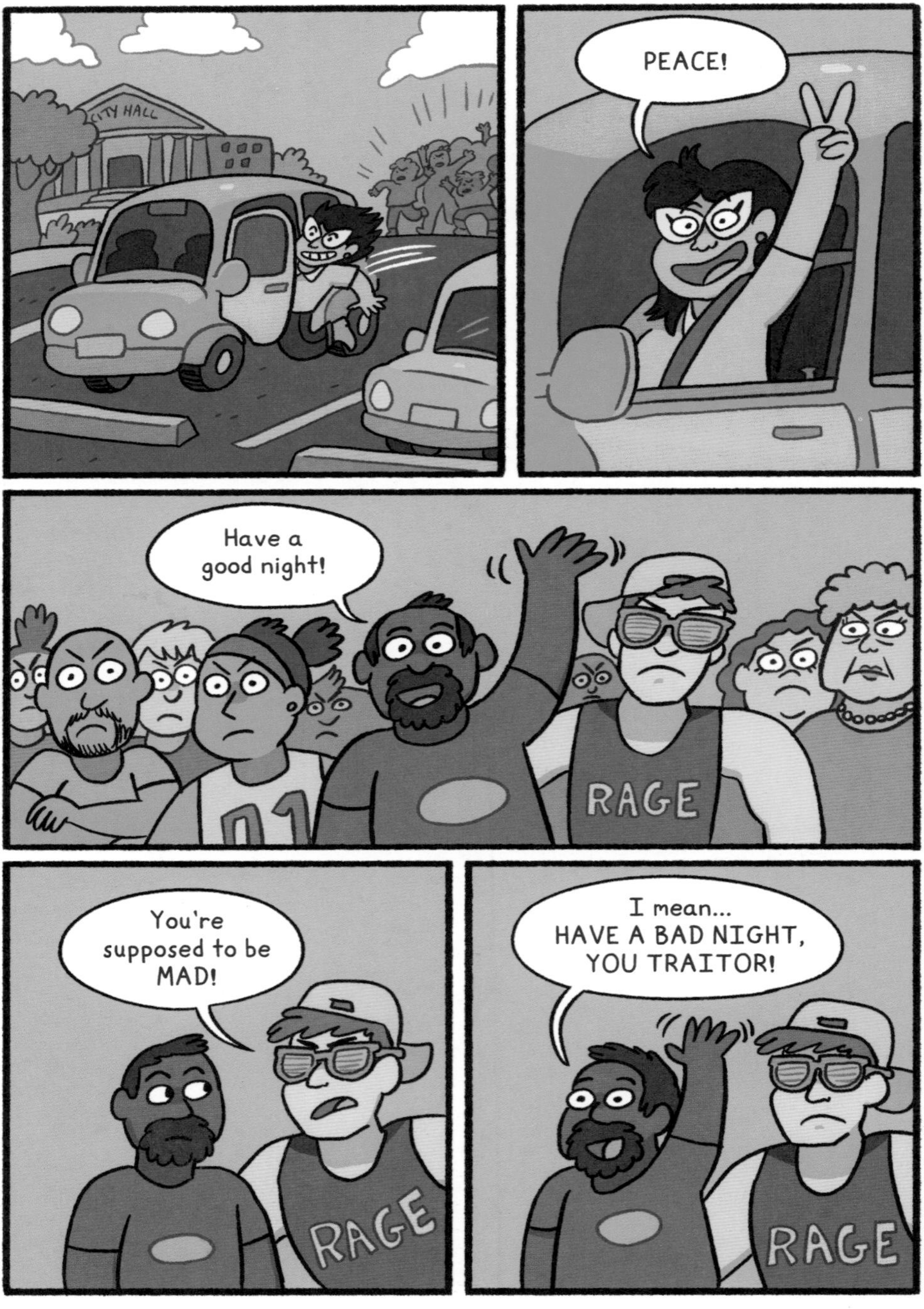
CITY HALL
PEACE!
Have a good night!
RAGE
You're supposed to be MAD!
RAGE
I mean... HAVE A BAD NIGHT, YOU TRAITOR!
RAGE

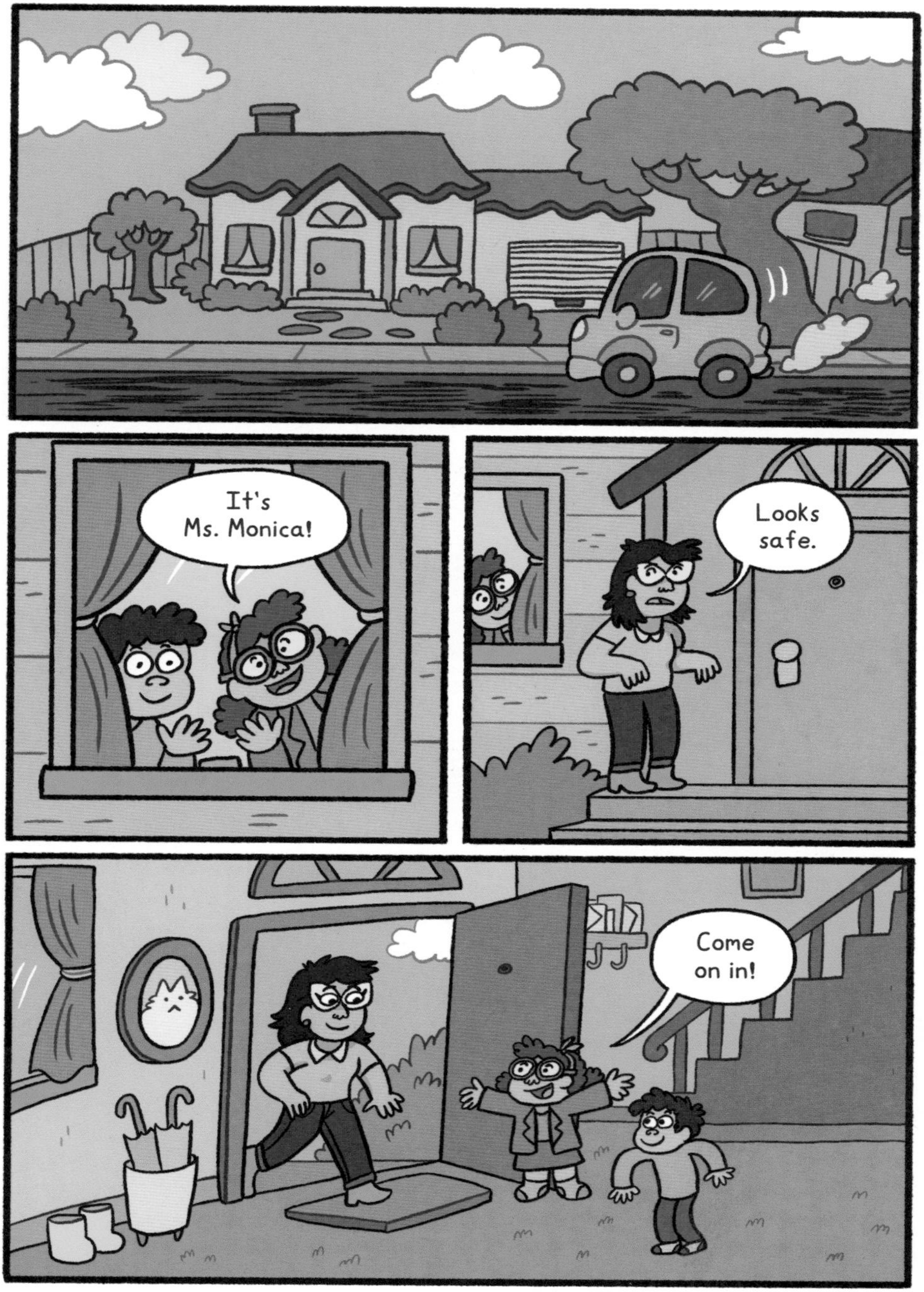
It's Ms. Monica!
Looks safe.
Come on in!

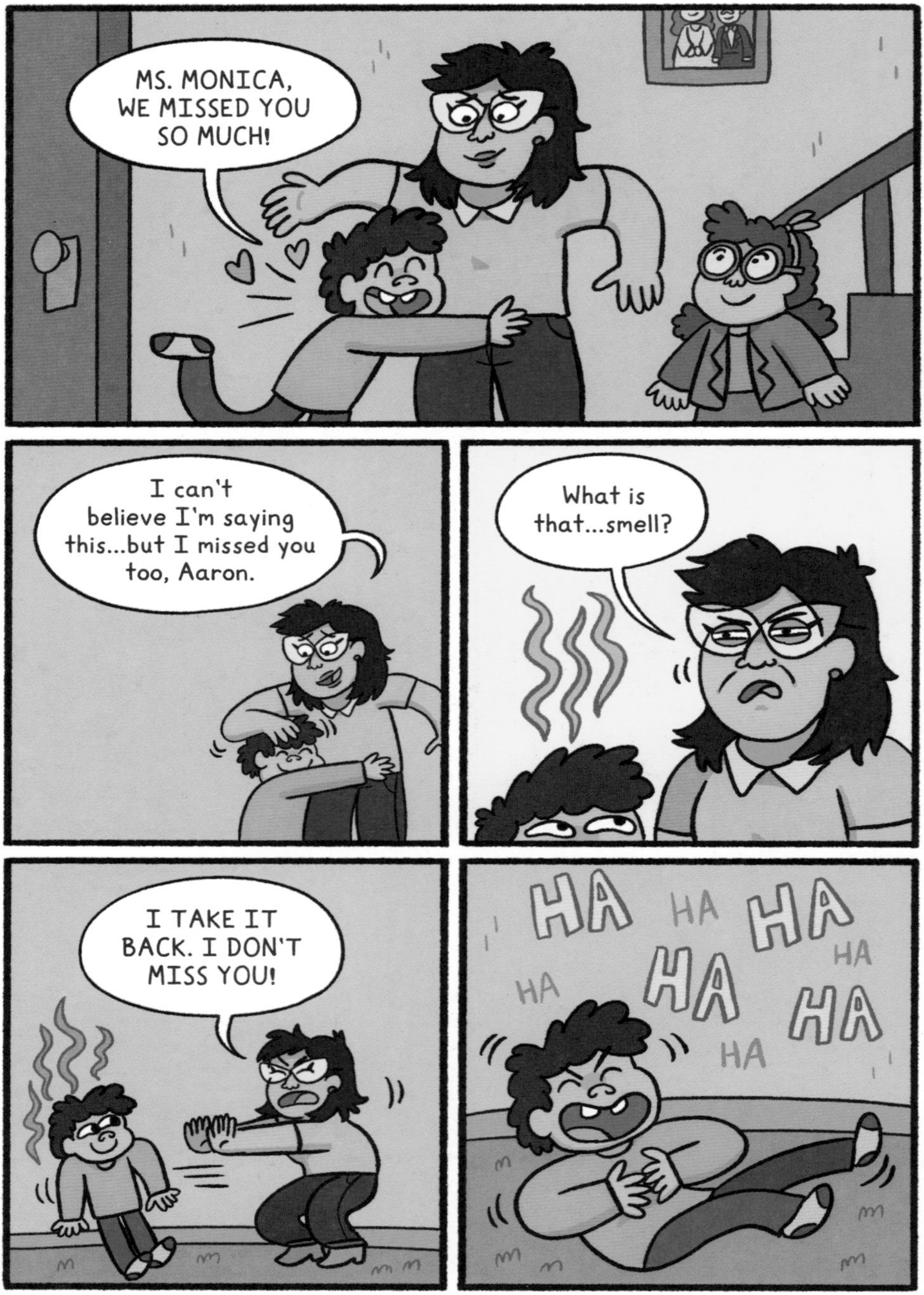
MS. MONICA, WE MISSED YOU SO MUCH!
I can't believe I'm saying this...but I missed you too, Aaron.
What is that...smell?
I TAKE IT BACK. I DON'T MISS YOU!
HA HA HA HA HA HA HA HA HA

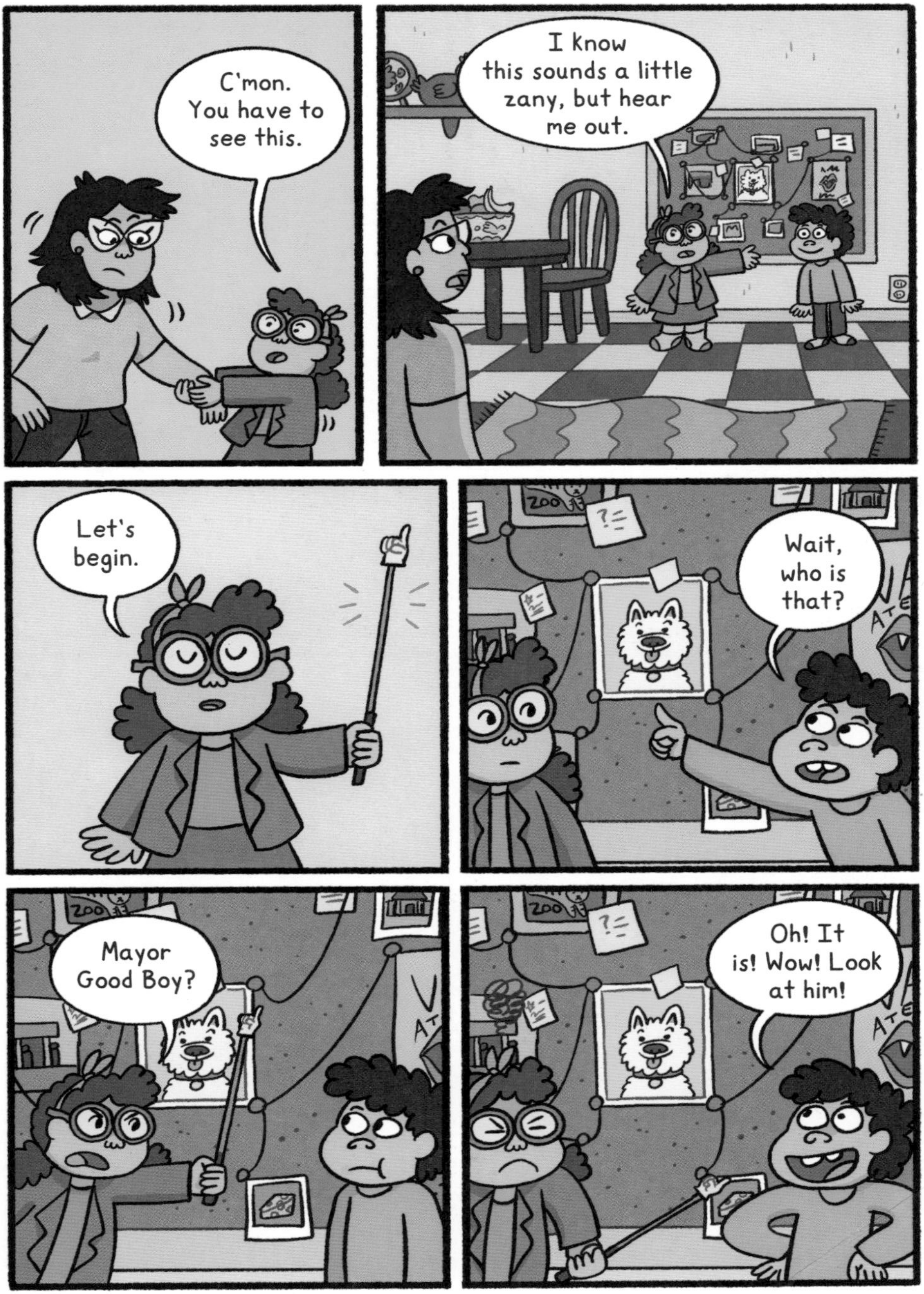
C'mon. You have to see this.
I know this sounds a little zany, but hear me out.
Let's begin.
Wait, who is that?
Mayor Good Boy?
Oh! It is! Wow! Look at him!

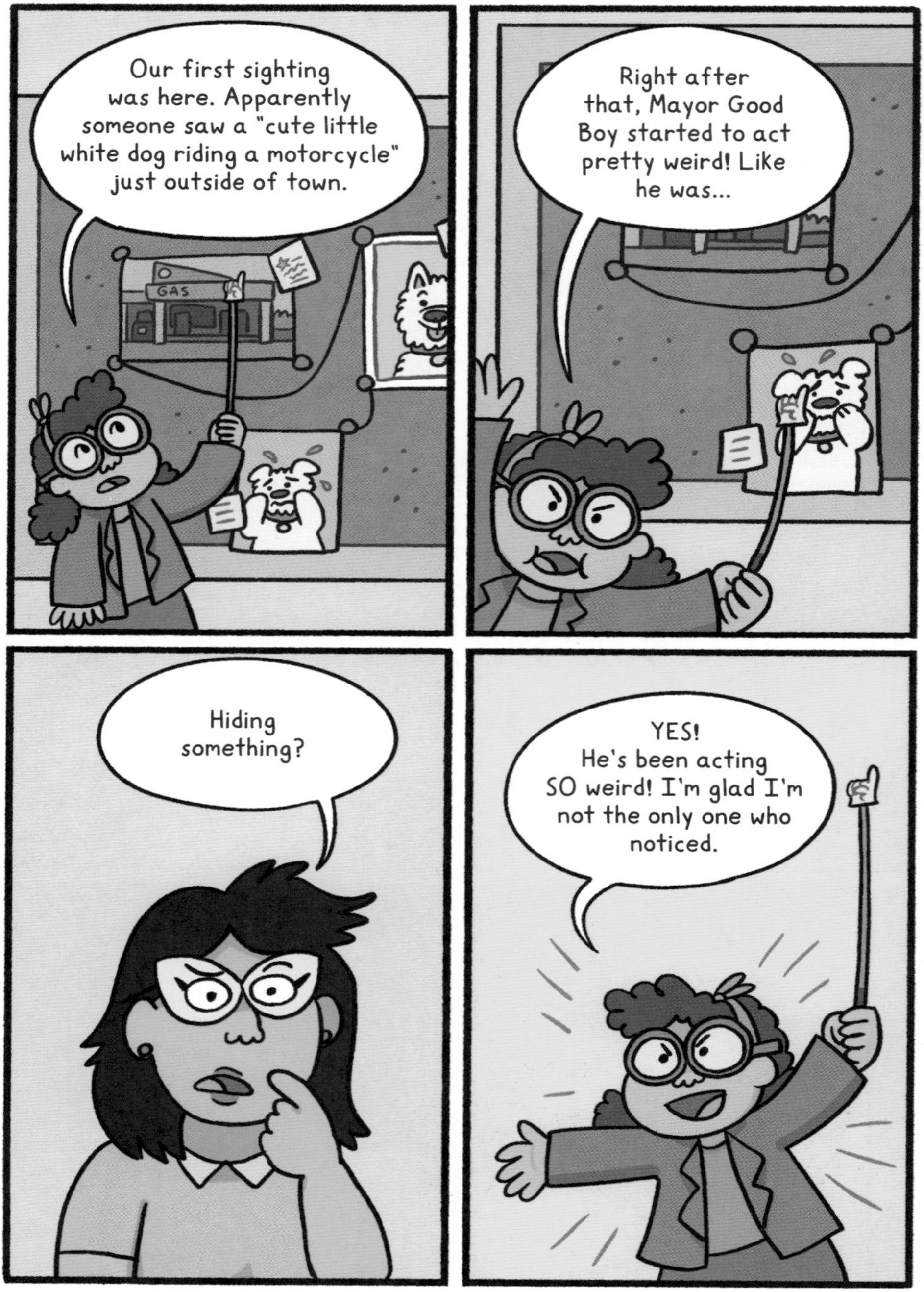
Our first sighting was here. Apparently someone saw a "cute little white dog riding a motorcycle" just outside of town.
GAS
Right after that, Mayor Good Boy started to act pretty weird! Like he was...
Hiding something?
YES! He's been acting SO weird! I'm glad I'm not the only one who noticed.

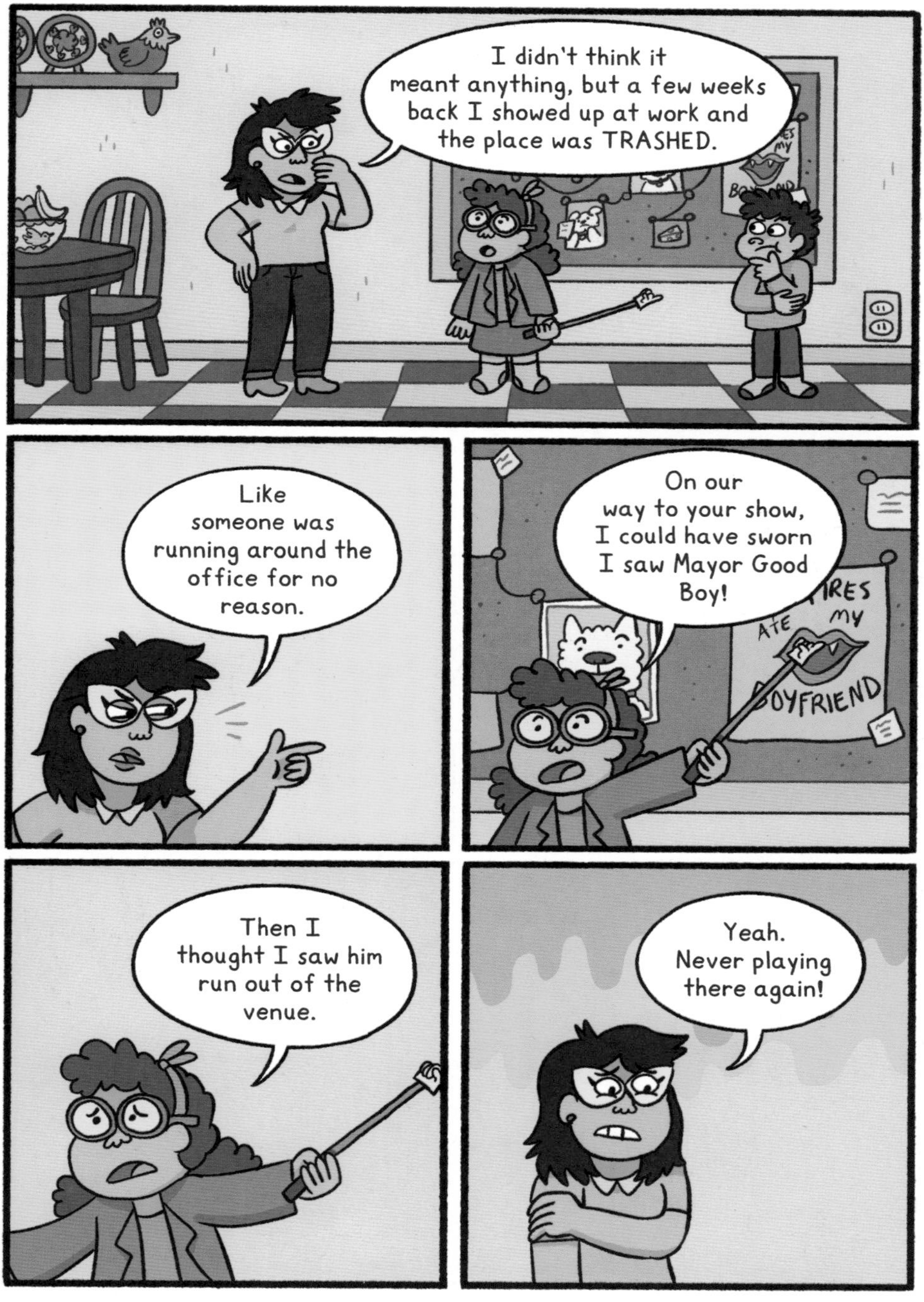
I didn't think it meant anything, but a few weeks back I showed up at work and the place was TRASHED.
Like someone was running around the office for no reason.
On our way to your show, I could have sworn I saw Mayor Good Boy!
Then I thought I saw him run out of the venue.
Yeah. Never playing there again!

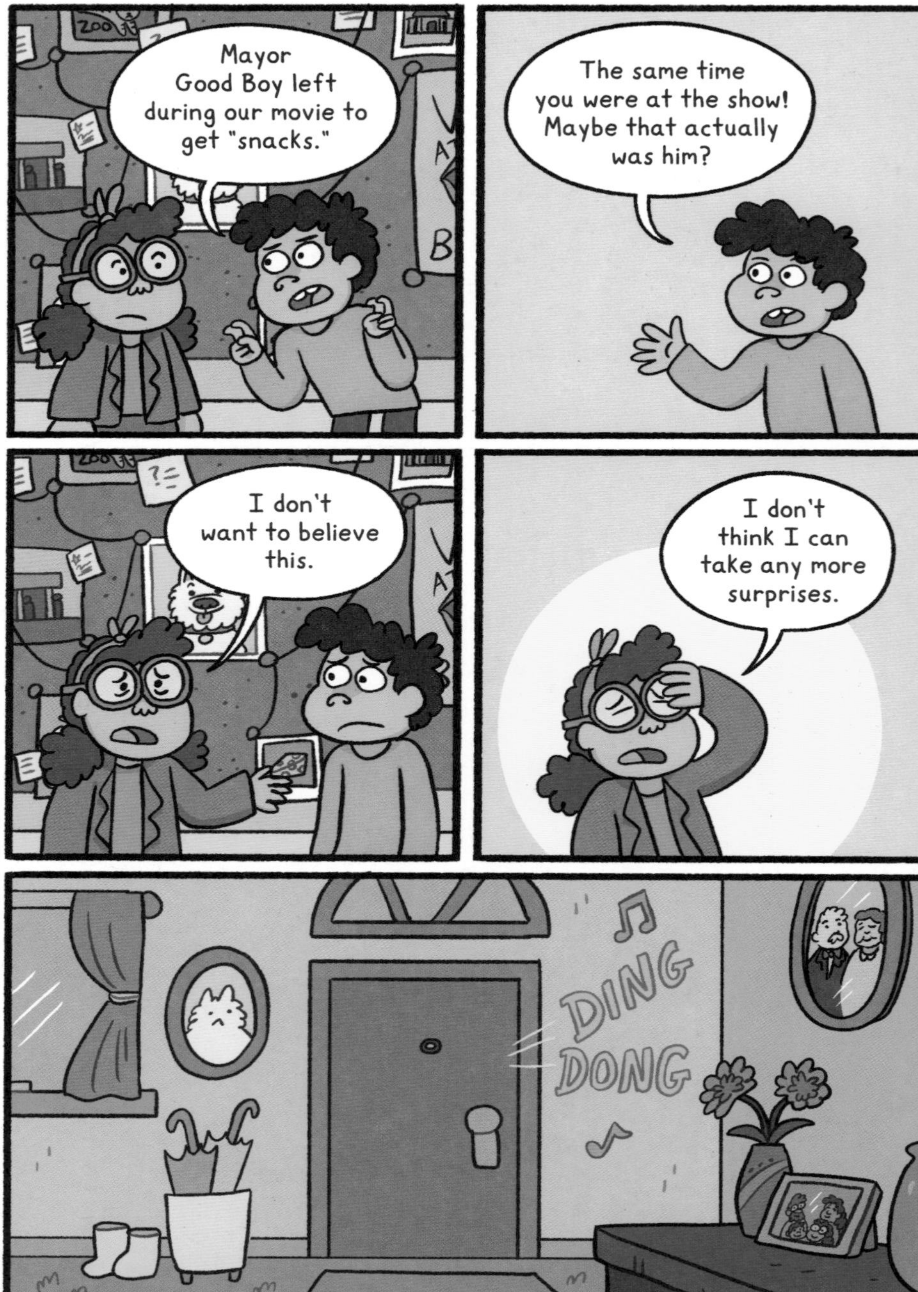
Mayor Good Boy left during our movie to get "snacks."
The same time you were at the show! Maybe that actually was him?
I don't want to believe this.
I don't think I can take any more surprises.
DING DONG

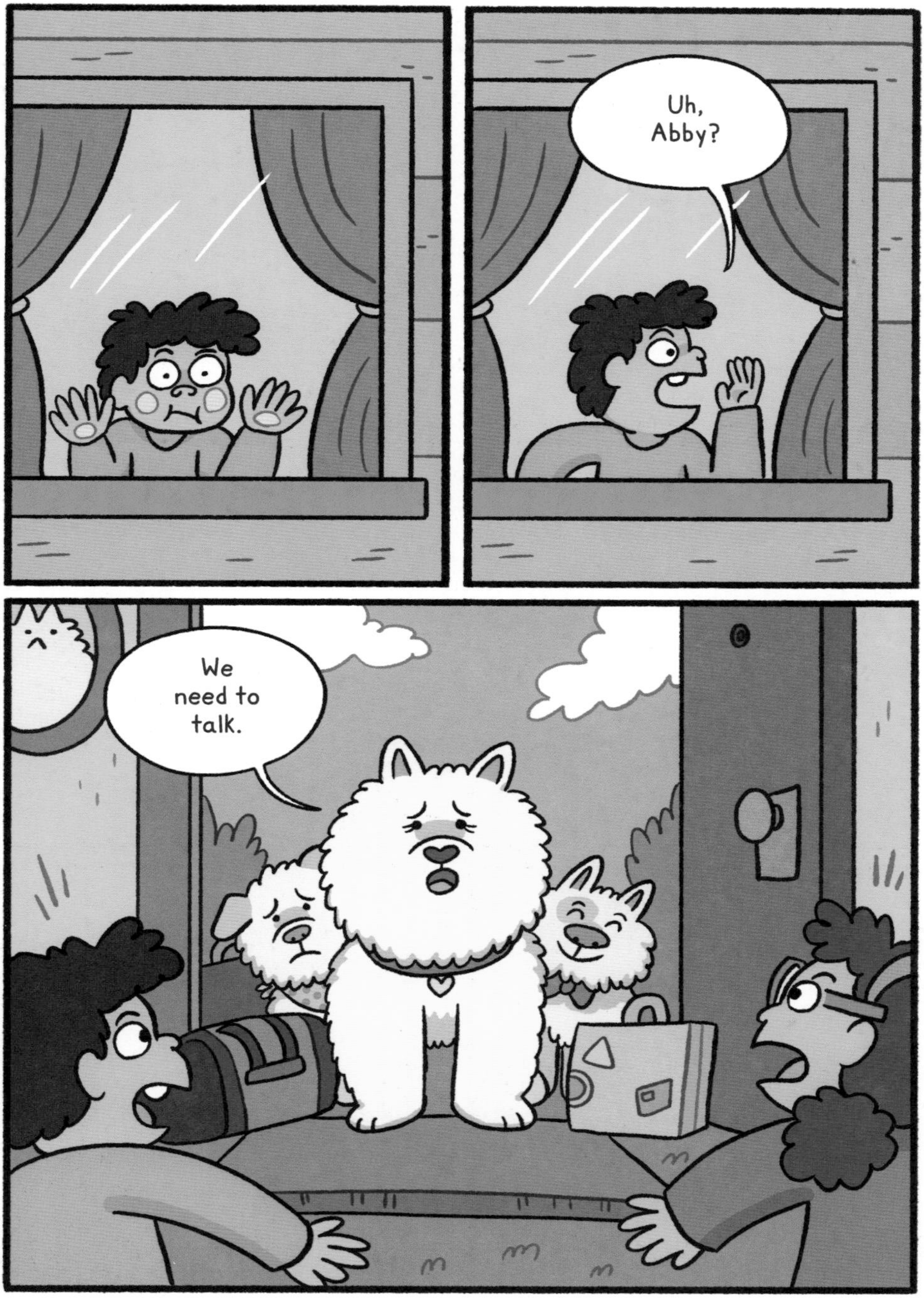
Uh,
Abby?
We
need to
talk.

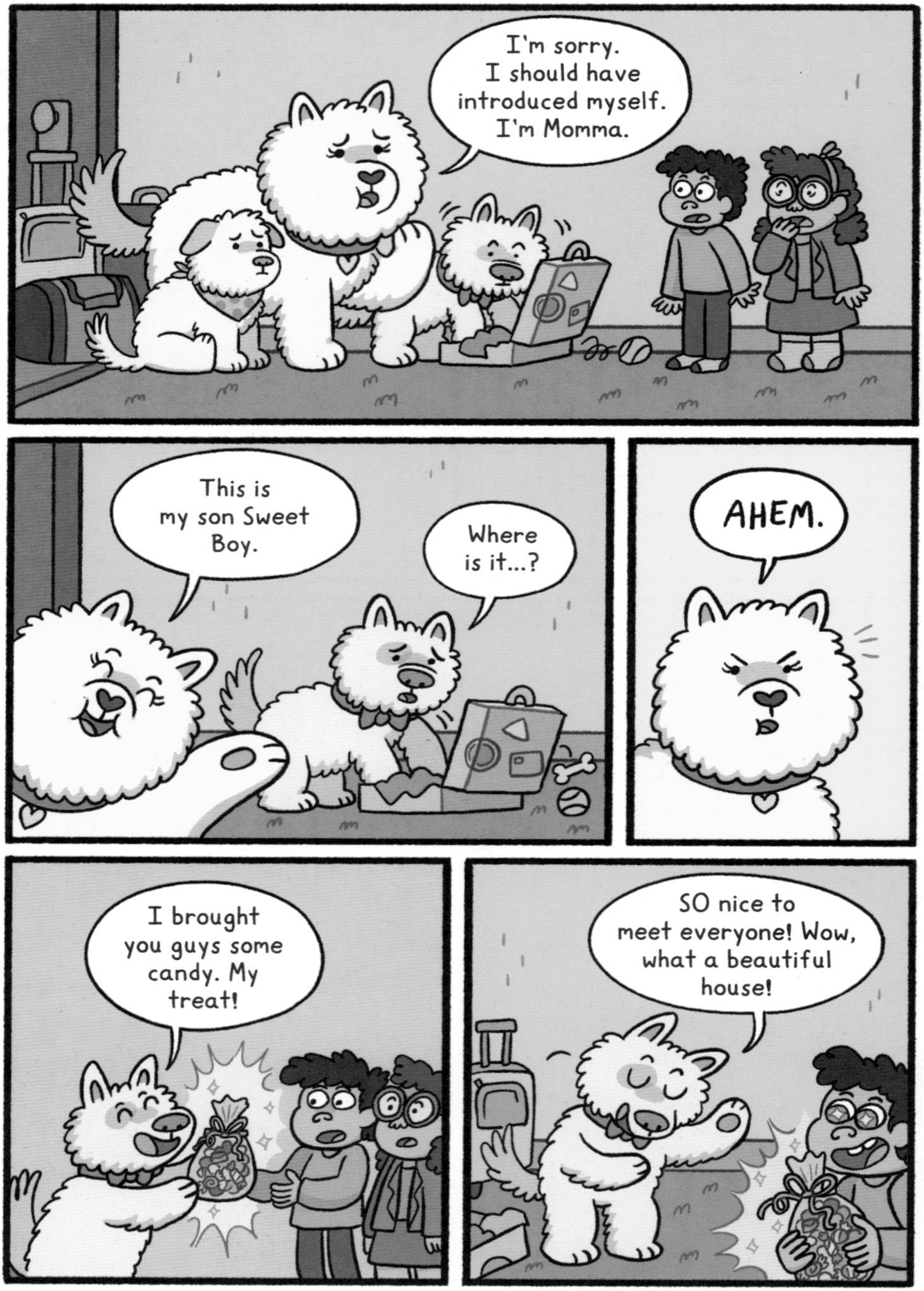
I'm sorry. I should have introduced myself. I'm Momma.
This is my son Sweet Boy.
Where is it...?
AHEM.
I brought you guys some candy. My treat!
SO nice to meet everyone! Wow, what a beautiful house!

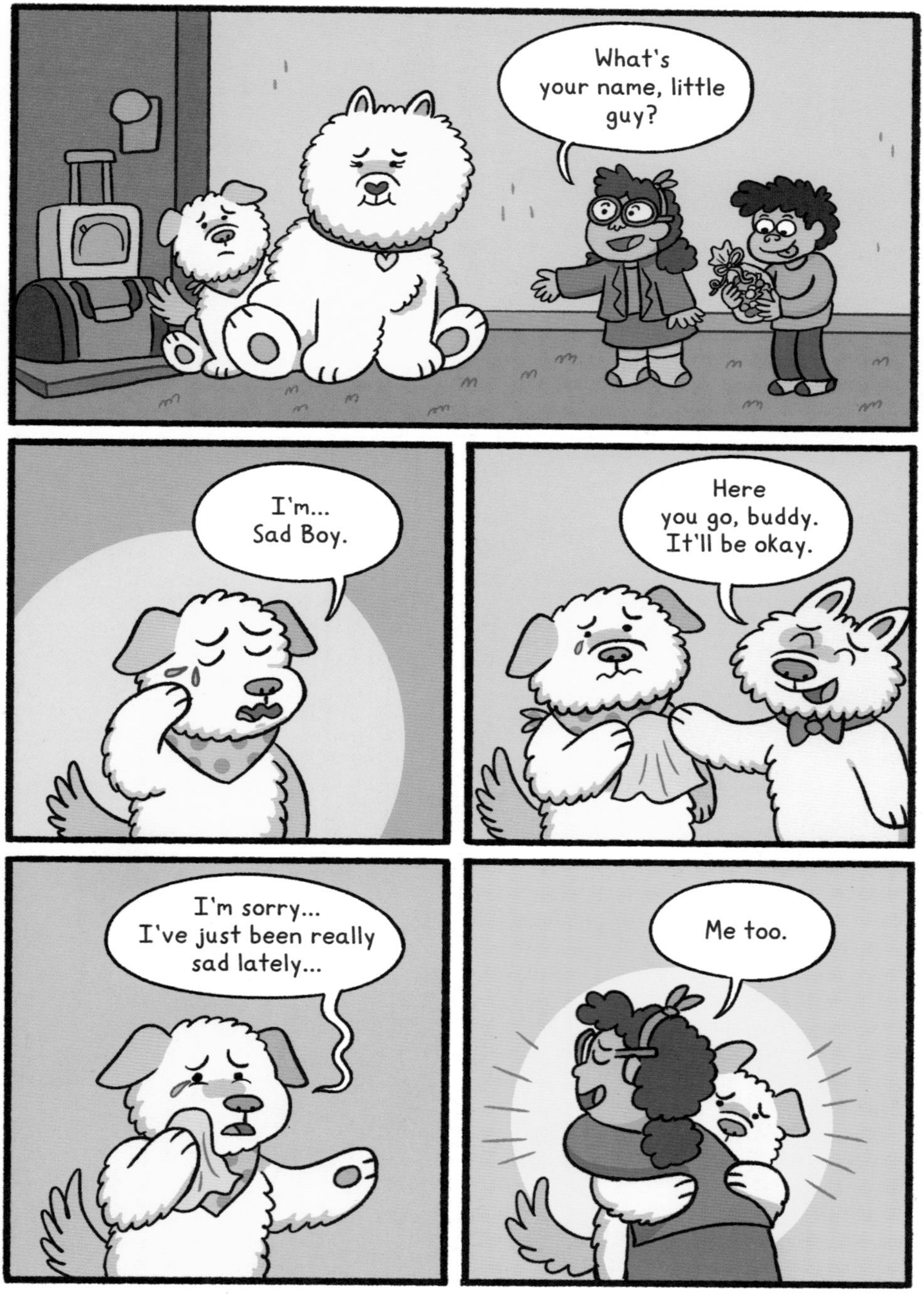
What's your name, little guy?
I'm... Sad Boy.
Here you go, buddy. It'll be okay.
I'm sorry... I've just been really sad lately...
Me too.

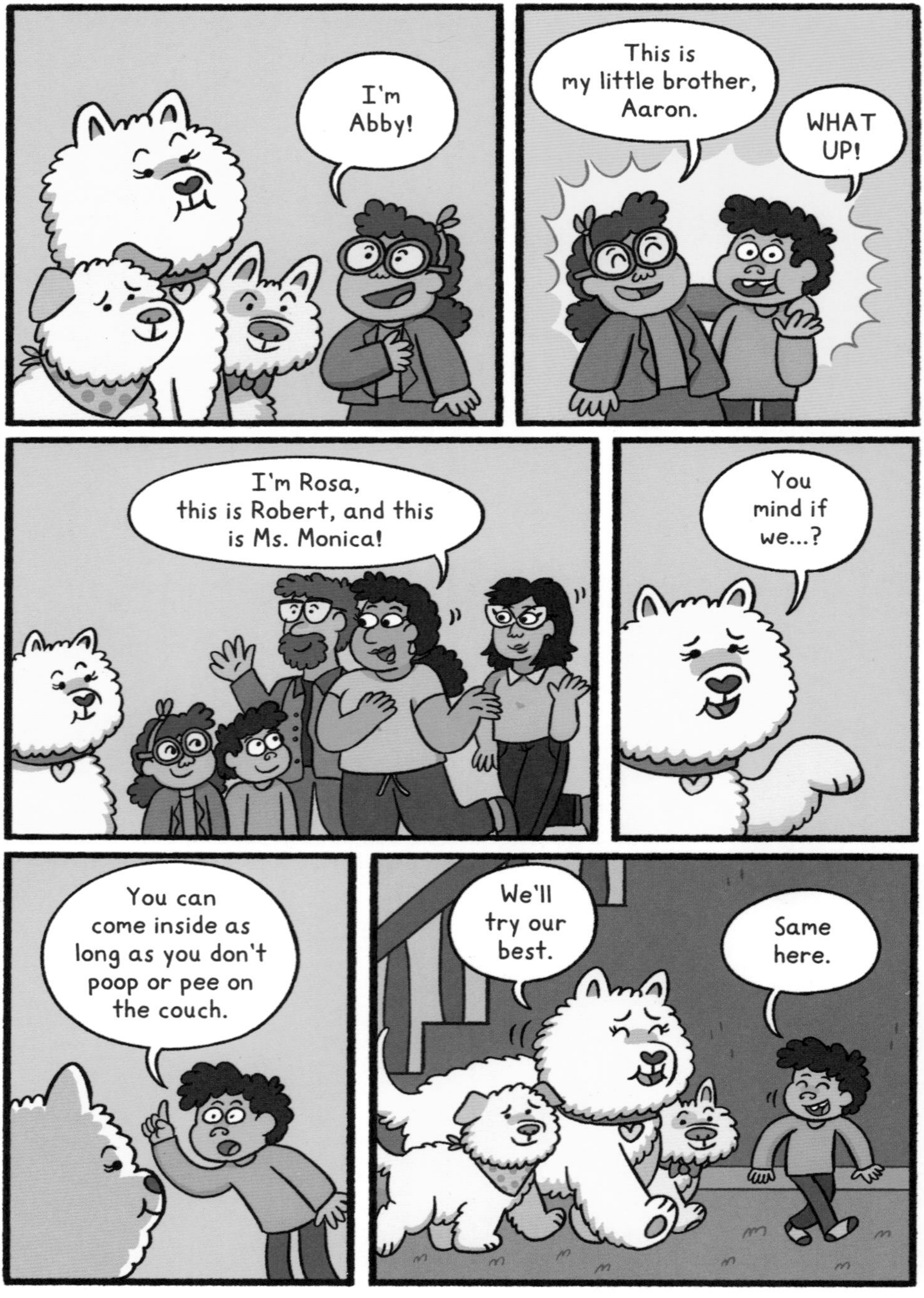
I'm Abby!
This is my little brother, Aaron.
WHAT UP!
I'm Rosa, this is Robert, and this is Ms. Monica!
You mind if we...?
You can come inside as long as you don't poop or pee on the couch.
We'll try our best.
Same here.

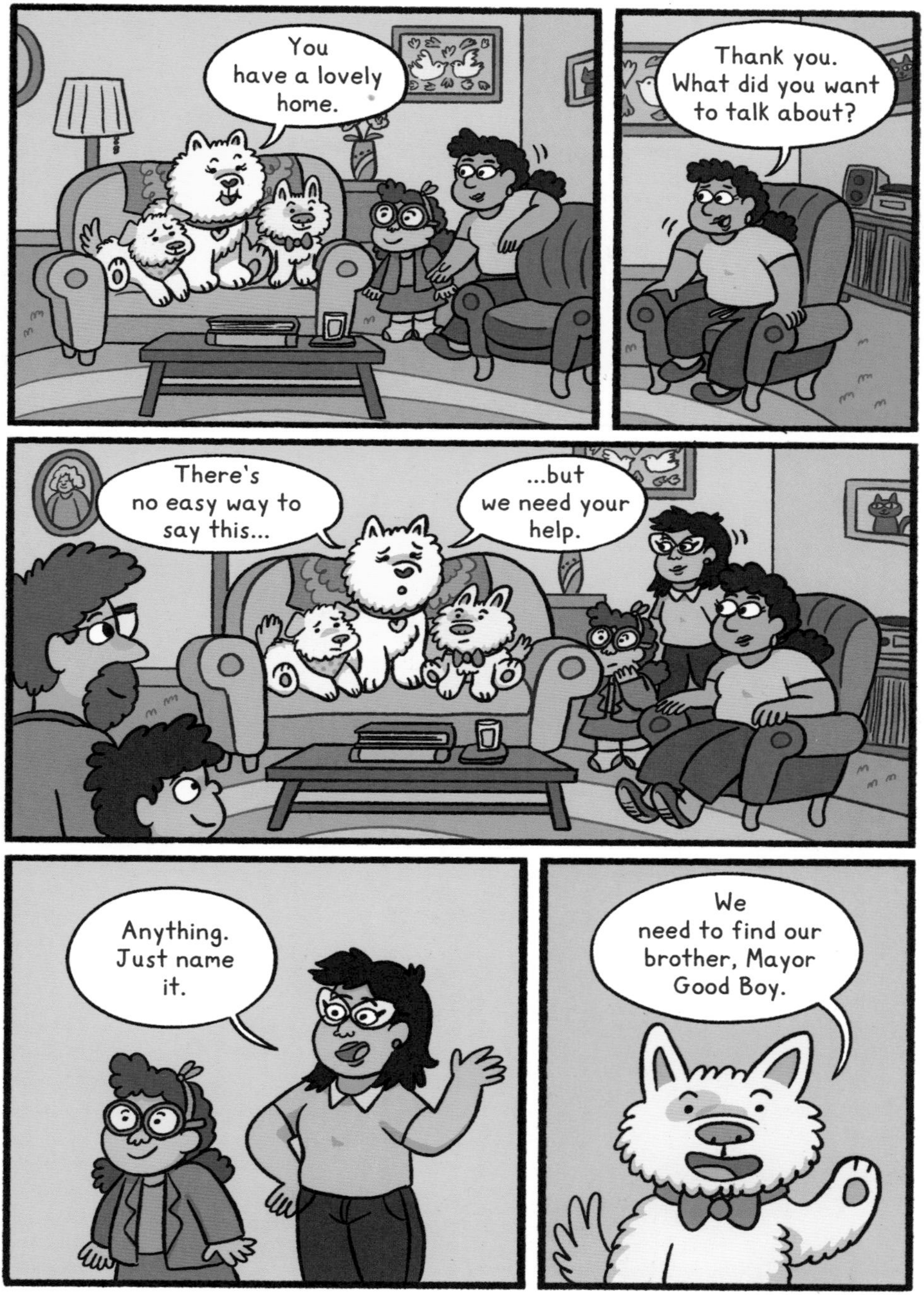

You have a lovely home.
Thank you. What did you want to talk about?
There's no easy way to say this...
...but we need your help.
Anything. Just name it.
We need to find our brother, Mayor Good Boy.

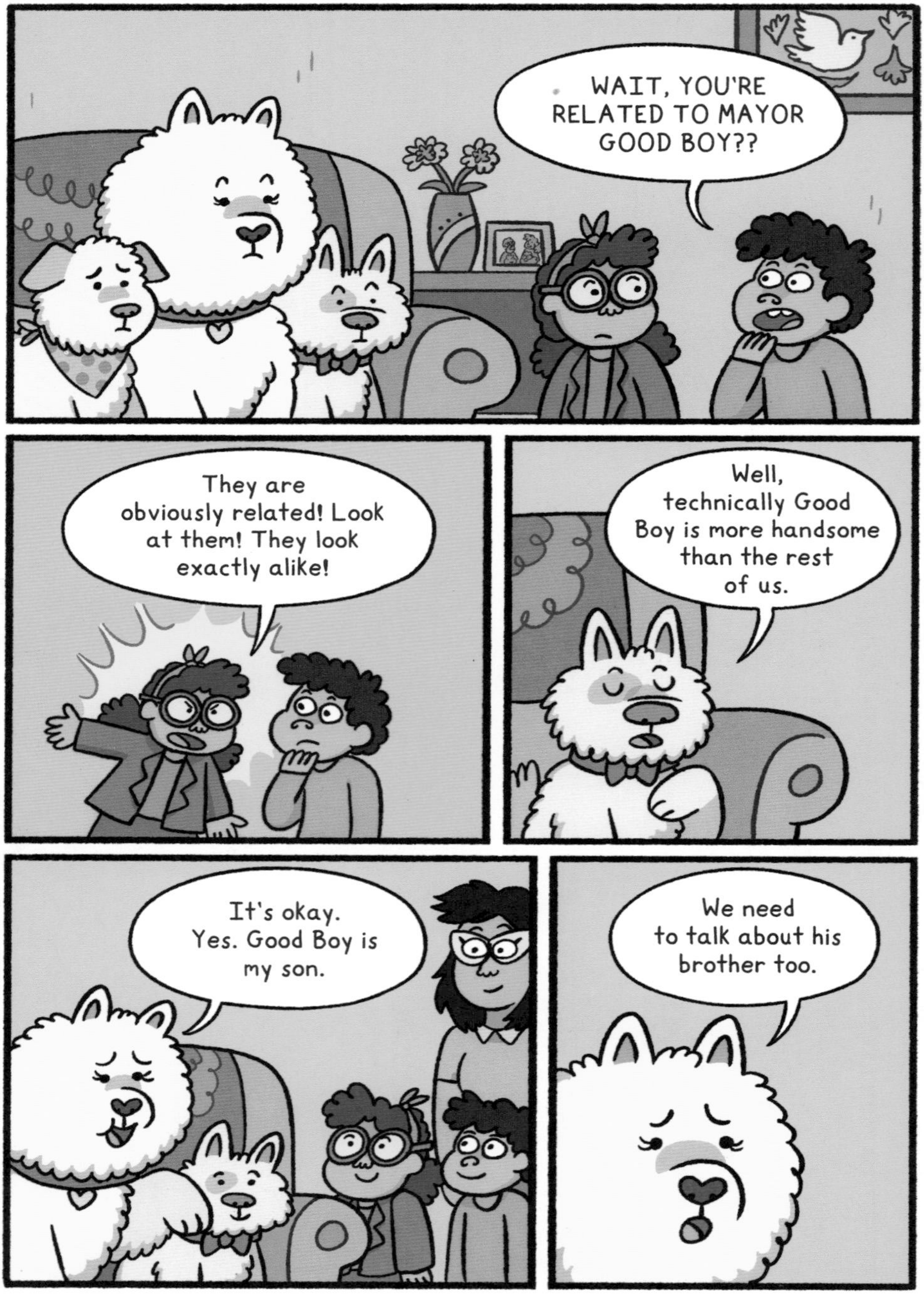
WAIT, YOU'RE RELATED TO MAYOR GOOD BOY??
They are obviously related! Look at them! They look exactly alike!
Well, technically Good Boy is more handsome than the rest of us.
It's okay. Yes. Good Boy is my son.
We need to talk about his brother too.

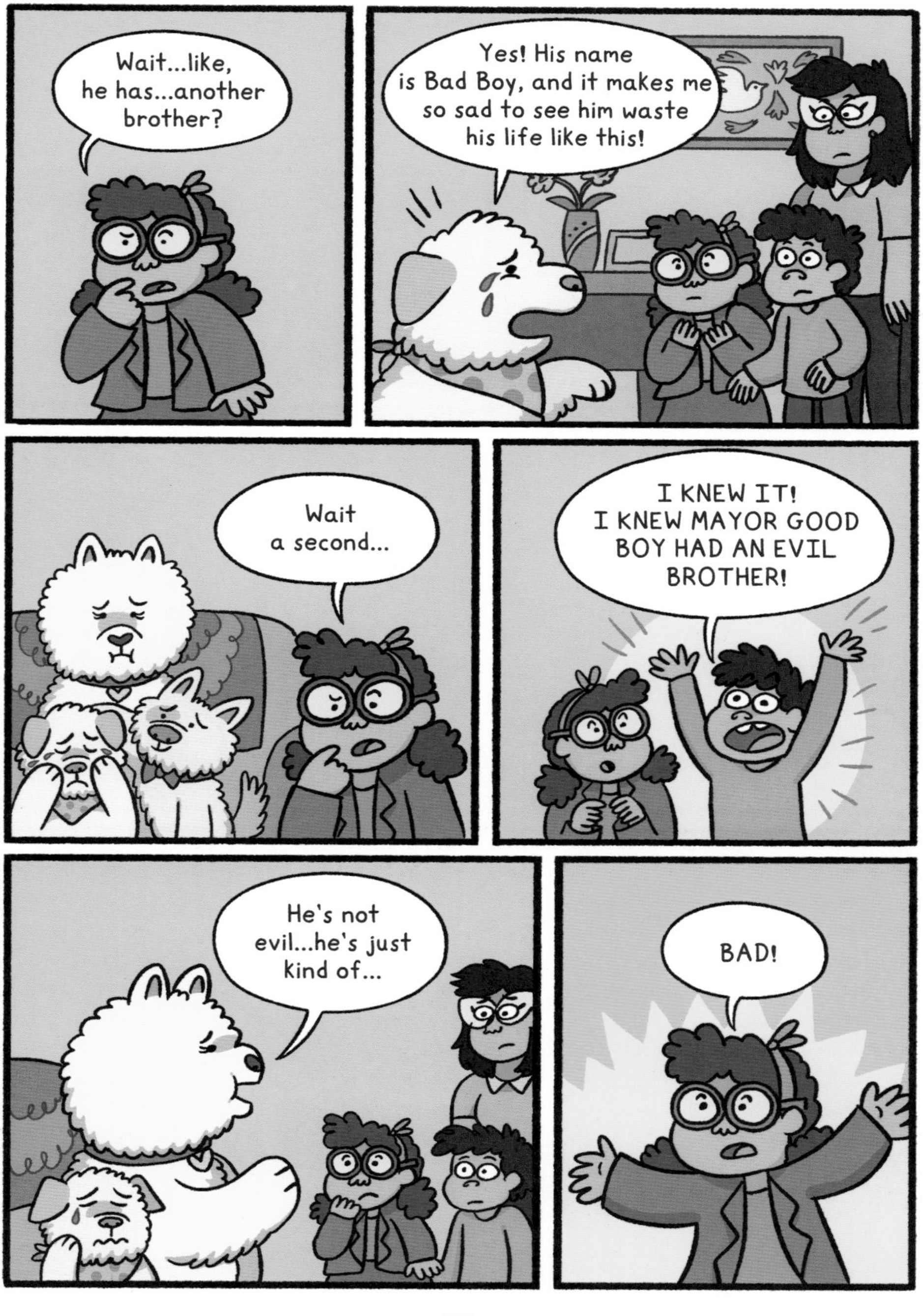
Wait...like, he has...another brother?
Yes! His name is Bad Boy, and it makes me so sad to see him waste his life like this!
Wait a second...
I KNEW IT! I KNEW MAYOR GOOD BOY HAD AN EVIL BROTHER!
He's not evil...he's just kind of...
BAD!

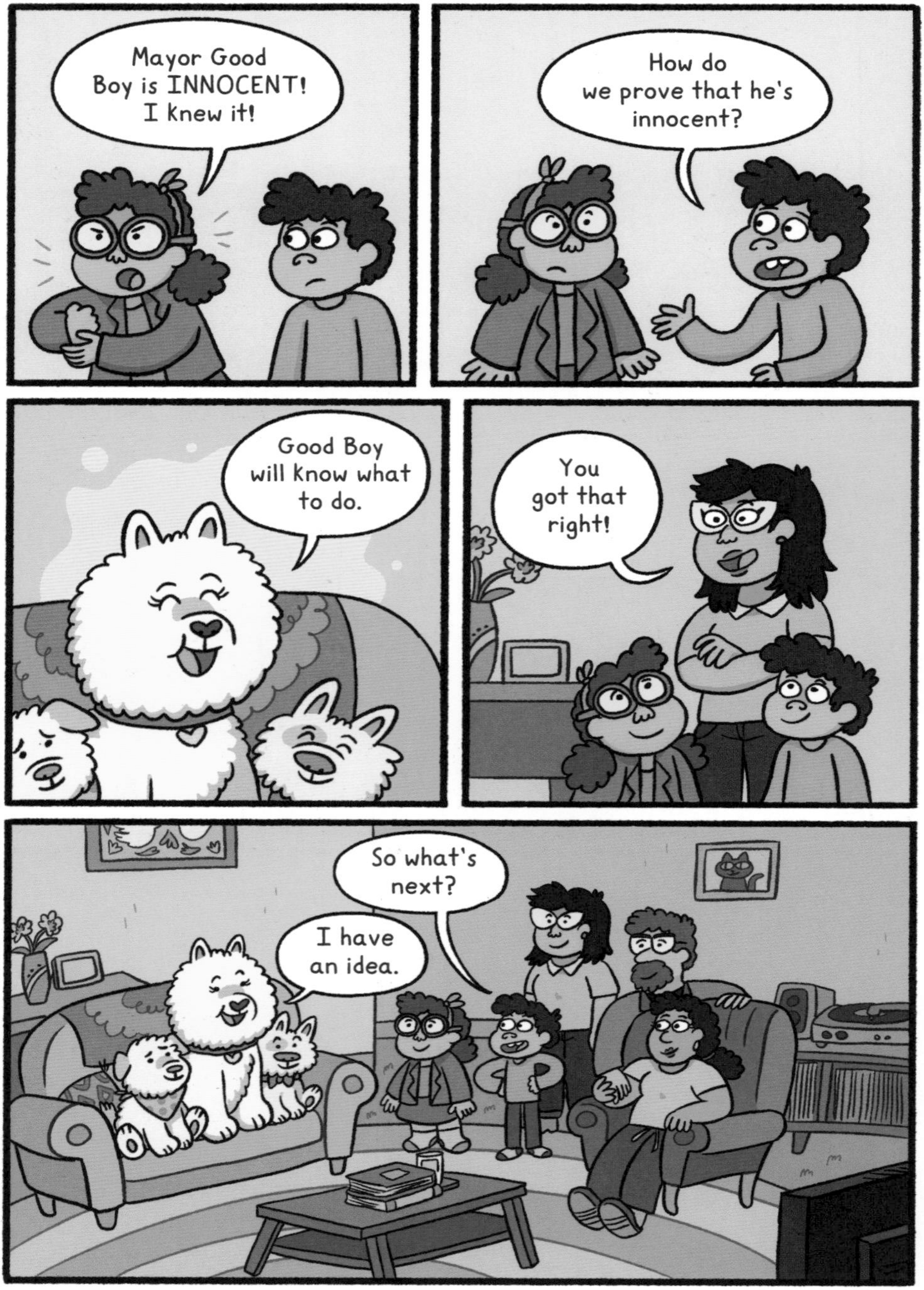

Mayor Good Boy is INNOCENT! I knew it!
How do we prove that he's innocent?
Good Boy will know what to do.
You got that right!
So what's next?
I have an idea.

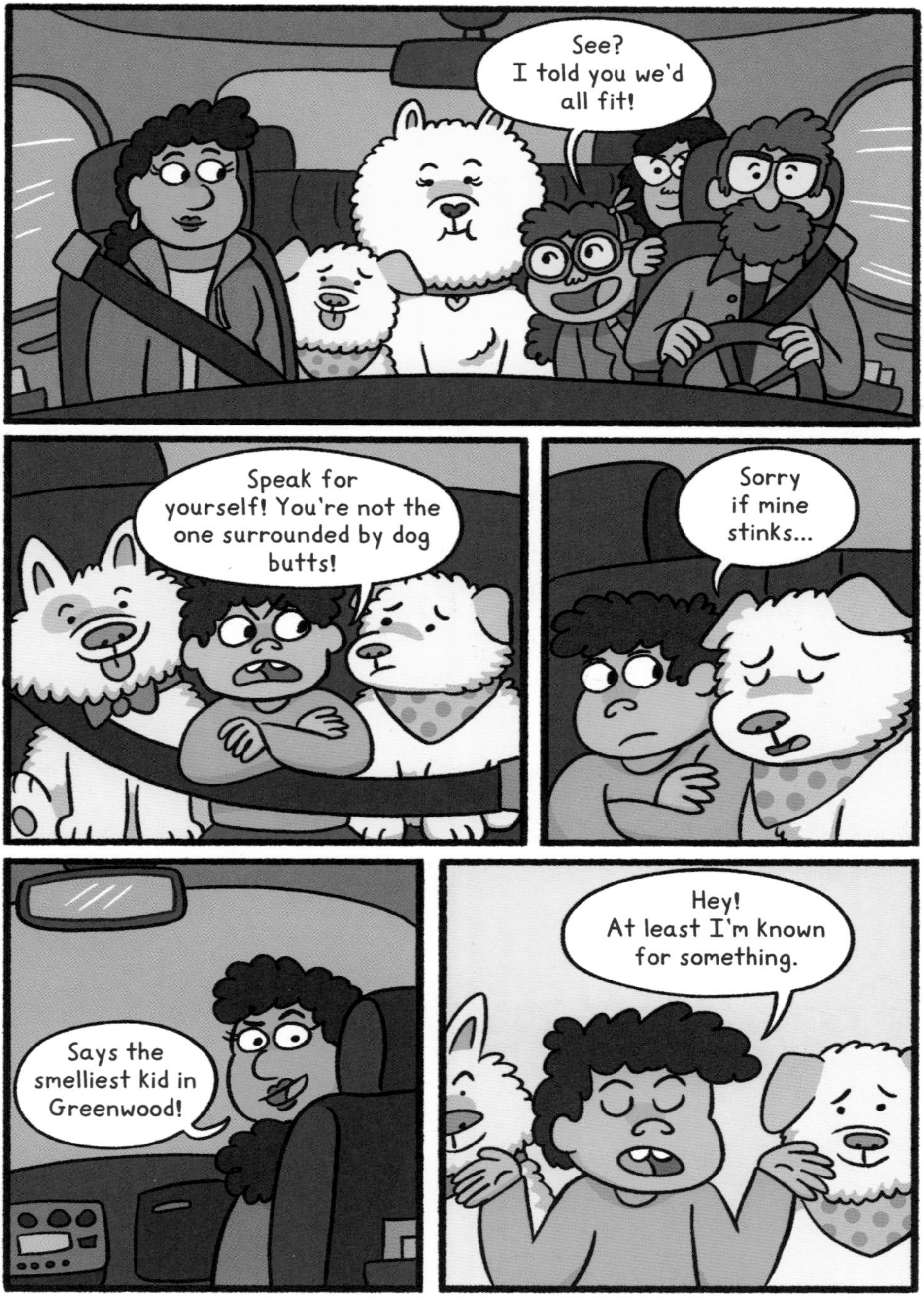
See? I told you we'd all fit!
Speak for yourself! You're not the one surrounded by dog butts!
Sorry if mine stinks...
Says the smelliest kid in Greenwood!
Hey! At least I'm known for something.

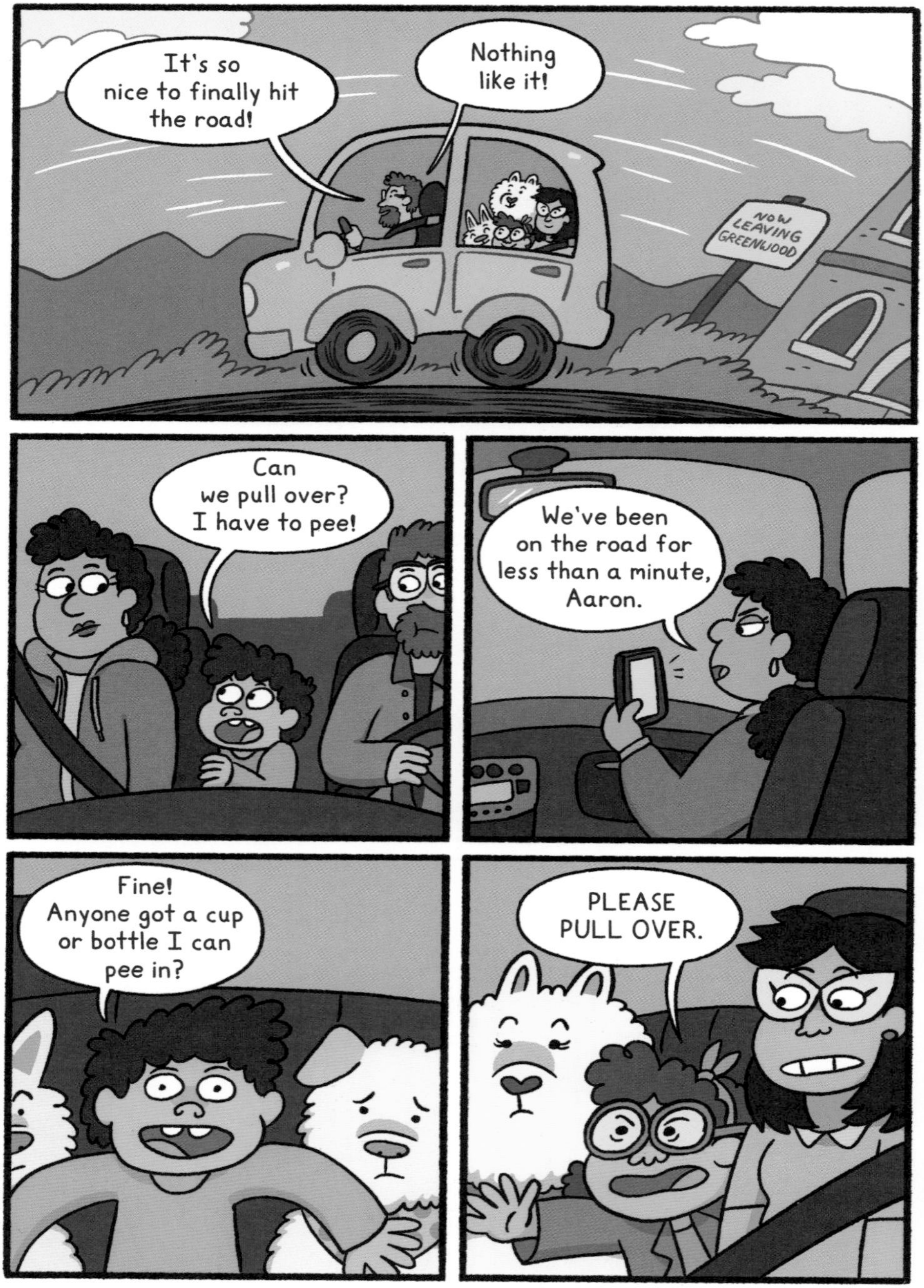
It's so nice to finally hit the road!
Nothing like it!
NOW LEAVING GREENWOOD
Can we pull over? I have to pee!
We've been on the road for less than a minute, Aaron.
Fine! Anyone got a cup or bottle I can pee in?
PLEASE PULL OVER.

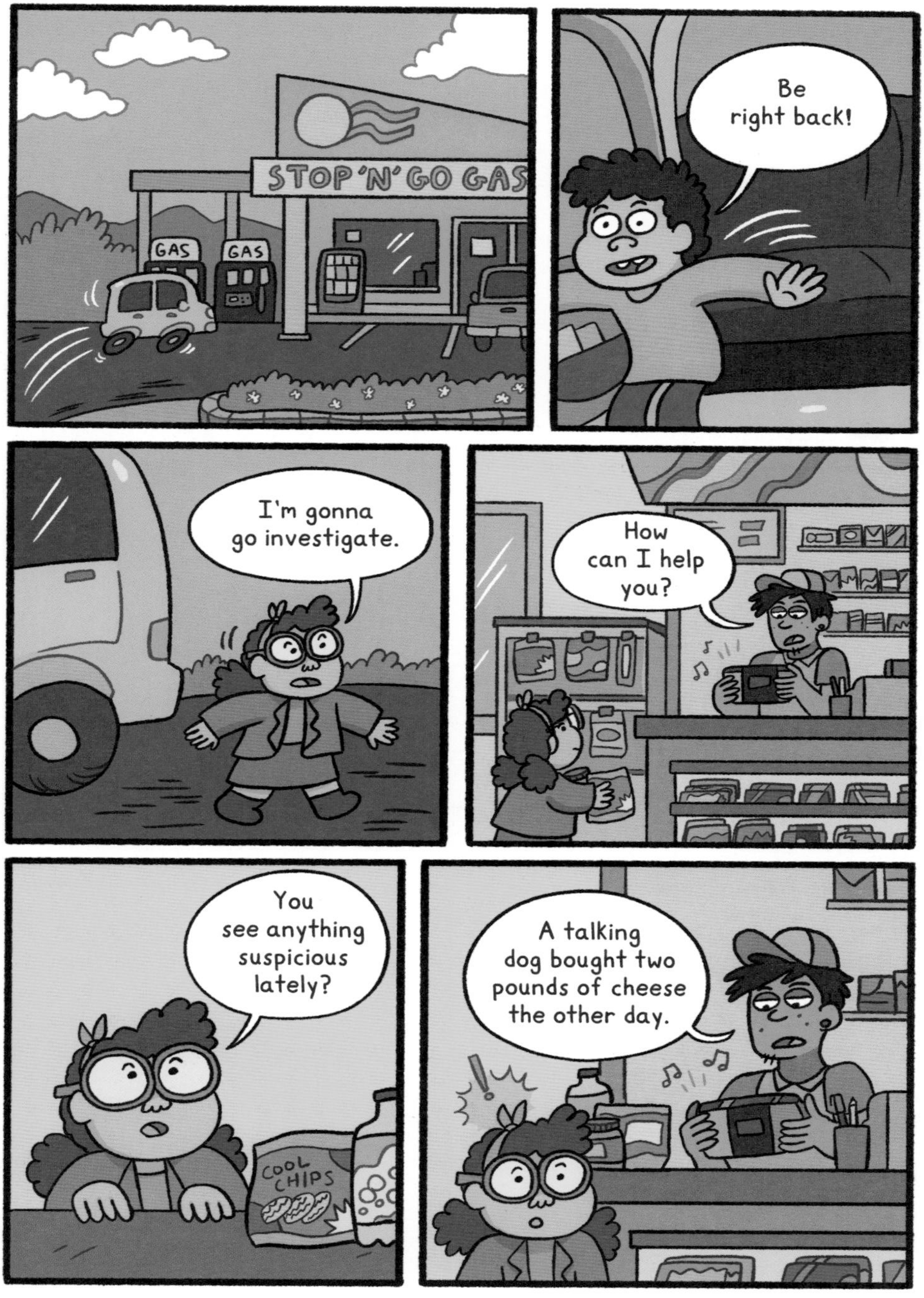

STOP 'N' GO GAS
GAS
GAS
Be right back!
I'm gonna go investigate.
How can I help you?
You see anything suspicious lately?
COOL CHIPS
A talking dog bought two pounds of cheese the other day.

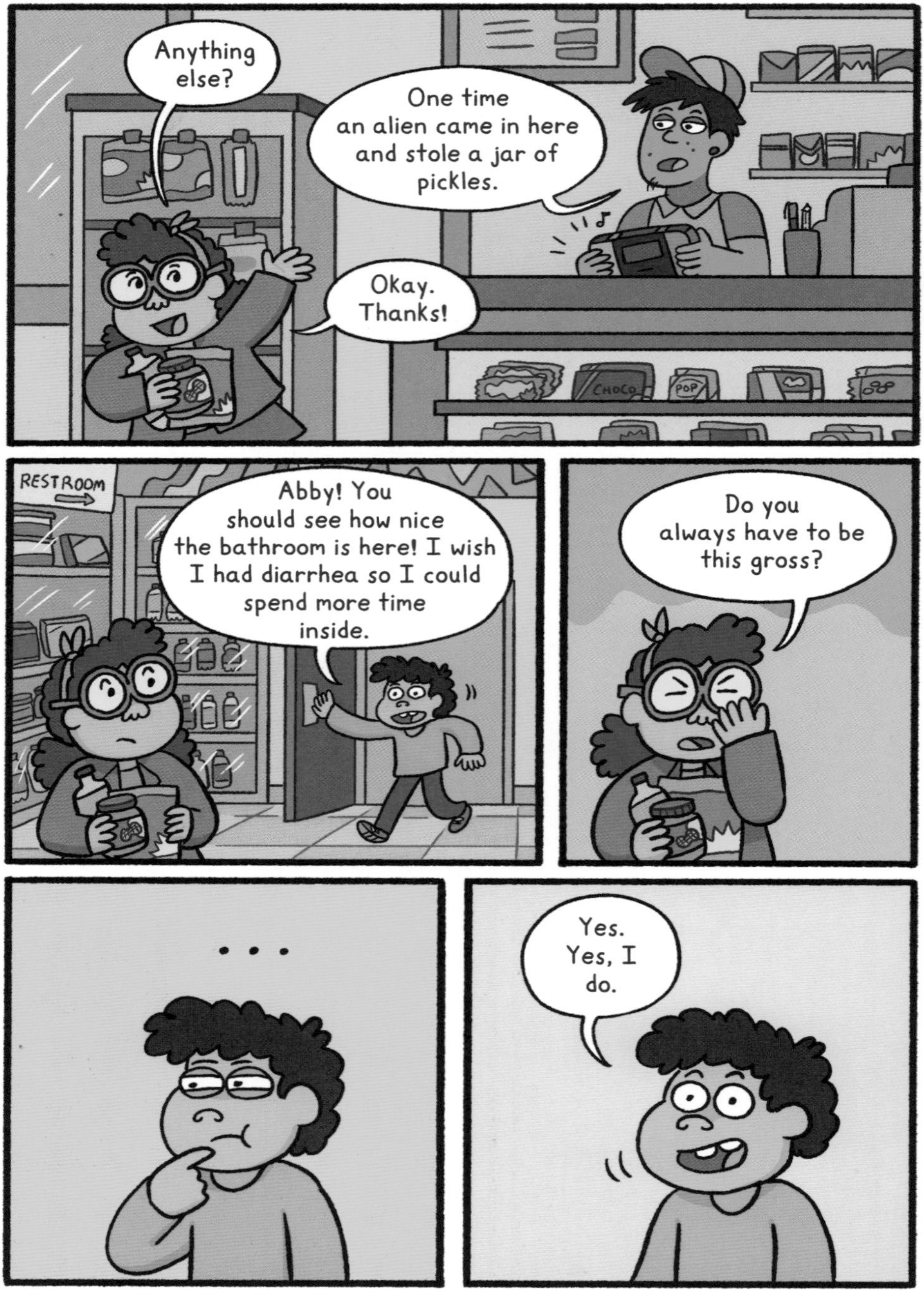
Anything else?
One time an alien came in here and stole a jar of pickles.
Okay. Thanks!
CHOCO
POP
RESTROOM
Abby! You should see how nice the bathroom is here! I wish I had diarrhea so I could spend more time inside.
Do you always have to be this gross?
. . .
Yes. Yes, I do.

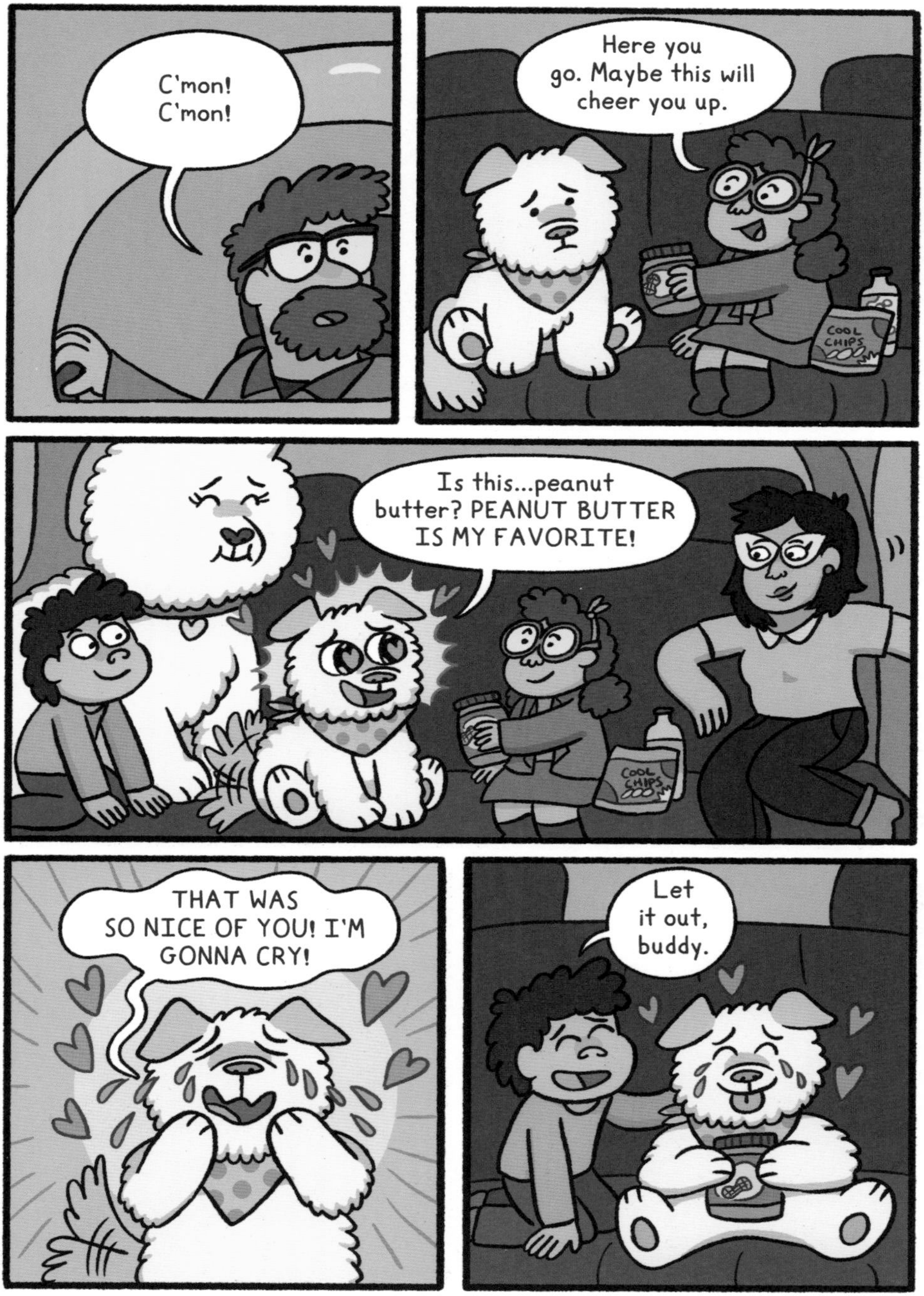
C'mon!
C'mon!
Here you go. Maybe this will cheer you up.
COOL CHIPS
Is this...peanut butter? PEANUT BUTTER IS MY FAVORITE!
COOL CHIPS
THAT WAS SO NICE OF YOU! I'M GONNA CRY!
Let it out, buddy.

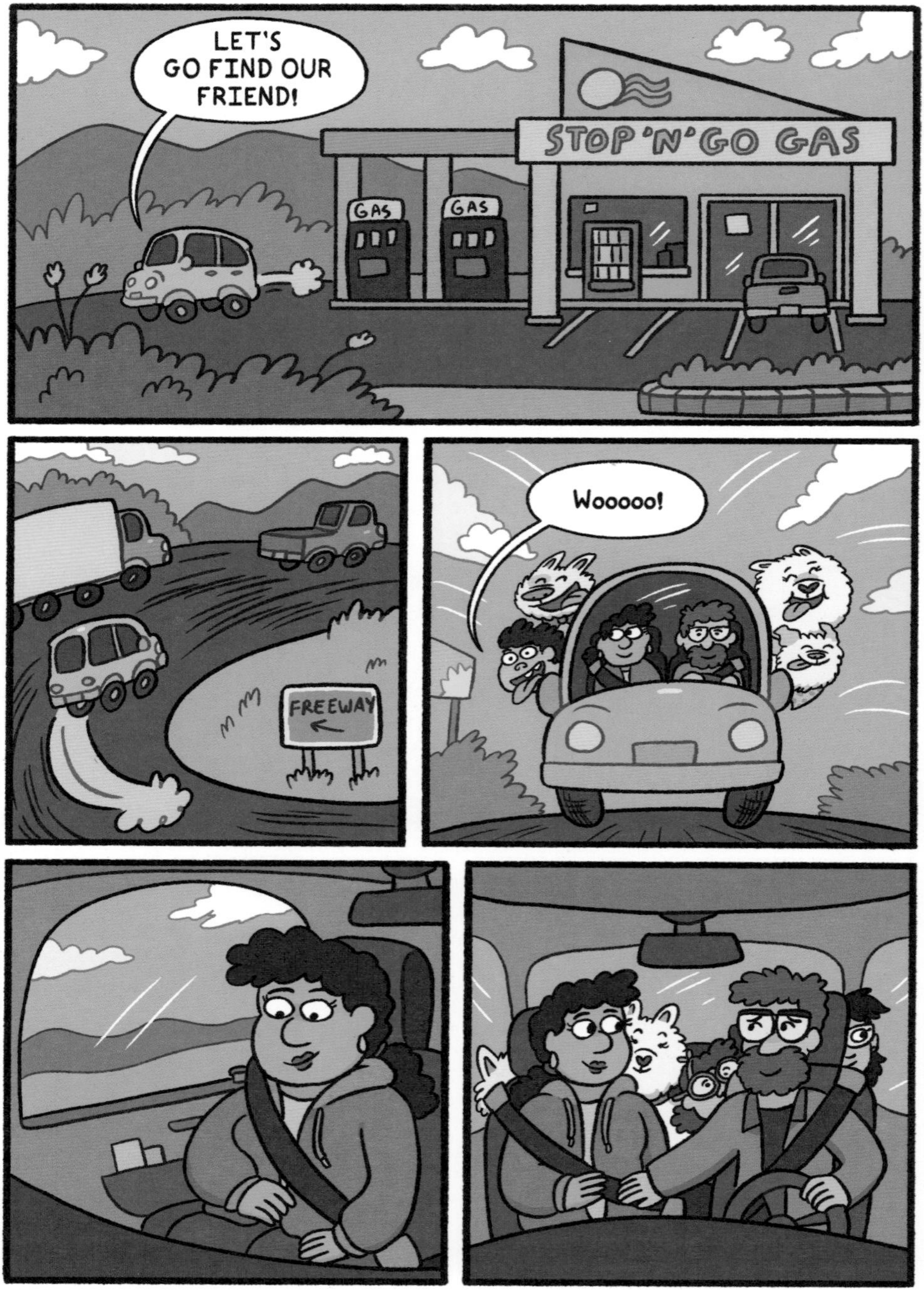
LET'S GO FIND OUR FRIEND!
STOP 'N' GO GAS
GAS
GAS
FREEWAY
Wooooo!

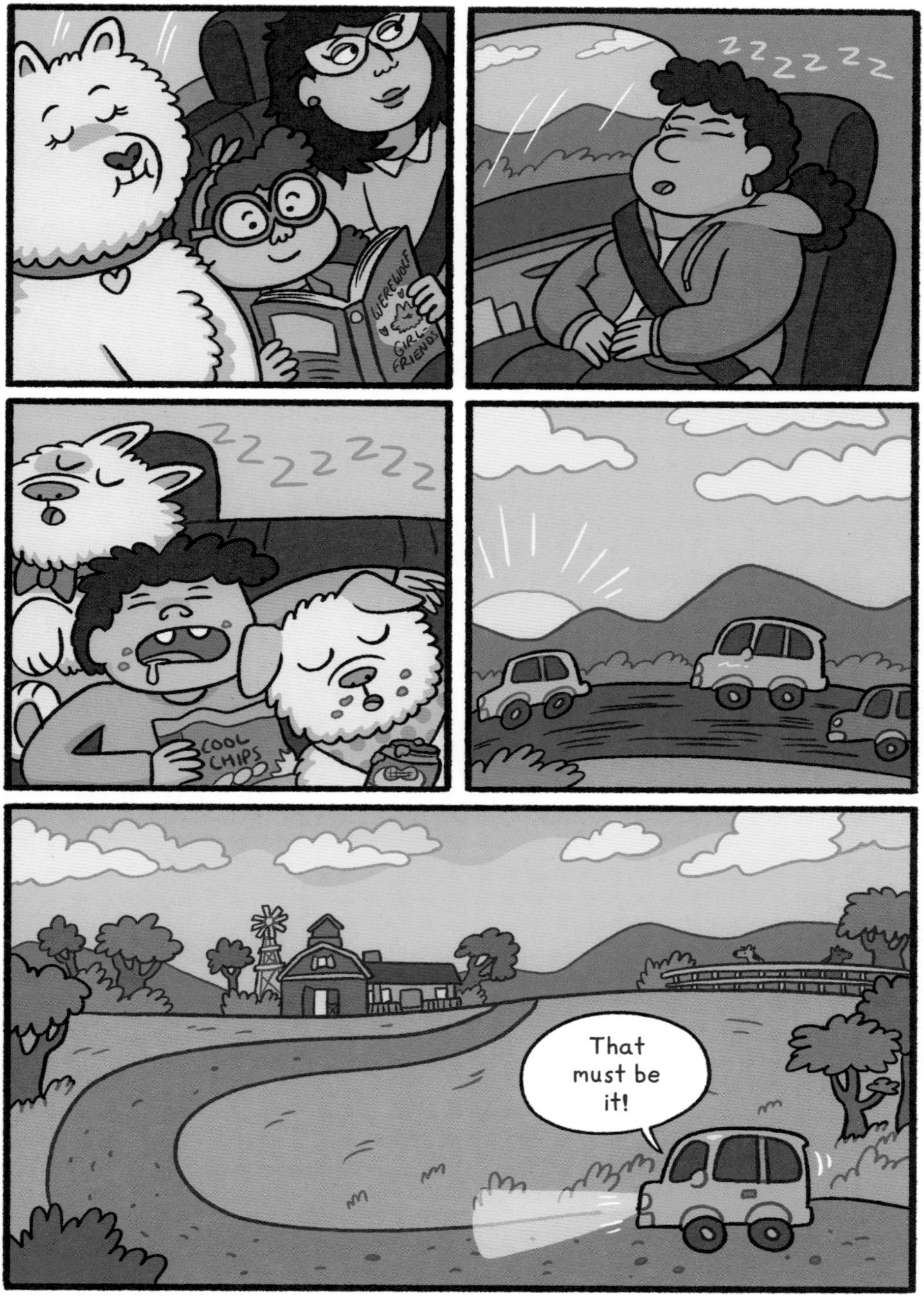
WEREWOLF GIRL-FRIENDS
COOL CHIPS
That must be it!

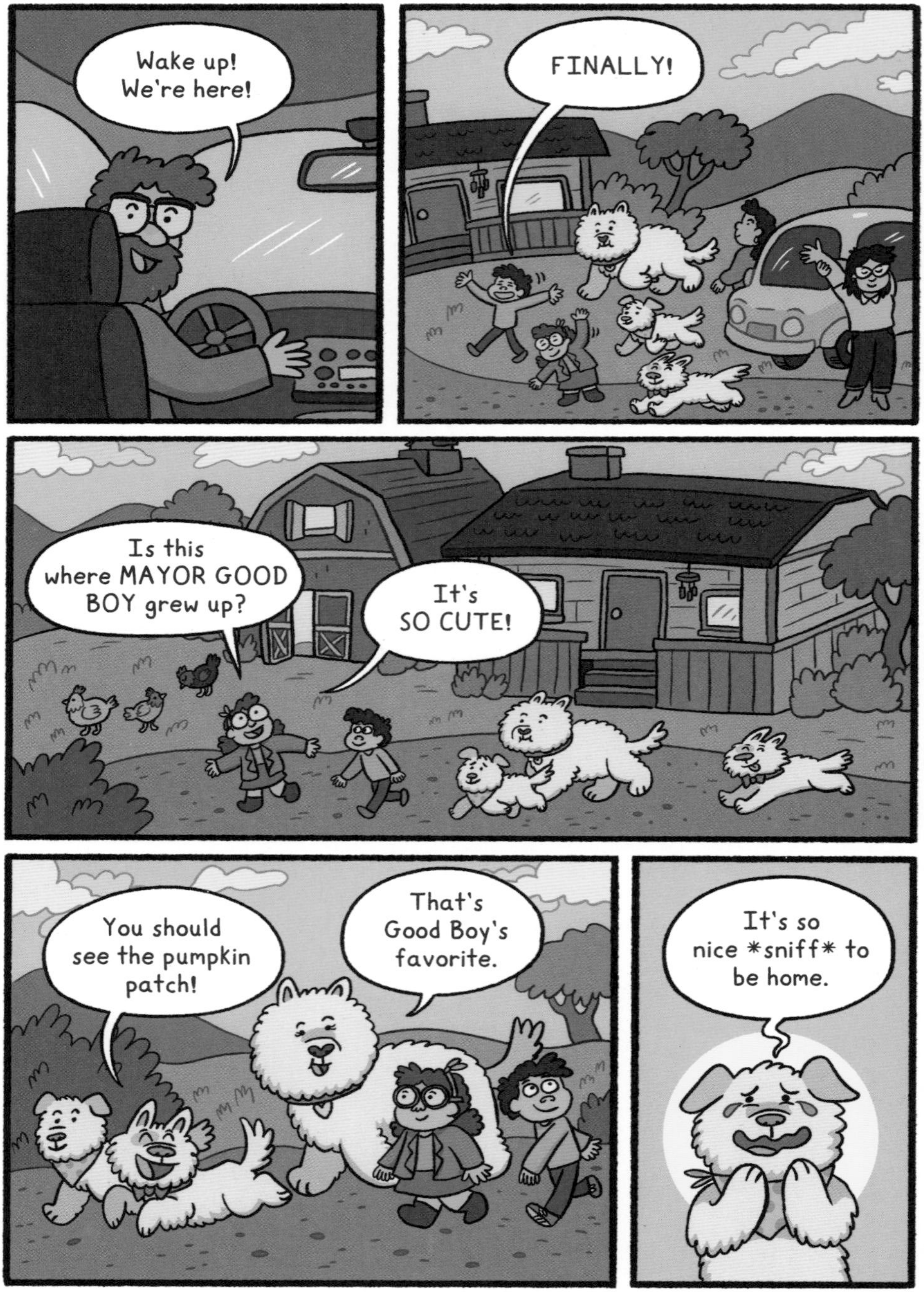
Wake up! We're here!
FINALLY!
Is this where MAYOR GOOD BOY grew up?
It's SO CUTE!
You should see the pumpkin patch!
That's Good Boy's favorite.
It's so nice *sniff* to be home.

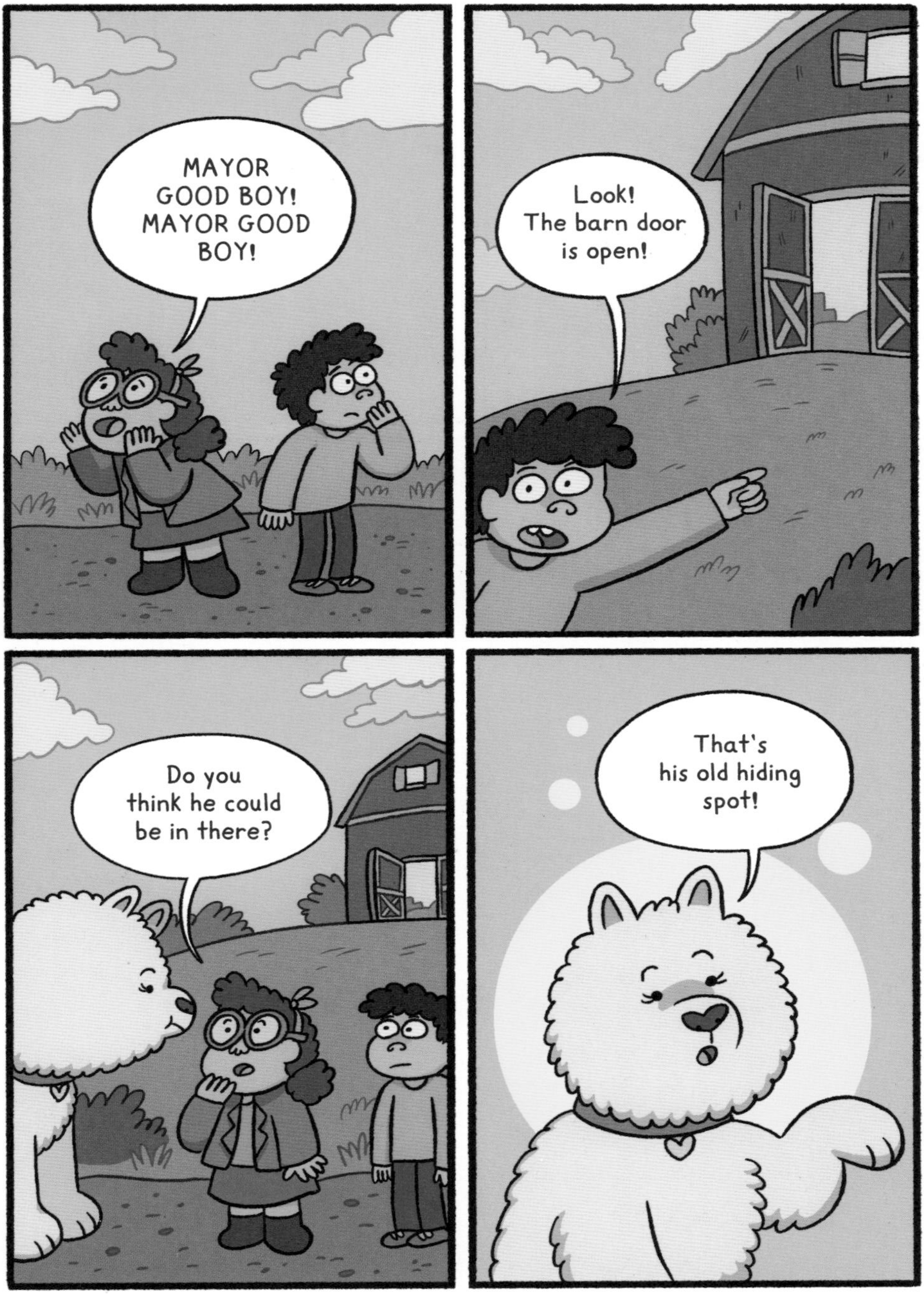
MAYOR GOOD BOY! MAYOR GOOD BOY!
Look! The barn door is open!
Do you think he could be in there?
That's his old hiding spot!

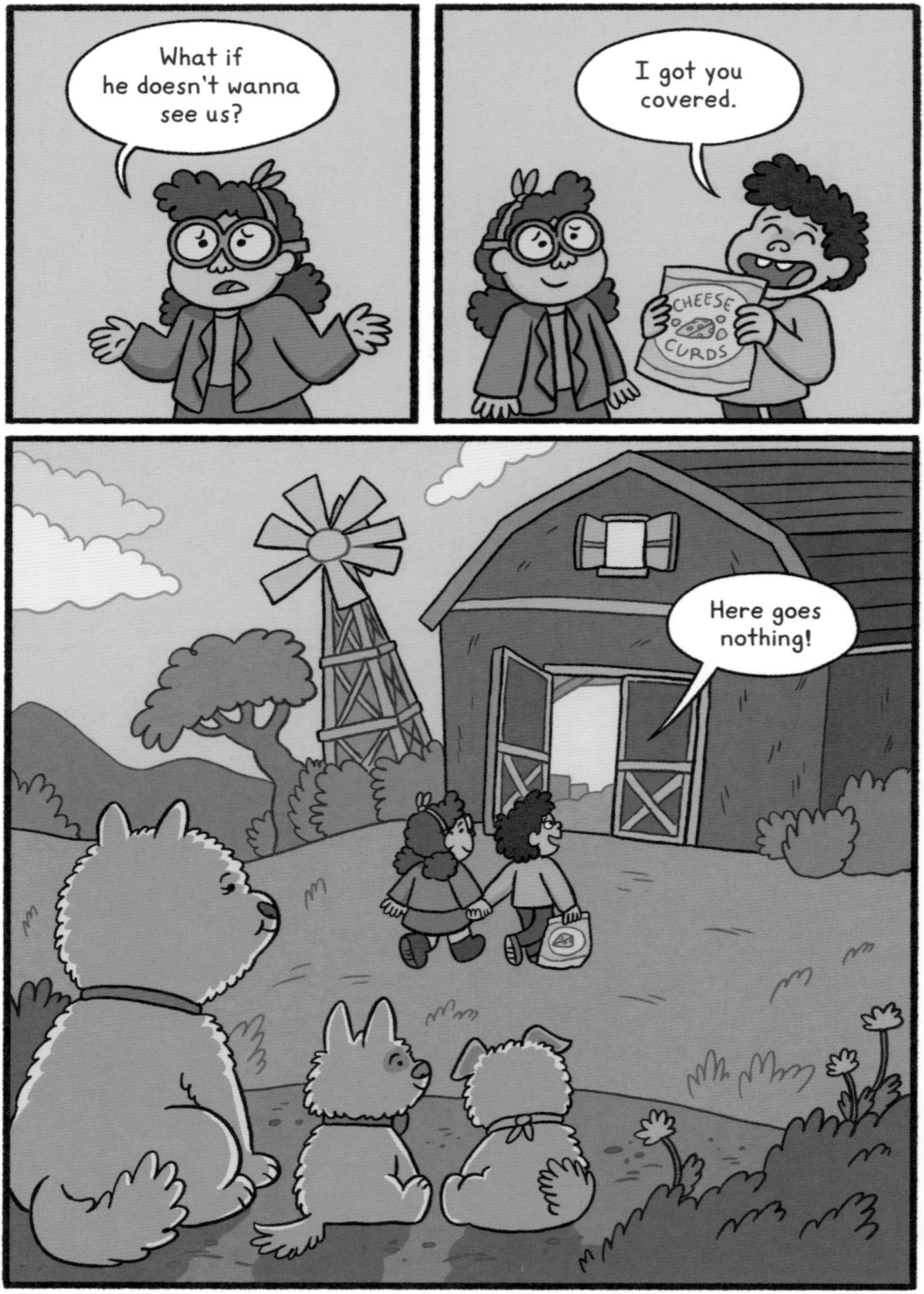
What if he doesn't wanna see us?
I got you covered.
CHEESE CURDS
Here goes nothing!

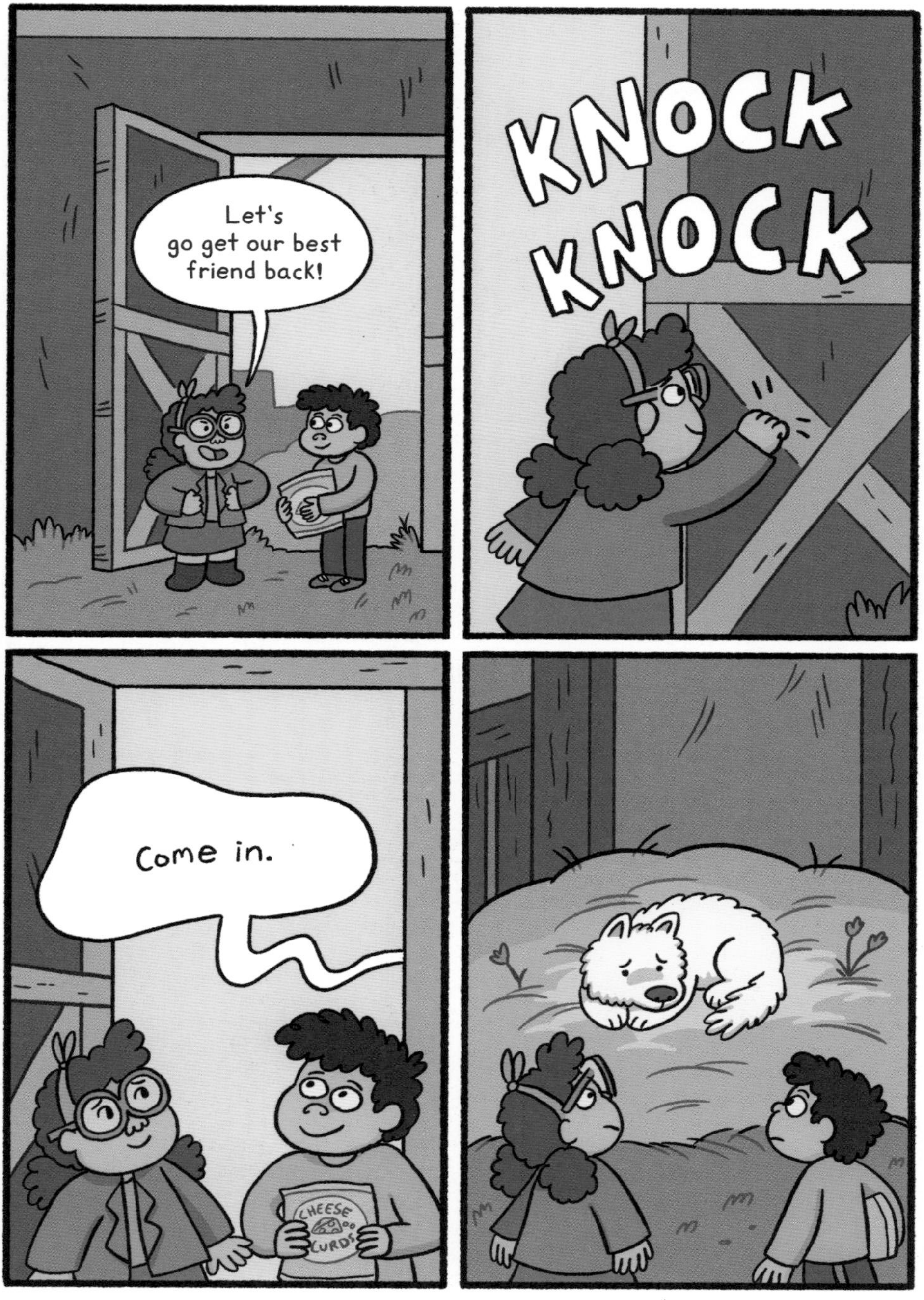
Let's go get our best friend back!
KNOCK KNOCK
Come in.
CHEESE CURDS

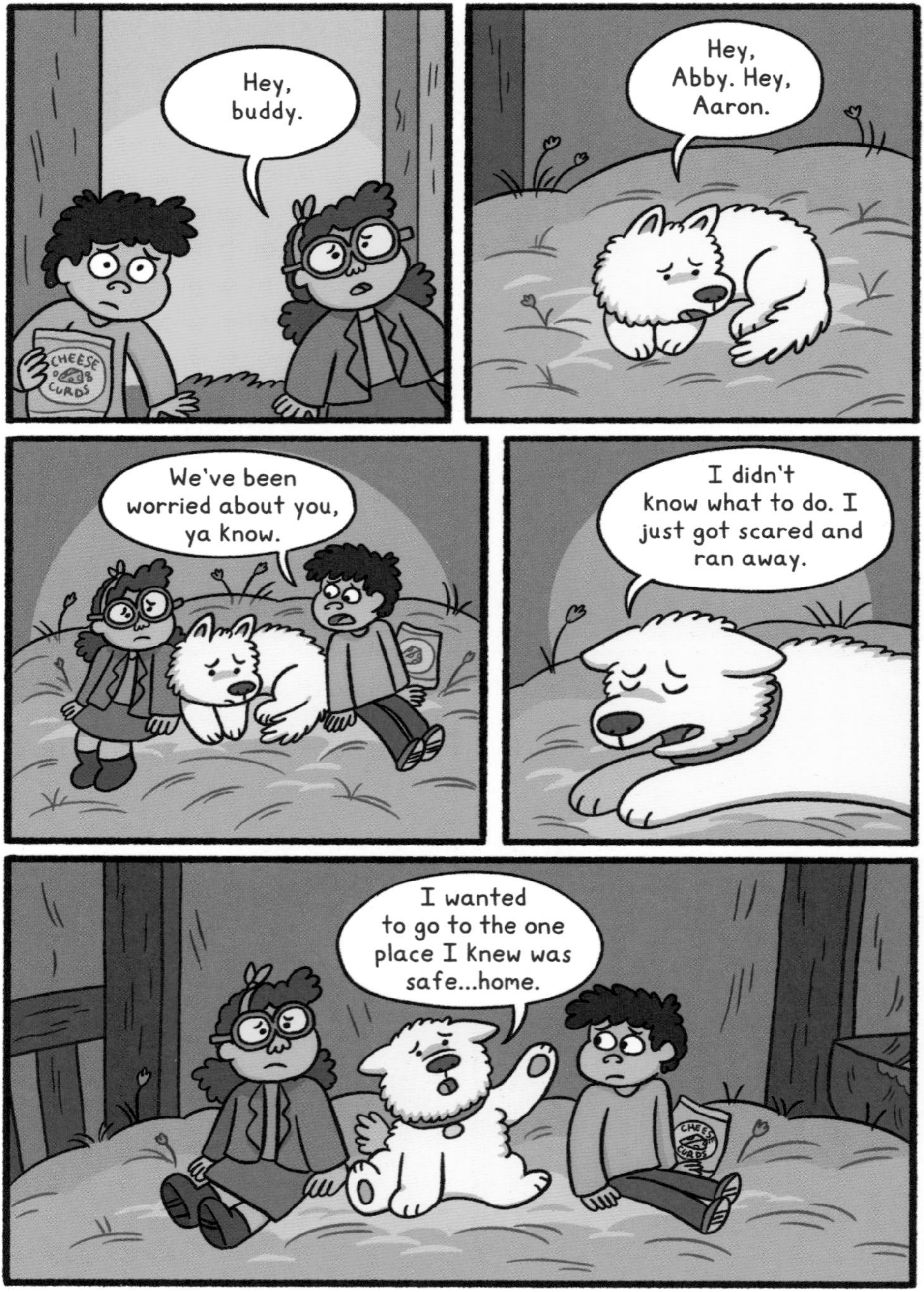

Hey, buddy.
Hey, Abby. Hey, Aaron.
CHEESE CURDS
We've been worried about you, ya know.
I didn't know what to do. I just got scared and ran away.
I wanted to go to the one place I knew was safe...home.
CHEESE CURDS

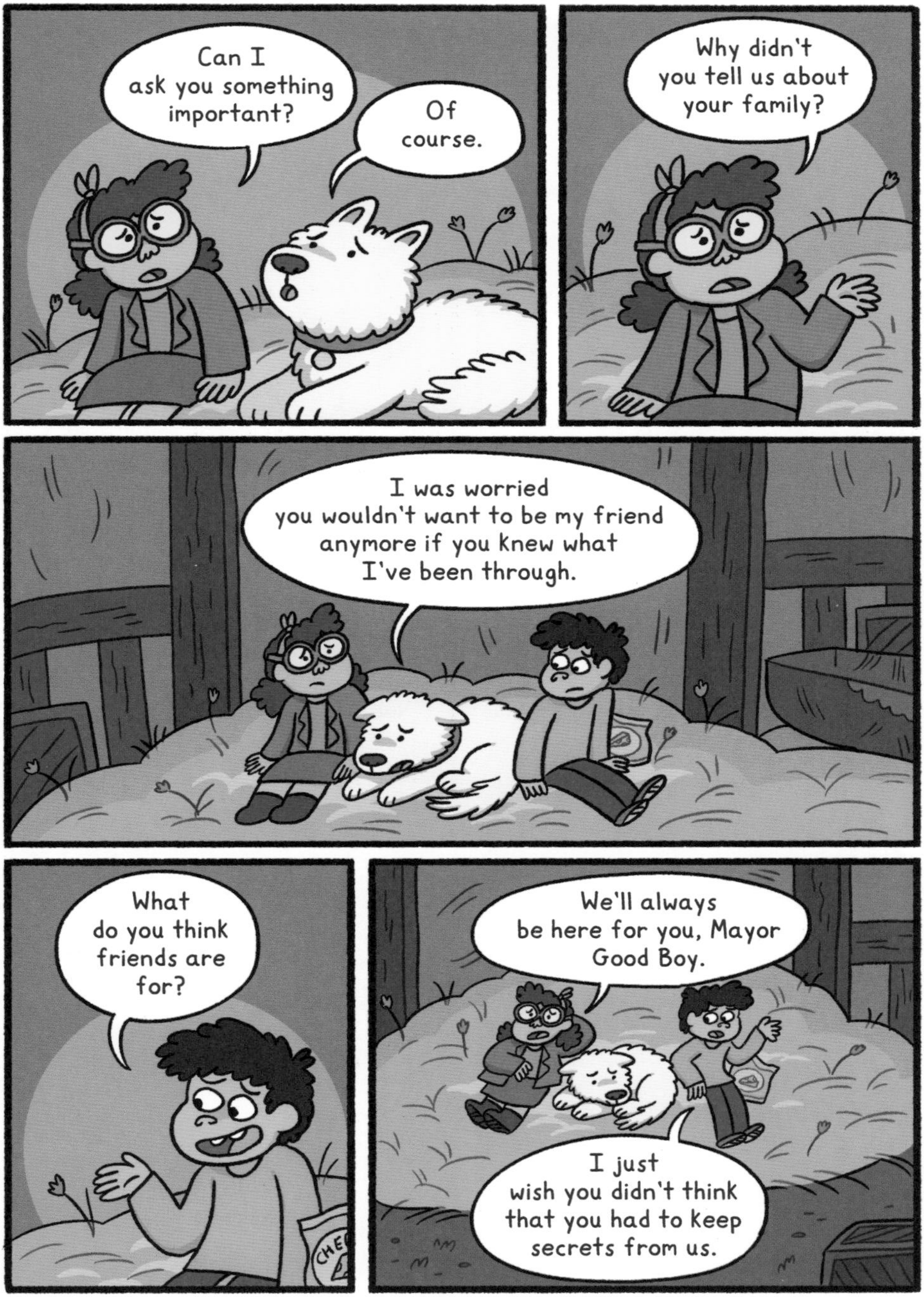
Can I ask you something important?
Of course.
Why didn't you tell us about your family?
I was worried you wouldn't want to be my friend anymore if you knew what I've been through.
What do you think friends are for?
We'll always be here for you, Mayor Good Boy.
I just wish you didn't think that you had to keep secrets from us.

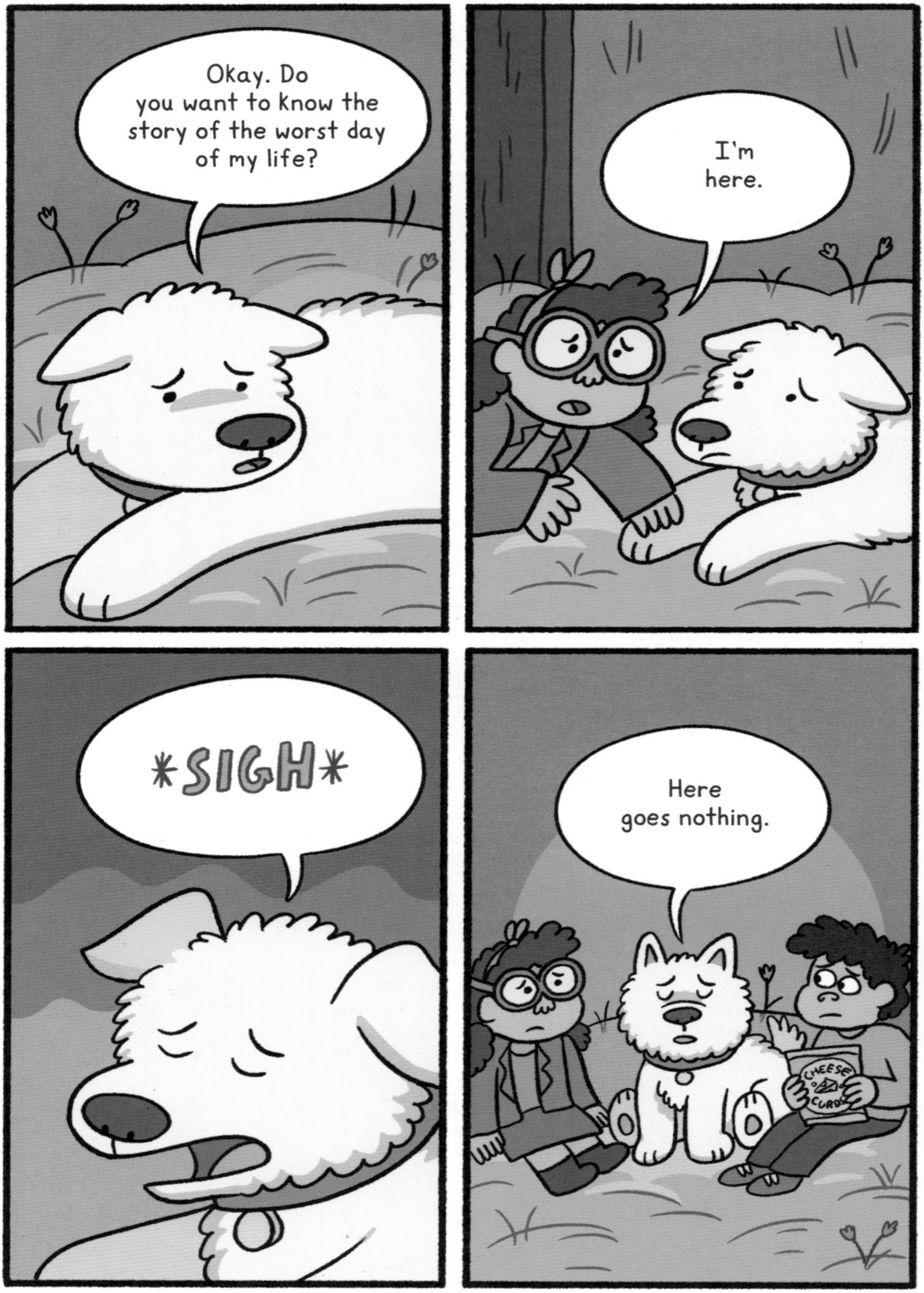
Okay. Do you want to know the story of the worst day of my life?
I'm here.
SIGH
Here goes nothing.
CHEESE CURDS

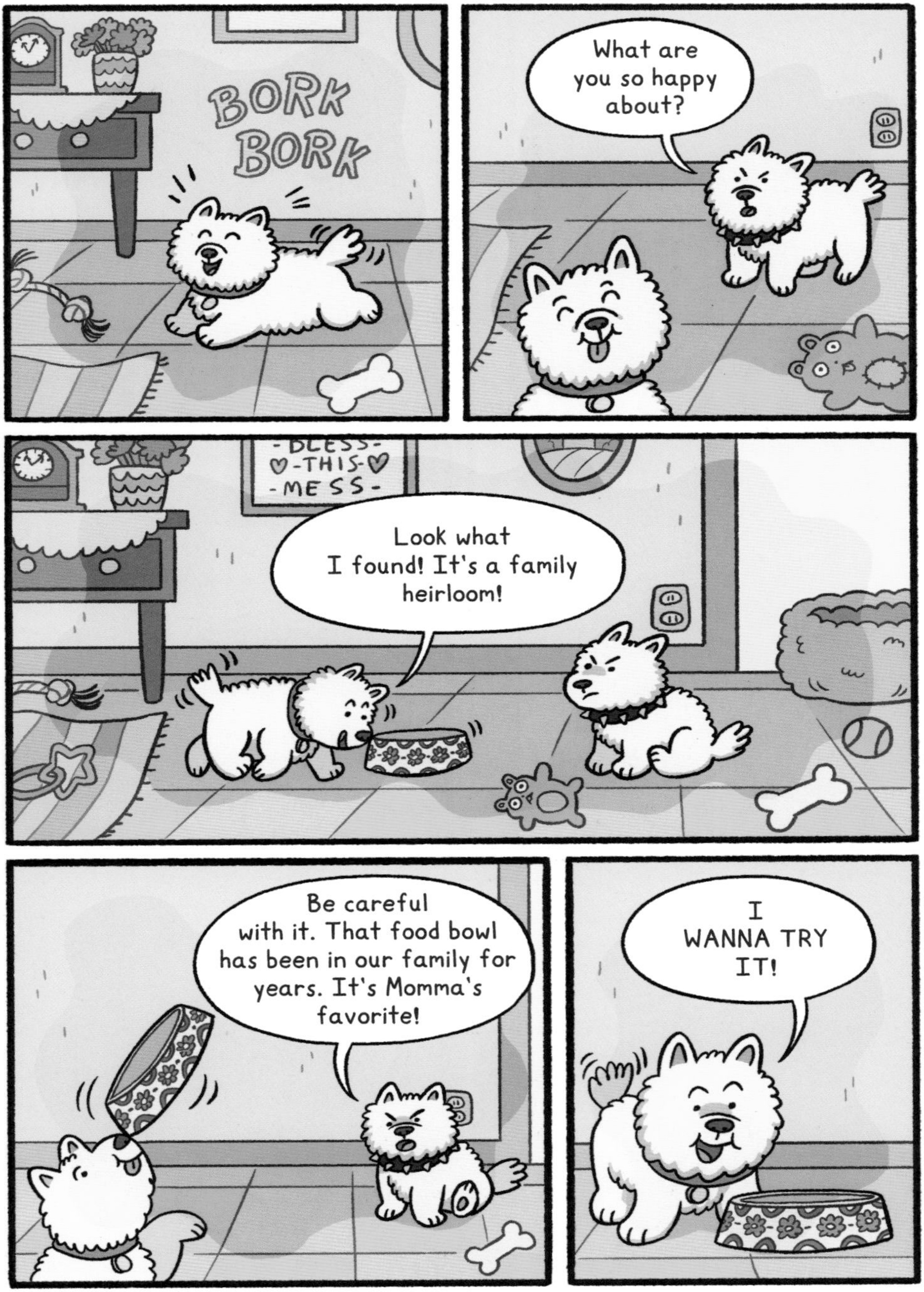
BORK
BORK
What are you so happy about?
-BLESS-
-THIS-
-MESS-
Look what I found! It's a family heirloom!
Be careful with it. That food bowl has been in our family for years. It's Momma's favorite!
I WANNA TRY IT!

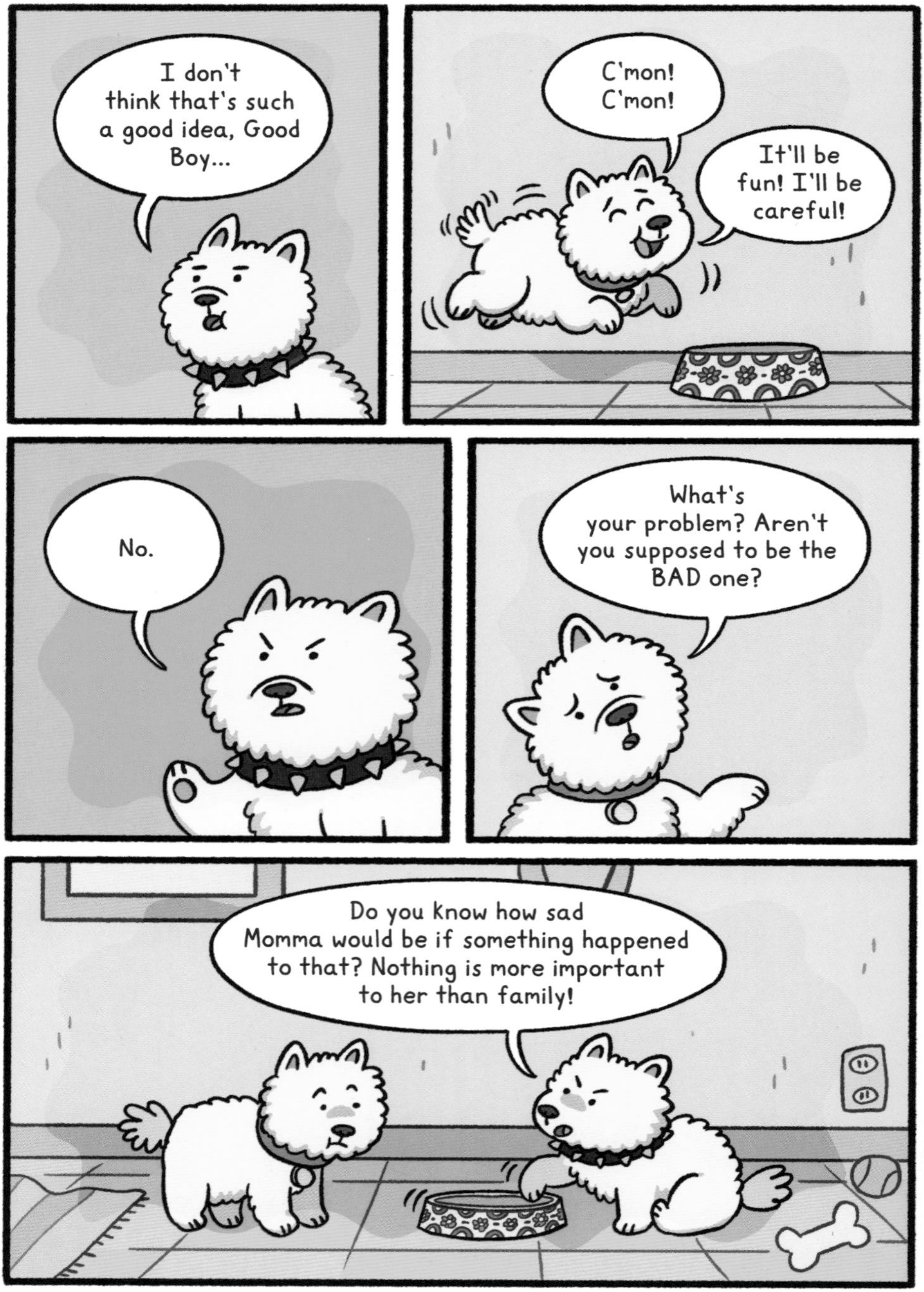
I don't think that's such a good idea, Good Boy...
C'mon! C'mon!
It'll be fun! I'll be careful!
No.
What's your problem? Aren't you supposed to be the BAD one?
Do you know how sad Momma would be if something happened to that? Nothing is more important to her than family!

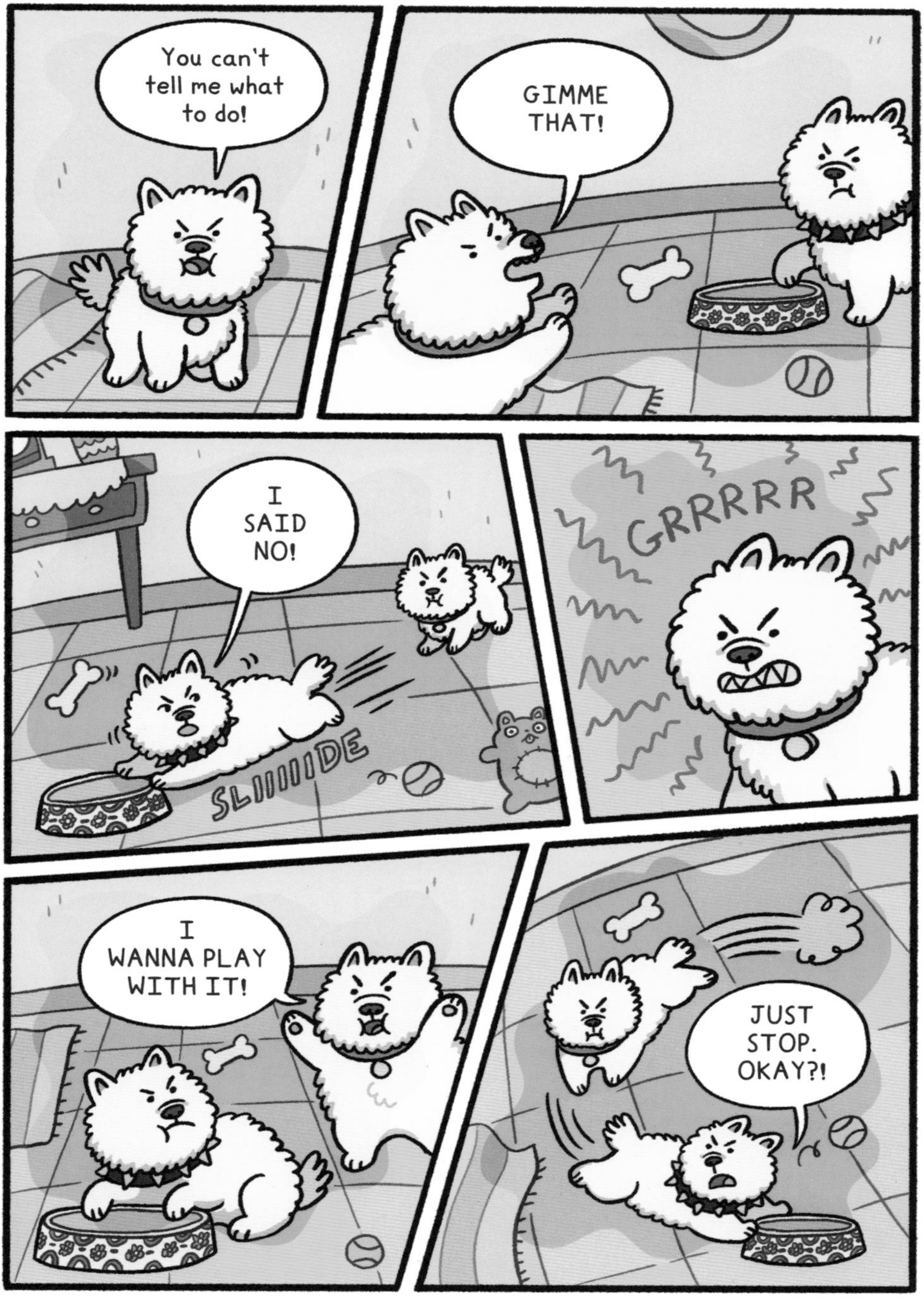
You can't tell me what to do!
GIMME THAT!
I SAID NO!
SLIIIIIDE
GRRRRR
I WANNA PLAY WITH IT!
JUST STOP. OKAY?!

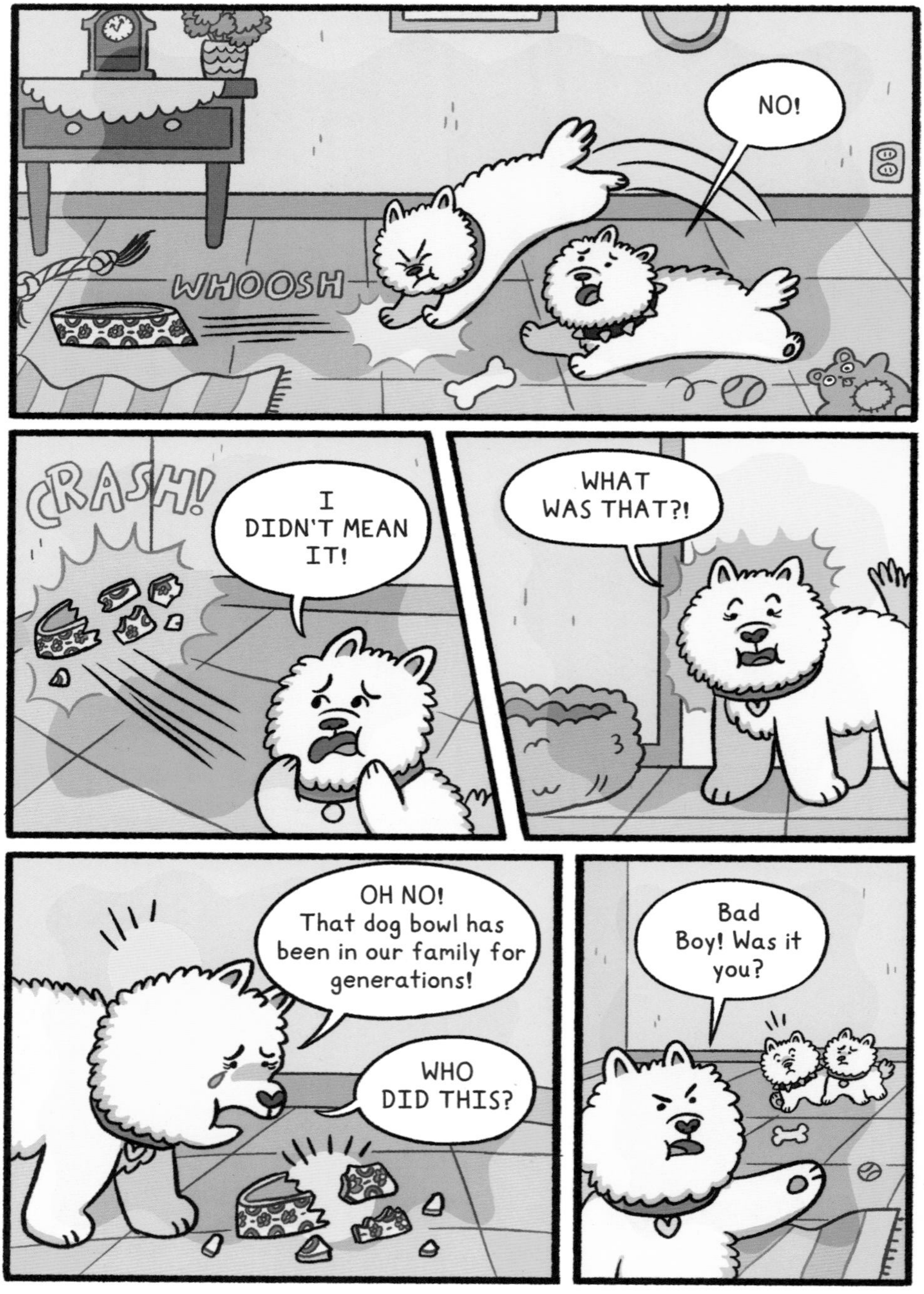
NO!
WHOOSH
CRASH!
I DIDN'T MEAN IT!
WHAT WAS THAT?!
OH NO! That dog bowl has been in our family for generations!
WHO DID THIS?
Bad Boy! Was it you?

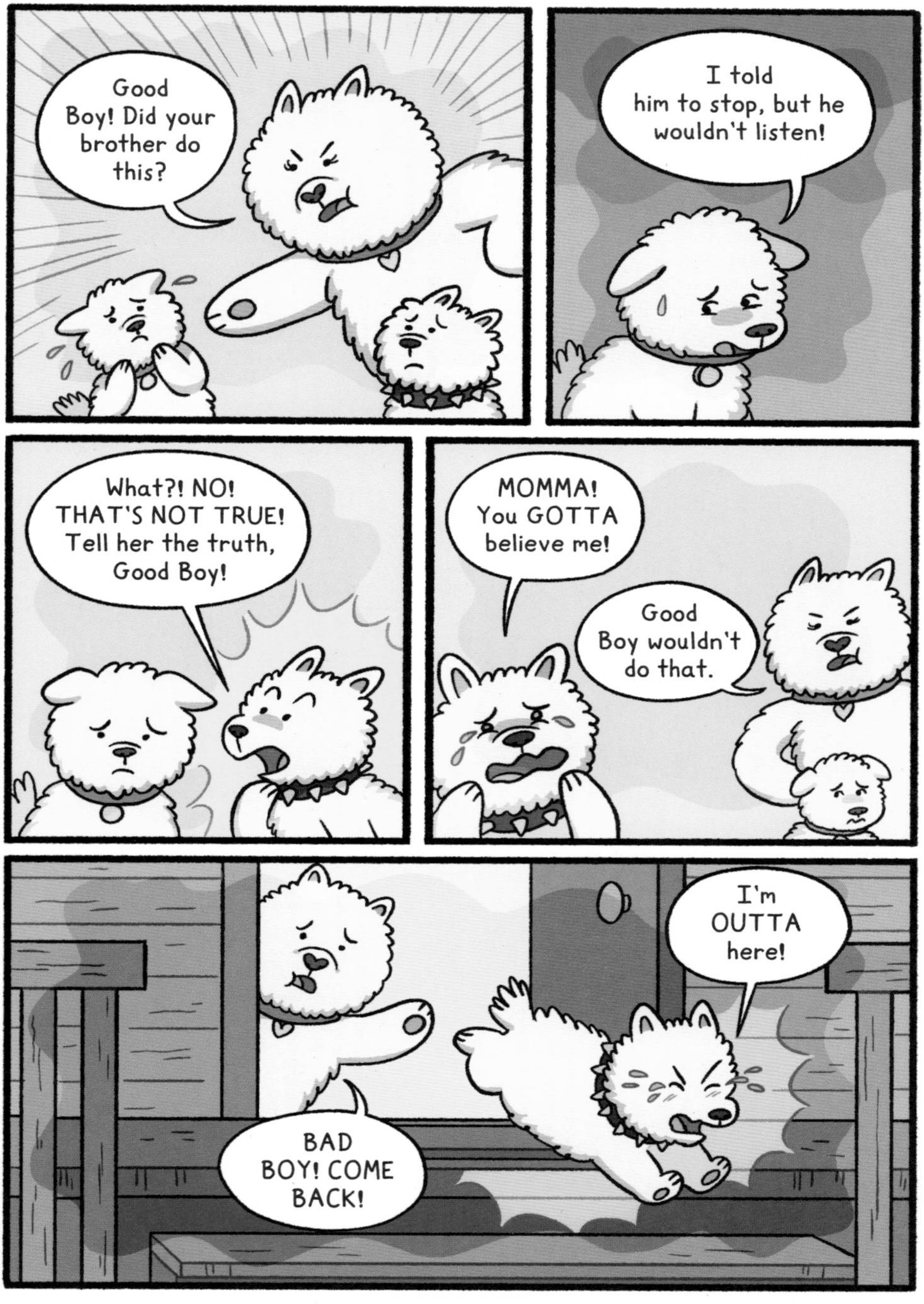
Good Boy! Did your brother do this?
I told him to stop, but he wouldn't listen!
What?! NO! THAT'S NOT TRUE! Tell her the truth, Good Boy!
MOMMA! You GOTTA believe me!
Good Boy wouldn't do that.
I'm OUTTA here!
BAD BOY! COME BACK!

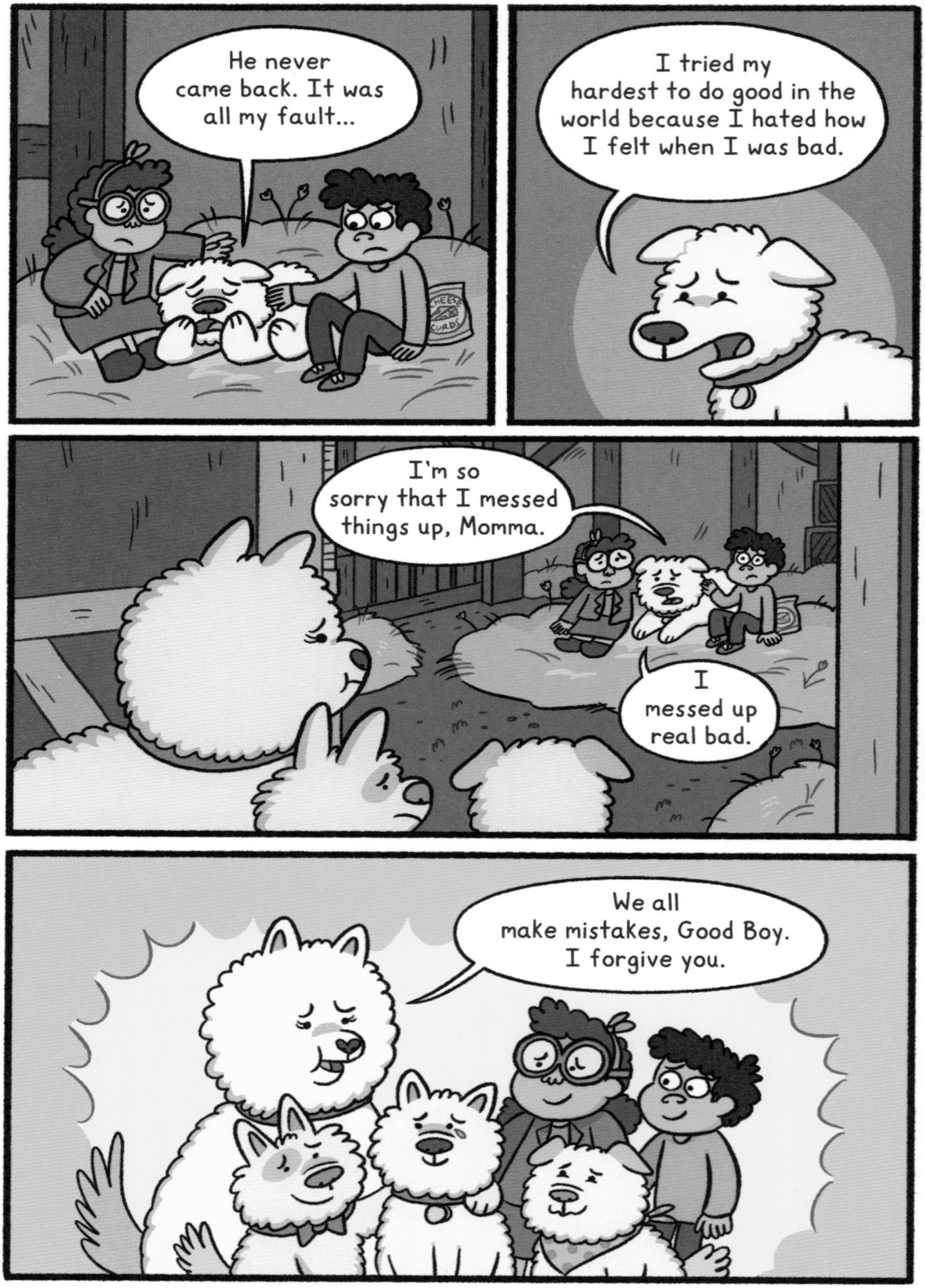
He never came back. It was all my fault...
I tried my hardest to do good in the world because I hated how I felt when I was bad.
I'm so sorry that I messed things up, Momma.
I messed up real bad.
CHEESE CURDS
We all make mistakes, Good Boy. I forgive you.

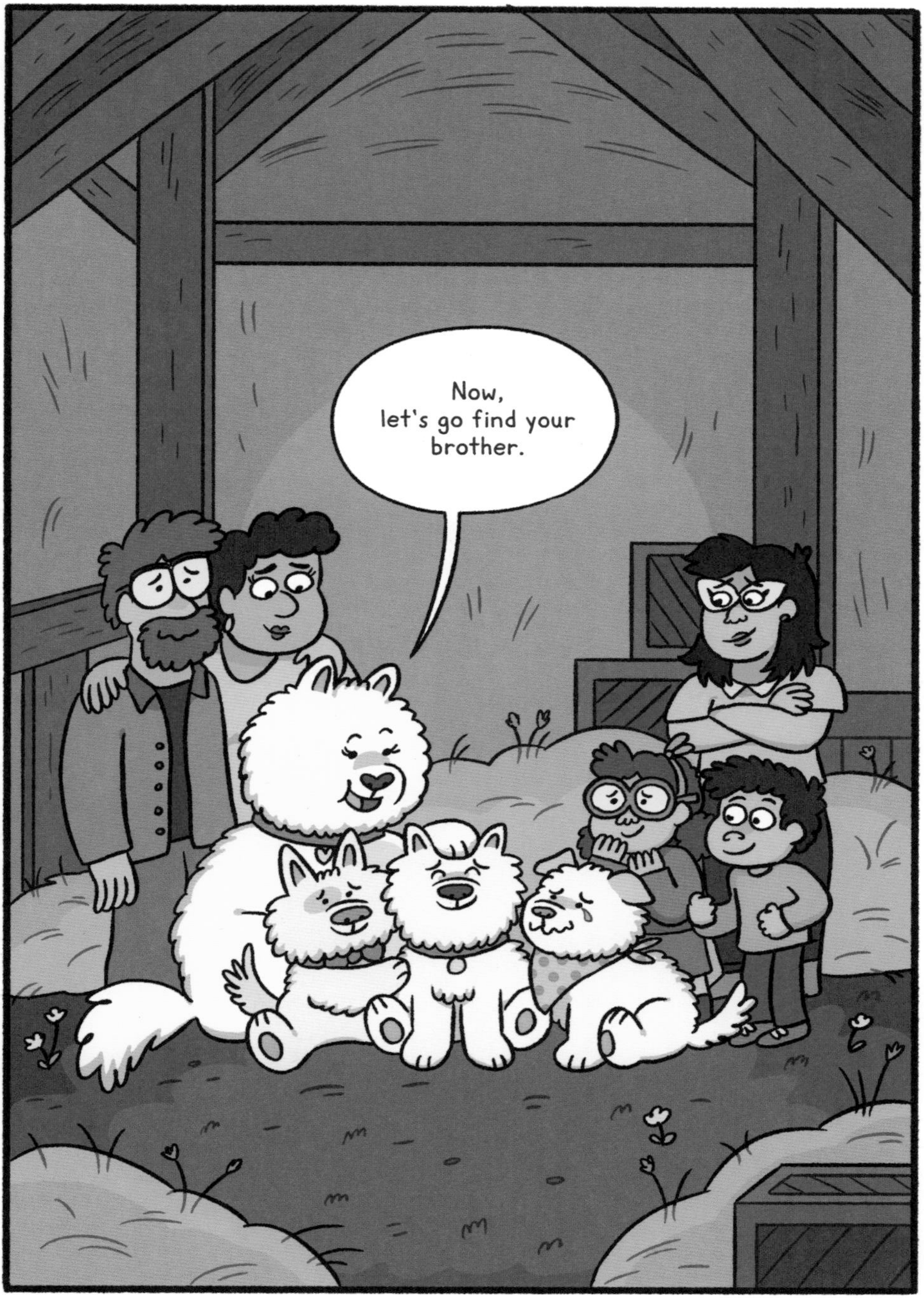
Now, let's go find your brother.

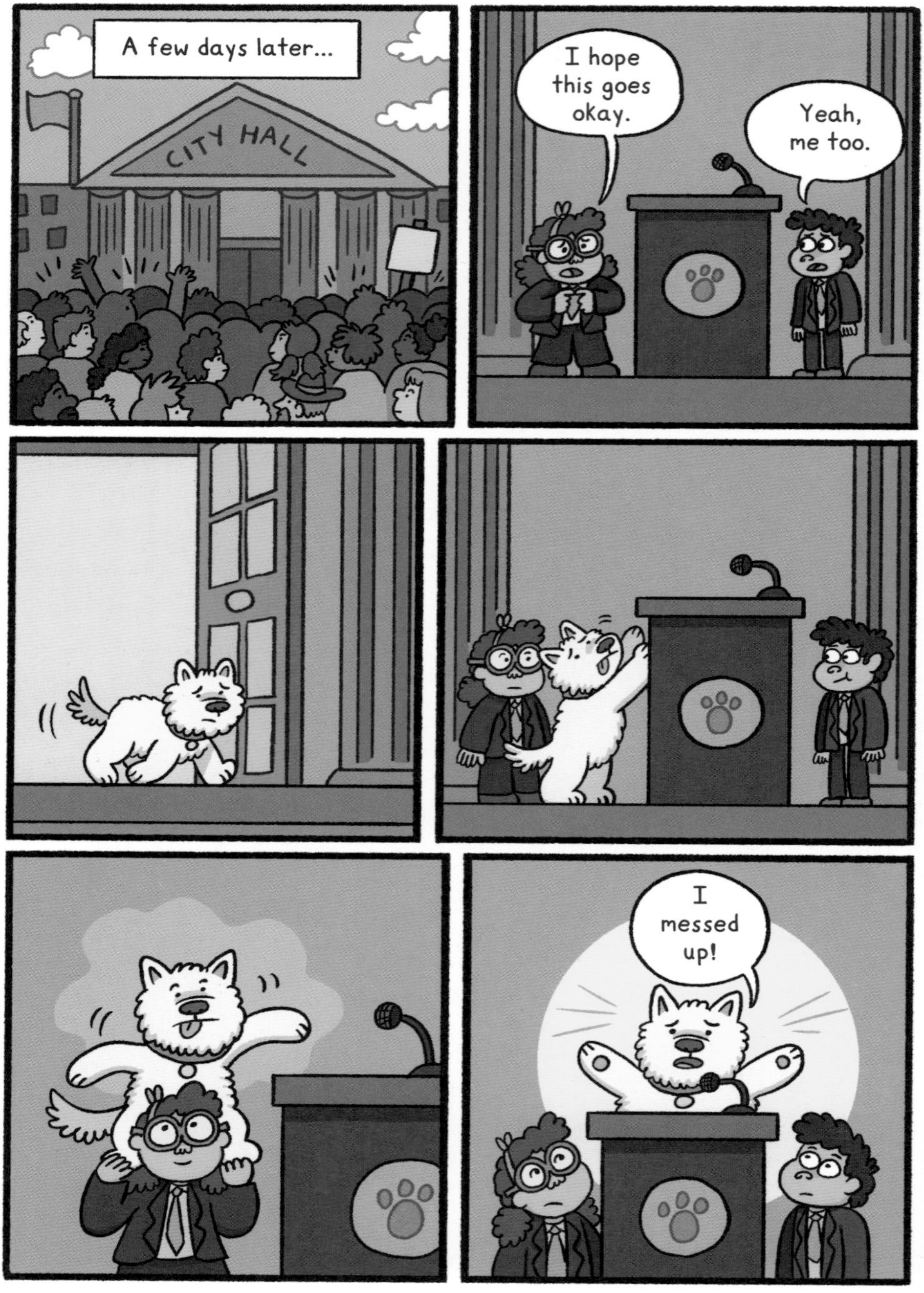
A few days later...
CITY HALL
I hope this goes okay.
Yeah, me too.
I messed up!

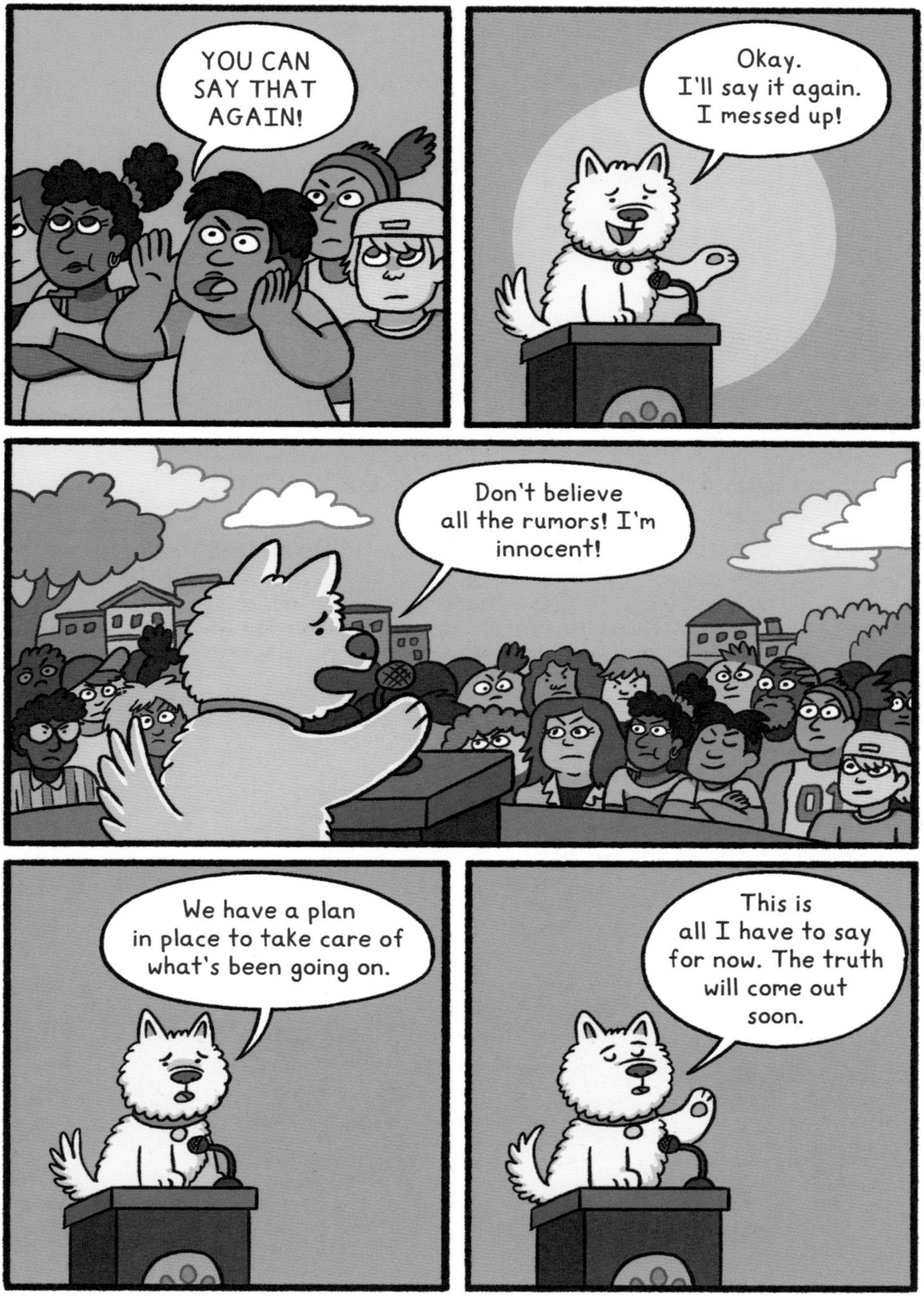
YOU CAN SAY THAT AGAIN!
Okay. I'll say it again. I messed up!
Don't believe all the rumors! I'm innocent!
We have a plan in place to take care of what's been going on.
This is all I have to say for now. The truth will come out soon.

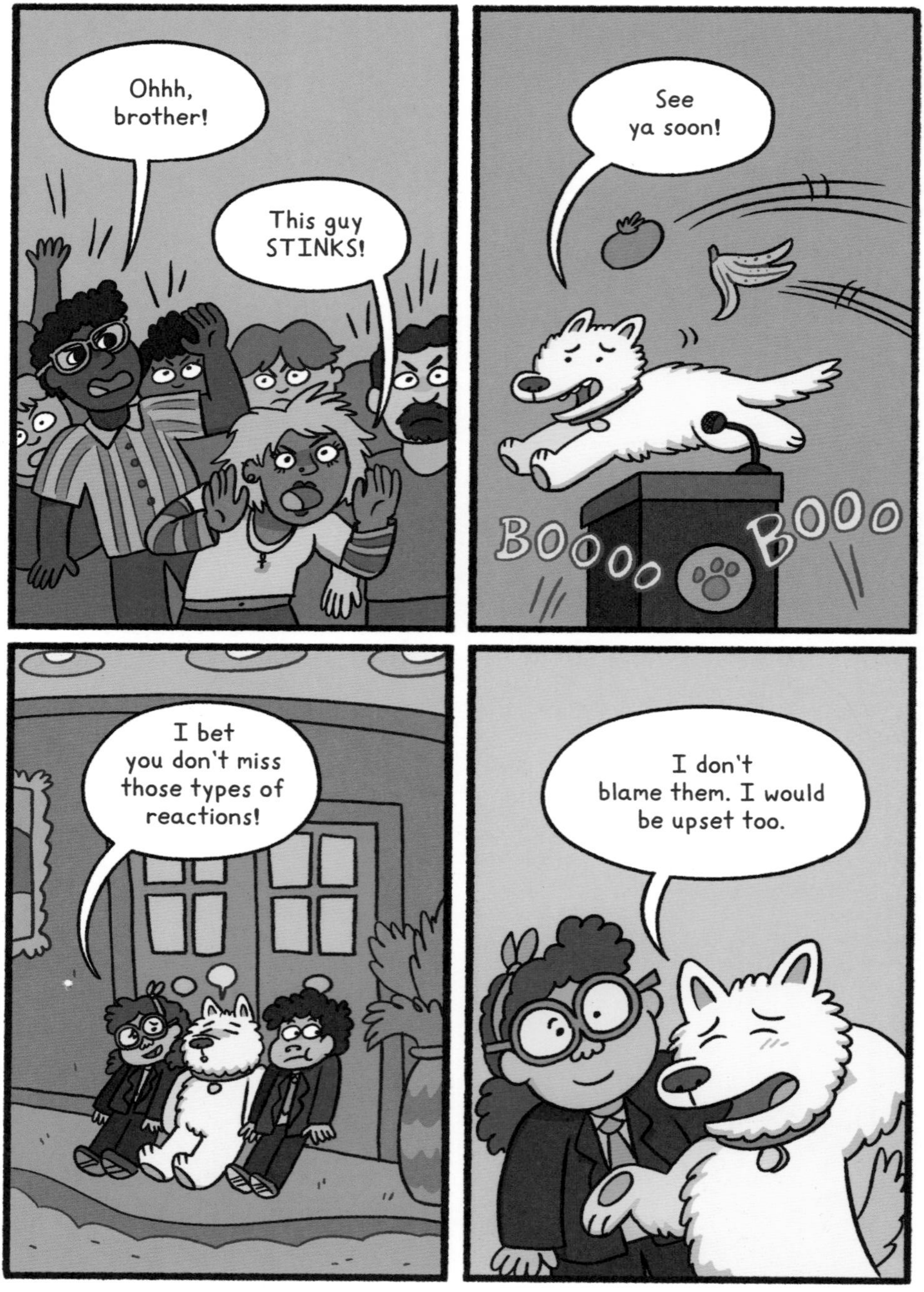
Ohhh, brother!
This guy STINKS!
See ya soon!
BOOOOO
BOOOO
I bet you don't miss those types of reactions!
I don't blame them. I would be upset too.

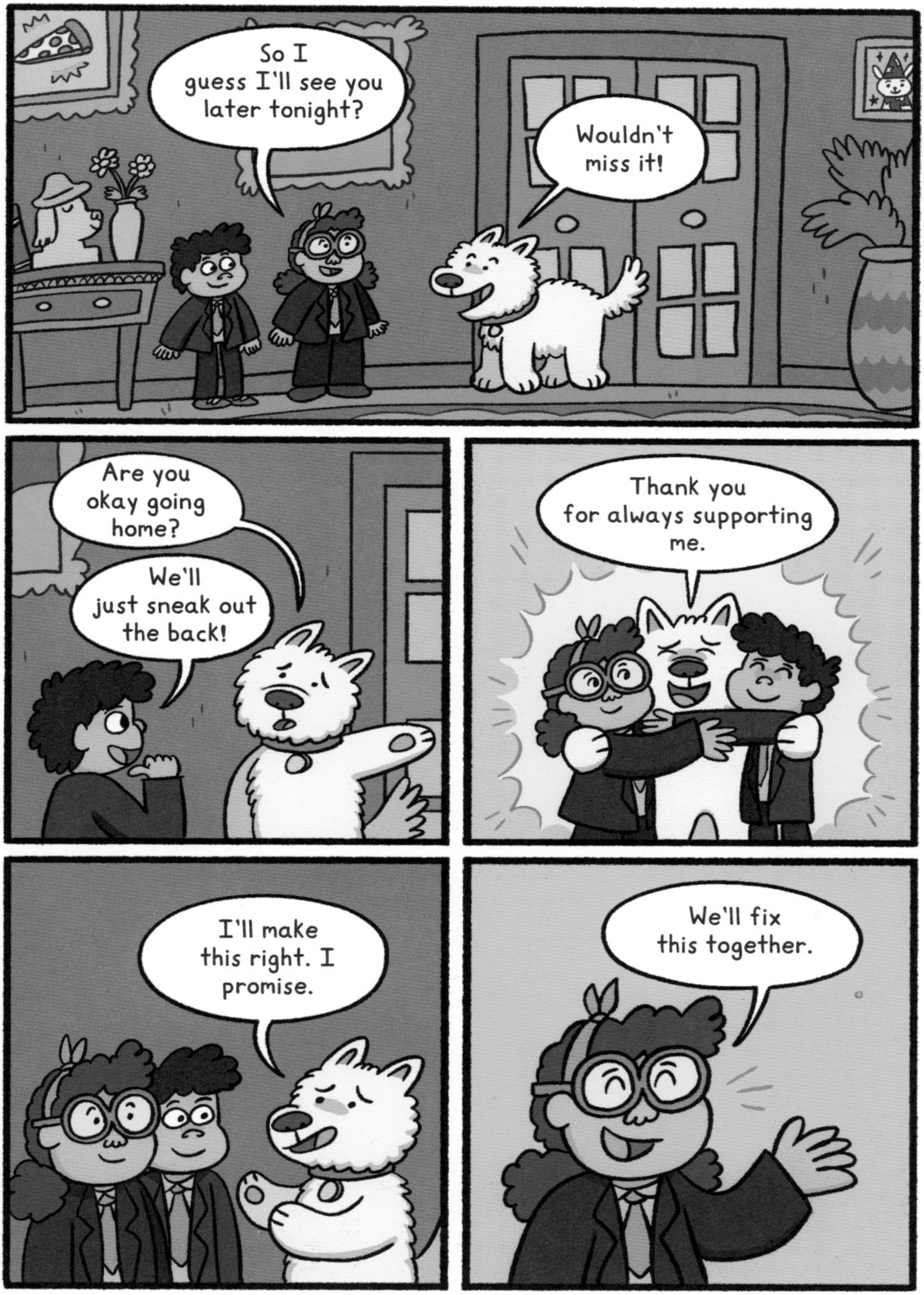
So I guess I'll see you later tonight?
Wouldn't miss it!
Are you okay going home?
We'll just sneak out the back!
Thank you for always supporting me.
I'll make this right. I promise.
We'll fix this together.

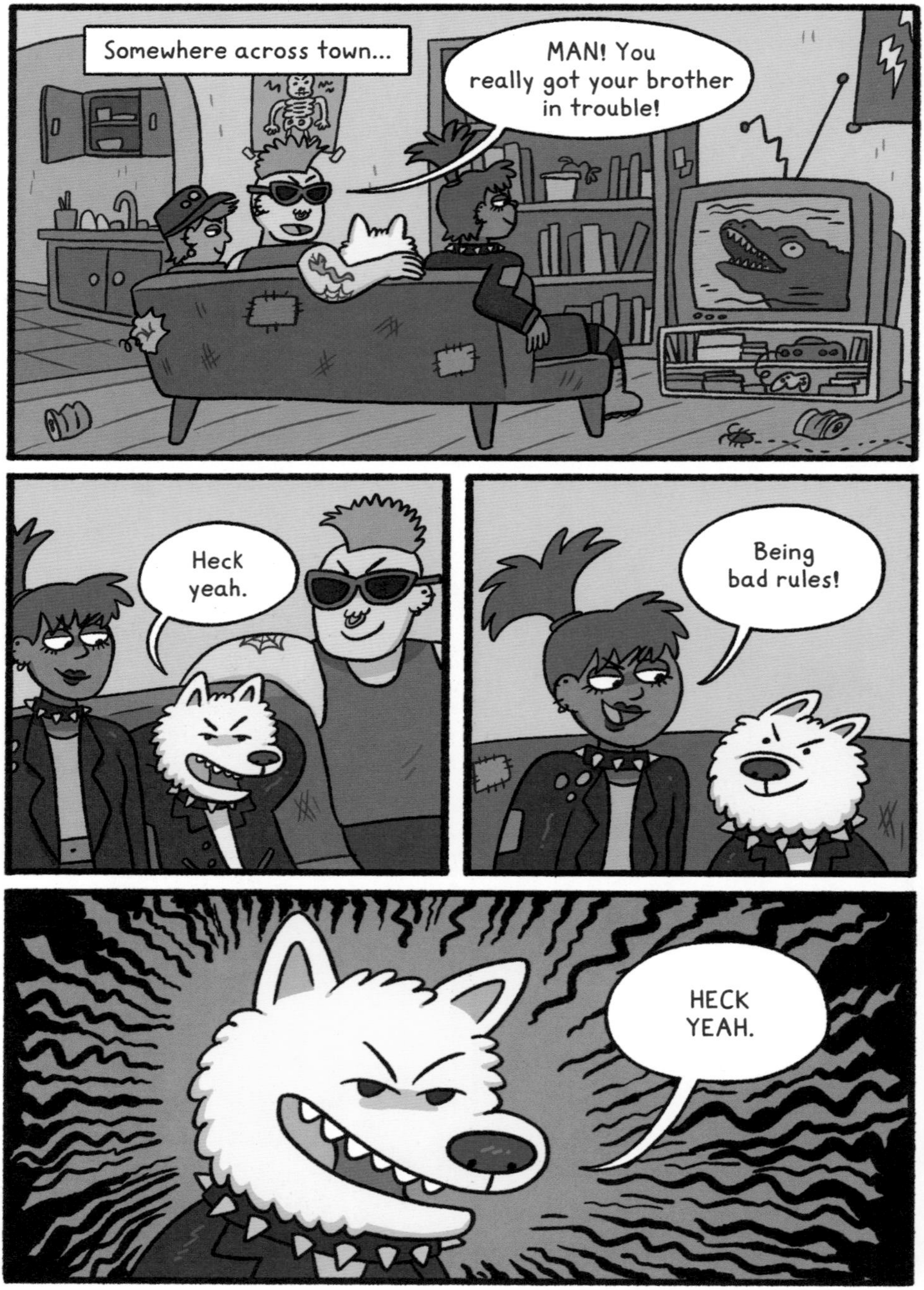
Somewhere across town...
MAN! You really got your brother in trouble!
Heck yeah.
Being bad rules!
HECK YEAH.

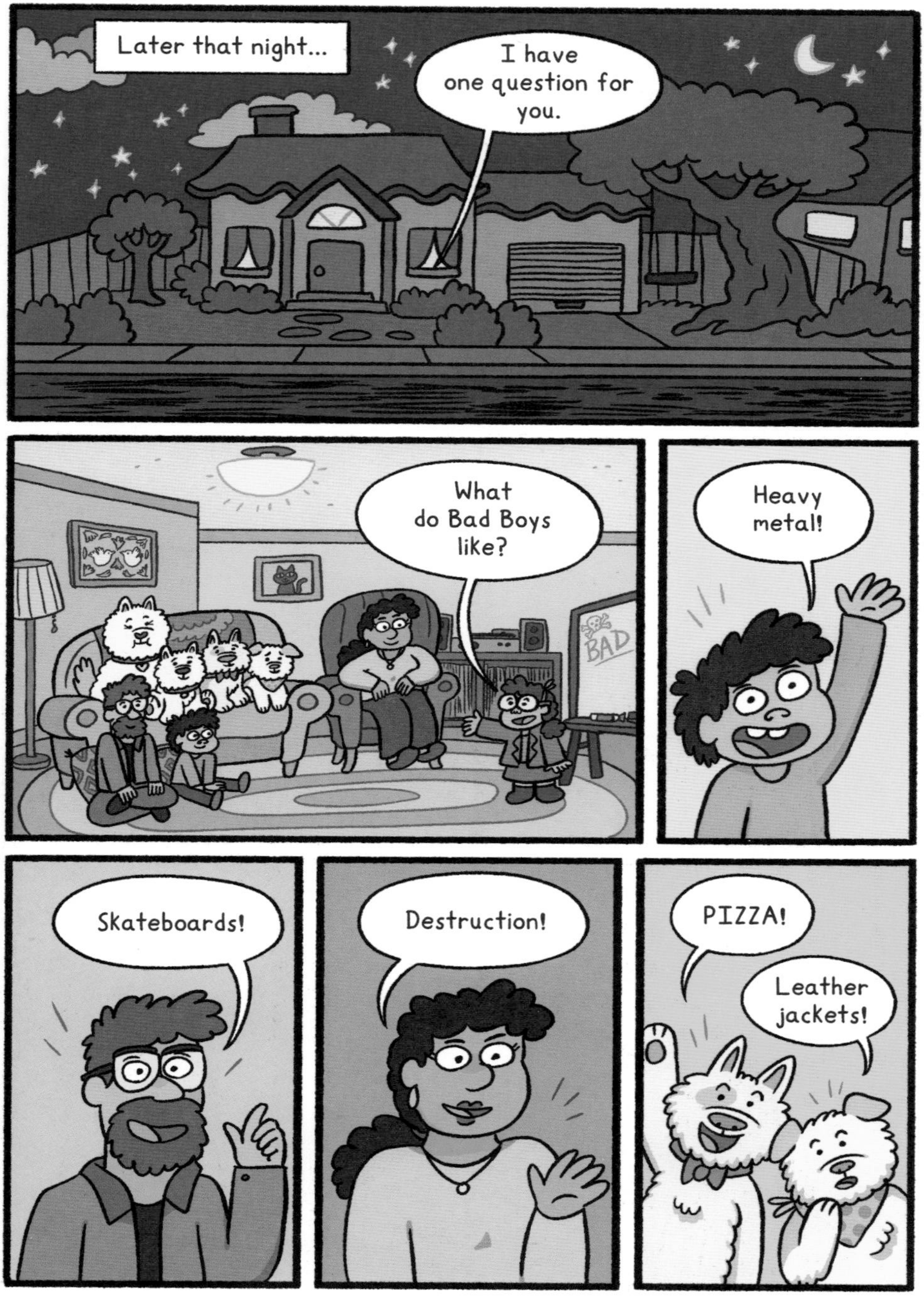
Later that night...
I have one question for you.
What do Bad Boys like?
BAD
Heavy metal!
Skateboards!
Destruction!
PIZZA!
Leather jackets!

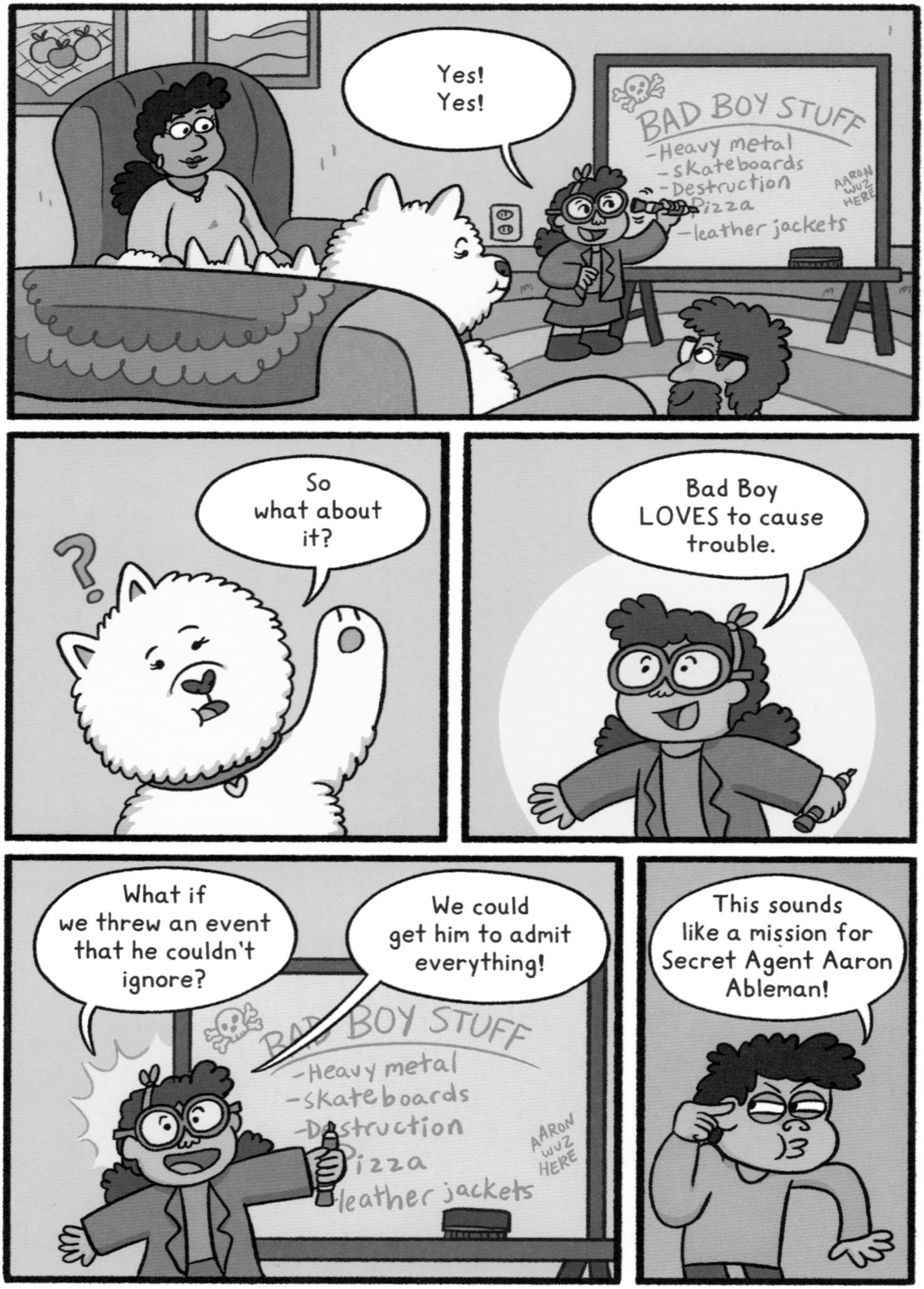
Yes!
Yes!
BAD BOY STUFF
-Heavy metal
-skateboards
-Destruction
-Pizza
-leather jackets
AARON WUZ HERE
So what about it?
Bad Boy LOVES to cause trouble.
What if we threw an event that he couldn't ignore?
We could get him to admit everything!
BAD BOY STUFF
-Heavy metal
-skateboards
-Destruction
Pizza
leather jackets
AARON WUZ HERE
This sounds like a mission for Secret Agent Aaron Ableman!

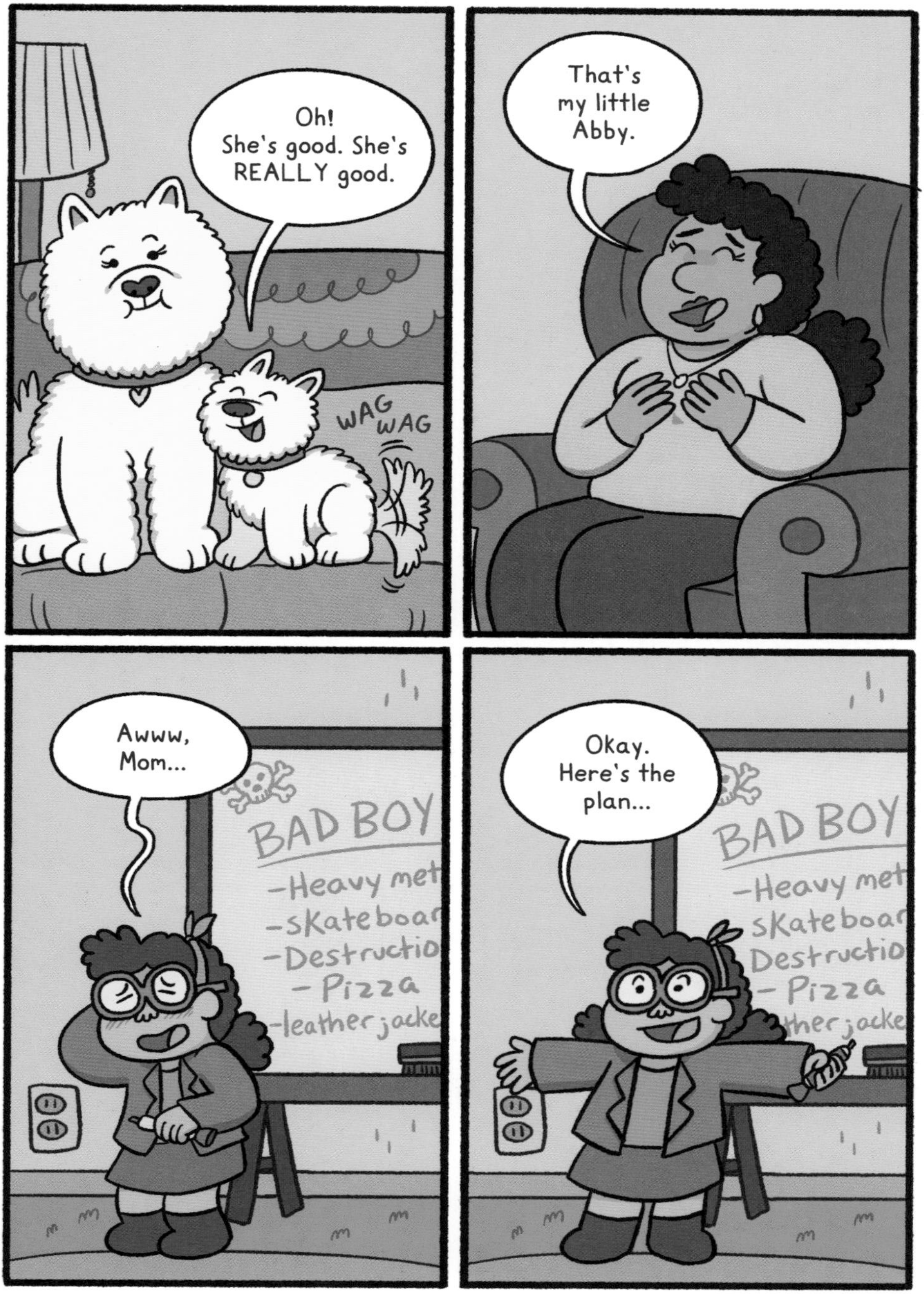
Oh! She's good. She's REALLY good.
WAG WAG
That's my little Abby.
Awww, Mom...
BAD BOY
-Pizza
Okay. Here's the plan...
BAD BOY
-Pizza

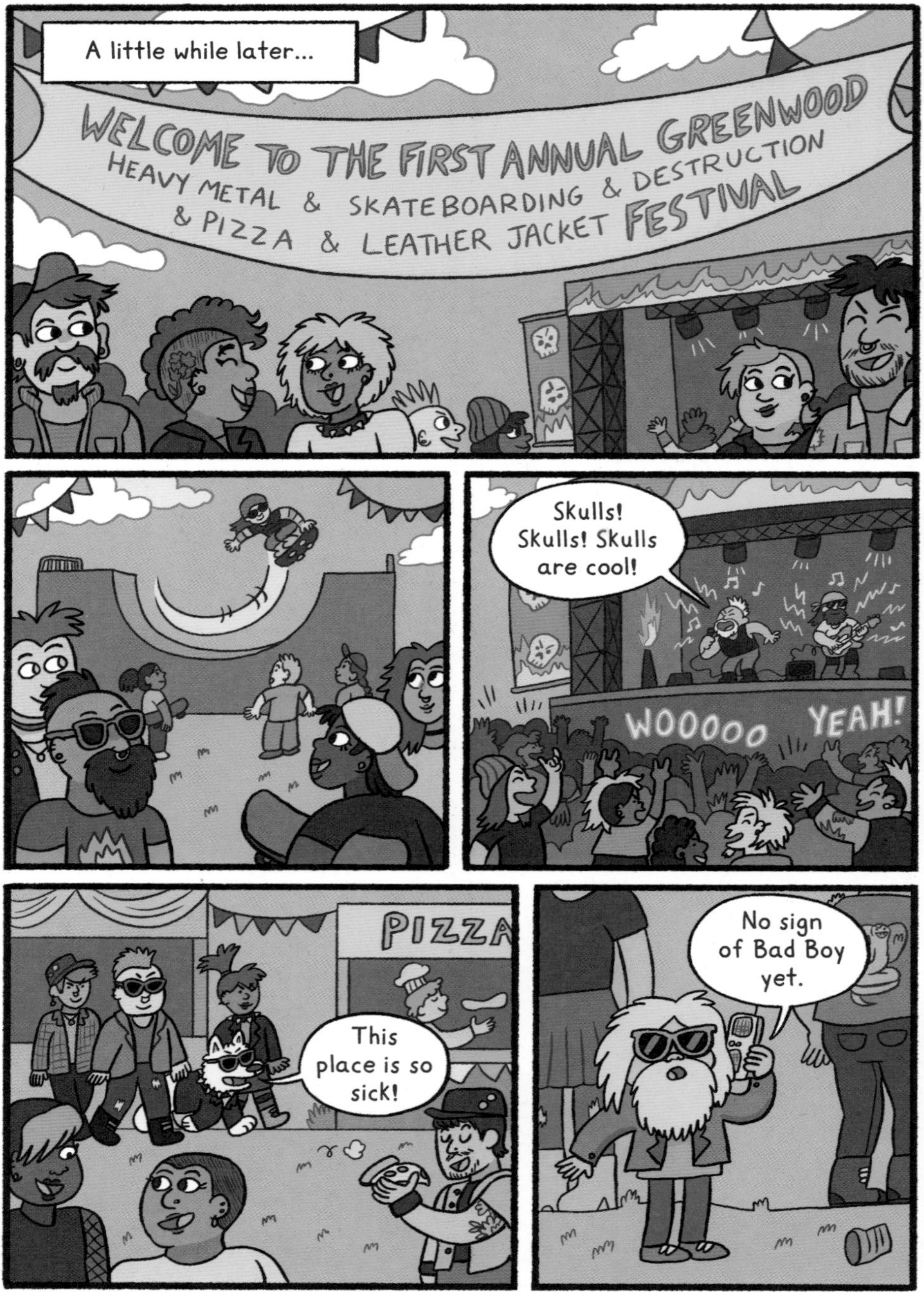
A little while later...
WELCOME TO THE FIRST ANNUAL GREENWOOD HEAVY METAL & SKATEBOARDING & DESTRUCTION & PIZZA & LEATHER JACKET FESTIVAL
Skulls! Skulls! Skulls are cool!
WOOOOO YEAH!
PIZZA
This place is so sick!
No sign of Bad Boy yet.

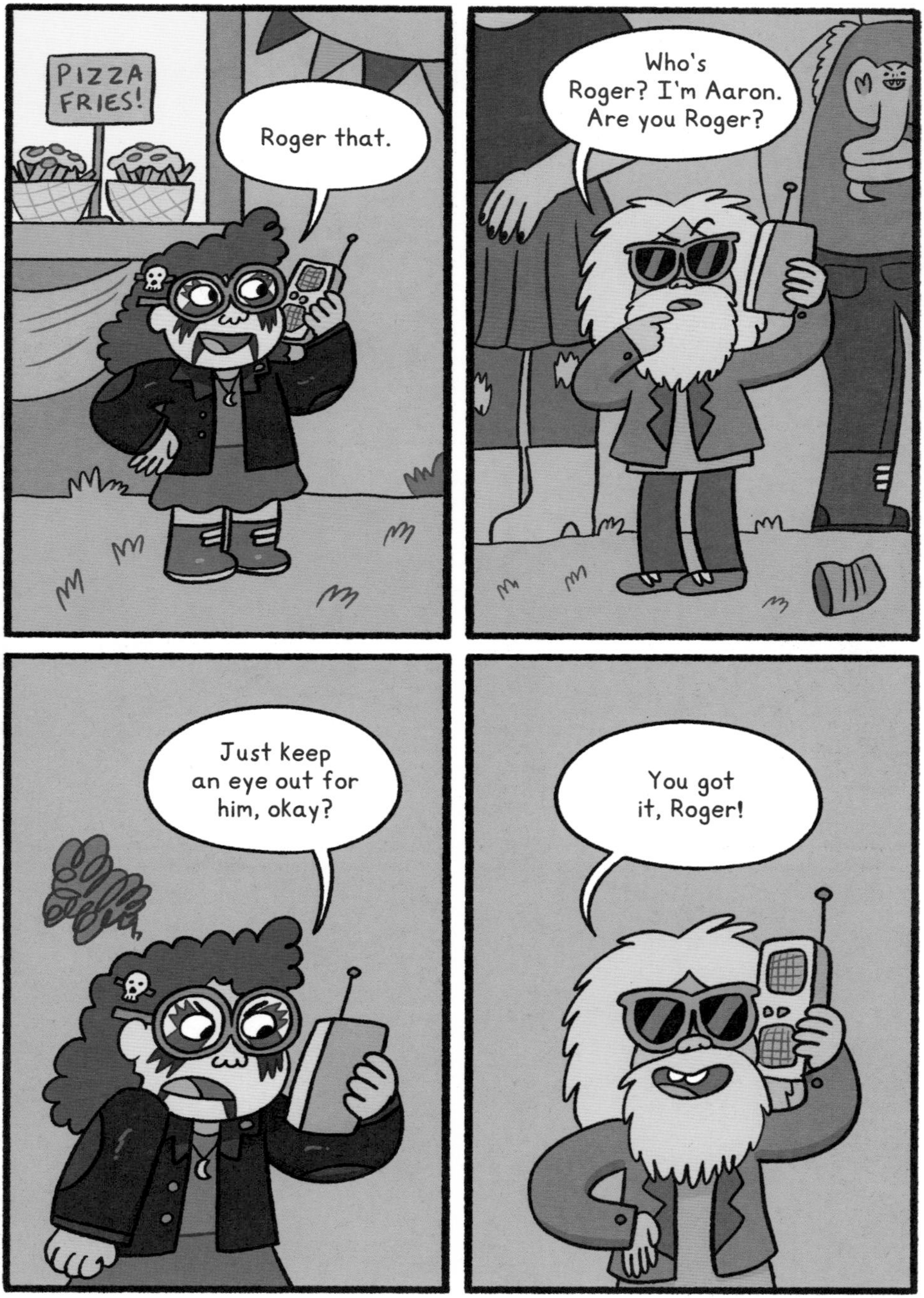
PIZZA FRIES!
Roger that.
Who's Roger? I'm Aaron. Are you Roger?
Just keep an eye out for him, okay?
You got it, Roger!

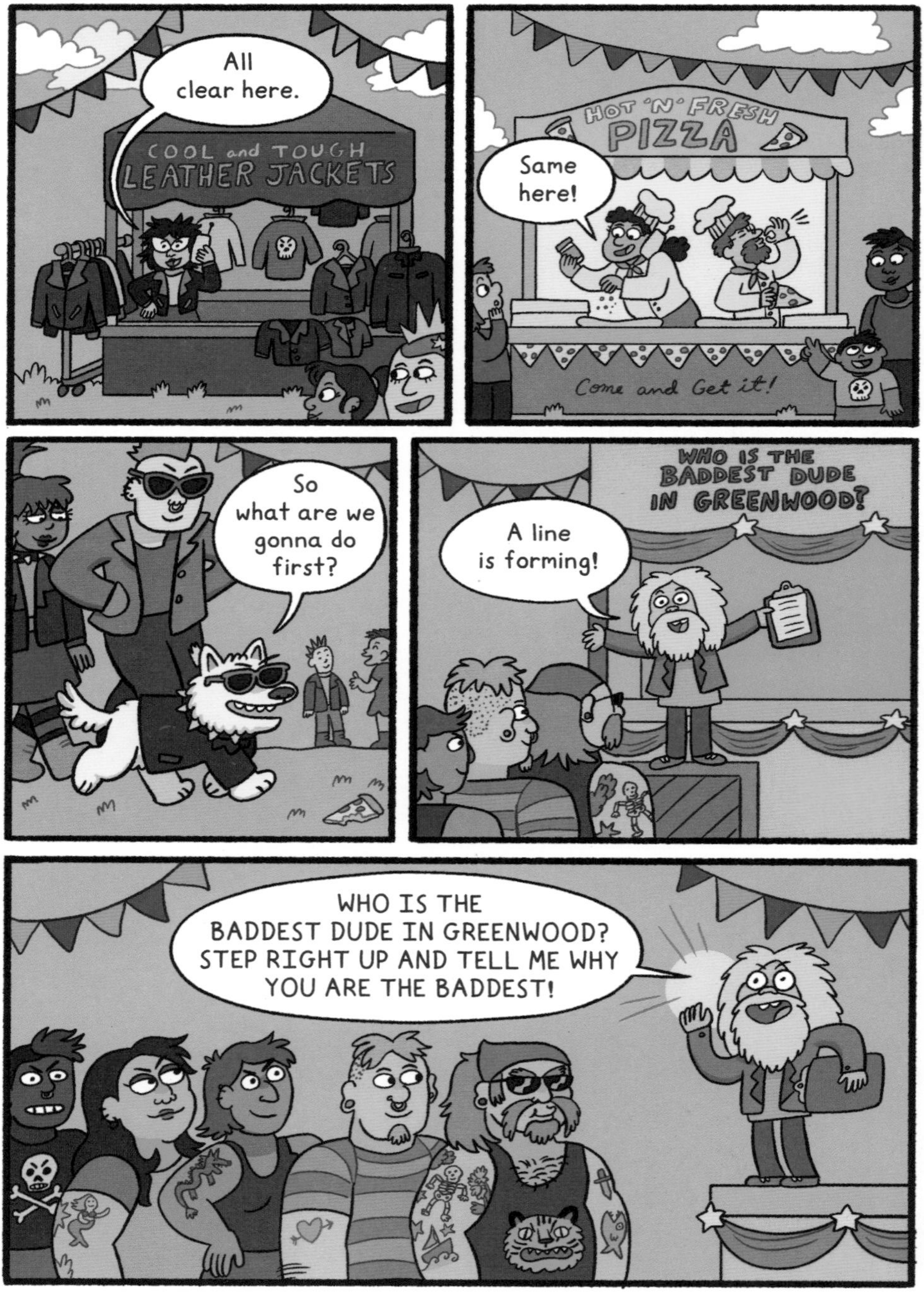
All clear here.
COOL and TOUGH LEATHER JACKETS
HOT 'N' FRESH PIZZA
Same here!
Come and Get it!
So what are we gonna do first?
WHO IS THE BADDEST DUDE IN GREENWOOD?
A line is forming!
WHO IS THE BADDEST DUDE IN GREENWOOD? STEP RIGHT UP AND TELL ME WHY YOU ARE THE BADDEST!

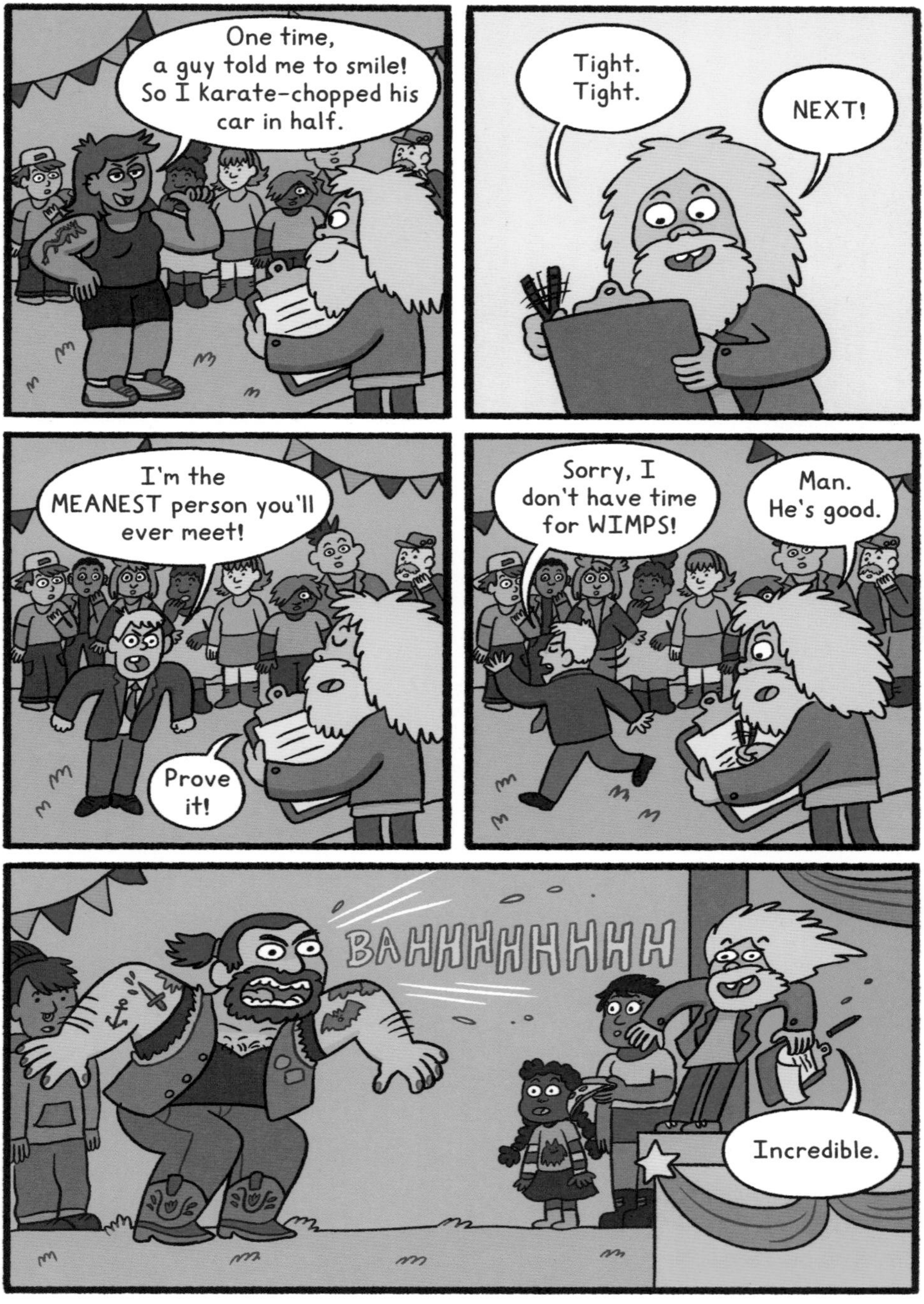
One time, a guy told me to smile! So I karate-chopped his car in half.
Tight. Tight.
NEXT!
I'm the MEANEST person you'll ever meet!
Prove it!
Sorry, I don't have time for WIMPS!
Man. He's good.
BAHHHHHHHHH
Incredible.

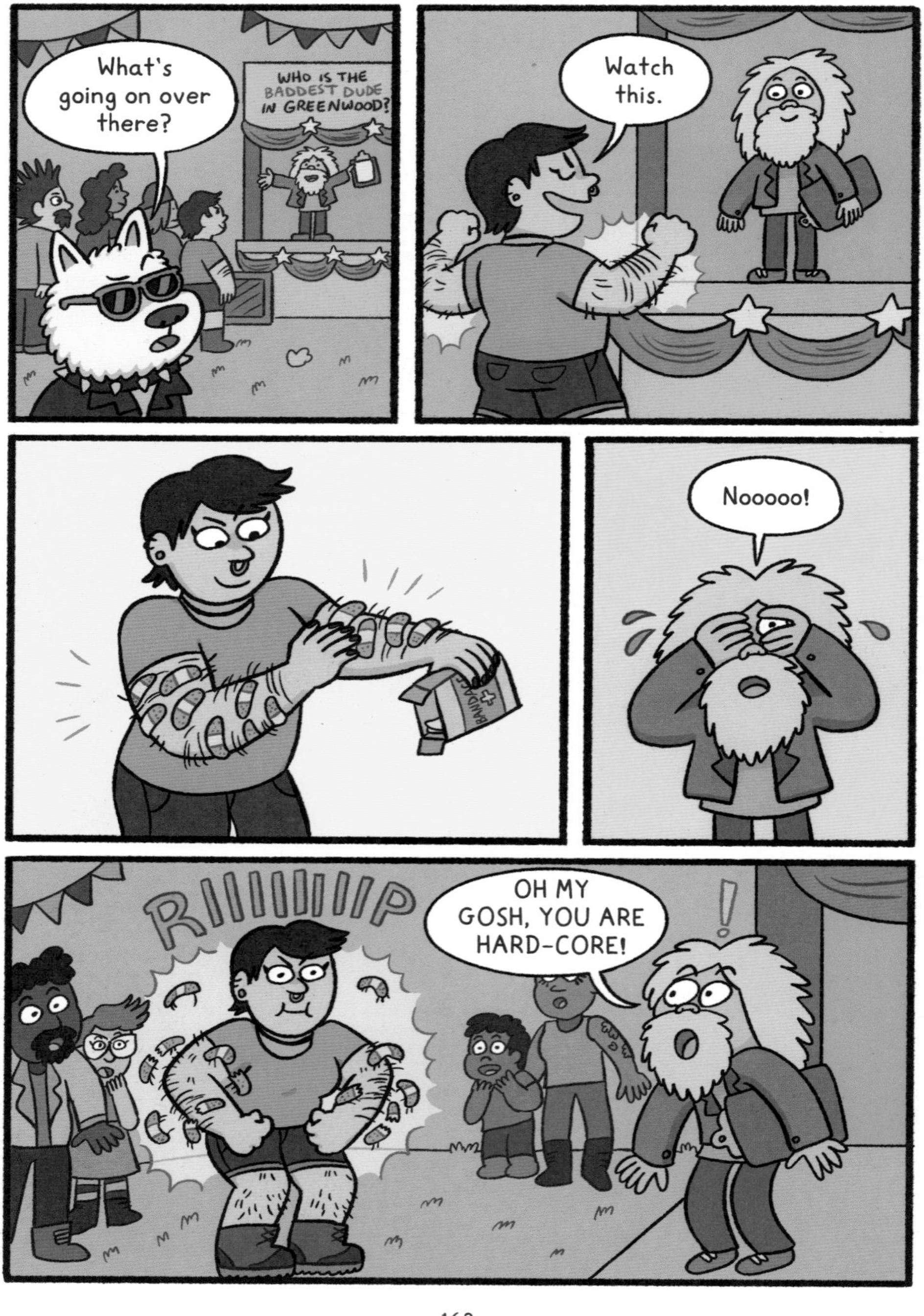
What's going on over there?
WHO IS THE BADDEST DUDE IN GREENWOOD?
Watch this.
BANDAGE
Nooooo!
RIIIIIIIP
OH MY GOSH, YOU ARE HARD-CORE!
!

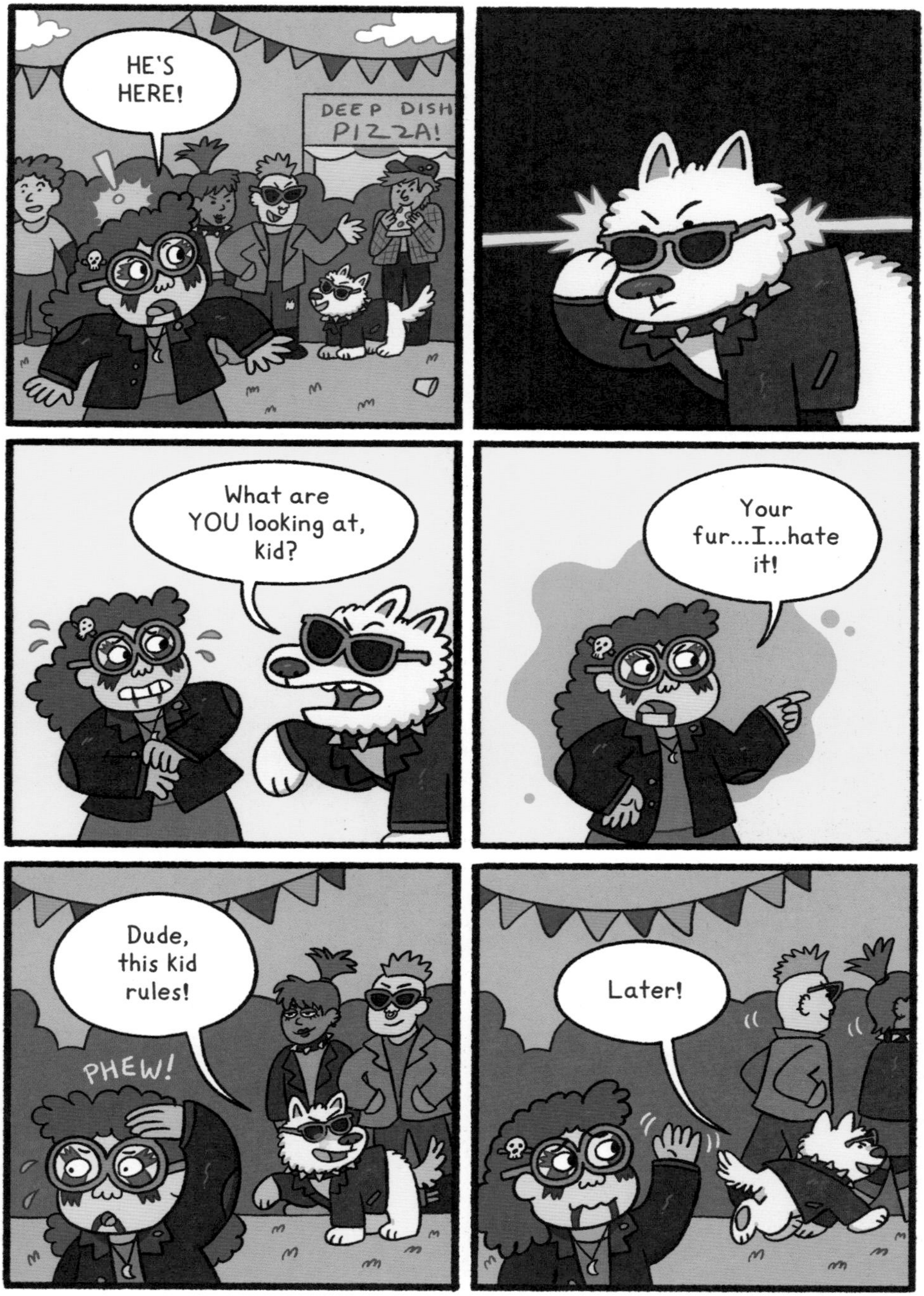
HE'S HERE!
DEEP DISH PIZZA!
What are YOU looking at, kid?
Your fur...I...hate it!
Dude, this kid rules!
PHEW!
Later!

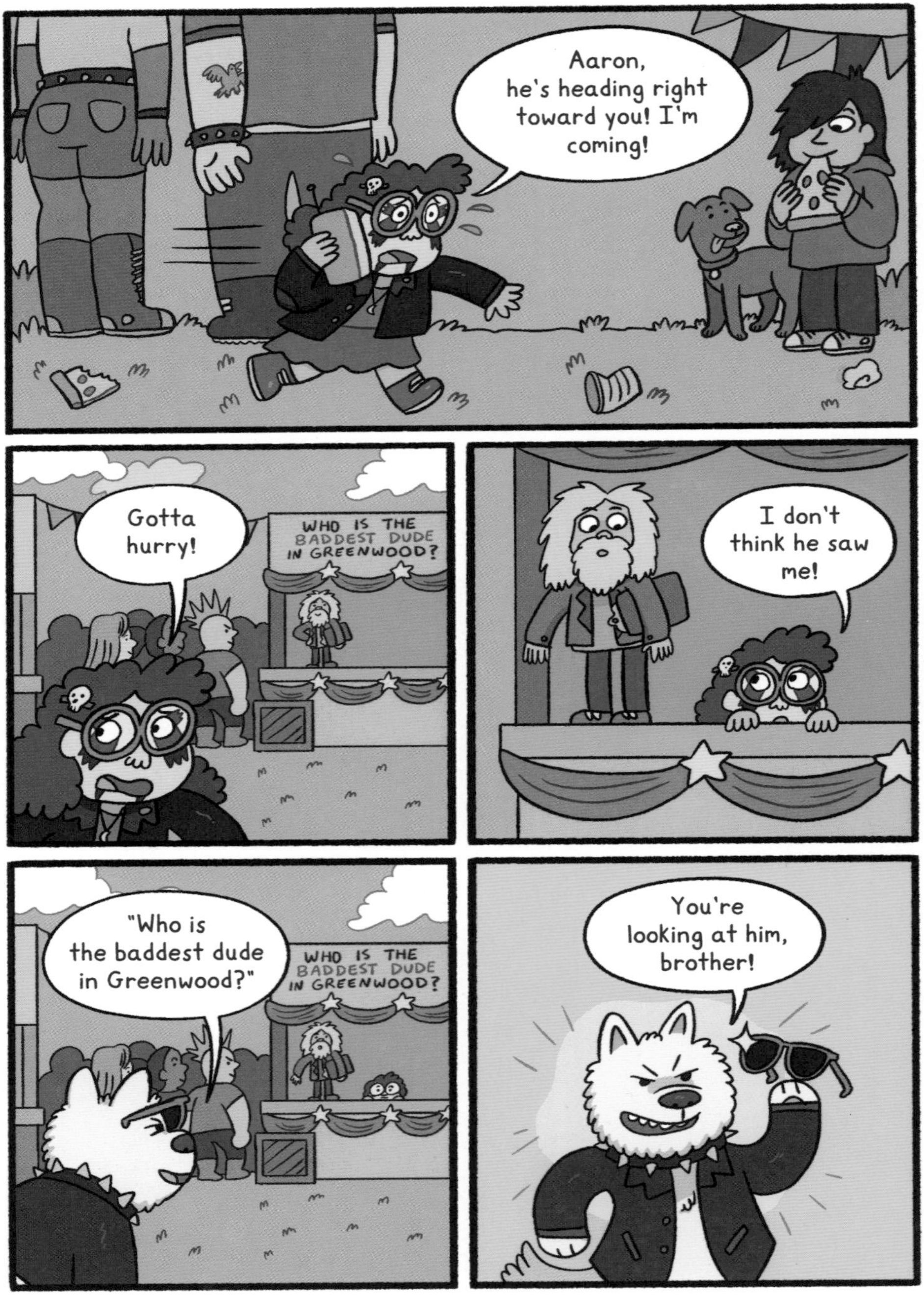
Aaron, he's heading right toward you! I'm coming!
Gotta hurry!
WHO IS THE BADDEST DUDE IN GREENWOOD?
I don't think he saw me!
"Who is the baddest dude in Greenwood?"
WHO IS THE BADDEST DUDE IN GREENWOOD?
You're looking at him, brother!

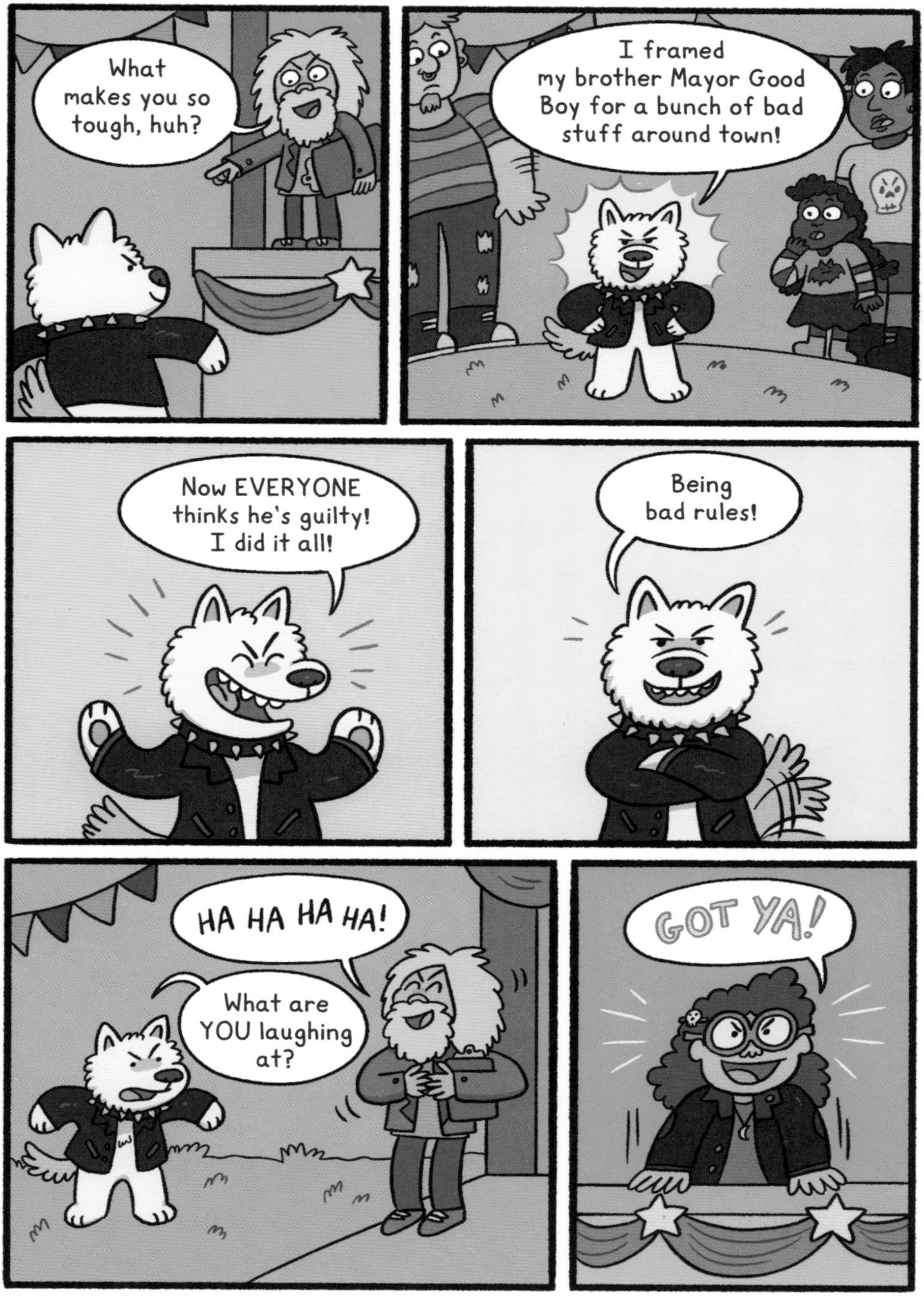
What makes you so tough, huh?
I framed my brother Mayor Good Boy for a bunch of bad stuff around town!
Now EVERYONE thinks he's guilty! I did it all!
Being bad rules!
HA HA HA HA!
What are YOU laughing at?
GOT YA!

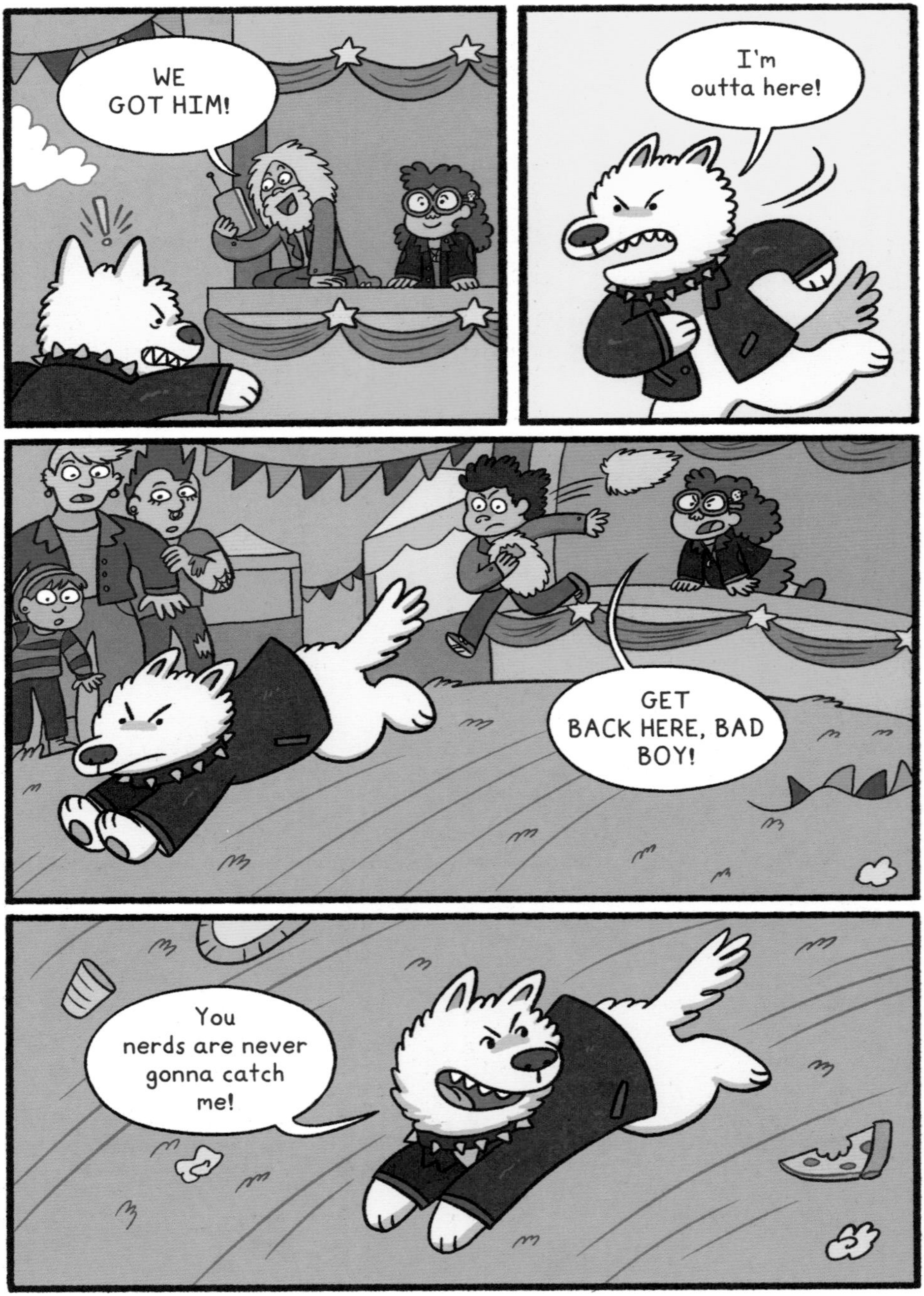
WE GOT HIM!
I'm outta here!
GET BACK HERE, BAD BOY!
You nerds are never gonna catch me!

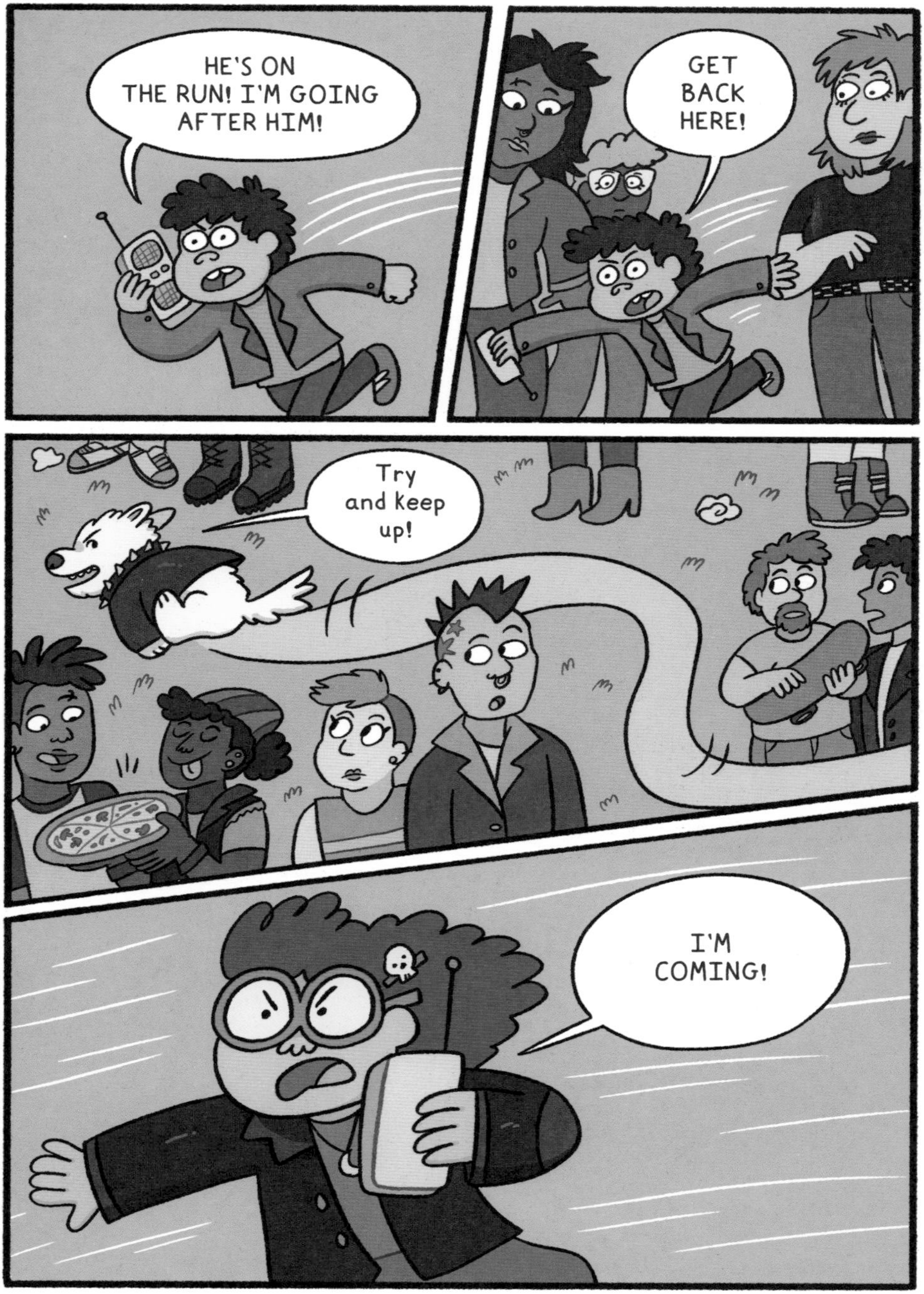
HE'S ON THE RUN! I'M GOING AFTER HIM!
GET BACK HERE!
Try and keep up!
I'M COMING!

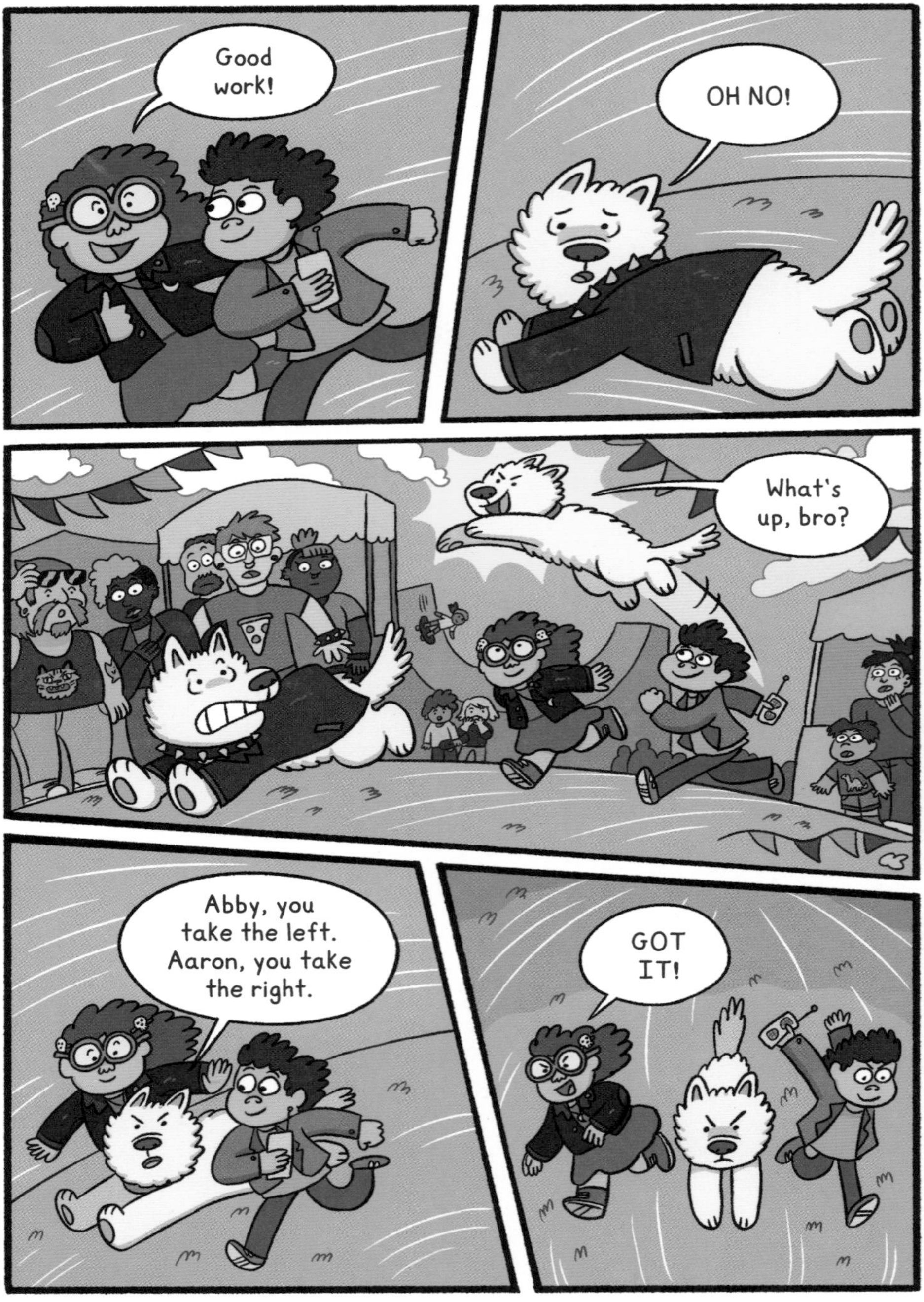
Good work!
OH NO!
What's up, bro?
Abby, you take the left. Aaron, you take the right.
GOT IT!

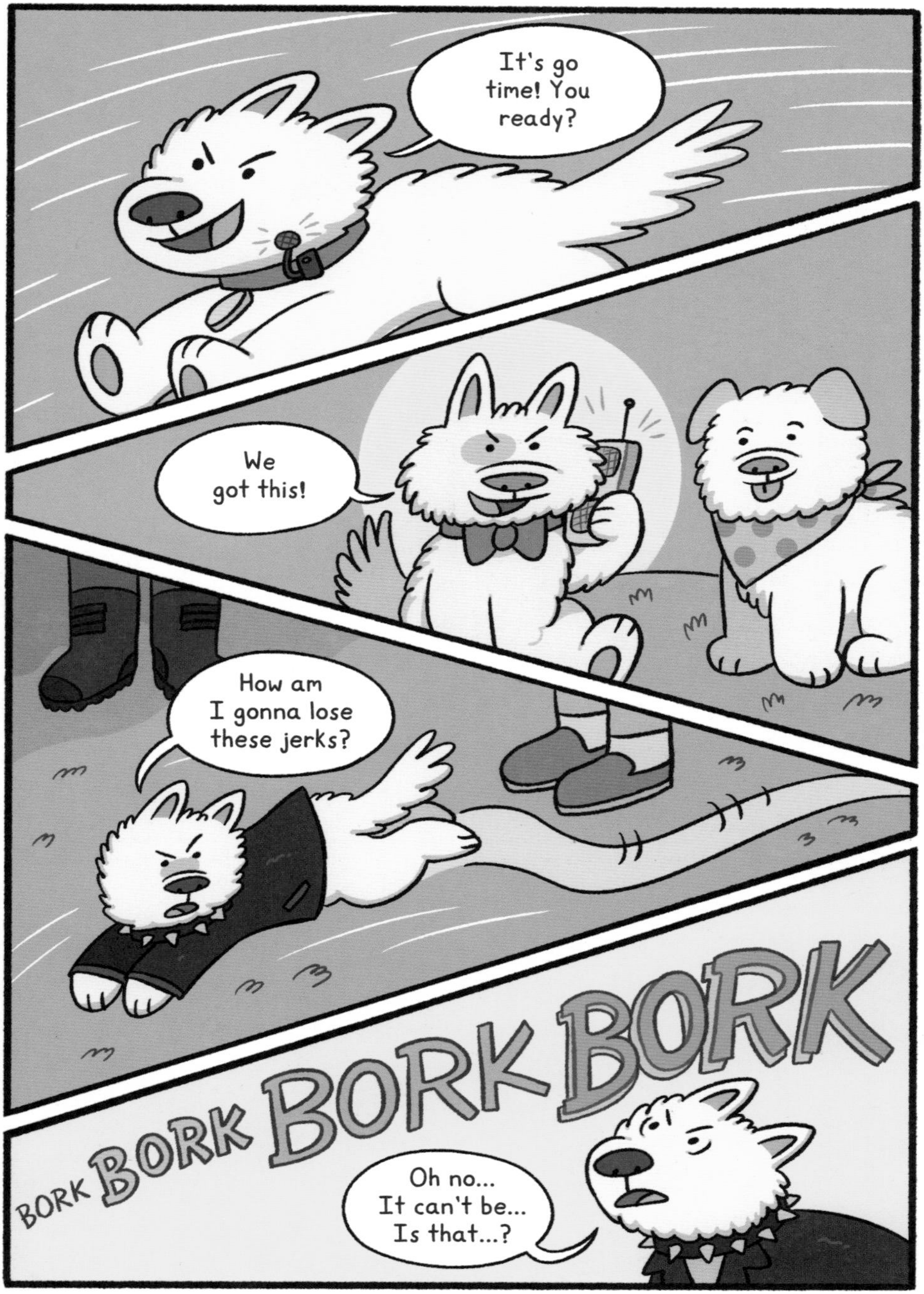
It's go time! You ready?
We got this!
How am I gonna lose these jerks?
BORK BORK BORK BORK
Oh no... It can't be... Is that...?

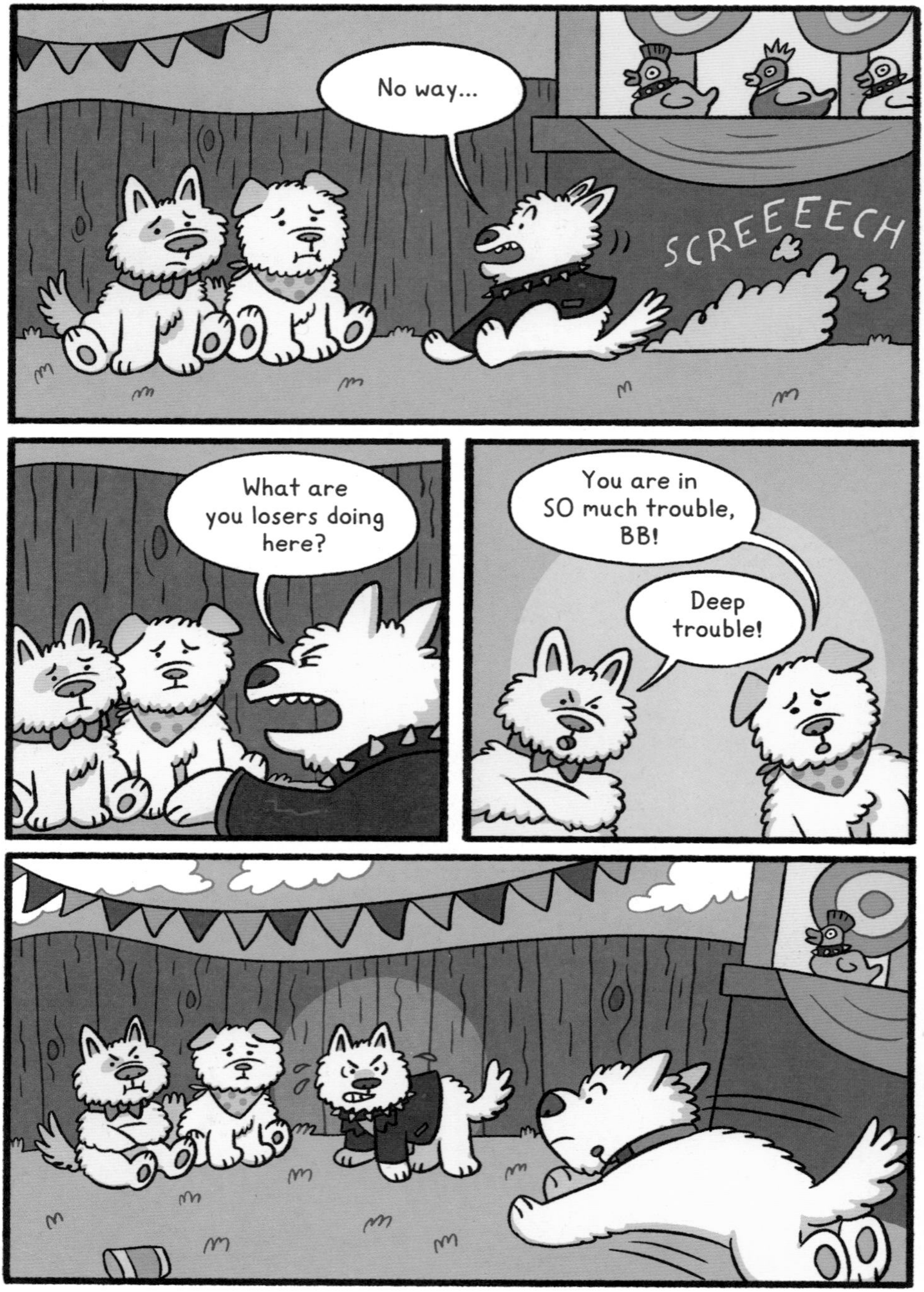
No way...
SCREEEECH
What are you losers doing here?
You are in SO much trouble, BB!
Deep trouble!

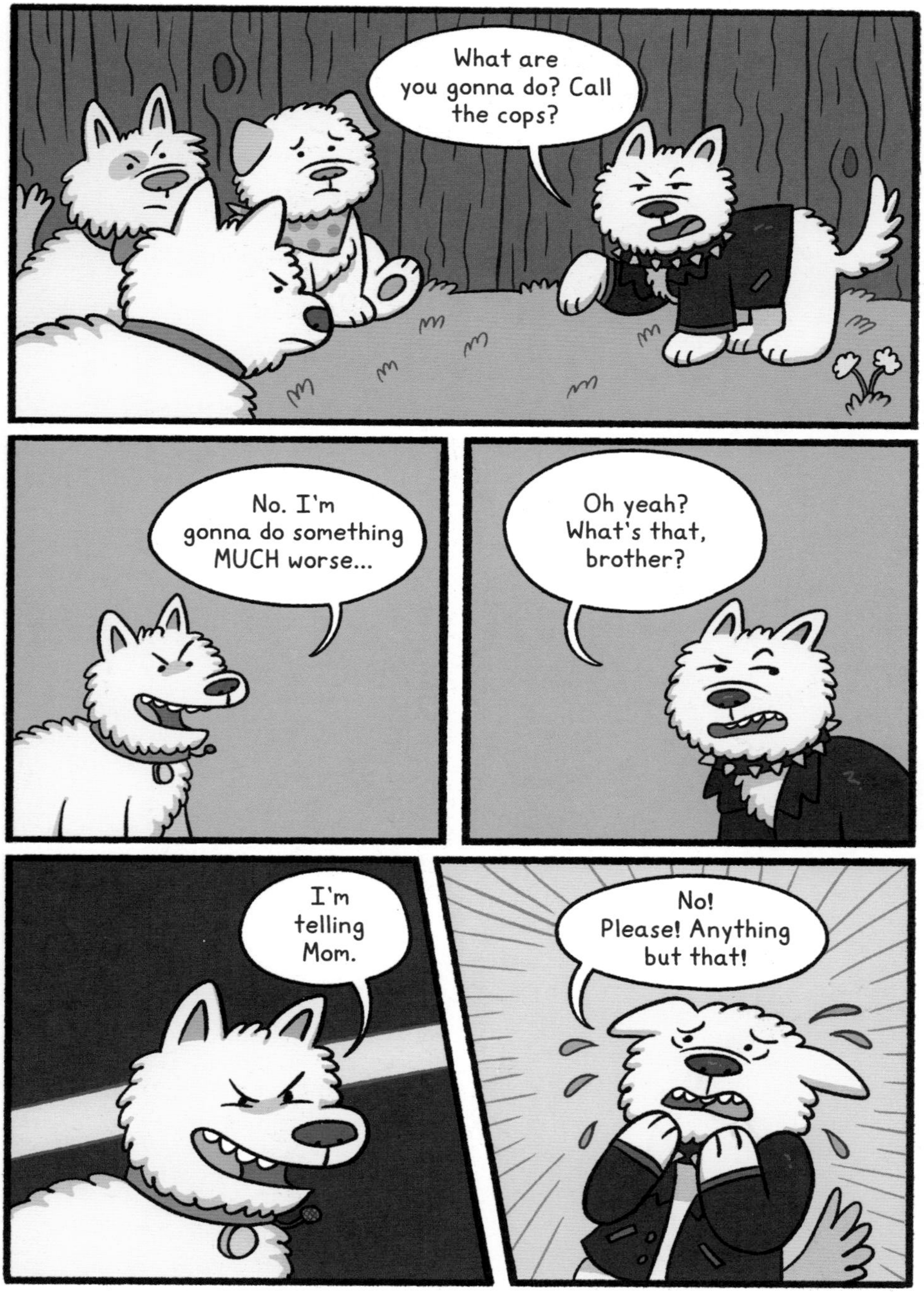
What are you gonna do? Call the cops?
No. I'm gonna do something MUCH worse...
Oh yeah? What's that, brother?
I'm telling Mom.
No! Please! Anything but that!

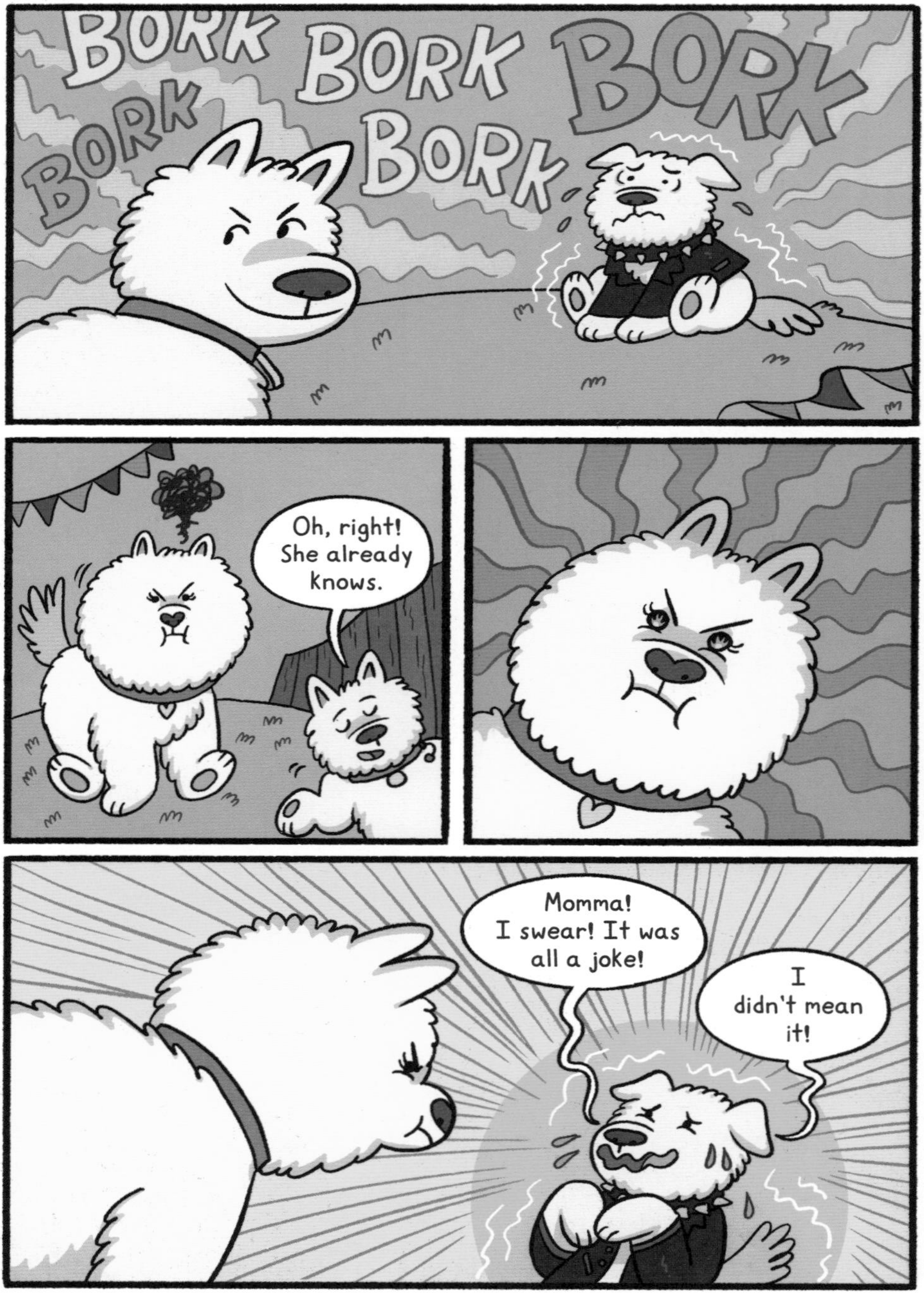

BORK BORK BORK BORK BORK BORK
Oh, right! She already knows.
Momma! I swear! It was all a joke!
I didn't mean it!

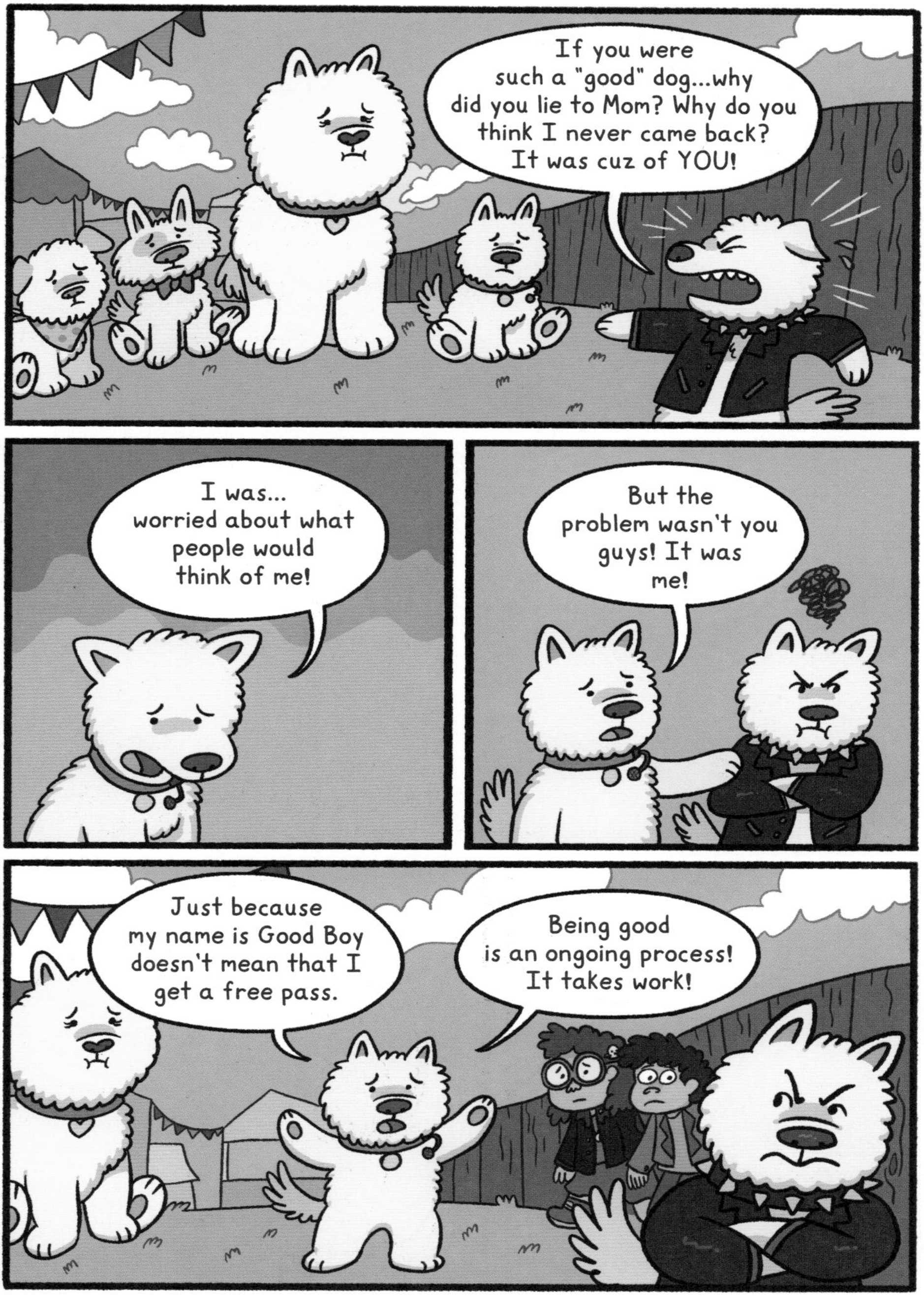
If you were such a "good" dog...why did you lie to Mom? Why do you think I never came back? It was cuz of YOU!
I was... worried about what people would think of me!
But the problem wasn't you guys! It was me!
Just because my name is Good Boy doesn't mean that I get a free pass.
Being good is an ongoing process! It takes work!

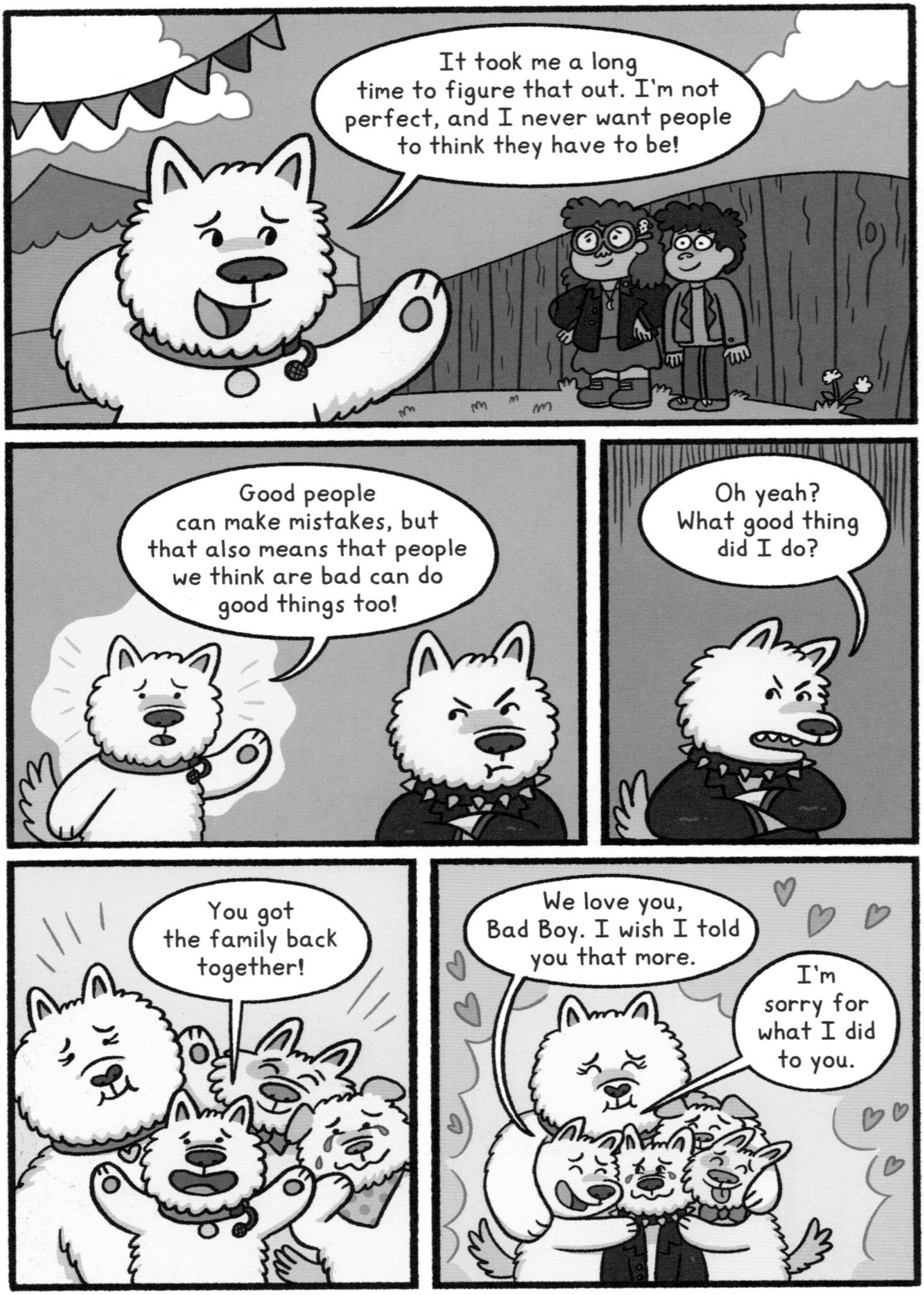
It took me a long time to figure that out. I'm not perfect, and I never want people to think they have to be!
Good people can make mistakes, but that also means that people we think are bad can do good things too!
Oh yeah? What good thing did I do?
You got the family back together!
We love you, Bad Boy. I wish I told you that more.
I'm sorry for what I did to you.

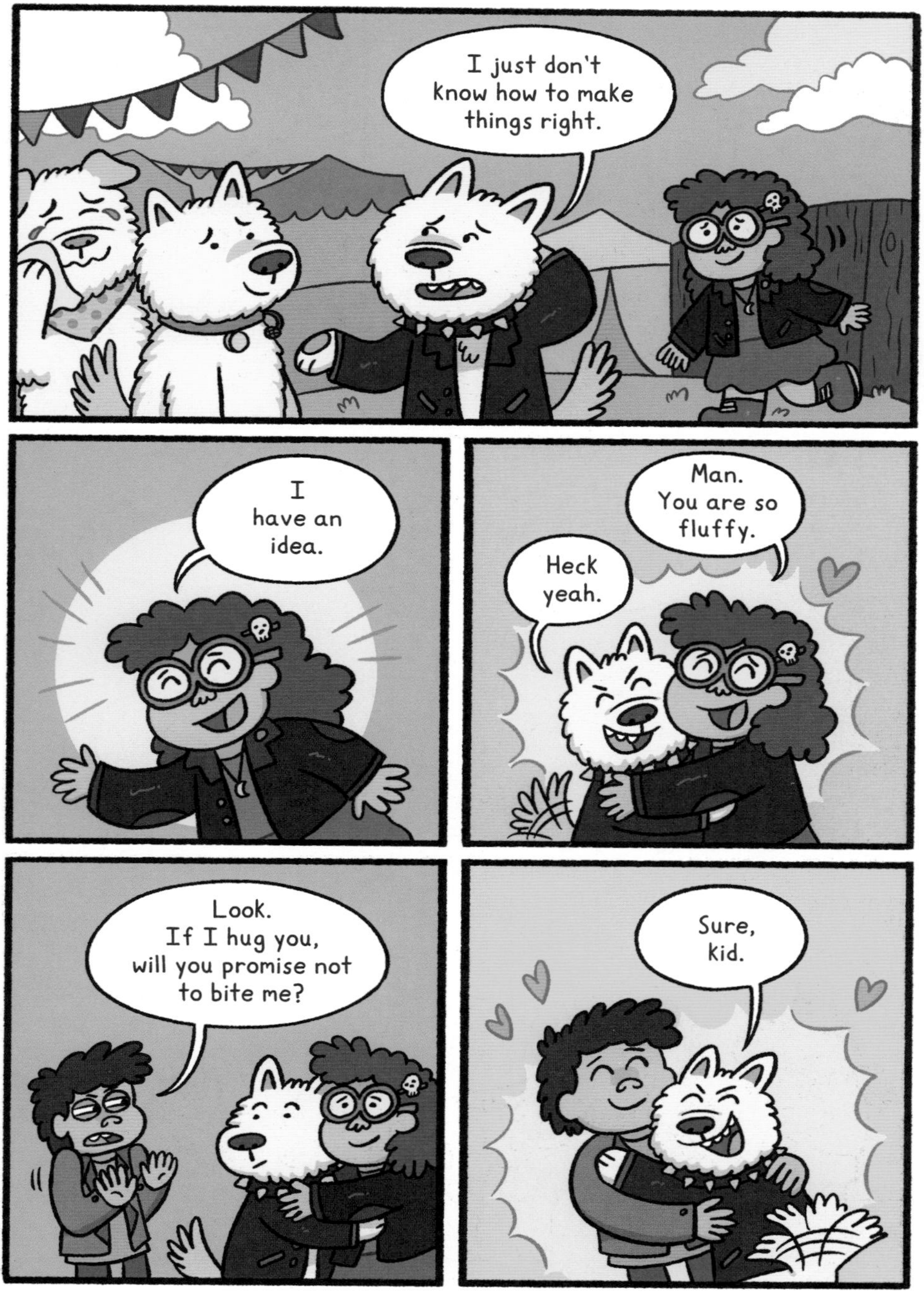
I just don't know how to make things right.
I have an idea.
Man. You are so fluffy.
Heck yeah.
Look. If I hug you, will you promise not to bite me?
Sure, kid.

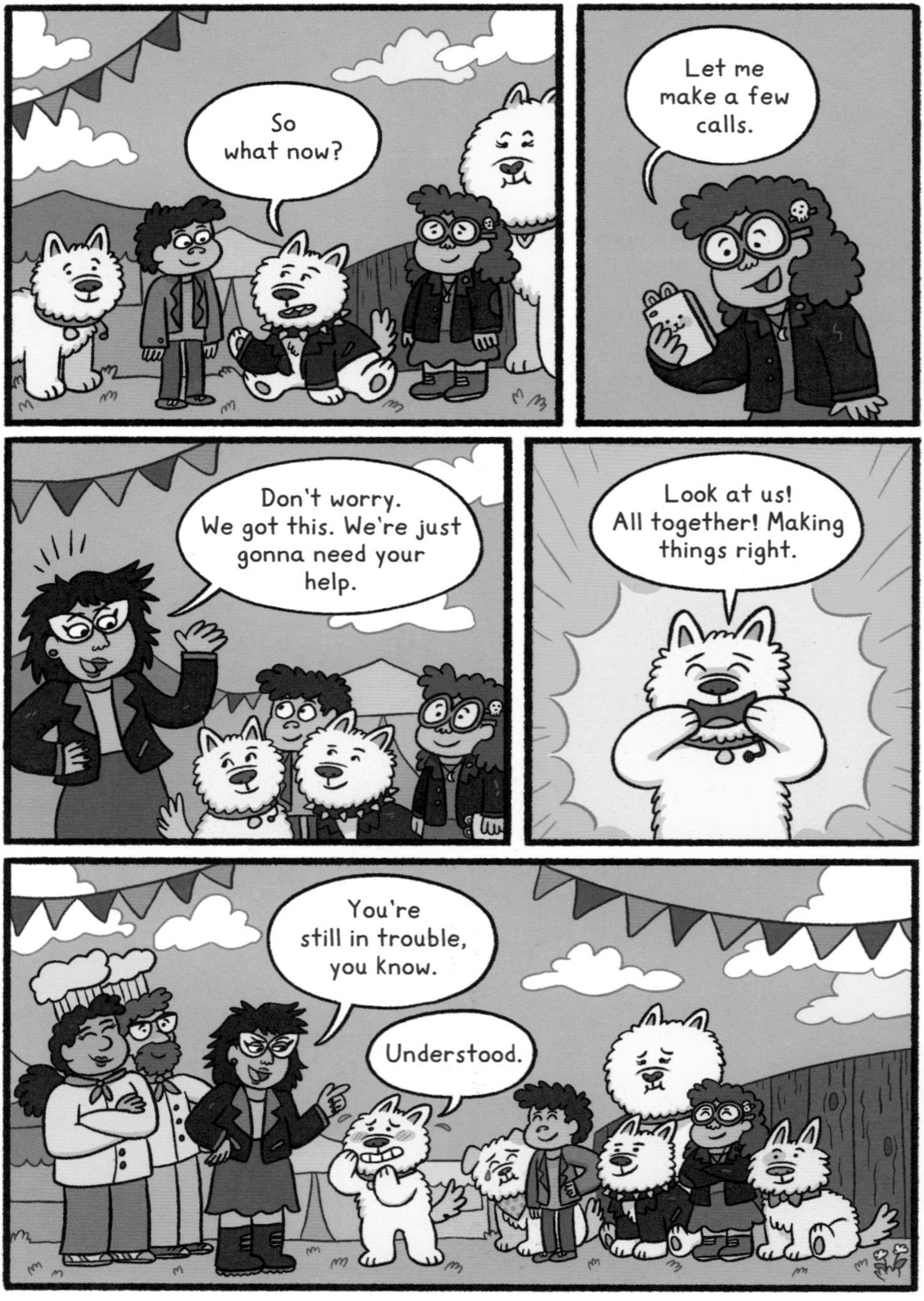
So what now?
Let me make a few calls.
Don't worry. We got this. We're just gonna need your help.
Look at us! All together! Making things right.
You're still in trouble, you know.
Understood.

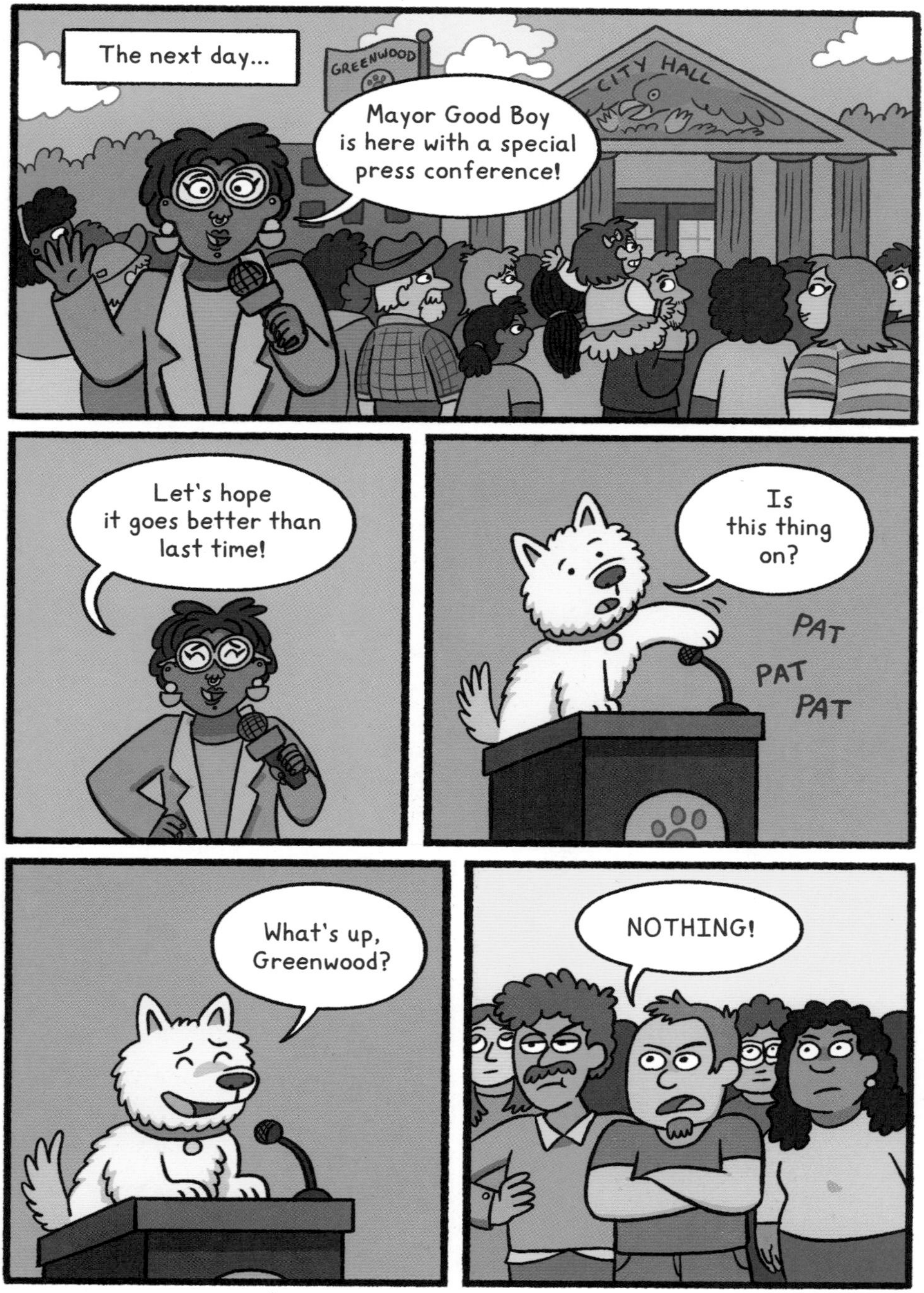
The next day...
GREENWOOD
CITY HALL
Mayor Good Boy is here with a special press conference!
Let's hope it goes better than last time!
Is this thing on?
PAT
PAT
PAT
What's up, Greenwood?
NOTHING!

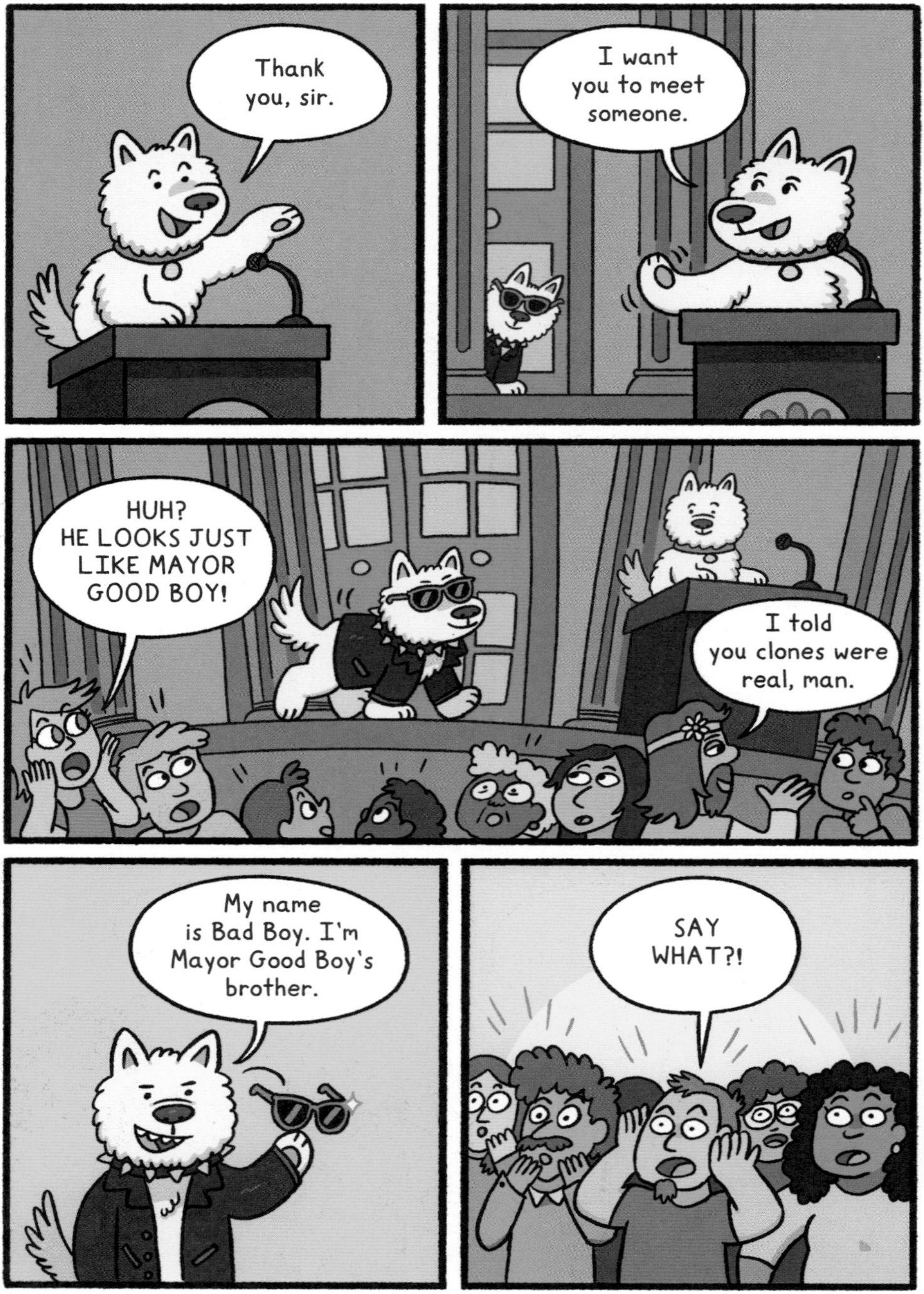
Thank you, sir.
I want you to meet someone.
HUH? HE LOOKS JUST LIKE MAYOR GOOD BOY!
I told you clones were real, man.
My name is Bad Boy. I'm Mayor Good Boy's brother.
SAY WHAT?!

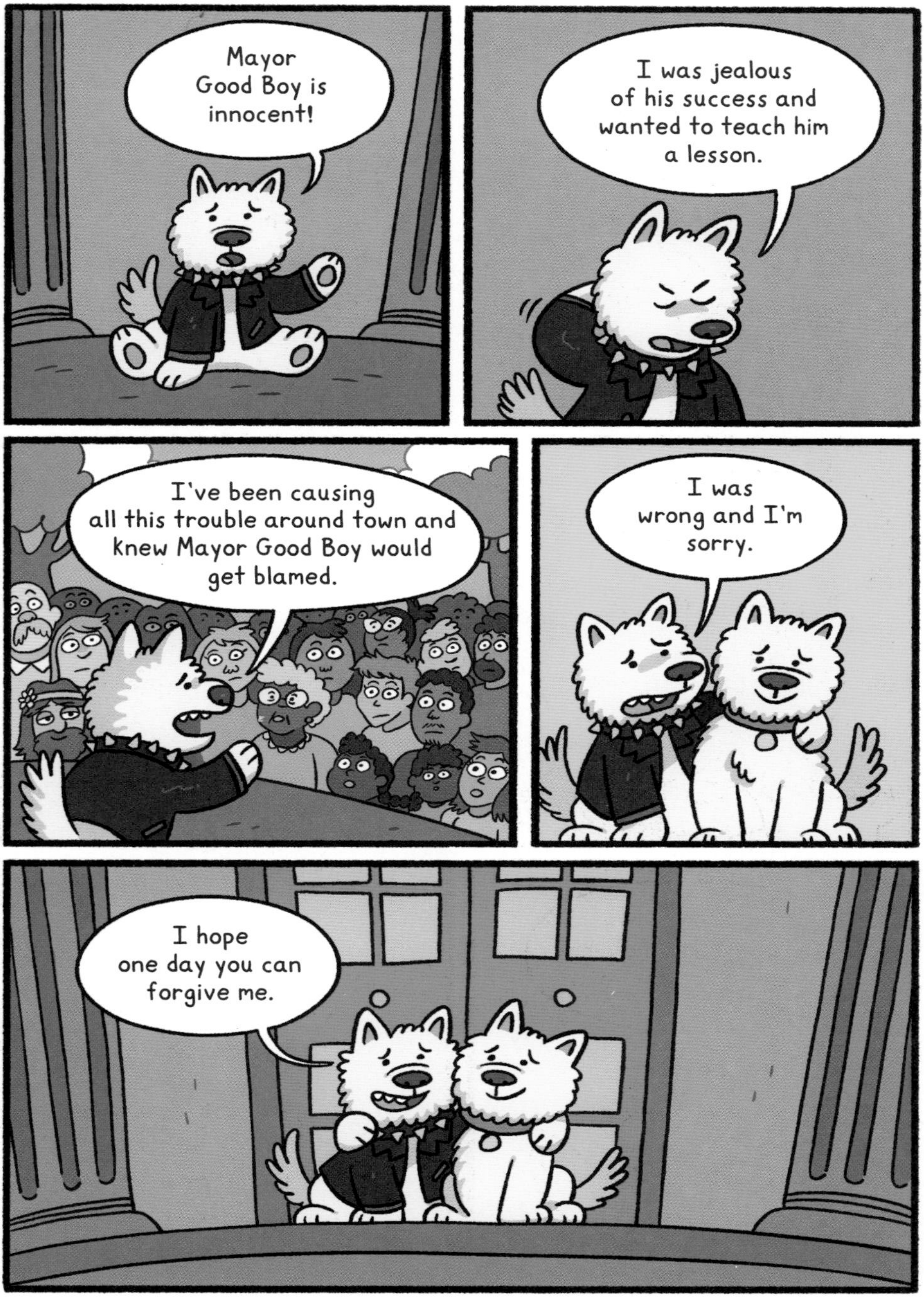
Mayor Good Boy is innocent!
I was jealous of his success and wanted to teach him a lesson.
I've been causing all this trouble around town and knew Mayor Good Boy would get blamed.
I was wrong and I'm sorry.
I hope one day you can forgive me.

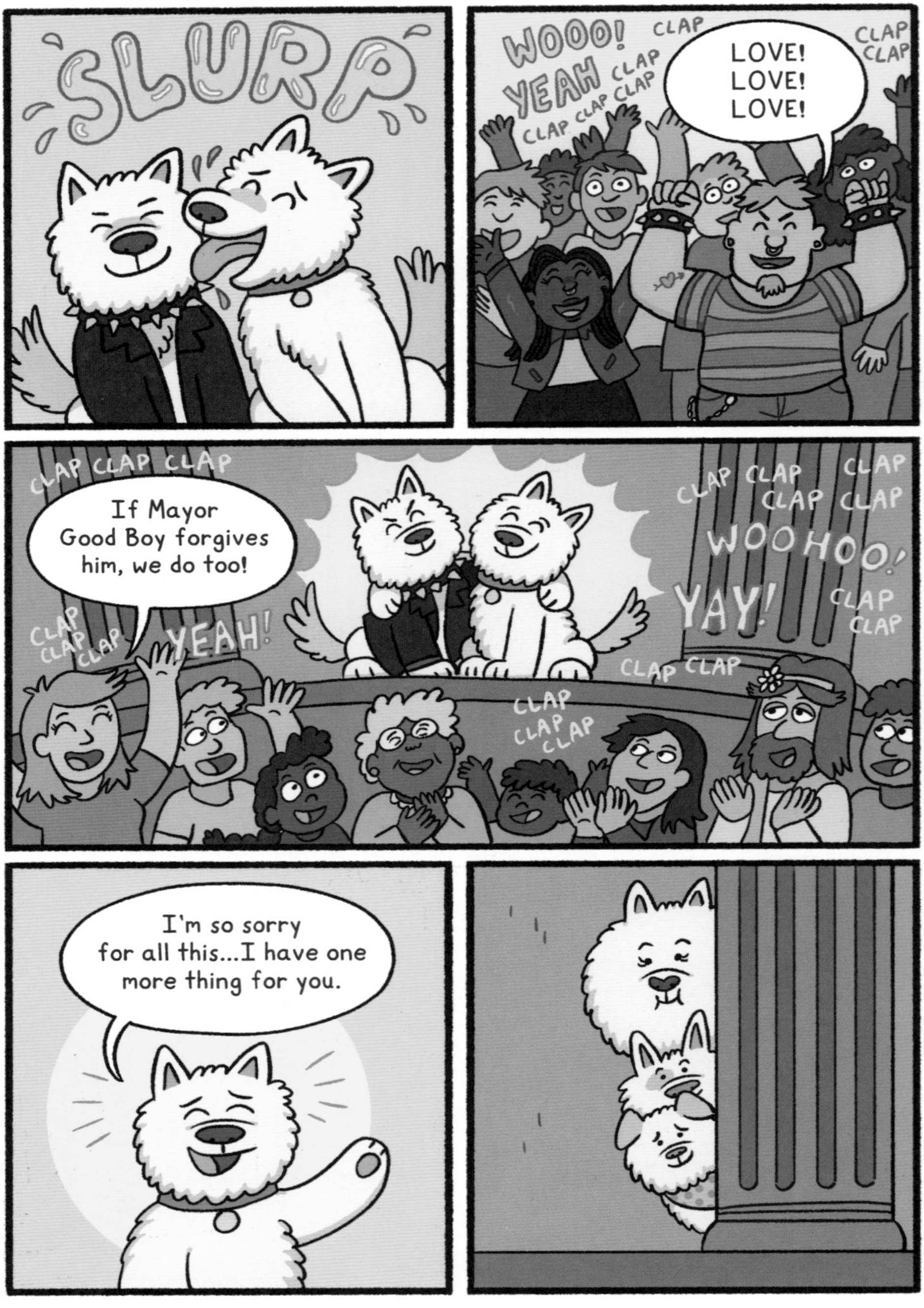
SLURP
WOOO! CLAP
YEAH CLAP
CLAP CLAP CLAP
CLAP CLAP
LOVE! LOVE! LOVE!
CLAP CLAP CLAP
If Mayor Good Boy forgives him, we do too!
CLAP CLAP CLAP
YEAH!
CLAP CLAP CLAP CLAP
WOOHOO!
YAY!
CLAP CLAP
CLAP CLAP
CLAP CLAP CLAP
I'm so sorry for all this...I have one more thing for you.

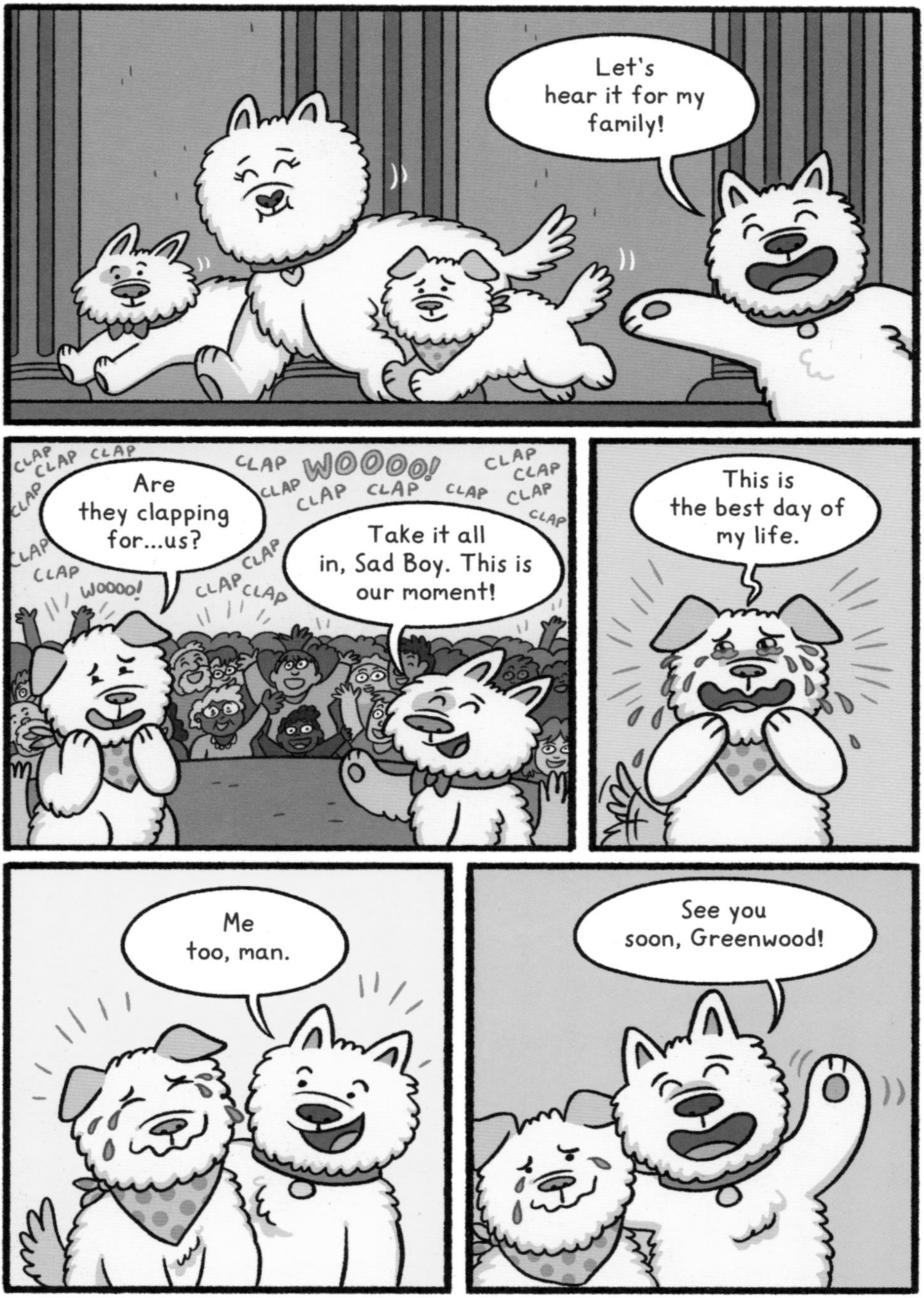
Let's hear it for my family!
CLAP CLAP CLAP CLAP WOOOO! CLAP CLAP CLAP CLAP CLAP CLAP CLAP CLAP CLAP CLAP CLAP WOOOO! CLAP CLAP
Are they clapping for...us?
Take it all in, Sad Boy. This is our moment!
This is the best day of my life.
Me too, man.
See you soon, Greenwood!

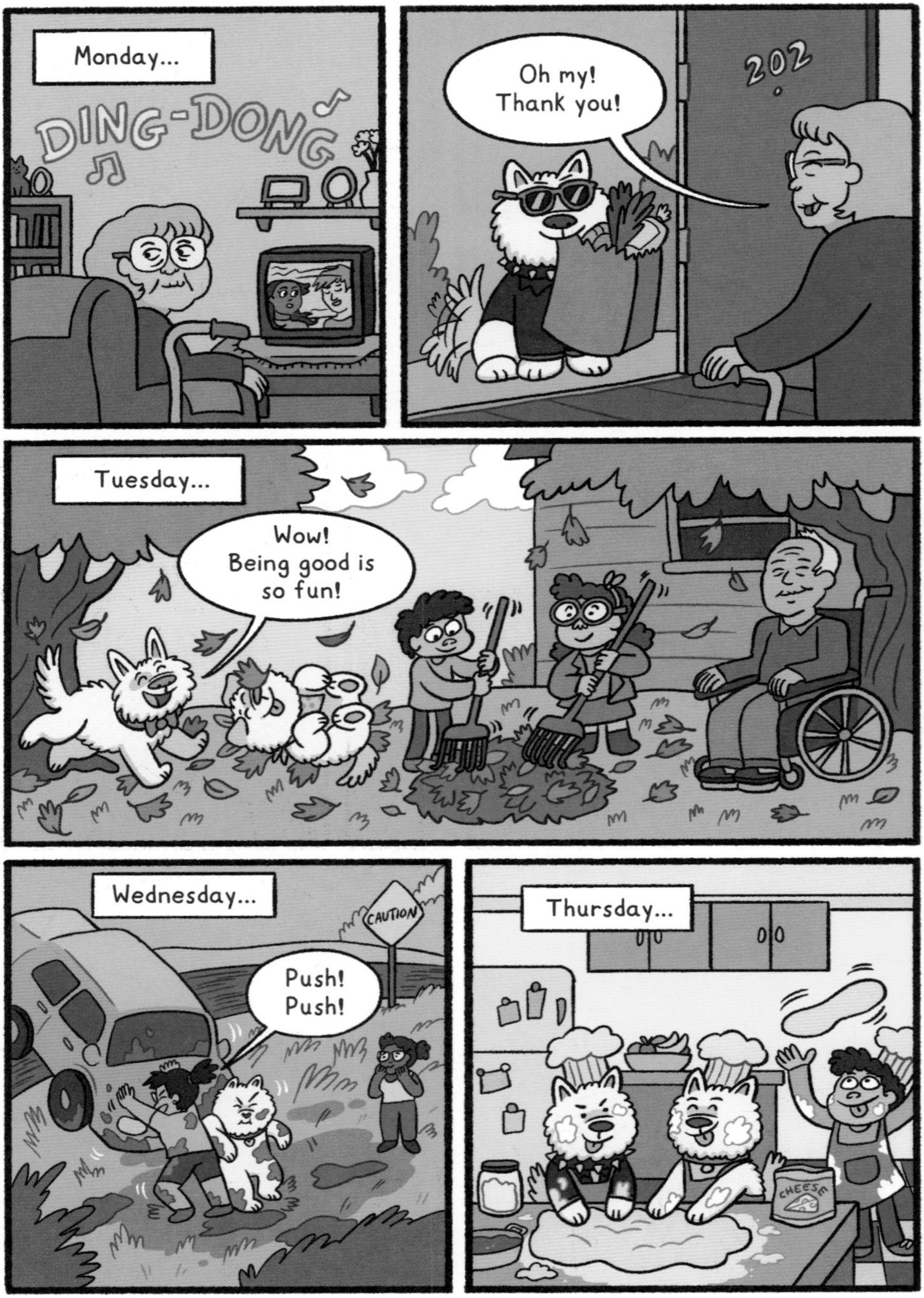
Monday...
DING-DONG
Oh my!
Thank you!
202
Tuesday...
Wow!
Being good is
so fun!
Wednesday...
CAUTION
Push!
Push!
Thursday...
CHEESE

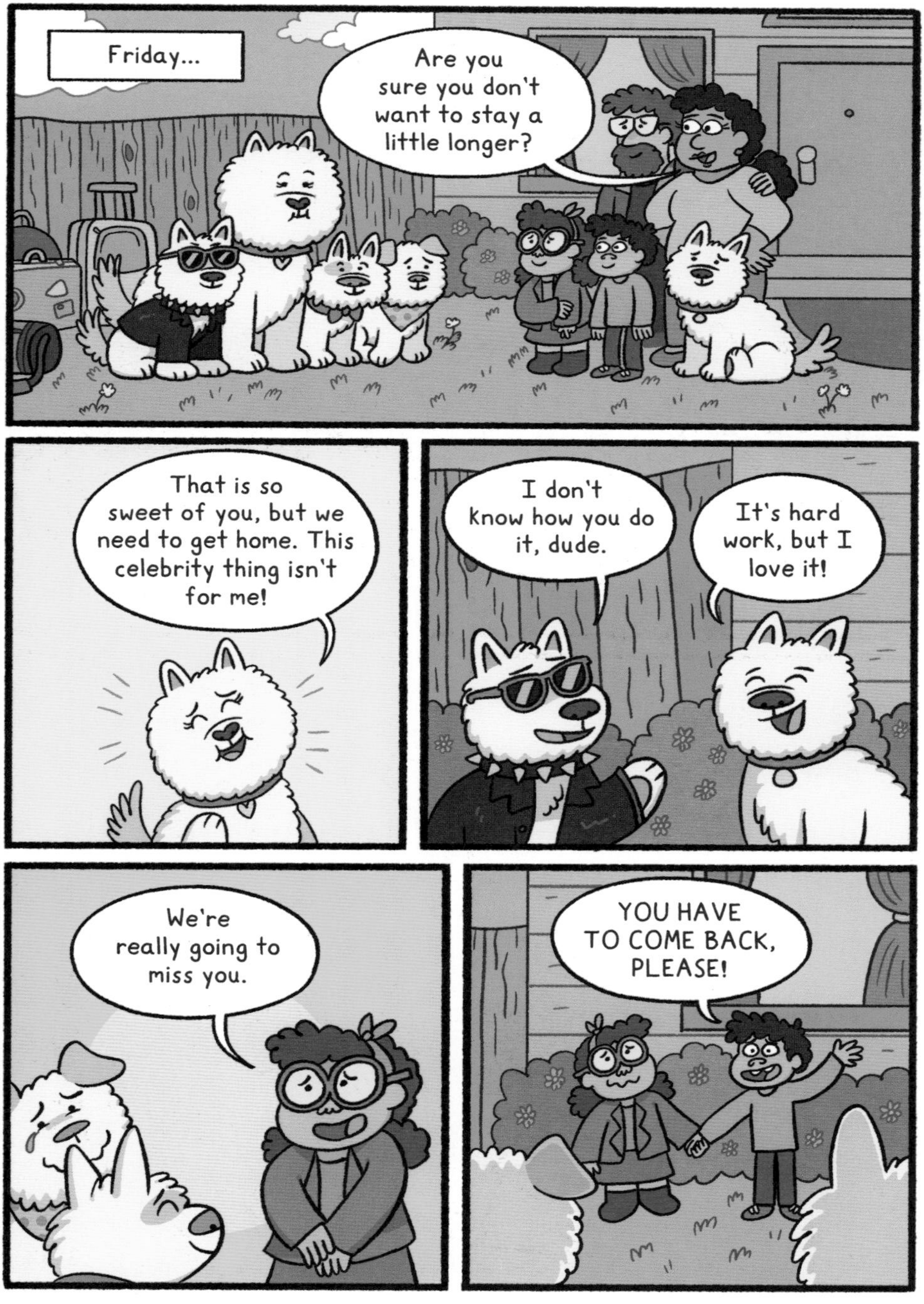
Friday...
Are you sure you don't want to stay a little longer?
That is so sweet of you, but we need to get home. This celebrity thing isn't for me!
I don't know how you do it, dude.
It's hard work, but I love it!
We're really going to miss you.
YOU HAVE TO COME BACK, PLEASE!

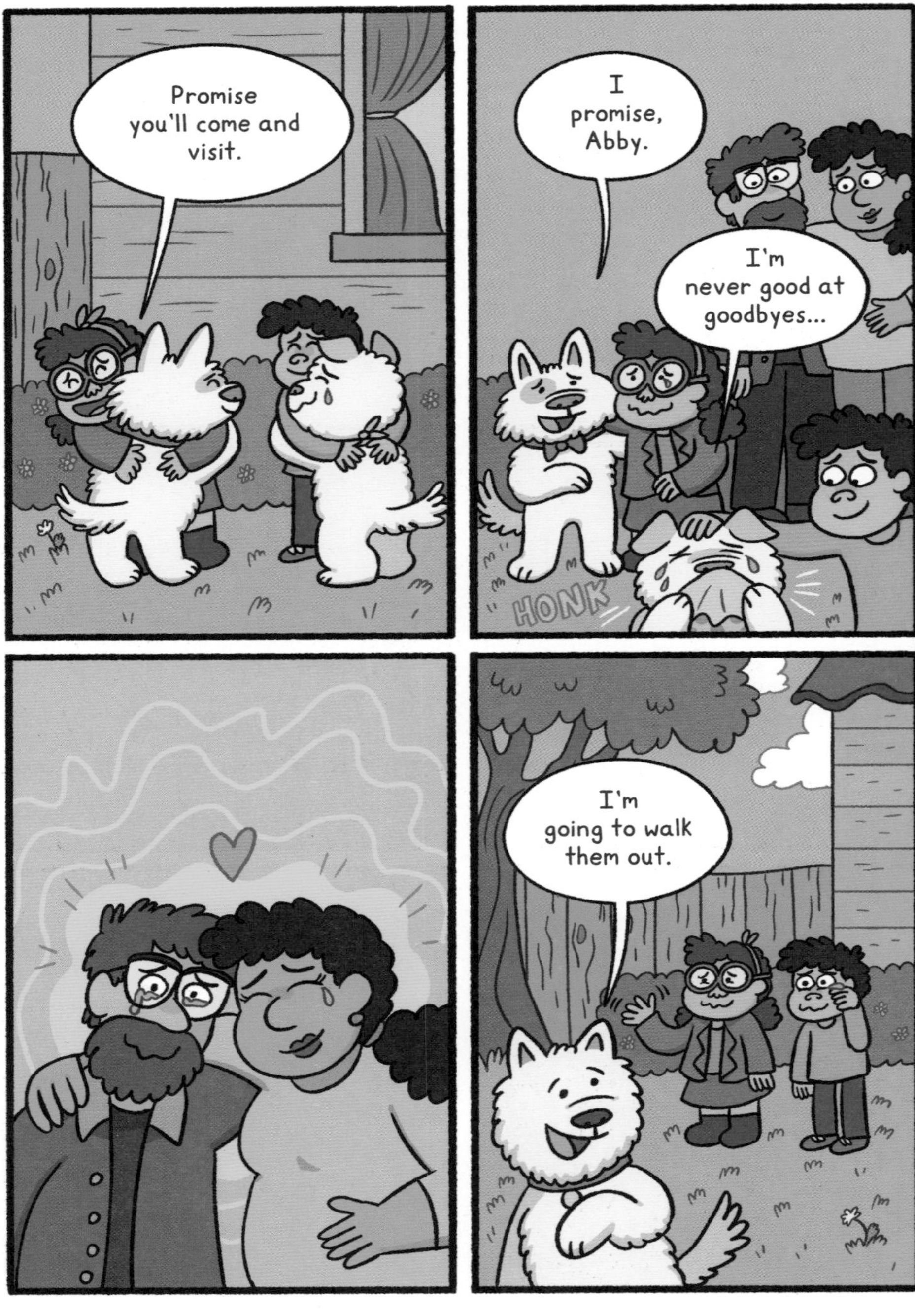

Promise you'll come and visit.
I promise, Abby.
I'm never good at goodbyes...
HONK
I'm going to walk them out.

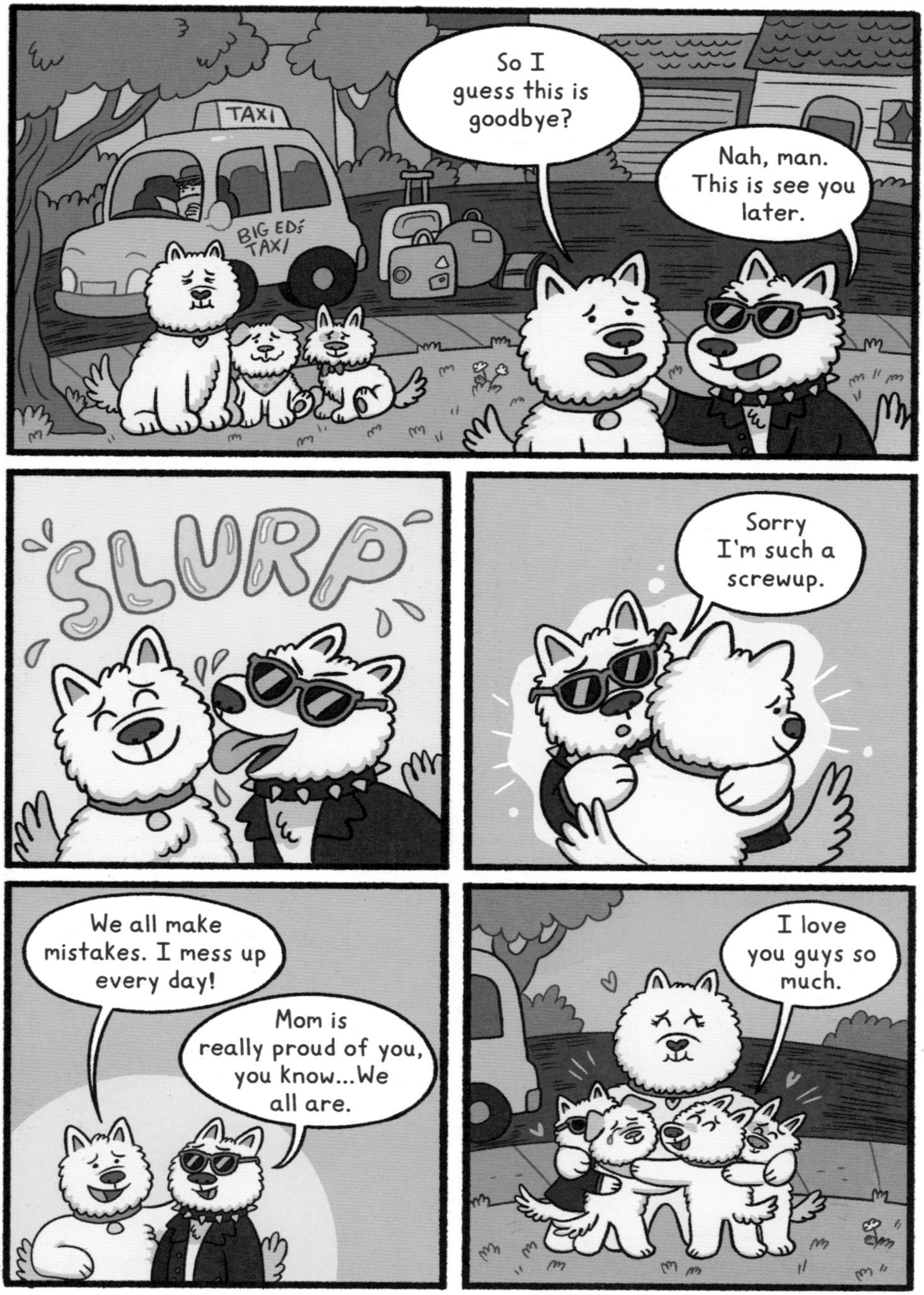
TAXI
BIG ED'S TAXI
So I guess this is goodbye?
Nah, man. This is see you later.
SLURP
Sorry I'm such a screwup.
We all make mistakes. I mess up every day!
Mom is really proud of you, you know...We all are.
I love you guys so much.

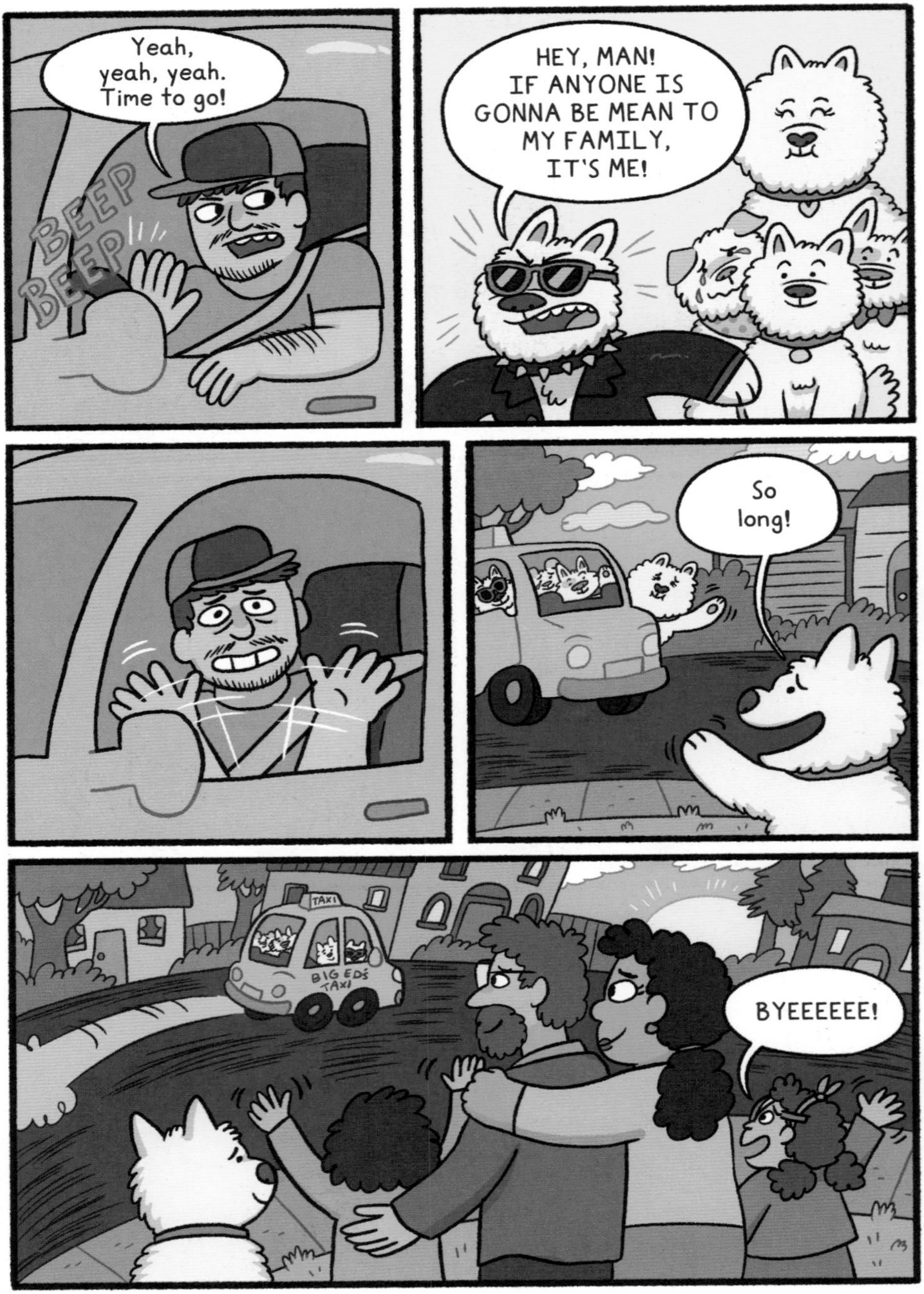
Yeah, yeah, yeah. Time to go!
BEEP BEEP
HEY, MAN! IF ANYONE IS GONNA BE MEAN TO MY FAMILY, IT'S ME!
So long!
TAXI
BIG ED'S TAXI
BYEEEEEE!

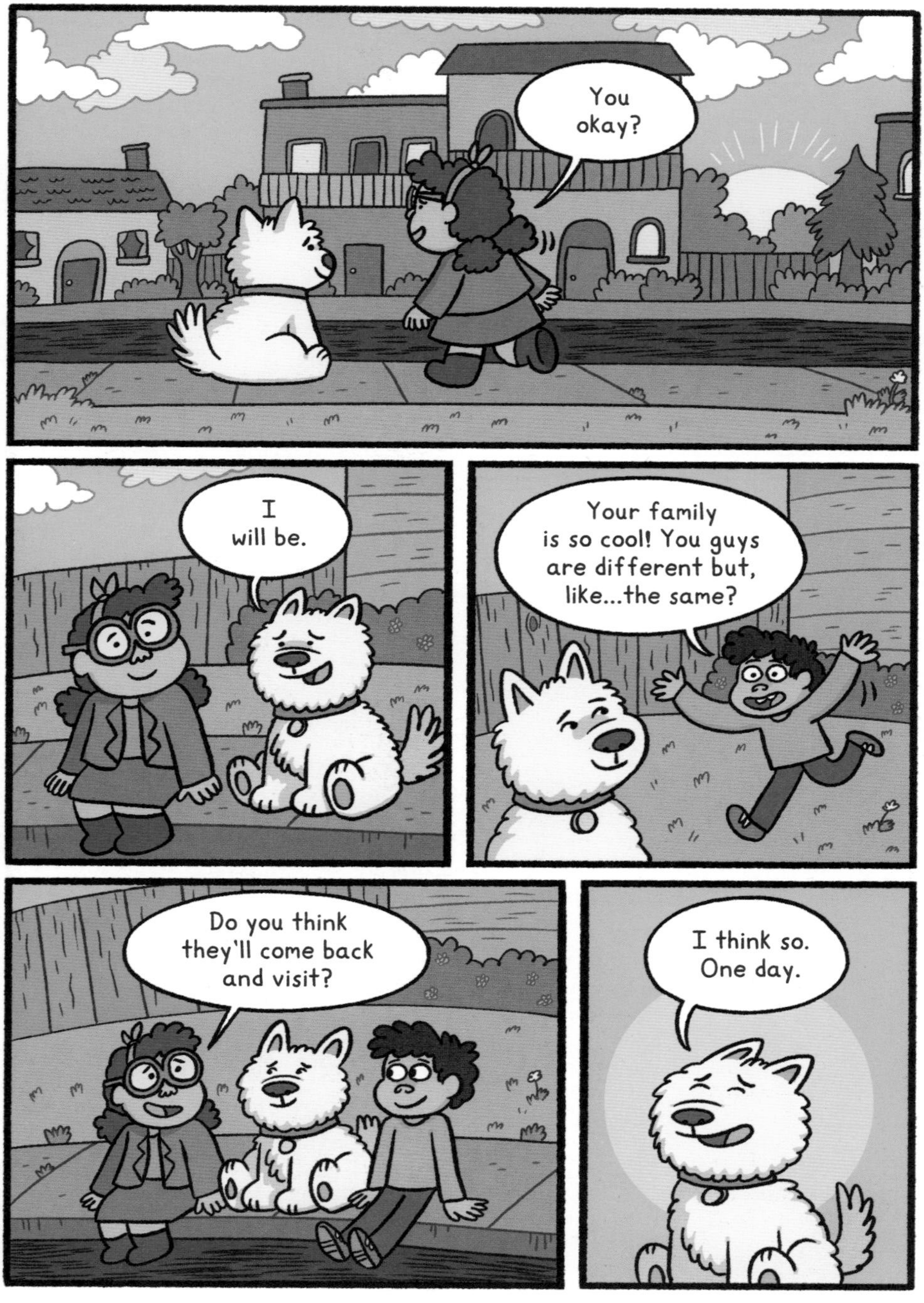
You okay?
I will be.
Your family is so cool! You guys are different but, like...the same?
Do you think they'll come back and visit?
I think so. One day.

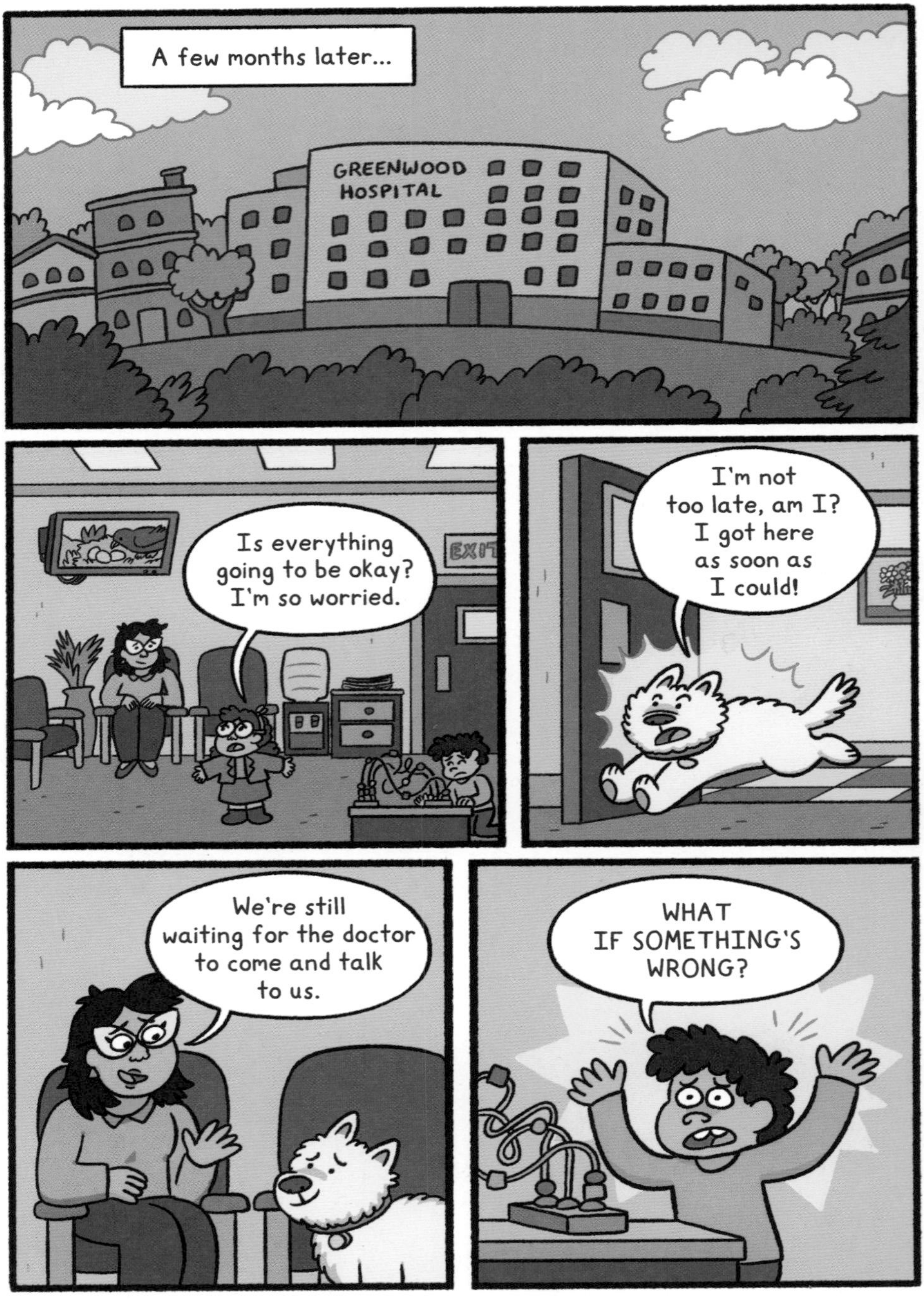
A few months later...
GREENWOOD HOSPITAL
Is everything going to be okay? I'm so worried.
EXIT
I'm not too late, am I? I got here as soon as I could!
We're still waiting for the doctor to come and talk to us.
WHAT IF SOMETHING'S WRONG?

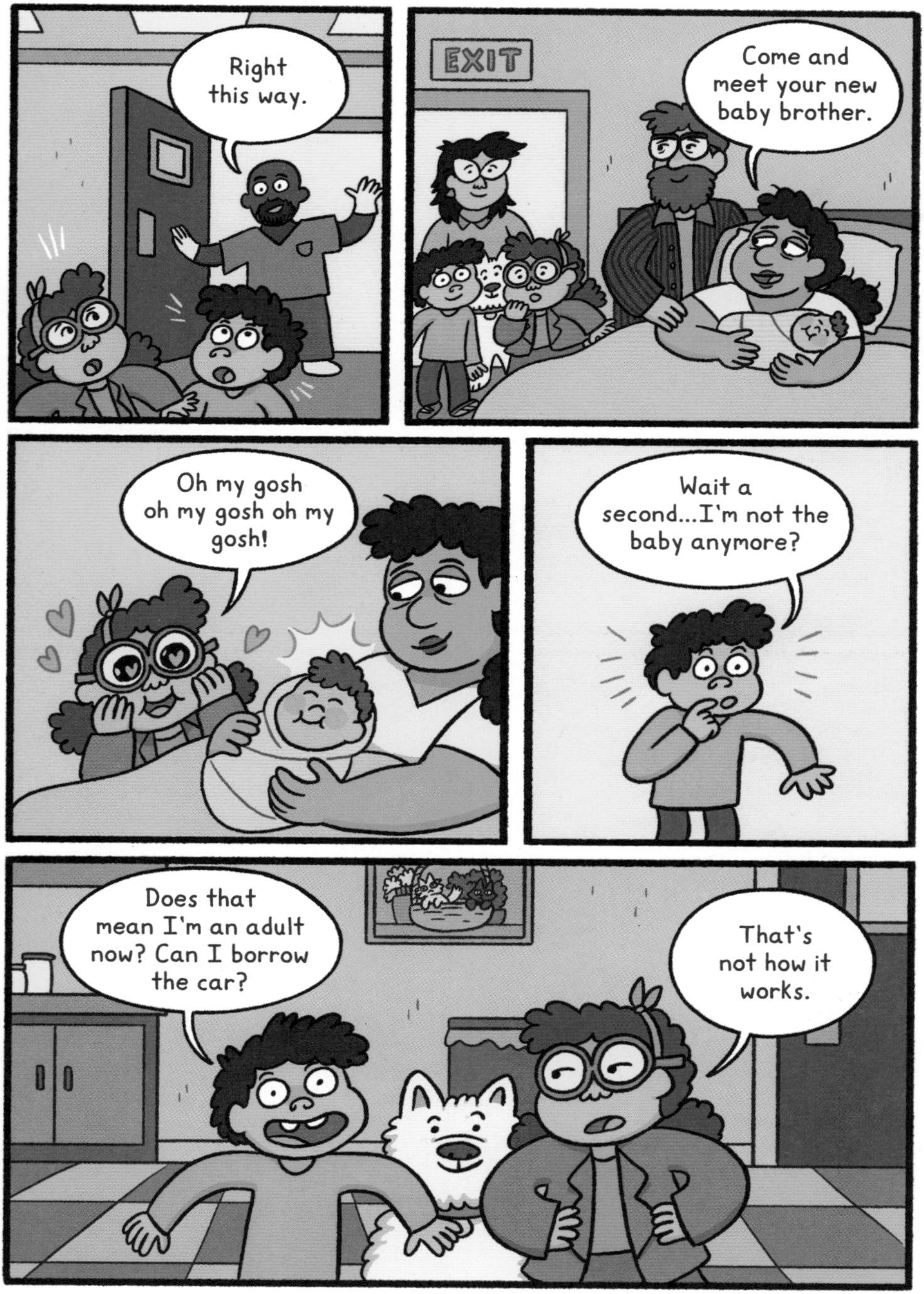
Right this way.
EXIT
Come and meet your new baby brother.
Oh my gosh oh my gosh oh my gosh!
Wait a second...I'm not the baby anymore?
Does that mean I'm an adult now? Can I borrow the car?
That's not how it works.

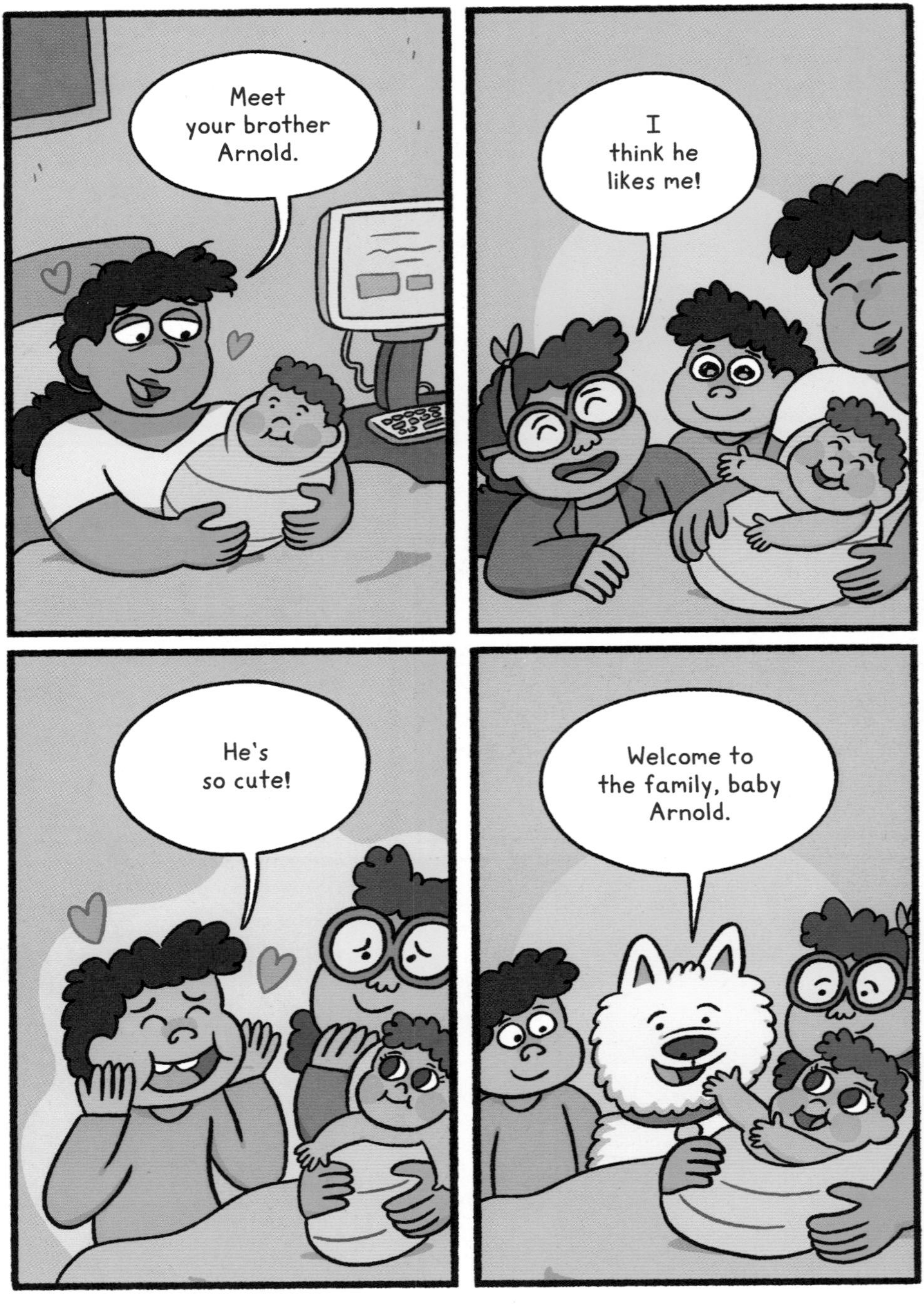
Meet your brother Arnold.
I think he likes me!
He's so cute!
Welcome to the family, baby Arnold.

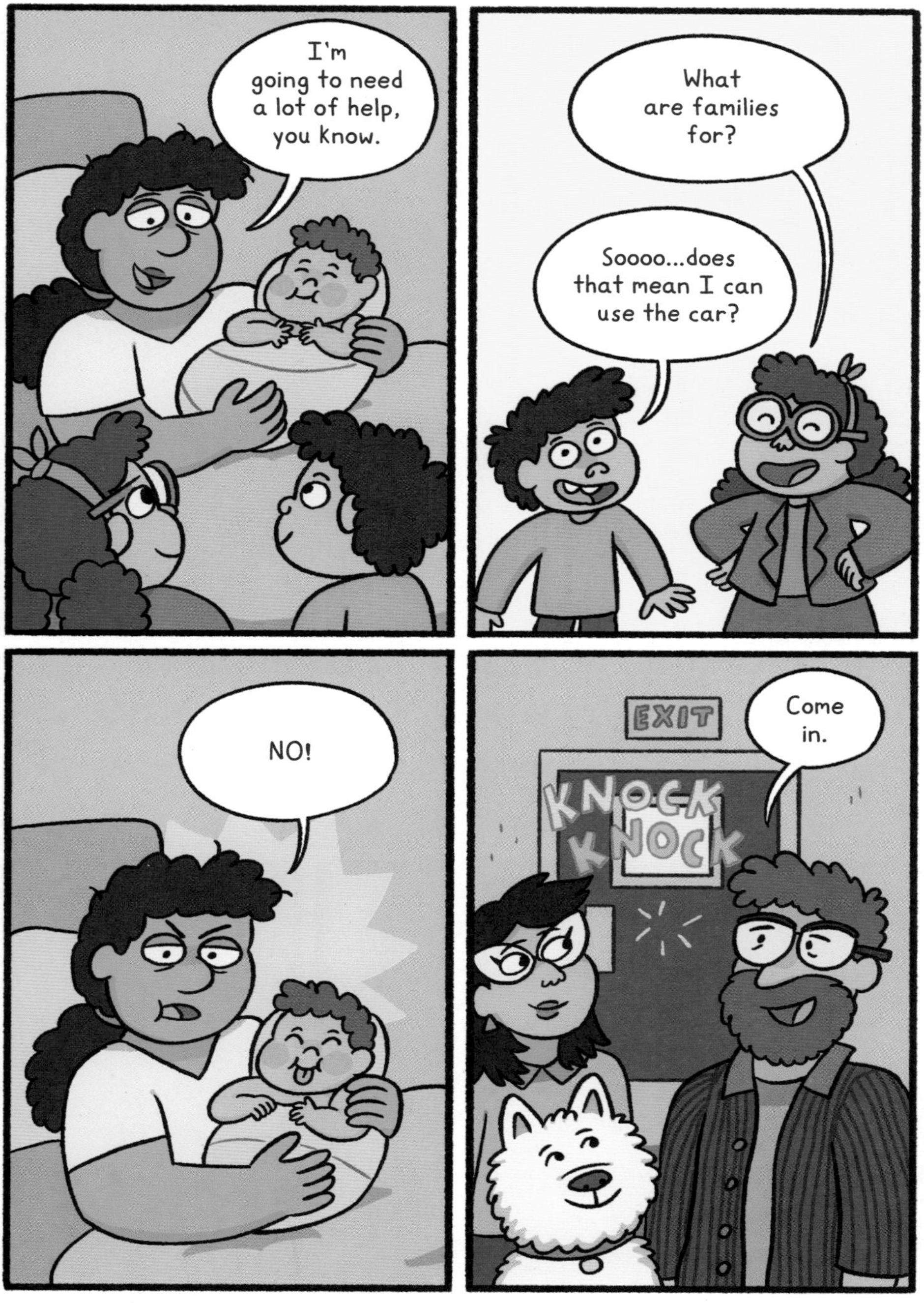
I'm going to need a lot of help, you know.
What are families for?
Soooo...does that mean I can use the car?
NO!
EXIT
KNOCK KNOCK
Come in.

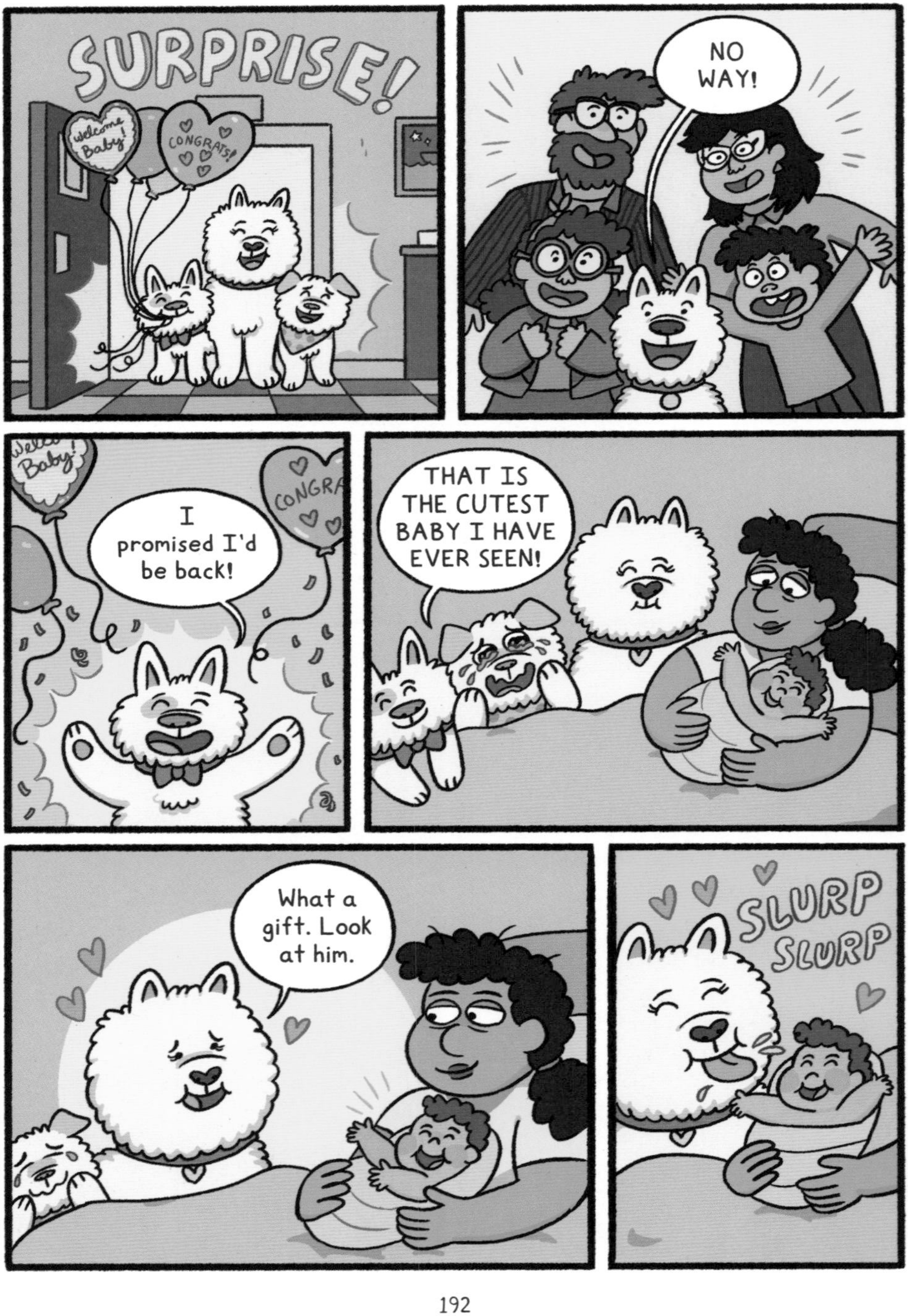
SURPRISE!
Welcome Baby!
CONGRATS!
NO WAY!
I promised I'd be back!
THAT IS THE CUTEST BABY I HAVE EVER SEEN!
What a gift. Look at him.
SLURP
SLURP

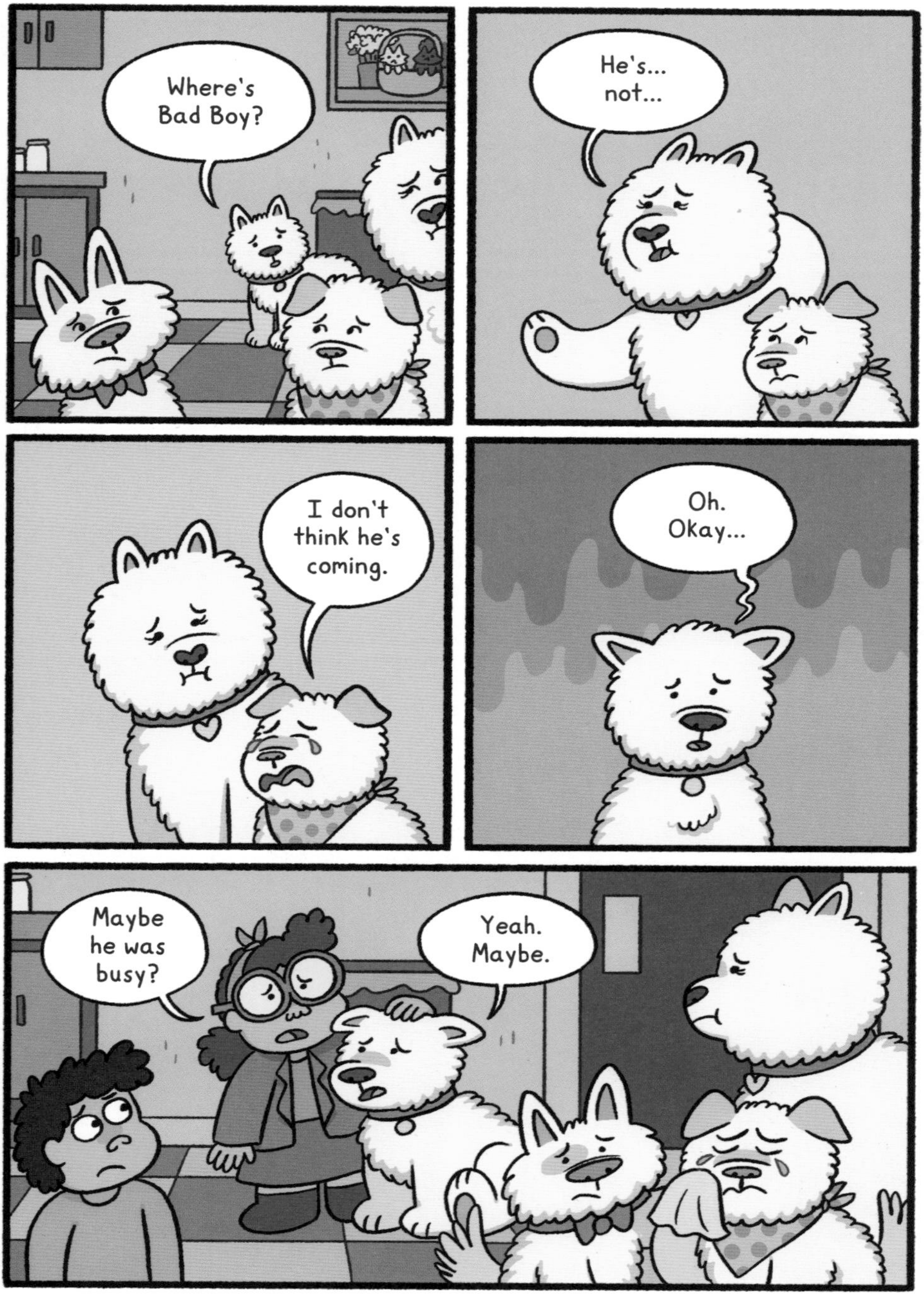
Where's Bad Boy?
He's... not...
I don't think he's coming.
Oh. Okay...
Maybe he was busy?
Yeah. Maybe.

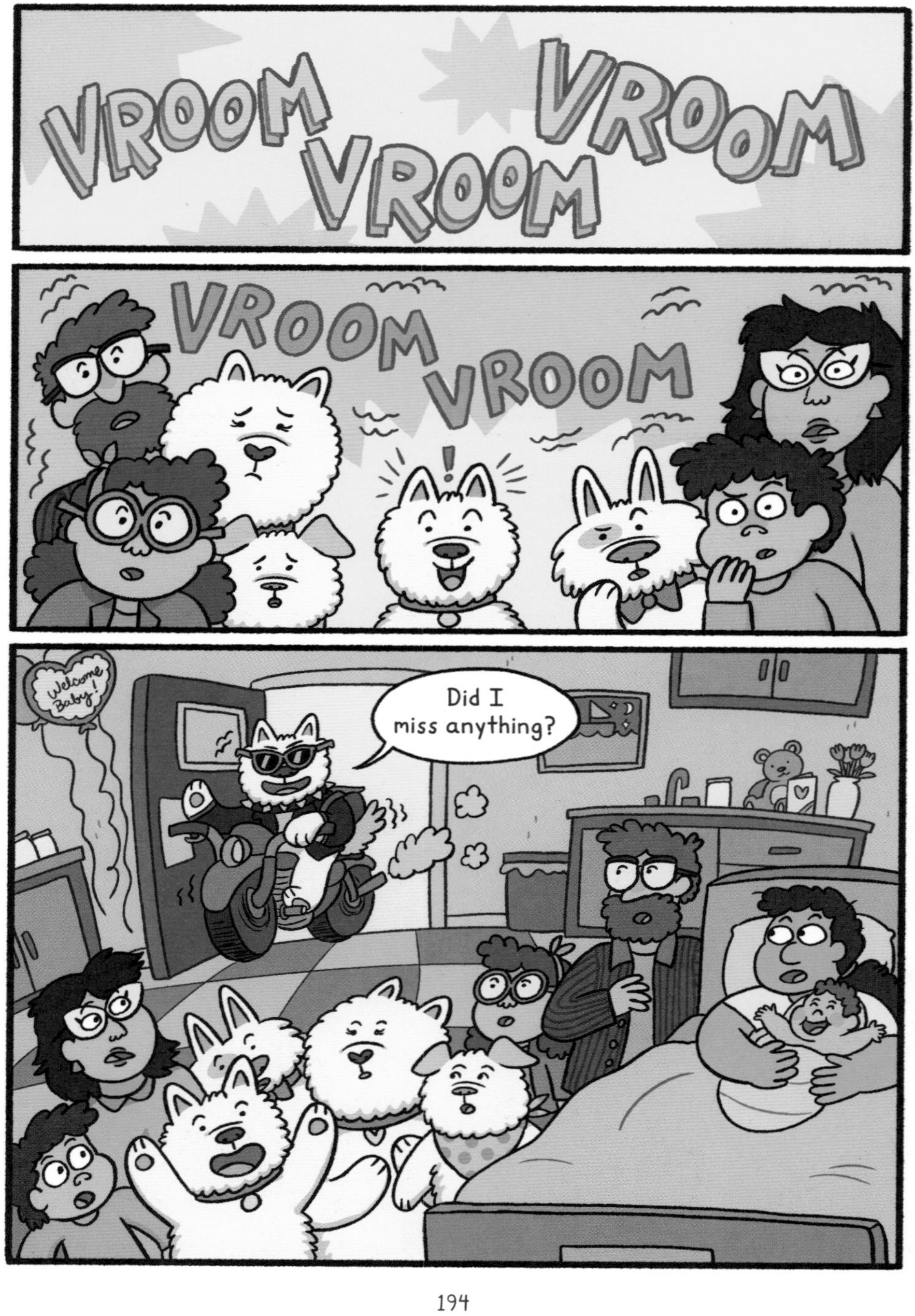
VROOM
VROOM
VROOM
VROOM
VROOM
Welcome Baby!
Did I miss anything?

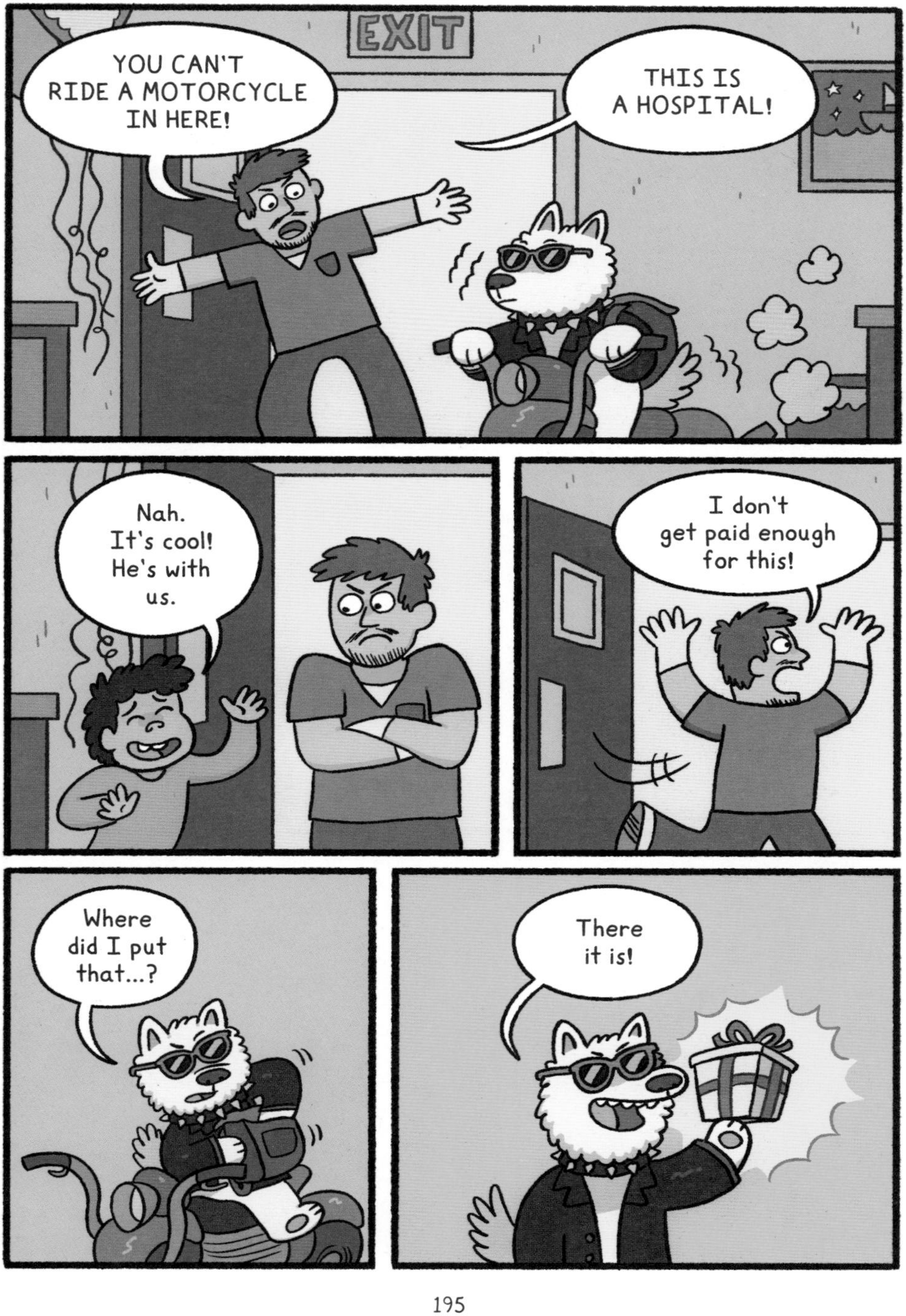
YOU CAN'T RIDE A MOTORCYCLE IN HERE!
THIS IS A HOSPITAL!
EXIT
Nah. It's cool! He's with us.
I don't get paid enough for this!
Where did I put that...?
There it is!

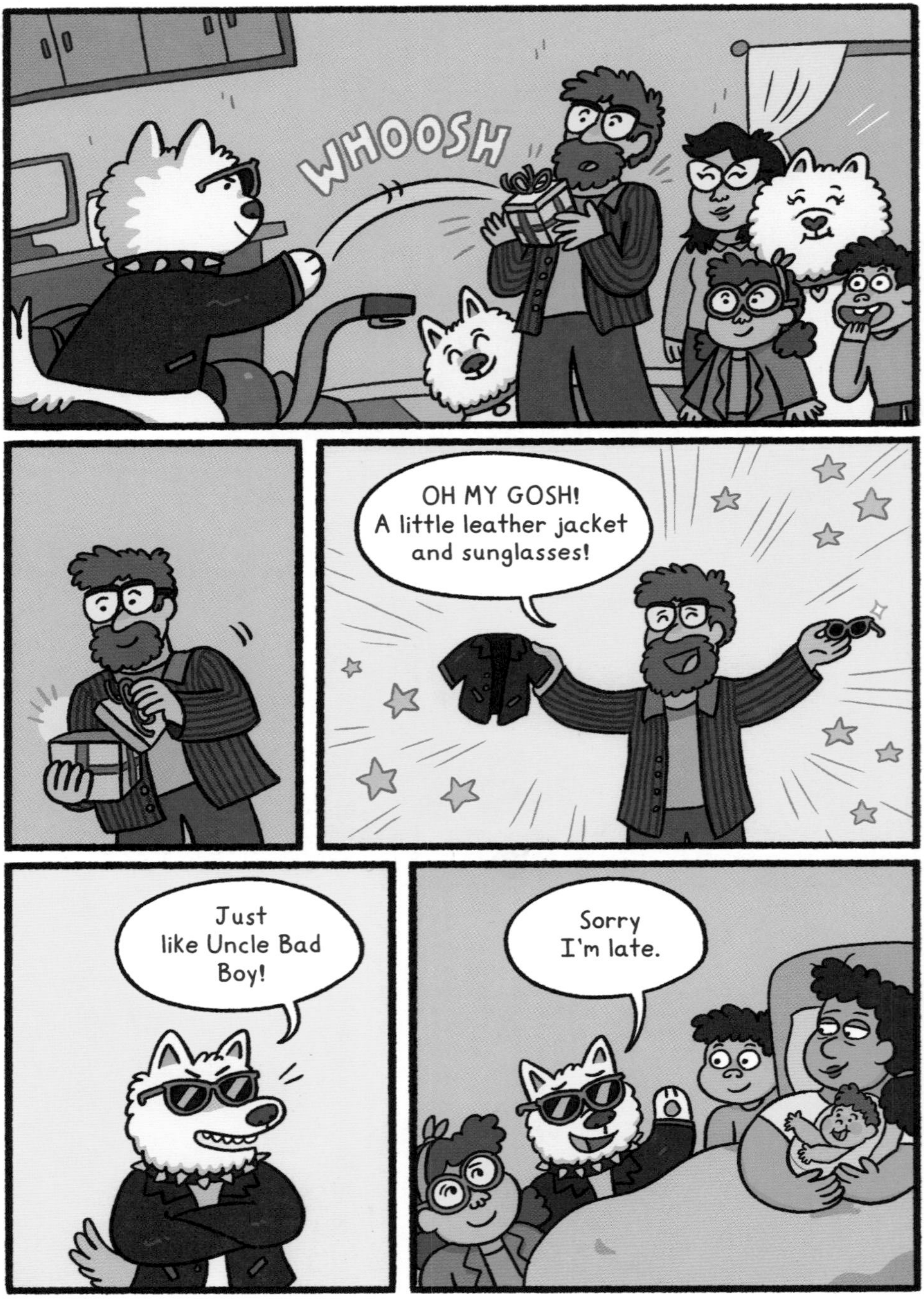
WHOOSH
OH MY GOSH! A little leather jacket and sunglasses!
Just like Uncle Bad Boy!
Sorry I'm late.

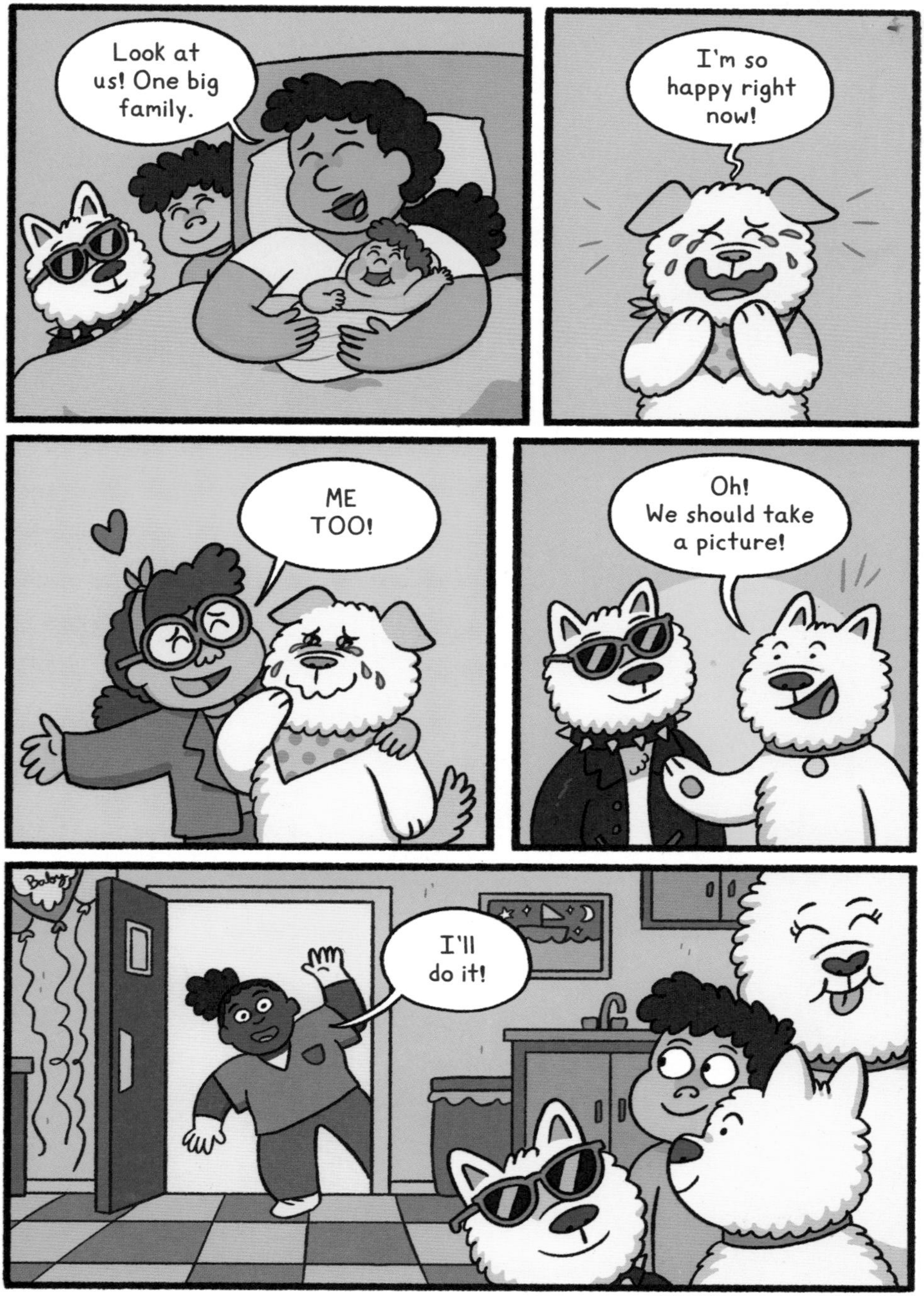
Look at us! One big family.
I'm so happy right now!
ME TOO!
Oh! We should take a picture!
I'll do it!

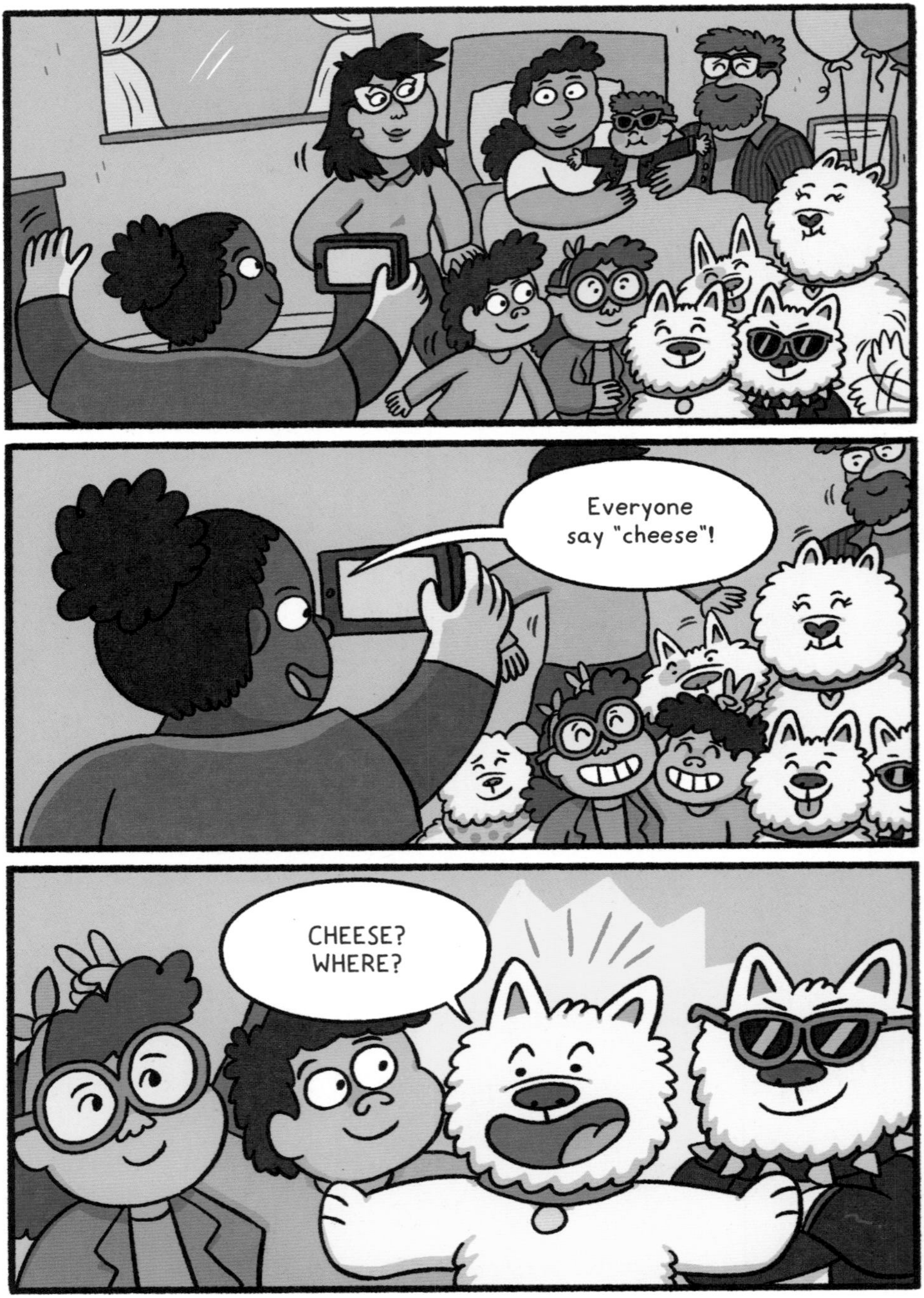
Everyone say "cheese"!
CHEESE? WHERE?

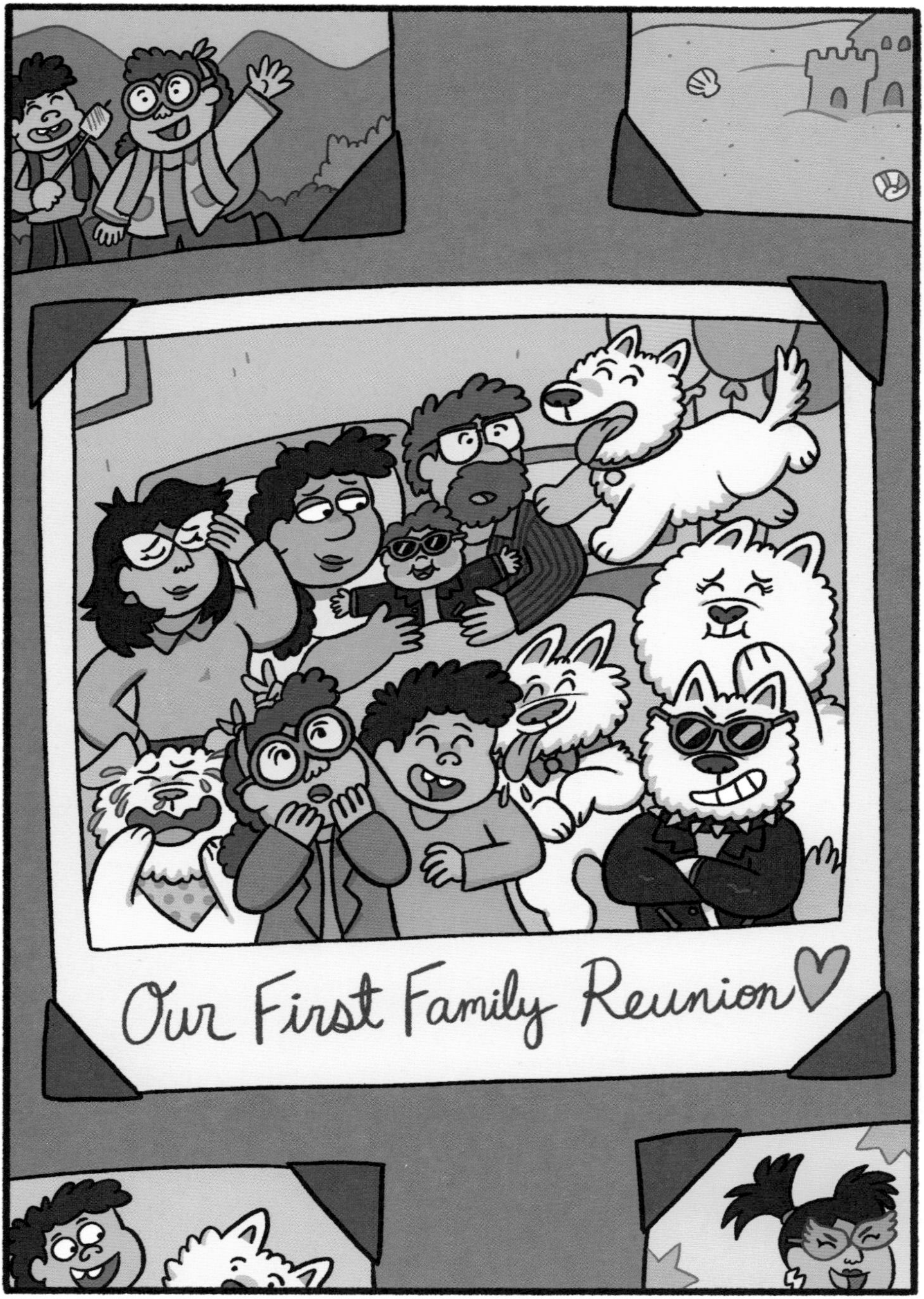
Our First Family Reunion

DAVE SCHEIDT is a writer from Chicago. When he's not writing comic books, he likes watching monster movies and eating snacks. He first started writing stories when he was ten years old and hasn't stopped since.

davescheidt.com

DAVE THANKS

I'd like to thank each and every librarian, teacher, educator, and bookseller out there for everything you do. I'd also love to thank each and every Mayor Good Boy fan for loving our books, laughing at our jokes, and supporting us. You mean the world to us, and it's an honor to craft these stories for you.

Andrea Bell
Tony Blando
Jenny Blenk
Gabe Bott
Mark Bouchard
Patrick Brower
Ryan Browne
Don Cardenas
Jimmy Clark
Patrick Crotty
Kevin Cuffe
Danny Diaz
Natalie Djordjevic
Julie Egeland-Hernandez
Bob Frantz
Jason Gibner
Casey Gilly
John Patrick Green
Alex Hernandez

Whitney Leopard
Demetrius McCraney
Scoot McMahon
Dana Marie Miroballi
Izzy Montoya
Kelly Nee
Charlie Olsen
Dav Pilkey
Sulma Rivera
Charles Schulz
John Siuntres
Silver Sprocket
Michael Sweater
Brandon Wainerdi
Larry Watanabe

AlleyCat Comics
Anderson's Bookshop
The Book Stall

Bookie's Chicago
Challengers Comics + Conversation
Chicago Public Library
Green Hills Public Library
Niles-Maine Library District
Skokie Public Library

I'd like to thank some of my favorite Bad Boys (and Girls):

Godzilla
Count Dracula
Chucky
Slappy the Living Dummy
Annabelle the Doll

MIRANDA HARMON

grew up in Oviedo, Florida, and now lives in Los Angeles. She graduated from Goucher College and studied comics at the Sequential Artists Workshop. When she's not drawing comics, she's usually baking, hiking, or sleeping. Even though she grew up with cats, she loves dogs too.

🐦 @MirandaMHarmon
mirandaharmon.com

MIRANDA THANKS

First, I'd like to thank my family, Mom, Dad, and my sister, Julia, for being so supportive from the other side of the country. Thank you for all your love and encouragement. Thank you to Tom Hart, Leela Corman, Justine Mara Andersen, and everyone else at the Sequential Artists Workshop in Gainesville, Florida, for your patience and guidance. I might not be making books now if I hadn't been given free rein of the SAW risograph machine for two years. Thank you, Eric Kubli, my loving and supportive partner, for making every day a good one. Thank you so much, Dave Scheidt, for coming to me with the brilliant idea for Mayor Good Boy, and for being a great collaborator and friend during the making of these books. A big thank-you to Whitney Leopard, Danny Diaz, Patrick Crotty, and everyone else at Random House for your invaluable help making this series. A huge thank-you to Lyle Lynde for coloring and adding so much life and dimension to our book. I feel lucky to be a part of such a great team. Thank you also to my agent, Charlie Olsen, for all your help. Thank you from the bottom of my heart to all my friends and peers I've met through comics, too many to name here, who have welcomed me into this industry and guided me for years. Last but not least, thank you to all the kids, parents, teachers, and librarians who have read and supported Mayor Good Boy. We appreciate you so much!